I0825215

Mrs. Benedict Arnold

Mrs. Benedict Arnold

A Novel

Emma Parry

NEW YORK

This book is a work of fiction. Any references to historical events, real people, or real places are used fictitiously. Other names, characters, places, and events are products of the author's imagination, and any resemblance to actual events or places or persons, living or dead, is entirely coincidental.

Copyright © 2026 by Emma Parry

Zando supports the right to free expression and the value of copyright. The purpose of copyright is to encourage writers and artists to produce the creative works that enrich our culture. Thank you for buying an authorized edition of this book and for complying with copyright laws by not reproducing, scanning, uploading, or distributing this book or any part of it without permission. If you would like permission to use material from the book (other than for brief quotations embodied in reviews), please contact connect@zandoprojects.com.

zandoprojects.com

First Edition: April 2026

Text design by Kevin Ullrich
Cover design by Lucy Kim

The publisher does not have control over and is not responsible for author or other third-party websites (or their content).

Library of Congress Control Number: 2026931585

978-1-63893-379-3 (Hardcover)
978-1-63893-380-9 (ebook)

10 9 8 7 6 5 4 3 2 1
Manufactured in the United States of America
LBK

For Antonia

. . . the enigmatic relations between André and Peggy Arnold [and] between Benedict and Peggy Arnold [are] perhaps the heaviest printed question mark of the American War of Independence.

—J. E. Morpurgo, *The William and Mary Quarterly*

It's a true account of how I imagine [it] to be.

—Nell Stevens, *The Paris Review*

Part One

Chapter One

Pennsylvania, 1777

I WAS ASLEEP WHEN THE FIRST SHOT CAME. DREAMING I WAS CROSSING an ocean, cold salt spray misting my skin, dread churning along with the restless swell. Conflicting updates arrived at intervals. A big win for one side. Their complete defeat. With no idea what to wish for, I searched the faces of older women for clues to their bewildering conviction.

A gun fired, a body slumped, and I woke with the report still ringing in my ears.

There was a second shot before I realized it was real.

I scrambled to crouch under the window I'd left open to the rain again, letting in the risk of rot.

Across the street, the Galloway house was in darkness. A porchlight exposed a tight mass of men's backs, the silhouette of muskets.

"*Committees of safety*" sounded deliberately sinister to me. The idea of citizens policing each other's beliefs had fear rising like water. Now they'd started targeting neighbors, even sleep was no relief.

My heart hammered as a sash was raised on the first floor and Mrs. Galloway appeared at the window, lit from behind. Impressively imperious, given her nightdress, and apparently immune to intimidation, the former speaker of the Assembly's wife demanded the men disperse. Raising her voice above their jeering insults like the practiced politician her husband had been, she insisted Mr. Galloway loved his country as much as any man among them. He'd accepted defeat and left the city, and there was now no more to be said!

The sash slammed shut, and with a sickening splintering the door downstairs was forced. Light moved about the house—glass smashing, servants shrieking—before the men emerged empty-handed.

Long after the men's footsteps receded, I kept queasy vigil, the only warped comfort that my brothers had been spared whatever was coming for us.

At first light, my father knocked on the door, instructing Betsy and me to be ready to leave in an hour.

"I am not without hopes that matters will subside. Until then, it's better we're out of the city."

As we began folding clothes to take to our country house, I whispered to my elder sister what she'd missed.

"We should offer to take her with us," I said with sudden conviction.

Betsy looked unconvinced but I went to find Father in his library, where he was volleying out letters to tenants, chasing late payments with his typical tact.

"Don't we have some obligation?" My voice dropped to a whisper. "You said it was a bid for peaceful reconciliation Mr. Galloway made, and he was only narrowly defeated?"

Father's skin, always quick to pink, flushed puce.

"The duty, Peggy, of every moderate-thinking man is to remain silent and inactive in these times."

I retreated, but not without wondering bolshily if it was.

We were all very quiet as we loaded only what one carriage could carry. Two Quaker widows, acquaintances in reduced circumstances, would be installed in our home to deter any committees thinking of requisitioning it. I was grateful to escape, and guilty at the thought we were leaving women with fewer choices to risk what we would not.

Rolling out of the city in a vehicle any mob could tip, the veneer of civilization seemed suddenly very thin.

It was a relief to feel the air cool as we reached Shippensburg, to see familiar oaks with their great green reach. Ignoring my mother's protests, I stuck my head outside the carriage, squinting as dappled sunlight flashed across my face and the breeze whipped my hair stiff.

At the mouth of the driveway, I climbed down from the carriage and waded alone through the wildflower meadow to the old stone house with its faded blue wooden shutters.

While my parents and Betsy went to rest, I set off into the woods. Out of sight, I could still run there—and I did, sprinting like an ostrich in my adult getup along the soft mossy paths I loved.

Javelins of sunshine pierced the woods, spotlighting trees which seemed to grow directly from the rocks. I saw a pileated woodpecker drilling holes like gunshots, a scarlet cardinal, a brilliant blue jay, eastern phoebes—one so far from shy she came with me, looping from one branch to the next along my path. Lichen, fern, mushroom, moss: Everything felt it had chosen to live there in that air.

At the waterhole, I shocked my toes in the cold dark green, water boatmen darting from my feet, and felt the long clench of fear release.

Initially, I was thoroughly taken with thrift. Wearing homespun clothes and eating only what we'd grown made me feel virtuous and romantic, somewhere between a picturesque peasant and a nun.

I scattered seed for the chickens, and collected eggs for Atty, but once I'd arranged the spices in alphabetical order and entirely refolded the linen closet, the days felt long, our seclusion stifling. Anxiety was compounded by all the guilt and grief which went unsaid.

My father took two papers, *The Pennsylvania Packet* and *The Royal Gazette*, and I pored over their pages trying to fuse the dueling perspectives—*The King is bent on our destruction / The Rebels will destroy us all.* I felt like a weathervane in a hurricane, and imagined a thousand grisly endings, the butt of a musket between my eyes, my flesh melting in flames. Any account of violence instilled fear of more. And it was apparently beyond me to read of suffering without imagining a worse what-next for myself. I looked up from the paper five times a minute to eye the driveway, alert for savage radicals or ruthless invaders—wondering truculently if my parents wouldn't have been wiser to keep the shutters shut.

When fear escalated to violent uncertainty—panic—I took unsteadily to the attic. The floor was so wonky we'd played pirates there as children, staggering on a listing ship. I began a secret index to monitor my dread levels, marking my anxiety like notes on a score, intrigued to see the most violently spiking crescendos didn't necessarily correspond with what I'd read. The grip of the worst fear was so strong I believed it must be reasonable, a premonition that would inevitably prove true.

I went to pester Betsy one afternoon, searching for escape from the endless nervy fretting.

"Don't you wish there were something we could do?"

"There's little any of us can do." She sighed, lifting the embroidery in her lap as a gentle exception. "We need to know our limits, Peggy."

To be told so was annoying.

"Why don't you make yourself a dress?" she suggested.

"There's nowhere to wear anything!"

"There will be, Peggy," she said, half-impatient, half-indulgent. "Make the dress and the occasion will come."

For all the tendency to rebellion, I liked doing what I was told, if I liked who was doing the telling.

I snagged an embroidered waistcoat of my father's and retreated to the attic to refashion it into a stomacher, using homespun for the skirt. I moved the fabric this way and that on the wide, warped floorboards, tilting the green-gold stitching to the low windows' light. I spent hours, all thoughts of radicals and retaliation forgotten, sketching and cutting and pleating, swinging between exhilaration—*this would be the best dress ever*—and dismay—*it was hideous, hopeless, and anyway I'd never get to wear it*—forging on until I felt inspired. Suddenly the dress was telling me where we were going, and if there's a better feeling, I'm still not sure I know it.

But as soon as it was done, worry weevilled back in. I was guilty of longing for something, anything, to break the tension.

Chapter Two

My father received the message in the middle of another miserable mutton lunch. Loss and worry had scored a pi sign between his eyes, which deepened as he read.

"It's William," he said. "Inviting himself to dinner."

My mother's head reared up. Uncle William had offended her at my brothers' funeral by asking if we children had not been inoculated, a question I could see had been tactless, but also felt fair professional interest, doctor that he was. He'd taken my face in his large, gentle hands to look for scarring, and I'd been comforted in the aftermath of the boys' dreadful suffering by the layer of protection he seemed to represent. Selfishly reassured too by his promise that Betsy and I should now have a degree of immunity from having been so exposed.

Father returned to the letter, his frown carved dark.

"He'll be bringing Neddy. Requests my help establishing our cousin in the legal profession after a spell in captivity—"

"Neddy was taken prisoner?" Betsy cried.

Father took another forkful.

"By which side?" I asked, as he swallowed interminably on.

"'Neddy,'" he read, finally, "'was prevailed upon by Johnny, Andrew, and Billy Allen to go with them to the British army, which he accordingly did, and was civilly received there by General Howe and the British officers. His companions soon after went to New York, and Neddy remained at Trenton. When the attack was made on the Hessians there, he was accordingly taken prisoner by our army'"—Father held that *"our"* as if between pincers—"'and carried with others to General Washington, who after examining his case and finding that he had taken no commission nor done any acts that showed him inimical, very kindly discharged him, and he is now with me.'"

"A reckless adventure," my mother said grimly, "ending in ignominy."

"It sounds so civilized!" I marveled.

Neddy's kind treatment by both sides was confusing. If allegiance mattered less than manners—decency more than winning—killing ought not to be an option. If all my dread was for a *game*, some kind of officer sport, that felt outrageous, but reassuring, too. Would war remain harmless for people like us? Was my anxiety destined to be melodramatic? I couldn't entirely hope so.

"He asks that I take Neddy on as my legal clerk, keep him from the temptation of further engagement, while William himself attends to battlefield casualties."

"A little company might be good, Mamma?" Betsy suggested.

"We ought at least to celebrate Neddy's safe return?" I tried.

"I can't look at him, the young man my sons should have become—"

Betsy and I exchanged a glance, and I appealed to my father for leadership.

"My dear," he tried, "I don't like it any more than you do. But perhaps our Christian duty—"

Mother cut that thread with tight lips. Church was persona non grata with her since the reverend said she shouldn't be attempting to summon the spirit of her dead children.

"A clerk would not go amiss." Father tried again. "I have neglected my practice since leaving the city, and something must pay for Atty, and our many bills."

Mother sighed in compliance. Betsy smiled in relief. I was giddy at the break in routine.

When I'd last seen him, Neddy had been navigating an awkward transition. Every inch of his skin harbored something hostile, an angry breakout or downy sprout of hair, nothing that would get a rasp from a razor. I had caught him in so close he was steaming the glass, sticking his tongue in his contorted cheek to get at some eruption. His wayward voice and scrawny body made it seem he'd been shackled to an unreliable animal.

* * *

He had come a long way. When he walked in the door, he made adolescence feel like enchantment. He was still Neddy, but he'd filled his frame and owned his height. And his skin—

"What were you thinking?" I asked, aware I'd been staring.

"Don't press him," Betsy said.

"I'm a soldier." He smiled. "I don't think. Do or die!"

William swatted him.

My uncle too was handsome and glamorous, crisscrossing the Atlantic six times already to learn from the best British physicians and treat the most interesting afflictions. He attended to aristocrats and attended Congress and had to have exacting standards. The room looked newly unkempt in our guests' presence. Family standards had lapsed. I spotted a cobweb on the gilt-framed reproduction of the King that reigned over the table with familial authority. Would William find the portrait offensive?

My father's greetings were more mannered than felt friendly. He shook hands as if assessing a threat. The brothers were near twins in features, with the same pale blue eyes and pink cheeks, but my uncle's skin was plump where Father's was thin. I watched sadly as Neddy tried, and failed, to warm up Mamma. She had been all our sanctuary lamp, but the light had died with the boys.

Neddy offered his arms to me and Betsy. "Heavens, cousins, how have you been?"

The reunion may be challenging, he seemed to say, *but nobody need get offended.*

William was rubbing my father's back, perhaps too heartily. "A government can rule only by the consent of the people—"

That sounded plausible, until I heard my father's mirthless laugh.

"I think you'll find all the better sort of people unite behind the King. Your cause, sir, is not legitimate—"

"There's honor in it you'll regret not recognizing, sir."

Why call each other "sir" once a sentence when contempt was clearly the message? Every assertion only fortified opposition. It was like watching bittle-battle wishing both players could win. Perhaps it was as it should be?

Two sides would always be needed—good sorts at each end pulling their weight—while everyone's happiness hung in the balance.

William's excitement had curdled into contempt. " . . . while the *British* threaten to make smallpox a weapon of war . . ."

I turned my head so fast I crooked my neck.

"They did it in the French and Indian War," William said, with something too like satisfaction. Did my uncle know what the disease did to people? He did!

Neddy shrugged apologetically. "Even if not intentional policy, Peggy, the British have herd immunity we colonies are nowhere near. It could be devastating. More dangerous than their navy—"

"The time for hedging bets is over, brother," Willliam said, taking the seat next to me and pulling my sketchbook onto his lap.

"May I?" he asked, his breath steadying as he flipped through my endless iterations of medieval figures. I found those lines soothing too.

"Who's this?" he asked.

"Joan of Arc," I said. "Convincing the Dauphin she could help him win."

"Very good," he smiled, handing the book back to me and raising his voice, "Now picture the British army being routed from another continent, closer to home—"

He winked, and I felt a guilty glow of benediction and conspiracy.

"William—" my father warned.

William ignored him.

"What did you make of the language of the Declaration, Peggy?"

I remembered my stomach tilting between elation at the rhetoric and fear of what consequences had been unleashed. I was further flustered by the proximity of Neddy, who was suddenly, inescapably, a *man*.

William was watching. "What say you, Peggy?"

I glanced at my father.

"What thinking reader could be unmoved?"

Lashing myself for sounding so mannered and bland, and showering sparks about Neddy, I splashed my face, hastily changed and raced back down for dinner, poking stray hairs back in place with a finger where there should have been pins. My mother's glance was a barbed dart. She and Betsy were pristine in muslin, backs rigid, while the soup was painstakingly ladled. Father confined conversation to Neddy's education, peppering him with questions about the relative merits of Princeton and King's College.

While I was grateful the sparring had stopped, wasting time on pleasantries felt rude to the universe, given we had only one evening with William and so much to learn. I wanted to hear about fashionable patients and extravagant afflictions and to marvel at all his pioneering new ways of doing no harm.

William spoke of how well Franklin had seemed on the crossing. My spoon splashed into my soup.

"Sorry—" I said to my mother, using my napkin to cover the stain.

"That grand incendiary," Father scoffed.

"Peggy used to dawdle in the passage by his printing shop in hopes of meeting him," Betsy said, returning the napkin to my lap.

"If I had, I'd have been too scared to speak—"

"You admire him?" Neddy asked.

I nodded. I was glad to be alive at the same time as him, but I couldn't say that. The only sounds were our creaking corsets and Father slurping soup.

"It's boring for the powerful if everyone they meet is cowed," William said. "What is it you admire, Peggy?"

That he can't look at a thing without thinking of ways to make it better? I didn't trust my thick tongue to get that out. I managed, "I like his writing—"

My uncle nodded politely. Neddy gave a slightly desperate grin. What I'd have said if I'd been ready was that he was so fizzing with creativity he didn't seem to worry about failure or waste one minute on doubt or deference. He could say the most brilliant thing one week and laugh about farts the next, which felt alien brave to me, still second-guessing every step. He liked himself, was what it seemed.

"When your time with such men comes, Peggy, listen. Keep your thoughts nimble and find the right time to pitch in. Never freeze, never fawn. And don't talk on and on, however fascinating you're being. Edward, you must take care your children don't become parochial. Peggy should travel at the earliest opportunity. Feel at ease with figures of consequence. You ought to take the family to London. Stay with me—"

"I don't believe now is the time for a sea journey, William."

"I'd love to go, though," I cried, before catching the set of my mother's mouth.

"So you shall," William said, refilling his wine glass and mine. "We're natural travelers in this family. Whatever happens between the mother country and the colonies, you'll always have the keys to both. Meanwhile, take comfort: Philadelphia is the one city in America all civilized Europeans know they need to see."

I liked that. Where it was at was where I wanted to be. And I loved America, its land and space; the freedom from persecution it had given our ancestors; the fresh chance it promised to expand all that people could be.

Still, Philadelphia had several impressive blocks. London had actual palaces, cathedrals! We colonies couldn't compete, not yet. I gave a quick genuflecting glance at the King.

Across the table, the brothers' jabs were getting sharper. My father was wagging a finger over his glass, preparing for sentencing, while William eyed him like a boil he would have liked to lance.

"Anything less than self-determination makes infants of us."

"What's childish, sir, is this temper tantrum rebellion—"

I wanted to believe the men were like wise and reverent chess players calculating many moves ahead, dueling politically to eliminate the real risk of conflict. As it was, I felt pinned in place while puppets bickered over me.

In a deferential, tentative voice Neddy addressed his plate, saying he'd seen there were fine, brave men on both sides, but while he would always feel the greatest respect for the King, reports from Lexington had fundamentally changed his thinking.

My father's eyes welled in question. I was beginning to worry about his health. Neddy took a deep breath and raised his head. He seemed to feel mine were the least difficult eyes to meet.

"Benedict Arnold's courage was indelible."

"General Arnold even you could not disdain," William said, almost affably. "Brave as they get. Fought for the King initially. Took a look at the evidence. Now an absolute Patriot. There's no shame in a thoughtful pivot, Edward. Not everyone's mind can be quick."

"His men would have done anything he said—" Neddy cut in quickly.

"A lot of dangerous nonsense—" Father harrumphed, but Neddy was forging on, lit with enthusiasm. He leaned toward me and Betsy, dropping his voice.

"When the fighting was done, he held a solemn ceremony. Each of his men signed their name to a vow he'd written—swearing they'd conduct themselves decently, soberly, obediently and expel any person guilty of behavior which might corrupt 'so great and glorious a cause . . .'"

It sounded as thrilling as a game we'd have played as children. He shrugged appealingly, and looked up at me from under thick brown lashes.

"Persuaded me," he murmured in his new, becoming rumble.

"I heard the rebels were savages in their way of killing—" father said.

William looked apoplectic. I felt a rising panic. My uncle lopped off limbs. He mustn't think us expendable. How could Father undermine what Neddy found inspiring, whatever the wrongs and rights? Betsy's polite agony, my mother's snide smile. The divide felt geological, a fault line running through us, chaos welling from the crack. Some instinct erupted. I threw my napkin back into my lap.

"But the conflict will end?" I cried. "It must! And when it does, all this"—I was now gesturing frantically, as if catching gas—"fuel spent fighting can push us forward. We'll progress, better than ever—"

I saw the set of my mother's mouth and returned my arms to my sides.

"I think we can all drink to that," Neddy said gamely. Slowly William and my father raised their glasses.

"Unusual, to find that one so intelligent should be as kind," William mused. "Aren't you lucky, Margaret, to have a child with a good head on her shoulders?"

It was an affront to talk to our bereaved mother of luck. There was a long sour silence in which I saw how irritating I had been, gabbing on rashly, relishing things I had no business to be.

Mamma stood to leave, and Betsy leaped up like a marionette beside her.

"Couldn't we stay, Father?" I tried. "Just a little longer. This once?"

"Women have no cause to concern themselves with politics," my mother said. "We must trust to those who know better."

Between the high feeling and the tight bodice, my breasts were brimming as I followed.

"I do trust them to know better, Mamma," I whispered urgently as we reached the small sitting room. "That's why it feels crucial to hear all they think—"

Betsy tried: "These things are beyond our power, Peggy. Willfully consuming news which puts one in a state of alarm might be thought morally wrong—"

"But what if it *were* in our power?"

"What if what were?" Betsy asked helplessly.

"Margaret Shippen, who do you think you are?"

My mother's contempt was so palpable, I felt slapped. I fled upstairs.

Betsy found me sobbing on my bed. She sat quietly with me until I finished with the ugly gulps and then brandished the familiar gold spoons with her funny, sommelier-like flourish. I pressed the cold metal to my eyes, and once the swelling felt it had subsided, raised my gaze for her approval.

"Better," Betsy said. "You'd never know. We only want to protect you, Peggy. Not all men have Uncle William and Neddy's patience for a girl of sixteen's ideas. Personally, I admire your stamina. I have heard enough about the Stamp Act and tea tax to last a lifetime."

I managed to go down to say goodbye to William. "I'm sorry—"

He waved that aside like chips on baize.

"Have you read Mr. Paine's 'Common Sense,' Peggy?"

I shook my head.

"High time. Have mine—"

I hugged my uncle hard and waved until he was out of sight, buffeted by all the high feeling and buffered too by a sense of expanding family.

Neddy wished me good night, murmuring with unnerving maturity how very good it was to be with us. As my mind scrambled in the pleasant precursor to sleep, I wondered if he might be my meant-to-be. Was marrying your cousin becoming a bit embarrassing? How questionable could it be if kings did it?

Chapter Three

After a year of so little conversation, Neddy was a godsend. Nothing I read in either paper was half as upsetting once it could be aired with him. My Dread Index dropped two octaves.

He proved a good legal clerk, with a knack for identifying cases involving interesting judgments which my father vaguely remembered but couldn't locate. He worked hard, too, around the farm, splitting logs and forking hay, shirtsleeves rolled, arms rapidly tanning and thick, chestnut hair shining in the sun.

Just as I thought I couldn't be better pleased with him, he flourished an invitation—and that afternoon changed everything.

Mrs. Cartwright was a childhood friend of Neddy's who had recently married an acquaintance of my father—a man, disconcertingly, twice her age. Betsy and I exchanged a reverent look of sympathy for her fate. Her note opened by trusting a resolution of the present conflict was in sight and closed in hopes we would lend our company to a small tea party.

"An occasion!" Betsy and I cheered in unison.

Atty helped me wash my hair and laid out the dress I'd made. I felt a pang for the whispering silks and taffetas we'd left in the city, but wearing domestic seemed the least controversial option. It was daunting, considering strangers' allegiances after so long in isolation. Worth it though, for the unaccustomed sense of purpose—the novel treat of somewhere to be! Plucking my eyebrows until my eyes were watering, I smarted to think I'd let anyone see them so unruly.

I met Betsy on the stairs.

"Do you think the Cartwrights incline more to the Patriot or the Loyalist side?"

"Hasn't it become bad manners to ask?"

My parents hadn't changed since breakfast.

"You're not coming, Mamma?"

"I'm not."

"Father?"

He shook his head. "Cartwright was hard to take before this marriage. Always on the make. He'll be intolerable now he's landed that girl—"

"Her and her ill-gotten gains," Mamma said.

"Oh?"

"Don't pester them with questions when you get there, Peggy. Remember your discretion."

I nodded but felt resistance rootling. This would be my first tea party since turning sixteen, and I wanted to feel free.

"Neddy can drive."

I smiled, excited at the idea of an unchaperoned adventure with him.

My mother's lips gave a little twist. "Your cousin should be equal to the responsibility, after his earlier heroics."

"I wish Mother wouldn't disparage him," I said to Betsy as we made for the carriage. "He could have been in a great deal of danger!"

"If she didn't believe Neddy capable of keeping us safe, she wouldn't let us go with him," Betsy said. "It's just her way."

"Well, I think it's a shame. He was brave. And to speak of Mr. Cartwright so harshly. What is a gentleman in trade to do but make money? That's surely what he's *for*. I don't see prejudice against the rich is better than any other bias. And we need a civilizing influence; my eyebrows were verging on feral. And Betsy, Father's beard!"

We were still giggling as Neddy drove us out into the lane.

Greeting us on the wide front step, the new Mrs. Cartwright looked bored and beautiful, cool, despite the September heat, in buttercup silk and a matching parasol. Immediately, the homespun felt misjudged.

She took my hand so lightly it was almost insulting.

"Did you make that yourself, Miss Shippen?" I felt my cheeks drenching red.

"Peggy's very clever with a needle," Neddy said. That felt a sorry tally of my skills, but I loved him for his loyalty.

"Since Neddy has been valiant, the least I can do is be useful."

Betsy shot me a warning look. I gave a slight headshake back, sure she was wrong to worry. Neddy's war story reflected too well on both sides to offend anybody.

"Don't you resent the way thrift's been elevated to some sort of patriotic gesture?" Mrs. Cartwright yawned.

I laughed awkwardly, a little shocked at her irreverence, but eager to meet her where she was. "Have you heard the ditty doing the rounds in Philadelphia? *Marry no man who'd wear London factory / No more ribbons wear, not in rich silks appear / Love your country much better than fine things—*"

"*—and grace your smooth locks with twine string!*" Betsy chimed in.

We laughed. Mrs. Cartwright smiled. "'Twine string'! As if."

"I hope you don't feel we're being self-righteous by wearing domestic fabric? Your own dress is beautiful—"

Mrs. Cartwright cocked her head and considered me languidly, as if I were an accessory she wouldn't mind trying, which I found fantastically flattering

The interior of the house was as perfectly groomed as our host. Liveried servants stood on hand to satisfy every little tyranny of taste.

Tea was laid on a stone terrace looking over the lake, where Mr. Cartwright was presiding proudly over translucent pink-and-white porcelain teacups soon steaming with fragrant Assam. There were sandwiches, the latest thing, with slivers of ham and cucumber, and a chocolate-and-berry cake. All the tiny niceties our beleaguered parents had found dispensable since leaving the city—ironed napkins, cake forks—in this household were holding strong. I smiled at Betsy. She looked perfectly calm and at home here. It would suit her, marrying into this order of glamour.

The table was set for one more, which allowed me to hope there might be a tantalizing bachelor brother, perhaps a wealthy reverend atoning for the family's ill-gotten riches, but the late arrival turned out to be a Mrs. Theodosia Provost. She was about twenty-six, with back-lit skin and the most beautifully cut gray linen dress. Meeting her all-seeing, warmly receiving eyes, I felt that absolute affinity one look between women can give.

It emerged her husband was a British captain serving in the Caribbean with whom she had five children and a house in New Jersey named the Hermitage—all of which sounded madly romantic to me.

"It is not a question of whether escalation is right, or necessary. It's a question of what is inevitable," Mr. Cartwright was saying. "If repressed, a younger energy will eventually say, 'Enough.'" He took a sip of tea. "Battle's not a bad thing, tests a man's mettle—"

"Isn't it possible a political solution could still diffuse the tension, without more violence?" Theodosia asked. "Galloway's pamphlets give me hope—"

"He won't be forgiven, whatever his earlier contributions," Cartwright said. "The radicals have the upper hand—"

"Are there examples in history of power changing hands without very long conflict?" I asked, feeling my skin flame at being so exposed but unable to resist the excitement of being in conversation.

"Always with the thinking, thinking, thinking," Betsy said, tapping her forehead. I felt embarrassed tears prick. It was too much feeling, not thinking, which undid me.

"That would take a coup," Theodosia answered me.

"And clemency from the new regime I think you'll find unlikely," Mr. Cartwright said.

"What about a comet so spectacular it would stun everyone into peace?" I wondered. "Superstition that was actually useful."

"There's a thought!" Neddy exclaimed cheerfully.

"The colonies have space enough—states enough now—to accommodate all persuasions," Theodosia encouraged.

"Could they set a date by which everyone has to choose their state? Solve it like musical chairs?" I asked, though I'd always found that game terribly tense.

"If a man's assets are threatened, if he's told to move against his will, sell up at unfavorable rates—" Mr. Cartwright shook his head. "You underestimate a propertied man's appetite for conflict."

"If it's an appetite, could it be checked?" I tried.

"With what incentive, Miss Shippen?"

"The greater good? Empathy?"

"Empathy's the last thing we need." Mr. Cartwright sat back expansively, spreading his legs. "The young are worryingly soft as it is. When you're defending against raids, it's not compassion that's wanted, it's more ammunition."

"Touché." His wife laughed.

My shock was too obvious. Betsy intervened with sandwiches.

As we walked through the gardens after tea, Theodosia fell into step. We were the same height, which I liked. And she was generous in letting me feel on the level.

"You don't agree?" she probed softly. "About war being the making of a man?"

"More like the end of him," I said stroppily. "I'm sorry, I know I sound facetious and naive, but they seemed to be *welcoming* violence in. Condoning it—"

"Her money's in munitions. Rumored to sell to both sides."

It hadn't occurred to me anyone could be so cynical. "Shouldn't there be laws against making money from war?"

"Tell that to every mercenary. I've always admired the Quakers," she said, walking on. "Principled pacifism."

"Is that an option if you're not altogether one? I like their silent congregation, but I don't think I could marry in. I couldn't do without music. And sitting out fighting without acting to stop it feels so pious it's almost belligerent."

"You'd welcome engagement?"

"Yes! If I had an outlet! I don't know what to do, beyond worrying from the periphery. There's nothing I can be, except a seamstress . . ."

She considered me. "An actress?"

"That always feels a euphemism for *mistress*, and a few gins from riddled on the street."

She smiled. "Women are considered players of economic consequence now, Miss Shippen. Where we shop, what for—"

"I do miss dressing for Philadelphia," I admitted.

"There's a store you should try when you're back. Joseph Stansbury. Tell him I sent you. He's good company, and a genius at cutting. He could do with a muse like you."

"I'll try him." I smiled, filing the name in my mind. "Thank you. But I'm not sure we have the sort of money I can make a war effort of spending—I'd like to do more."

"It's nice you'd think to try."

We took wide, grassy steps, perfectly trimmed and flanked by huge terra-cotta pots of begonias, down across the lawns.

"What would happen if a woman stood in front of every solider, insisting the enemy first kill her?"

"You've read your Aristophanes?" Theodosia asked.

"Yes!" I said, blushing. "What if the married ladies of England and America were to conspire together?"

"Men can't all be capable of rape—"

"They wouldn't dare!"

"For us to stage our answer to *Lysistrata*, it would take an extraordinary female leader. I have to hope this war will end faster than I can imagine a woman coming to wield sufficient influence."

"We've had such women before—"

"Have we?"

"Gwendolyn?"

"Legend has it—"

"Queen Elizabeth?" I tried, worrying it was excessively Royalist even to mention her. "You must miss your husband, so far away?"

Theodosia laughed. "Speaking of enforced abstinence? Between the French and Indian War and now this, we have lived very separate lives. I've been on my own since last year—trying to keep the New Jersey authorities from seizing our house by entertaining the Continental Army, while avoiding alienating Loyalists by hosting Tories too. It's a lot of maneuvering—"

"It sounds exciting!"

"It helps it's necessary." Theodosia smiled. "Five children and a husband out of the picture. But my mother pitches in, and we do enjoy it. I like the daily validation, the momentum to rising every morning."

We stopped to rest on a bench set back within a yew hedge and smiled at each other. She was the first older woman I'd wanted to be.

"What do you tell your children?" I asked. "Hard to insist it's wrong to fight or lie when war shows them constantly it is not? You must want to keep them forever too little to leave—" I thought of my brothers then, and it took a moment to be sure I would not cry. Always that frailty, when it was brave I wanted to be.

Theodosia frowned sweetly. "I try to help them see the decency in everybody, and to imagine what might have made a temperament become unpleasant. I try to show them an honest life, even though I'm currently playing all sides. I want them to see how to live and really be alive. I say all this as if we've got everything in hand, but there is no end to the mistakes I make, the constant course correcting. On the way here I was worrying I've been remiss not to teach them how to skin squirrels. All the courtesies I've drilled in, but not how to fix dinner in a pinch."

"It may come to trapping animals, but children will still need manners."

"To thank the rabbit for his meat?" We were giggling by then.

I loved the way Theodosia's hands animated her conversation, the line between her eyes which showed she was thinking. She gave me a feeling like relief that I could tell her anything. She was too self-deprecating, too thoughtful to be mistaken for shameless, but she had a very likable defiance, more freedom from boring underconfidence than anyone I'd met.

I sighed. "We should get back."

"You're right." Theodosia climbed to her feet.

"Don't become bitter, however bad it gets?" I suggested, as we took the stairs back toward Betsy and Neddy on the terrace. "That's one rule which can stick?"

"Yes." Theodosia smiled, touching my back as if sealing a deal. "Here's to never being bitter. Life hit us with what it will."

* * *

Waiting for the carriage to come around, Neddy bent his head to catch something Betsy said and in her answering glow, I saw with sudden certainty the two were in love.

What an idiot I was! Blinkered, and arrogant. All those times I'd seen him smile at something I'd said, stand as I came into the room, oblivious to the far greater attention he must have been giving Betsy.

And no hint from her that she was falling for him! That seemed a sad thing to say of sisters. It couldn't have happened if we'd still been in the city, sharing a bed.

But Betsy was steady. She would wait to say a thing until she was sure of it. She didn't need to take people's time trying on her every thought for size. Of course, Neddy would prefer her lovely, restful contentment. It took some rearranging of hopes though, and I was grateful for the faff and fluster of lost gloves and leave-taking to give me a moment to get over my dismay.

As Neddy helped my sister into the carriage, I smiled at them both, my head to one side. Betsy answered the question with a deep, sweet blush. Neddy grinned and took her hand to his lips. I felt a last little stab of hurt and loneliness, but seeing their happiness, told myself not to be feeble. Theodosia's example would be my armor now.

Still, I had a new factor to calculate in my Index: the risk of being a sad old spinster forever dependent on our parents. Betsy's impending departure made an urgent question of my own happy-ever-after.

Chapter Four

From there things moved at a precipitous pace. General Washington rallied twelve thousand men to intercept the British advance on Philadelphia before being outflanked, allowing General Howe to march his fifteen thousand troops into the city and take over all our beautiful government buildings at once. The Patriot Council evacuated to Lancaster, and the British drove home their victory with successes at Brandywine and Germantown.

My father folded the newspaper like an argument won, announcing we'd be returning to the city. Since there had been skirmishes along our intended route, we'd travel in convoy with the Cartwrights.

I said a mournful goodbye to my attic sanctuary, string section welling in my head as I trailed a finger over the windowsills and chairbacks; goodbye to my quilted bed, from which I looked into the dense green treetops; farewell to the flagstoned kitchen, where the light through the leaves at teatime made a dappled dance on the walls. I hugged each plump, fussing hen in turn, as dust motes whirled in the great God-rays slanting through the hatch in the barn. So long to the miraculous soft moss that carpeted my paths, to the infinite varieties of green, the rushing brook and staggered waterfall, the life teeming in the waterhole and all the woods' shady shelter from whatever horrors awaited in Philadelphia.

There was a festive tinge to our nerves as we assembled that September morning, comfort in being in company. Neddy, Betsy, Atty, and I were in one carriage, our parents in a new phaeton behind. For all my anxiety about what trouble we'd meet on the way and find on arrival, there was no resisting Neddy and Betsy in their bubble of love. Their joy was infectious, and I couldn't not smile in the face of it. It was one of those crisp early autumn days too, when the colors feel useful, they're so beautiful. It took effort not to remark on the splendor of every falling leaf.

Nearer to the city, the flow of traffic picked up, the roads coursing with carriages and families on foot trudging in both directions. I saw men missing limbs, others limping, and wagons charred from burning. The convoy came to a halt, and I glanced nervously at Neddy. He jumped down to assess the situation and returned with the relief that there was nothing worse than paperwork behind the wait.

The splendidly mustachioed face of Abraham Carlisle appeared through the carriage curtain. What a welcome friend to find manning the gate. The master craftsman responsible for much of the city's finest carpentry, Abraham tilted his chin and squinted at everything as if measuring dimensions with his mind. He had always been kind to me, building houses out of matchsticks to keep me happily distracted in Quaker meetings—adding every miniature timber with miraculous balance.

Abraham asked after our time in the country, and sizing up Betsy's romance with a glance, gave a smiling salute to Neddy before nodding to the long line stretching behind us and cheerfully waving us through.

Redcoats were everywhere, marching in well-dressed formation on the green, patrolling on gleaming horses. There was reassurance in all the order—and comfort in no visible resistance. That scarlet uniform had a trick of making fighting feel unthinkable—beneath it—an impression compounded by the weird ease with which the British had taken the city—as if the enemy had simply immaterialized.

Every block we passed was layered with memories, the burial ground where we'd laid my brothers, the beauty of Carpenter's Hall and the State House, our market with its bantering traders and gleaming banks of freshly caught fish, the pretty simplicity of the Friend's Meeting House and St. Peter's, and, at last, our lovely brick house on Fourth Street between Walnut and Spruce.

As we spilled inside to find everything looking exactly, thankfully, as we'd left it, my father's forehead augured well. Dread Index low.

The morning after our return, as we were moving Betsy into our brothers' old room, a concession to her elevated status my mother now felt able to make, we received a first invitation from British headquarters: thick engraved cards promising music and dancing. My father worried it might not be wise to fraternize with the occupying forces, the war not being officially decided. I asked if there wasn't a risk we'd endanger ourselves by declining, given we were now under their rule?

"Besides," Betsy said happily. "Neddy will be with us."

My mother warned me there was danger in moving to music, with soldiers who'd been drinking, and it would be particularly easy for me to get a name.

Was that fair? I'd hardly been in the presence of men.

Neddy said kindly, "It is shocking how quickly a malicious story gets hold. Soldiers are terrible gossips—"

I said I'd be careful, though the threat felt sillier than others we'd weathered.

Our dresses had been stuck in locked closets while we were gone, so there was a lot of wafting at windows and spritzing with lavender water before we were ready to leave. I still smelled mothballs when I moved, but I was too excited to be back in satin to let that dent the fun.

The party was only four blocks away, but we took the phaeton as it wouldn't do to dirty our shoes. Climbing the thickly carpeted stairs of the Masters-Penn House, flanked by my father, smooth shaven again and taking tentative pleasure in the occasion, I was happy and proud that his bet on the British, and the timing of our return, had apparently been proved so wise.

We were welcomed by a plummy and ruddy General Howe and suave Henry Clinton—names so big in the papers it was thrilling to see them real men.

The rooms were richly lit and hung with crimson paper edged with gold. I glimpsed a Florentine triptych hung to one side, and on the other, a daring depiction of San Sebastian.

Surrounded by the languid accents of expensively educated officers, the gold braid of epaulettes and silver hilts of swords gleaming in the candlelight, every detail was designed to signal our privilege in being present, and ensure, perfectly politely, that every guest knew exactly where their loyalties should lie.

A handsome servant in General Howe's livery, his features so perfectly sculpted they looked carved, lids discreetly lowered, offered coupes of champagne from a silver tray, while footmen gently steered the guests toward the terrace. Torches burned brightly from sconces on the brick wall, and roses were clustered in crystal on tall tables, their scent making a magical confection of the air. In the garden below, a pond was covered in floating candles and late-season water lilies, which looked to have been placed there in flower that day. A lantern-lit path ran from the shimmering pond through formal gardens to a hedge maze beyond.

We were embraced by Abraham Carlisle and his wife while trading stories of our friends and neighbors. Abraham assured me Mrs. Galloway was safe and well, her husband back from New York, newly appointed superintendent of police and ports by General Howe.

I was looking in every officer's face for a feeling of recognition, some glorious chord of fate announcing the man meant for me. The fact I was prepared to meet every pair of eyes which chanced across me quickly made me a magnet. Men flocked to our side, the boldest murmuring with their eyes the things they'd do if they could. I felt the interest I excited, and I liked it.

I told myself to stop smiling so brazenly. Perhaps it was true I had a tendency to abandon. Temptation was not impossible to imagine. If I stayed out of the darker parts of the garden, I couldn't be in danger of more than dancing though, however wanton the music might make me feel. These men were officers, overseen by their superiors, and every respectable family in the city present. I was my parents' daughter, and I would behave.

I was determined to savor every detail though. Rural seclusion had made me grateful, whatever else. The stirring orchestra. Faces animated by candlelight and anticipation. Cold glasses beaded with condensation. After all the mead and muddy reds in the country, the wine was fine and crisp, in ever-replenishing supply.

To be dancing, without fear, passed hand to hand between endless officers, was the biggest luxury and dizzy, sweet relief. Such a celebration must mean peace.

"When did you become so fun?" Neddy asked.

"When I became happy, I think?"

"You are casting a wide spell, Peggy. That last fellow you left standing looked abject!"

I danced until I was giddy, damp tendrils escaping the hair pins at the back of my neck.

As I cooled off on the balcony, a figure emerged through the parting crowd of scarlet. Lean legs in long boots, a tapered waist, great shoulders, and finely chiseled features. I felt like champagne when his eyes met mine.

He introduced himself as Captain John André, taking my hand and bowing, looking teasingly up at me along the length of my outstretched arm. I was warm and still a little breathless from the cotillion.

His cool, dry lips brushed my skin, his eyes scanned mine, and for a fraction of a second it was as if all thought were on pause. Then sound rushed in, the world moved forward, and I found I was full-force smitten. It was everything I'd feared and everything I wanted to happen.

"You're becoming quite a star, Miss Shippen."

"That was an impressive entrance yourself," I said, idiotically.

"May I?" He led me back to the dance floor, and as the rush of my butterflies subsided, I found he danced exquisitely, moved like nobody else alive.

"Why do I feel we've met?" he asked. "It's not possible I'd have forgotten?"

"Perhaps I remind you of someone else," I said.

"I can't think of a reply which you wouldn't dismiss as flattery."

André had a low, even, cultured voice with no discernible accent. That is, you knew at once he'd been educated, but there was nothing condescending about him, no class or regional notes, only the lightly worn influence of generations of good taste. I felt a headrush of destiny and tried to rationalize. There was a fascination with the uniform, and to find a man of action as sensitive and intelligent and charming as André, was bound to have an impact. However much I wished there were no war, I couldn't be sorry there were soldiers.

I must not let my fear of being the spinster sister make me fall for the first plausible man.

But he was so much more than plausible!

"The waterlilies are pretty," I said as we danced past them. The furthest thing from wit. He undid me.

"Aren't they? Poor things."

"Are we to pity the lily, Captain?"

"They might have lived twenty years left in their pond in peace—"

"Oh. That is sad—"

"And yet, would you have such beauty living in obscurity, before declining unseen? Life is short and full of cruelty. I want beauty where it can be seen, Miss Shippen, and where it can share its scent and movement. I choose full bloom."

"Though it means death—"

"Perhaps a plant is expendable, even a very pretty one, when winning hearts and minds."

"Is our opinion so important, Captain André?

"Miss Shippen. Your good opinion might hasten the end of hostilities."

"Mine?"

"And your city's—"

I laughed. When his eyes were on me, I felt liquid, at once invincible and limp in his grip. I couldn't take my eyes off his lips.

"Have you found comfortable lodgings in the city?"

"I am Benjamin Franklin's tenant."

"Are you really? It must be so inspiring to live among his things—"

He dropped his face alongside mine, gave a fleeting glance at his commanding officers, and admitted, "It is—"

When Neddy cut in, for decency probably, André looked as if he considered protesting before dropping his head in regret and elegantly conceding defeat. Neddy moved me with his cheerful, slightly clumsy command across the dance floor. He laughed to see me struck.

"Shall I tell you everything I know about him?" Neddy teased, and I could only nod dumbly as he turned me.

"Well, he's fluent in multiple languages. He's an artist. Paints and draws beautifully, I'm told. He is a prolific writer. An officer on a rapid ascent and called the most handsome man in America."

I finally found my voice. "I haven't met the man to contradict that."

He laughed. "Now, it's only fair to mention that there are also rumors of a thwarted love story in England. A beauty who dismissed him, but to whom he remains devoted."

I was too far gone to find a tragic entanglement anything other than enticing. It was hardly as if a man like that should be free.

We went to sit with Betsy and Father, who had been joined by May Chew, a girl I'd known since childhood. Her father had given shelter to British forces during the recent battle of Germantown and the house had been heavily shelled as a result—winning her a lavish supply of gallantry from the officers. I felt a base stab of jealousy. She was perfection in inky blue, with a sapphire big enough to land a prince at her clavicle. Although grateful for the ballast of knowing her family, I couldn't help feeling I'd sink in anyone's eyes beside her. We chattered animatedly, self-consciously about the party while I willed André to return.

Lord Rawdon was introduced. He was tall, smooth, attractive in that aristocratic way, a hint of cruelty in his well-shaped lips. I was relieved to see him commandeer May's attention.

I noticed the glamour of the room was now more relaxed, the service a little less prompt. Officers were draped over chairs. Dawn wouldn't be long. A servant lit a cigar for Rawdon, and he blew the smoke sideways from his face, keeping his eyes on May, left hand between his tightly crossed thighs.

Suddenly I felt André's presence at my back like heat. The tiny hairs on my nape stood to attention and blood rushed to my face. *For God's sake, Peggy*, I scolded myself, *activate some restraint*. But my body refused to obey; everything in me was glimmering.

"You fit in very quickly, you Redcoats," I told him, half turning. "You've made the city your own."

"We have an old affinity," he answered, "the British and Philadelphia."

"We're one people," General Howe said, arriving at our side with Clinton, and André instinctively straightened his back.

"Sir. Have you met Miss Shippen?"

"On arrival," Howe said, bowing slightly at me, though his eyes didn't leave Clinton's for long.

"The Crown's direct deputy in the colonies," André explained.

"Thank you for coming," I said stupidly.

"Couldn't consign you to societal breakdown." Rawdon yawned wolfishly. "No fuel, no candlelight, a cold winter ahead."

"Perish the thought," Clinton said dryly.

May, sensibly, said nothing and smiled. She really was divine looking. If I had that face, I would have stuck to smiling myself.

"To order being restored—" André raised his glass.

"To peace," I said, and our glasses chinked. I felt that at any moment my arm might make a violent start, there was so much electricity in me, and I kept my full coup close, the bubbles tickling my chin.

Howe was laughing with the Lorings, his eyes only on the wife. Clinton surveyed him and the scene, his constantly moving eyes and mind assessing susceptibilities his smile suggested only he could see. He guarded himself so intently I had the sense there was no territory, even in conversation, he'd be willing to concede. It was intimidating, his complete lack of interest in me. Watching him, I was embarrassed to find I'd raised an empty glass to my lips.

"More champagne?" Clinton asked me, eyes like a blade as he summoned a server with a casual click of his manicured fingers.

I raised my refilled glass. "To your recent successes, General."

He inclined his head, unimpressed and intent on monitoring the room. His skin was evenly tanned and unusually flawless. André was engrossed in talking to May, so after an awkward silence I persevered.

"How did you learn what to do? To take command in a foreign land?"

"Royal military academy. Maps. Most things worth knowing have now been printed, even in this city."

I wanted to tell him I'd rather hear it from him. The only military history I'd ever read confounded me. Why the excess of indigestible details? No one could accidentally be that uninteresting. I suspected deliberate obfuscation, priests using Latin to keep congregations at bay.

"Do you read Latin and Greek, Miss Shippen?"

"Only a little, though my father was generous with my education."

"We don't need any more Colonials reading about Rome," Rawdon drawled.

"I think any ambition excited by learning about a republic would be checked by the fate of that experiment," Howe quipped.

Clinton refilled my glass again. The hand a lash from mine had probably been as close in turn to the King's. I glanced at the signet ring—one of those oddly elongated English lions—and was disconcerted to find his cool grey eyes again waiting for mine. I smiled to apologize for staring and Clinton dismissively turned to Rawdon.

The pair began a conversation about the function of government, a subject that, between the champagne and the hour, was beyond me. I wondered if the citizen of a republic would still be considered a government subject, and if I might be drunk. Noticing me looking foolishly for an opportunity to weigh in, Clinton asked archly what the function was of Miss Shippen.

"Miss Shippen's function is decorative," Rawdon asserted.

The group laughed. I was a little flattered, but more humiliated it was obvious I had nothing to contribute. I couldn't hope to, not without the handle on history this set had. My father soon came to gather us home, merrier and more relaxed than I'd seen him in years.

André looked at me intently.

"Until the next occasion. I hope we'll talk more."

In the carriage back, I was glad of the predawn darkness. Minute to minute, I was beaming as I thought of André's smiling lips, cringing over what I'd said, unbelievably excited to have met him, and terrified he'd be taken by war or the virus or May Chew and I'd never get to see him again.

I lay in bed until late morning with a copy of Herodotus open and unread on my lap, nursing the little flame that meeting him had lit.

Chapter Five

THERE WAS NO LINGERING IN BLISSFUL REPLAYS OF MOMENTS WITH André though, not when he was so far from mine. I was spurred from bed the following morning by the worlds I needed to know. I had Hume propped on the shelf above the pitcher as I washed my face, Paine on the chair beside me as I put on my shoes, and a pile of books by the bed, mostly making me feel a fraud for not finishing them.

At lunch I gabbled happily about the party, trying to capture the extravagance for my mother.

My father rubbed my hand. "It's lovely to hear your descriptions."

My mother stood abruptly. "If we are to have you married this season, you'll need new dresses. I gather from Mrs. Frankie you face stiff competition. I'll see about a fitting. Half a dozen should do it."

"Thank you, Mamma!" That was generous, though I was hurt by the need for haste and unnerved her dependable informant sounded so unsympathetic to me.

"Oh, but could I try the dressmaker Theodosia Provost recommended, if he's not more expensive?"

"My dressmaker is no longer good enough for you?"

My father reached for her. "My dear—"

"No, never mind. She'll do as she likes."

She left the room. There were more of these occasions when she lashed out—telling me there were no more candles, when I knew that not to be true. Swearing she'd summoned me to lunch but I'd been too busy in my books, when she had not.

I saw in my father a dim gleam of recognition that in the immeasurable extent of her loss, something unhealthy had got in. He followed after her, and after five minutes of sharp pitch and soothing rumble behind the door, he returned to tell me I must be a better daughter and pour on more love before retreating abruptly to his library.

For a long time after my brothers died, I'd wake with senseless urgency, as if to a sudden summons that they needed me, and cry with fresh loss that they were gone. Seven years on, some days I'd forget for a second. And then I'd remember, and feel the weight all over again, the horror and the loss. It saddened me, the thought I'd keep losing them week after week by further degrees, and I reached for little details, the dimples on James's knuckles, the whorl in Edward's hair, as if I could keep them snug at my hip as I had when I'd lugged them around the house. Seeing their room transformed for Betsy, I realized I couldn't any longer capture the sound of their laughs. I decided I'd take the last of our fall flowers to their grave on my way to the dressmaker.

I walked briskly, hood pulled low, relishing the freedom of being out, alone, on city streets.

My arrival sent a crow cawing from the gnarled yew.

The curved headstones had taken to tilting inward, as if the boys' small shoulders were still bent over the same book. I sat, hands splayed in the soft grass that tucked them in. My parents' impossible double blow inscribed in a soft, sloping font.

I set the asters in place and stood up, grateful to inhale the clean breeze off the river and feel the sun on my face.

"Hello, Peggy."

It was the English accent of Esther Reed, a woman a little older than me, with a neat figure and features, married to a man my father knew from the Assembly. Her eyes were alert in their bony sockets.

"How are you and Mr. Reed?"

"General Washington has recently requested my husband serve at his aide de camp."

"What a great honor!"

"He declined several times, feeling far from fit for it, but the commander did insist."

"You must be very proud, Esther. Will you join him when you can?"

"I have affairs to concern me here—"

"I hope all is as it should be?"

"Except for being all wrong?"

"I meant only with your house—"

"I'm more concerned with the alien invaders than with domestic comforts, Peggy."

It felt we were moving rapidly through a hazardous maze. It was unsettling, the feeling of threat, when her manner oozed intimacy.

I tried to be sympathetic. Everyone was contending with such a lot.

"I was sorry to hear about the horrors of Brandywine. Washington's loss of a thousand men—an unthinkable number. You must worry—"

"The King lost five hundred—"

"Yes. Terrible. All round. I was only thinking of your worry for Mr. Reed. He must have seen awful casualties. All those poor families—"

"Their proud sacrifice? Think of Deborah and Judith and Esther! The mother of the Maccabees, giving up her sons to die before her eyes!"

I felt my smile become a little alarmed.

"Well, I hope Mr. Reed himself remains safe and well—"

"It is his privilege to avenge our dead countrymen. Very much so," she said, watching me with unattractive intensity. "Indeed, he's in excellent spirits. Very high on the triumph at Saratoga. Horatio Gates and Benedict Arnold trounced the Loyalists there, and the much-touted General Burgoyne was forced into a most humiliating surrender. The British will realize seizing this city did not bring an end to their troubles, and the French have now seen the Patriots can win—"

My heart sank at the idea of the conflict expanding.

"Will the French really risk provoking the English, so soon after finally finishing the Seven Years' War?"

"They've been throwing their weight behind these United States for some time," she said. "Plausible deniability as yet, but you'll see. Keep your eye on reports of New York."

"I will."

I felt as tired as she seemed jubilant. The idea seven years wasn't enough for the French, when two years of this anxiety was already, surely too long.

The clock struck the hour.

"I should go," I said. "Dressmaking appointment."

"We must renounce excessive ornament, Peggy. This is no time for vanity."

I was irritated now but gave a noncommittal smile.

"The weakness of our constitution," Esther said, "and prevailing opinion might stop us from marching for glory, but I would throw myself into the flames rather than submit to the disgrace of humiliation before the enemy—"

"Let's hope it doesn't come to that—"

"I am considering a number of ideas, Peggy, useful schemes for ladies who wish to be of service and preserve their virtue."

"Excellent, Esther," I said, already moving rapidly away, "count me in."

Joseph Stansbury's store was a converted carriage house, brick with white trim. His initials were elegantly carved in white oak, the discreet sign swinging from a wrought iron brace. A bell rang softly as I stepped in and closed the door behind me. The small store was a fantasy of fashion: polished wide-plank floors, the prettiest ceiling moldings, hats on stands at rakish angles, and mannequins constructed from white oak and taut beige linen sporting fabulous corsets. The store's double-height back wall was fitted with cubbies containing bolts of fabric in every conceivable weave and color, with a ladder on wheels attached. My Index was elevated after the encounter with Esther, and that shop felt a sanctuary.

Stansbury himself was a spry and appealing figure in his forties, in beautifully tailored shirtsleeves, measuring tape about his neck, and breeches cut a shade tighter than felt respectable. He greeted me with elegant flair, and settled me with a cup of coffee while he finished attending to a customer.

A much younger man, lean and dark, was perched on a high stool, wearing a dummy jacket marked with pins and penciled darts. He gave me a disinterested once-over before returning his attention to a slim volume of poetry, one hand on an empty coffee cup, his brow creased by an attractive frown. I'd never met a more daunting pair.

Nerves were making my cup rattle audibly in its saucer, and I was forced to set it down without risking a sip.

Stansbury sealed the lady's purchases in crisp brown paper, tied with lilac, before flourishing the blunt edge of gold scissors to curl the ribbon tips into bouncing coils and guiding her from the store with a hand hovering over her back.

I introduced myself and explained Mrs. Provost had recommended him.

The dark man's attention shot up a notch at mention of Theodosia, and Stansbury introduced him as Minister Jonathan Odell, a vicar, and poet, from Princeton.

Stansbury sent me behind the screen to strip to my shift and measured me in a reverie of efficiency while mining me for information. Within seconds he'd established my father's profession, the exact location of our houses, and the friendship with the Cartwrights which brought Theodosia into my life. He scribbled down numbers and appraised me without any suggestion of impertinence or desire. "Perhaps a narrower profile to the skirt?"

"Whatever you think," I said. "I'm very happy to trust you."

"Subtle expense is the effect du jour. Self-denial must be seen to be believed in this era. What a time—"

He gave a brisk shooing motion as if he could whiff all conflict gone.

"Your family were spared, I hope, the more persecuting energies which preceded the British arrival?"

"We left town—"

"Half the city did," he said airily.

"The half who could," Odell said from outside the screen.

I looked at Stansbury. "You were not so lucky?"

"Odie and I endured a brief imprisonment."

"That must have been very frightening." It felt impolite to ask on what charge.

"We refused to take the loyalty oath," he explained, dropping his voice.

"The idea of being coerced into saying anything is intolerable—"

"I'm not sure I believe it's a hill worth dying on a second time." He smiled, but his eyes gave a hint of what he'd weathered.

"Our ancestors escaped England to avoid government force," I said, outraged on his behalf. "Belief is a matter of conscience, not coercion. That freedom is what the colonies are for. To dictate what another mind thinks or speaks, on pain of imprisonment—"

"Or worse—"

"I can't fathom it. The British surely have put a stop to it?"

"If the British fear their presence hasn't quenched the rebel threat, they may exact oaths of their own. And I'm afraid the attempted assassination of Washington in New York, and the very presence of occupying forces, will only encourage extremists of every stripe. There are those longing to hunt dissidents like game on both sides. It's all a long way from over."

He left me dressing with shaking fingers, while I heard the well-oiled wheels of the library ladder sliding back and forth. As I emerged, he pulled a length of rose pink from its roll with a rumble and held it up to my face.

"Meanwhile, we must do our part—"

I looked at him for guidance, but he lifted my chin to the light, and the right.

"An angel from every angle, but that," he said, resting the back of his hand on my left cheek, "is irresistable. You know the Chews too?"

"It was Miss Chew's blue that made me realize I need you."

Odell looked up in brief amusement, which felt a small victory. Stansbury promised to give me a dress to relegate anything she wore to irrelevance, whisking away the pink and switching it for green, then cream, then heather. He was strong, for all he was small. With a shrug from Odell, the six dresses were settled.

Stansbury's gold scissors sheered through the cloth with pleasing ease. He billowed and folded the fabric; deftly bundled and cut matching thread for the sleeves, stomacher, and white underlining; and again securing the minister's sardonic approval for each choice, picked out trimming and lace for the necklines and cuffs.

"It seems an awful lot—"

"Reason not the need, or if you must, consider it that your custom is helping war victims," Odell said, nodding at Stansbury. "Little income with half the city missing. None at all in prison—"

"No, although not that much profit in law lately, if you're avoiding defending plaintiffs of either side—"

"Your father is investing in your future security—and his own reputation for invincibility."

"He is considered one of our most moderate countrymen," Odell confirmed.

"What if I don't deliver the necessary return?"

"In these?" Stansbury gestured at the fabric, as if I'd insulted him. He was teasing, which was new to me. He smiled. "You could be married nine times within the week, Miss Shippen. Certainly, this season—"

"You might like to sit out a round until the victor's decided," Odell advised.

My stomach lifted on another swell of fear and impatience. Stansbury heard my intake of breath.

"The British have it," he affirmed, with reassuring conviction. "Power the world has never seen."

"And the pink will look good whether you're dancing with scarlet or blue," Odell added.

"The whole red/blue business makes it feel like some sort of staged entertainment, or tournament," I said.

"Tournaments do end in death," Odell observed.

"To a purely ornamental tournament then, Odie," Stansbury said stubbornly. "And a worthy winner for Miss Shippen."

Chapter Six

Theodosia was in town seeking the British administration's assistance, and we met at Stansbury's, her "home from home," for tea while I had my next fitting.

She revealed she was in the city for help locating her husband, who appeared to have gone missing in the Caribbean.

My hand flew involuntarily to my mouth.

"I'm so sorry!"

"We've lived independent lives a long time," Theodosia reminded me kindly, as if I were naive to think being without him the worst thing.

"What do you think happened?"

"The virus, pirates, enemy fire, his own soldiers' revolt, a shipwreck, or slave rebellion . . ." She thew up her hands at the panoramic hazards. "Though I tend to think if anything very dramatic had happened, someone would have shared the story."

"He may yet be safe and well then? A letter might be lost in transit—"

"Or he could be holed up with a beautiful Creole riding out the war—"

"Leaving you and the children?"

"I think he knows I'm capable of holding the fort on my own."

I loved the courage and lack of posturing in that.

"Perhaps your competence put him to shame?" Stansbury asked.

"He didn't seem the sort of man to find neediness more attractive than self-reliance, not when we married. But it's true too I've changed. I did sometimes worry how we'd reintegrate after all this time."

"Does the not knowing make you more vulnerable to New Jersey authorities, or less? Now it's not clear you have a husband working for their enemy?"

"I'm hopeful my friendships within the Continental Army will defend me from Patriot rage. I'm a little more concerned about British reprisals, now it appears I don't have a husband active on their account. Hence coming here to pay my respects to Clinton. But tell me about you, Peggy Shippen, have you met anyone special? Word of your dances with Captain André reached me in New Jersey—"

I should have guessed they'd know each other too. I felt myself grow red.

"Oh, there are so many impressive officers." I abandoned the attempt at nonchalance. "But yes."

"He does cut a notably fine figure," she said.

"Ravishing," Odell confirmed.

"If your dancing partner is the social director of the British army," Stansbury said, "this dress must slay from every angle. There's nobody meets him doesn't love him. It's quite extraordinary. Even Odie hasn't a snide word."

"He's admired from both sides," Theodosia said. Odell laughed, and she shot him a scolding look.

"Is that his official role, social director?" I asked.

"He is the perfect embodiment of an English gentleman—" Stansbury reflected.

"Not excessively English though, thank God," Odell said. "Fair amount of French."

"Yes, but does that mean it's his job to dance with me?"

"Not four times in one evening!" Theodosia laughed, and I blushed again.

"Your intelligence is impressive," Stansbury remarked archly, and she raised her cup to his.

"Is it true the French are now officially supporting the Patriots?" I asked.

"It's not that simple," Theodosia said.

Would anything about this war ever be?

"But you're right about André. Rare to find such a natural manner so close to power."

"People close to power need charm to stay there," Odell said.

Stansbury raised an eyebrow. "Then I think we need to adjust this cut . . ."

"What about Rawdon for you, Peggy?" Odell asked. "He's attractive, and rich."

I made a face. "Isn't he a bit lascivious? For all his reassurances the British army are here to defend us, something in his combination of lust and disdain felt dangerous. Reminded me a little of Aaron Burr at fifteen. Impeccable manners with mothers, but you wouldn't want to be left alone with him."

Theodosia laughed. "If we're entertaining thoughts of the other shore, what about Hamilton for you? He's as good-looking as André, fast on the rise, and as widely liked—"

I felt the old hot confusion, an instinctive, stubborn refusal to admit the outcome was still in contention. I wanted this conversation settled, the war in all our rear view.

"Losing the battles they have, can they really rebound?"

"We'll see if Washington survives his leadership challenge. They're deviled by infighting now," Theodosia said. "And he'd already nearly lost Hamilton for want of promotion—"

We looked at her alertly. She shrugged.

"They all need to let off steam. Occasional ranting and railing, a bit of weeping, all par for the course. But if you listen, even when they're in their cups, you learn something."

"Have you met Washington?" I asked.

"He uses my house as his base in the area."

"He's not a drinker?"

"No, Odie. More a hot chocolate man. Gets jolly on one Madeira. Unlike Hamilton and Lafayette, who can really dig in." She shook her head, smiling at the memories, and I felt my world expanding in happy admiration.

"Franklin?"

"Not yet."

"How's that?" Stansbury said, taking my hand and spinning me from him.

"Fit for a Philadelphia duchess," Odell declared, with faintly scathing charm.

Theo smiled. "The duchess of Pennsylvania. I like that for you."

"Have I been sounding pretentious, taking on airs?"

"Never," Stansbury said affectionately. He was fast becoming my fairy godfather. "Something in your bearing. The point is there's no one to whom you couldn't be introduced."

"And no end to the good she wouldn't do," Odell said, winking at Theo, and unnerving me again with the loaded dice he threw.

It was wonderful to have the promise of Theodosia's company at the next dance. For all the cladding Stansbury's skill lent me, I found entering parties excruciating. The sudden pressure to win a man and marry quickly meant the girls I'd been raised with were thrown into relief as rivals. If a room erupted in laughter as I arrived, I was convinced I was the laughter's target. The sweeping assessment of older women, hostile mothers of other daughters, and the omnipresent and terminally unimpressed friend of my mother's, Mrs. Frankie, left me riddled with doubts about what unsuspected misstep I'd made in my dress.

I had a typically literal nightmare about looking down to find I'd arrived in shoes with a collapsed sole, the heels worn bare of leather. There were so many routes to what felt like unrecoverable embarrassment: a scuffed toe or unstitched hem, a recognizable refashioning an old outfit, arriving in a dress which resembled another's enough to encourage uncomfortable comparisons. Too much variety betrayed vanity and extravagance. Too little suggested limited means, which might taint the family name—and then there were infinite calamities to be had with hair.

I went in for one vertiginous creation I regretted before the party even started. The city was in the grip of an insane inflationary experiment with hair, piles of powdered curls getting higher all the time. It wasn't unusual to see women with their heads sticking out of carriages their wigs wouldn't fit in. Making the concoctions strong enough to survive an entire evening meant welding them together with an itchy, gluey brew of gum arabic, animal fat, and flour. The whiff had to be overcome by strong perfume, which meant a headache, as well as pain in the neck from the weight. And inevitably, after any very vigorous dancing, the pile would topple or tilt.

"Theodosia's parties at the Hermitage are legendary," André said, as we shared an ice together later that evening. "She has a reliable formula: good music, wine and food, and complete freedom from conversational restraint."

"That sounds liberating. Venturing any opinion feels it might spring a trap lately."

"Not with me, I hope, and certainly not with her. There's no end to the license in a good game of Crambo."

"What's that?"

"A game. One player begins—"

"There's no point explaining. I can't even remember the rules of whist one Christmas to the next—"

"You'd soon learn by playing. It starts simply," Theodosia said. "But once everyone is drinking and riffing, the virtuosos emerge, improvising ingenious satirical couplets about public figures."

"In rhyme?" I said, aghast.

Theo laughed. "I'm the first to admit I have no gift for it, but we have a lot of fun trying. A distraction from whatever unpleasant realities might be waiting the next day. And it can be exhilarating to listen, when the best get underway. Odie, you can imagine, raps out scandal—"

André dropped his chin and voice, so that I felt his breath on my neck, and I discreetly directed my gaze to Lord Howe as he recited:

Sir William, he, snug as flea,
Lay all this time a-snoring
Nor dreamed of harm, as he lay warm
In bed with Mrs.—

His voice dropped to mouth "*Loring*"

I laughed, happily scandalized, glancing at Howe and his married mistress.

André was distracted by the arrival of a posse of young women fanning out from the top of the stairs.

"Forgive me," André said as he excused himself to greet them. "Theodosia, come back tomorrow morning. I'll be sure Clinton sees what can be done about locating your errant husband and securing that nice house of yours." He dropped his voice in an aside for me, "We should all spend an evening at the

Hermitage together some time." I glowed at the idea of a future plan involving the three of us.

"You must excuse me, Miss Shippen," he murmured, *sotto voce*, releasing my hand reluctantly. "You know I'm obliged not to leave ill will in the British Army's wake."

"For King and country." Theo smiled as we watched him captivate the new arrivals. "He plays his part well, but it's a waste of his talents. Have you seen one of his plays?"

"Not yet."

"He's the creative intelligence behind every performance, writing scripts, painting sets, engineering special effects, deflecting praise so likably he's a one-man masterclass in appealing genius . . . Let's take a turn around the room," she suggested, laughing. I'd been gawking at him again.

"I suppose she comes with an enormous dowry?" I said of the elegant young woman in his arms.

"I'm afraid so," Theodosia said. "But I see the way André looks at you. You don't need to fear being replaced as favorite, not as long as the British hold the city."

Again, I felt dismay that willing it over wasn't making it so.

"How can war be both boring and horrifying? I wouldn't have thought it possible—"

"And yet the bad news goes on and on."

I described the conversation with Esther which had depressed and unnerved me.

"I do wonder what schemes she has in mind for women wanting a war effort."

"She sounds unhinged! Stay well away, I say."

"How is it, when everything about war ought to be unacceptable, questionable on every possible level, the minute we're in it, there's this weird pressure to submit? To defer to the men who started it and trust they'll know when to stop? The consensus is so coercive it goes without saying. We can read about battles, give to charity, economize, agonize—only we must fall in line, concede to our superiors, that is, the men willing to kill. It's as if war were a natural force, or act of God! And women, bound by some colony prerogative—an insect's instinctive obedience—not to do everything, anything, to stop it! I sometimes feel I'll go mad, listening to ladies' polite pieties about keeping up soldiers' morale, when it's so monstrously wrong boys are at risk at all—"

"Quiet resistance—discreet influence—can be a powerful thing," Theo said, touching my cheek with the back of her hand. "Trust God made you the way he did for a reason." She encouraged me to while away the slow-ticking hours sipping tea and sorting ribbons by practicing gathering intelligence about what mattered to me, without giving up anything of my own.

It was only after arriving home that I realized my hair was completely askew. I cringed to think of having ranted on, while above me loomed the Leaning Tower of Pisa. I'd imagined Theo's head had been cocked in interested attention, but she had only been tactfully taking her angle from me.

Next time we were invited to tea with the Chews, I resolved to be a little less forthcoming, more watchful, but not obviously withholding. We had been back and forth between Cliveden and our house since before I could walk—my father enjoyed talking law with Mr. Chew as much as he did anybody alive—but the house never became less impressive, with its handsome Palladian design and distinctive Wissahickon schist sparkling in lime. The entrance hall was enormous, big as a ballroom, it had seemed to me as a child. I still marveled at the towering cabinets on the top landing, with drawers wide enough to hide in and shelves so high they needed a custom ladder to be reached.

It took effort to pretend I wasn't listening. I made my eyes vacuous and set my shoulders in what I hoped was a convincingly oblivious attitude while our mothers moved from the weather and rising prices to bad romances.

"We'd have liked to have a match," Mrs. Chew was saying of a niece, "but he turned out to be that silly sort of man who perhaps did not know the incumbrances on his estate."

Mrs. Frankie relished a catastrophe from her own family. "I fear nothing will prevent that charming girl from rushing into destruction."

I felt my usual anxiety at the sound of any dangerous fate (and at their scary judgments) but continued impassive as I scanned the elegantly redecorated sitting room for any hint it had been so recently under siege. I believe I appeared impressively incurious until I heard Mrs. Cartwright ask, "Is Captain André thought to be in love with the lady he left in England, or is she a convenient shield to keep insistent female attention at bay?"

At which point I immediately flushed. My mother and Mrs. Frankie exchanged a freighted look.

Mrs. Chew revealed he'd written her daughter verses and insisted May fetch and read them, to her daughter's mild embarrassment and my complete torment.

"Quite the cultured lover." Mrs. Frankie laughed.

I tried to sound amused. "May, that's so funny, can I see?"

His handwriting was beautiful too.

May seemed oblivious to my agony. Was it real disinterest, or a successful mask? Probably she was unconscious of any threat. I asked her what she thought the truth was behind the rumors of André's attachment in England. She gave a careless shrug, "For all the marked attention, do you believe he's in earnest with either of us?"

Mrs. Chew saw my dismay and said tactfully that though she saw more art than ardor in his letters, the captain was naturally enchanted by us both. A pity then he had no fortune of his own and a mother and sisters dependent on his salary.

I was glad to hear my friend warned off, but not at all sure May would be deterred. She, after all, had galleons of money to support the man she married. It didn't occur to me to mind André's lack of wealth for my own sake. He was indispensable to Clinton, which made him practically a favorite of the King and surely with all that talent he would rise. I realized May might still expect an answer.

"I think Captain André has too much to give—too much to do—to settle his attentions on any one lady yet. He's considerate of all of us because it's the wish of Clinton. It's the general who has his devotion."

If that was the truth, I wasn't ready to concede it to myself. My mother of course saw all things—a knack I found more unnerving since she and Mrs. Frankie were back to convening with my departed brothers.

"Your mother does not share your affection for Captain André," Father told me that evening.

"Oh?" I said, disconcerted to feel I was not among allies at home.

"And then I'm obliged to mention, given your liking for nice things—"

"She was begging the favor of good silk for her nightdresses from the age of eight!" Mother cut in.

"I'm afraid I can't settle money on you myself—"

"I didn't expect—"

"You are making a spectacle of yourself to no end, Peggy," Mother said. "This entanglement is drawing unhelpful attention to yourself and the family, alienating the Quakers who disapprove of the British pleasure dens and endangering our relations with the Patriots."

I looked up in alarm. If my parents were worrying about pleasing the Patriots again, my Index had been trending lower than it should.

"We had hopes of peace; they appear to be blasted," Father said.

But the invitations from the British kept coming that winter, invitations we were encouraged to accept, whether for ice skating parties or sledding or dances, lulling me into believing their tenure would never end. I'd occasionally see Esther standing to one side of the steps as we entered, or glimpse her disapproval, as I careened past on skates; she never joined in. I introduced her to André once, on the sidelines of ice hockey on the lake, and he invited her to join us for hot chocolate with what seemed to me irresistible charm, but she gave a small, tight smile and declined.

I wrote to Theodosia almost daily, hoping Clinton had been able to help locate her husband and protect the Hermitage, sharing my hopes and worries about André.

It didn't surprise her he was dogged by gossip, she said; he had a face the world would always want to watch. He'd told her how highly he thought of me, and she believed he was being clever in courting May to deflect attention from our growing closeness.

"He is wise, isn't he? Finding a role in the army that makes sense of his strengths."

"I'd like to see what he'd do freed of obligation to military hospitality," she said.

"Oh yes," I rushed to agree. "That light and quickness in pure service of art."

It was exhilarating picturing him liberated. All of us, free of fear.

"If women did have more influence, Theo, do you think the horror would stop? How will we ever know when our ambition can only be furtive (which in itself can hardly be healthy)? How do wars ever end?" I asked the wisest woman I knew.

"Well, eventually the parties have to start talking."

"I believe you've met our duchess," Odell said, as I turned up for my next fitting to find André lounging against the counter with a glass of wine.

"I certainly have," he said. "Doesn't our meeting in September feel years ago? It's the endless consequential developments, making a month of every day. When this war is over, I'd be happy for nothing at all to happen, for decades. One of my favorite of Franklin's many illustrated inventions is kite swimming. What do you say to scudding across a warm bay on our backs, wind in our little individual sails?"

I sighed. That did sound like heaven. He smiled at me. He had a gift for that too. Appreciative, but no hint of a leer.

"So, are we to call you your Grace?"

"No, we are not."

"I have always had a soft spot for the aristocracy," Stansbury said. "It's pleasant to think of men ascended beyond drudgery and corruption, with wealth so old it's timeless, free to make heirs and spares and tend to landscapes."

"The length of those lineages does lend a certain divinity," Odell said.

"I was always confusing the King and God in my mind as a child," I said.

"Quite right," André said with that unbuttoning smile.

"It's easier to like a man reluctantly inhabiting an inherited position than a scheming up-and-thruster looking to usurp it," I said. "Though perhaps scheming is never appealing."

"An audacious heist might be quite exciting?" Stansbury suggested.

"None of what's said here goes any further?" Odell was smiling at me, but serious.

"No, certainly. You can trust me, Reverend Odell—"

"Odie."

"Odie." I laid my hand on my heart.

"The King doesn't have a choice," André said. "In that he's like those of us who must work for a living."

I was hotly self-conscious suddenly of my own idleness.

Stansbury saw my unease. "Your work, Peggy, is to be your usual lovely self."

"Before marrying a man of character and fortune," Odie ended.

"We were talking about the merits of royalty," I said, gauche in my embarrassment and dismay.

"The masses happily distracted by palaces and princesses, while efficient functionaries like André do the actual work," Odie said.

"I'm not sure there's a rational defense of royalty," André said. "But there are worse ideas than catering to a spoilt lord. Up to a point. As with anything, you weigh what harm, what gain—"

"We in business appreciate the stability, certainly," Stansbury nodded.

"And he's not a bad King. No princes in the tower," Odie said. "Of which we're aware."

He reached to top my glass but reluctantly I stopped him.

"I should get home," I said.

"My dear," Stansbury cried. "You mustn't go anywhere. You're the glue of this little gathering."

"One last toast?" André pleaded, gesturing to the world outside the studio. "Keep it all offshore a moment longer?"

I accepted Odie's refill and we all raised our glasses. I thought how my heart had raced and hands shaken ahead of venturing to bring a cup to my lips when I first met these men, and how happy I was now to be trusted, and asked to linger.

"To freedom," Stansbury said.

"And friendship," André said, meeting my eye as the wine reached our lips.

Chapter Seven

In May, the French officially declared war on England.

Sir William Howe, the commander in chief in North America, announced he intended to step down and hand control of the colonies to Clinton.

"That means advancement for you, John," Stansbury said.

"Yes, they place more faith in me daily," André said sardonically. "There's talk of a ball."

"Would you rather be on the front lines?" Odie said sharply.

"Did you never enjoy it? Active service?" Stansbury asked, as he tailored André's new jacket. "Like this?" he asked, pinching the fabric to the waist. I loved the license that gave me to look directly at his frame.

"A little tighter, Peggy?" Odie laughed. I turned back to *The Gazette*, breastbone burning.

"I was not in my element," André admitted good-humoredly. "It was only five minutes before I was captured."

We laughed.

"Truly, and I'd happily have stayed prisoner longer, but Benedict Arnold was far too full of energy and decency to keep me captive long. He was looking for a prisoner swap and to move on."

The name resonated as celebrity will.

"The legend of Lexington treated his captive well then?" I asked.

"With great civility. Now that's a natural warrior. Watching him in action I admit I was guilty of believing the Patriots would win."

"Not anymore, though?" I asked.

"I hear he's crippled. His horse got shot out from under him, and one leg was basically flayed. It can't be likely he'll survive more action. The Patriots ought to pension him, but they can barely agree on funding a standing army. They don't pay soldiers what they need to keep their loyalty. And besides, it's my job to believe, to see, the British will win. We will. The imbalance in resources is just too great."

"Why is Howe leaving now?" I asked. "Why not stay and enjoy the victory?"

"I'm not saying it's imminent. It is hard to pace one's hopes at times. Sometimes success feels a breath away—sometimes the wait and the work feel they'll never end. But eventually we will win—"

Eventually. The weight of misery, the pain and maiming, the waste was all too much. The pressure in my chest felt it might ignite.

"I wish I could do something!" I burst out. "I'll feel terrible if I'm swanning and lolling about while everyone else risks dying. Would you let me know? If there is some way to help. Without getting in the way?"

"In all sincerity?" He smiled at me. "Thank you."

"Well, I mean it. I'd give everything, do anything, to bring an end to all this."

"Beauty queen dreams of peace," Odie teased.

"Anything?" Stansbury's fond eyebrow cocked.

"I'm not going to bring children into this war. And I want children! One day. But not unless it stops. I swear it. I refuse."

"Peggy," André said, pushing my hair back behind my ear, "you'll be the death of me."

A few weeks after Howe's announcement, André called on my parents.

My heart stopped as I heard him being let in. Was he here to ask my father?

I smooshed my ear between the banisters trying to hear more than the low hum of their conversation, until Atty took pity and went in to offer tea, leaving the door open so I could eavesdrop.

André was calling me his protection against blunder. "It's quite a diplomatic feat, sir, and I believe Peggy's equal to it. She has your same delightful tact, that ability to win friends of every political persuasion—and your taste and sensibility, Mrs. Shippen. She'll help ensure the ladies' costumes are as elegant they ought to be."

"We're talking about a party?" Father said doubtfully.

"A themed party, conceived to usher in a new era of unity," André said. "A splendid send-off for General Howe—and a celebration of Clinton's new tenure. I can't say much, though I know you, sir, we can trust. Perhaps it's enough to hint the King has high hopes for the success of Lord Carlisle's peace delegation, making its way across the Atlantic even now with every concession the Rebels ever sought except outright independence. There should be much to celebrate soon, God willing. So many people just want to be told what's what. Let's help them see the relief in British victory."

"Surely a party is guaranteed to stir resentment among those not invited; rage from those already inclined to retaliation. You'll be escalating tensions just as shortages are getting worrying—"

"If we can restore confidence, there will be less hoarding, which will help with prices and supply. And with peace, of course, embargoed goods will again flow freely."

Into the silence, he mentioned the party's location was Walnut Grove, the country seat of Joseph Wharton. "I believe an old friend of your family?"

He sensed my parents' softening and pressed ahead.

"Please believe me: my intentions are professional. My only goal is advancing peace in the colonies. Peggy will be quite safe. I have an entire regiment of chaperones."

Father was persuaded. Atty and I danced silently upstairs for joy!

Clinton's own carriage came to fetch me to Franklin's house. I'm not sure I'd ever felt more excitement than on my way to work with André, in the house of the most inventive mind alive. Approaching the front door, my unguarded smile was checked by a lurking stranger clearly monitoring my arrival.

"Was I just surveilled on my way in?" I asked André as he took my cloak.

"The man in the bad wig?" he asked. "Yup. Selectmen from the Committee for Observation—I've taken to waving at them. Let me give you the tour—"

The entire house was a cabinet of curiosities with wonderful devices on every surface. André showed me a copper bath shaped like a slipper, kitchen contrivances to carry off steam and smells, a glass harmonica of Franklin's own devising which made what sounded like the music of the spheres. He showed me human bone through a microscope, a divided bowl to stop soup sloshing on a sea crossing, insulated stools to keep soldiers on Winter sentry warm, electrical apparatuses, and those instructions for kite swimming!

Stansbury and Odell were shown in.

"Is it wise to be convening here?" Stansbury asked, visibly rattled by the militiamen outside.

"I'll see you're safe."

"Predatory behavior of the sort the Council went in for before you got here would only help the British peace commission," Odie said.

"Let's hope it doesn't escalate before they get here."

I pulled a chance book from the shelf, *Essays to Do Good* by Cotton Mather, clearly a well-thumbed favorite. Skimming the amiable exhortations to the reader not to shirk any opportunity to do every positive thing in one's power—amazed to think my eyes were following Franklin's own as I read!—I took it as a blessing for our peace initiative.

We sat around the large table, each of us with paper and colored pencils, so that the undertaking felt the best sort of play.

How to make the party feel unprecedented? A name was needed. To call it a ball, André thought, would conjure British assembly rooms, the old order, and this was no time for lions and unicorns. We needed something to honor the rich culture of Philadelphia, its peaceful origins, the success of our melting pot, a diversity beyond anywhere else. Nothing too French, obviously. A dash of Italian perhaps, to offset British superciliousness? We riffed on possibilities, until André landed on the word Mischianza—from the Italian for *mixture*, with a dash of extravaganza.

"It's not ridiculous?"

"It's perfect!"

"We need to promise dazzling invention. Win the city's affection! We want romance and extravagance, a fantastic mash-up. We will celebrate with such insistence the war will end when we stop!"

We laughed at lame ideas, clapped happily at inspired ones, and it was established the party would be an immersive performance, borrowing elements of opera, royal pomp, chivalric traditions, and music from the world's best composers.

Working alongside each other felt like reaching on a keyboard for the perfect chord—an unanswerable harmony. My longing for peace was bound in with my longing for him and both were becoming my obsession.

There was endless revision to the party's playlist. André would sing a phrase. Odie and Stansbury would harmonize. Anyone else at that might have been nauseating, definitely fair game for parody, but they were just too good.

It would be a Royalist-Loyalist spectacle in love with the colonies, a celebration of American energy defined by the precise execution of pageantry at which the British state excelled.

"The entire production should underline what we're capable of," André said, "while deflecting attention from the darker side of empire—"

"How sinister could all that bunting ever be?" Odie asked archly.

André's long tapered fingers were moving rapidly over fine sheets of paper, sketching a regatta, jousting knights. I kept track of progress over his shoulder, fighting the urge to kiss the back of his neck. Soon, a rustling pile of paper slid from every chair in the room. Each sheet was like fine flaky pastry, marked by the looping pencil strokes that made up his designs. There were layers of scrunched, throwaway ideas on the floor and smoothed out keepers pinned under mugs and jugs throughout the library.

I loved our rapid back and forth—"Where are we with the wine? The glasses? The guestlist?"—and the satisfaction of having to hand what was wanted.

"You process delight in a very distinctive way," André said, watching me steadily. "Like fireworks."

"Let's have fireworks!" Stansbury exclaimed, gesturing spirals from his temples.

And then we were drawing pictures of starbursts and comets and flocks of fireflies before André summoned the engineers to realize our designs. Seeing the respect and affection they felt for him, having my ideas considered, listening to their earnest and informed explanations of pyrotechnic logistics, I had never felt such luck or fun.

"Could I borrow it?" I asked André. "*Essays to Do Good*?"

"I should think so, if, as our host would say, 'you return it, clean and soon.'"

Over the next weeks we swung from extravagant hopes for the peace the party might bring—and a cramping sense of the risks. Apart from the goodwill of the city, André's professional life was on the line. He confessed he'd dreamed he was walking a tightrope over the London skyline. The dome of St Paul's below. The tightrope had sagged and collapsed, and he'd fallen into what felt like flight, but he knew would be death.

Stansbury kneaded his friend's shoulders before giving them a brief slap and returning to his scissors. "Well, yes. Any misstep would be a massive embarrassment for the King and Clinton and professionally devastating for you. That's why you've enlisted the best."

I was determined my contributions would give him confidence. I cared for Andre's reputation like my own. Hoped of course it would be.

All the medieval clothes I'd drawn as a child informed the costumes I designed for the men. So many things I'd learned from history finally felt applicable, and it was a thrill to have company in making lateral leaps. The Field of the Cloth of Gold could be a model—a splendid performance to put a stop to combat!

"French and English kings sought to outlaw war forever with that spectacle—"

"Let's get it right this time."

A new ship from the East brought silks and jeweled veils, which tipped the theme more exotic still. Stansbury joined us in pushing the outfits to outrageous frontiers.

"This will mean a considerable windfall for all the occupier's favorite suppliers," André said.

"What a good war we're having," Odie said. His deadpan excelled.

The ladies were to be dressed as if from a Turkish harem, with cloth so sheer, our lower backs and stomachs would be discernible. André had me model his prototypes, and I loved the shy light that came up in his eyes when I stepped out from the screen. Daring choices eclipsed the real ongoing dangers. Or perhaps fear had become so normal, the stakes so high, that worrying about modesty seemed indecent now.

Unwrapping a reem of fine rose-gold fabric, André bent to smell it, and Stansbury smiled and said, "I think we have the stuff of your suit!"

Once his outfit was done, and André turned to face us, a young man as beautiful as any in history, I caught Stansbury and Odell exchange a glance. My attraction to André was running rampant. I gave a smile of shy defiance: Nothing had happened . . . we had never been alone.

"You burn too bright, John," Odie said.

André walked to the door. Three militiamen could be seen, making no secret of being armed.

"They're getting bolder," he said.

"If they're winning support, it's because people don't trust them not to seize their homes. Fear, not affection—"

"French ships spotted off Staten Island—"

"Unconfirmed."

All talk of war only made the work more urgent.

"Word is the British will be leaving for New York within the month," Father said grimly, as I came in the door.

"Oh no, that can't be true," I insisted, hanging my cloak. "The British have spent a King's ransom on this party. André and all his officers have donated money of their own. They won't leave before the peace commission can arrive and the Mischianza work its magic—"

"Mischianza," mother derided. I checked the salty drift of my thinking.

"Their evacuating makes me uneasy, Peggy. The British will leave a vacuum only the most ambitious Patriots can fill. Meaning a whole new reckoning with collusion."

I held on to the wooden banister, willing what I was saying to be true:

"If they were leaving, I think Captain André would have told me. Rumors of a British departure are probably intentionally seeded, designed to sharpen the city's affection, tip it toward peace."

I could have asked André outright about Clinton's plans post-Howe, but I didn't have the heart to hear what he might say. I told myself it was an unhealthy temptation, reaching for tomorrow rather than sitting with what was known of today.

As it was, I willed myself oblivious.

Chapter Eight

WITH A WEEK TO GO WE MADE A SITE VISIT TO WALNUT GROVE. IT WAS a beautiful old house, modeled on the grandest British estates and surrounded by old-growth oaks, rolling lawns, and parkland studded with deer.

On the wide, flat terrace in front of the house, officers on horseback were rehearsing the jousting with blunted lances. It was something to see the training and choreography, the way horse and rider fused, making art of mounted combat. With more of my petulant defiance, I privately railed again at why men must fight at all when sport sorted winners from losers so well.

I couldn't linger to admire the discipline and rippling muscles for long, not with a hundred details to which to see. I loved working alongside André, glimpsing the team we could be. It felt outlandishly privileged, to be tasked on a breezy day in May with arranging entertainment fit for a King. It was satisfying just to be spending his money.

We'd decided we'd line every inch of the dining room with glinting mirrors, four walls of light, reflecting the candles and the silver, the chandeliers and the china, along with every person present in their finery. A phalanx of reflections, inspiring thoughts of peace and abundance for infinity.

It was like having a magic wand—my wish my command—and André and his team to make it so. We were soon driving around the leafy outskirts of the city in Clinton's carriage, followed by a procession of carts, securing the loan of mirrors from dozens of families. My task was to defuse hostility from those not so delighted to find a British captain at their door. We went to the Chews at

Cliveden, the Carlisles, the Robertses, the Cartwrights, and most of the people who owned houses with big-enough mirrors. I knew, too, whose participation to mention to preempt misgivings elsewhere.

Seeing André's eyes close to mine in sunshine for the first time, I almost forgot our script. When he smiled, his irises changed with the light, going from gray to amber-green, gold flecked, and indecently inviting.

I loved watching him talking to my parents' friends. Loved watching the back of his neck, the band of pale skin beneath the crisp-cut collar. The lines of his uniform had been so refined by Stansbury he felt unassailable.

As each door was opened, I wrenched my gaze from him, launching into our double act. "We're hoping to include you in what is going to be the most wonderful party. So and so, your neighbor, was kind enough to loan some glass and mentioned you had some mirrors of your own you might let us borrow? Don't let his uniform fool you. You have every right to refuse!"

But nobody did. I was in love, and on a mission, and I felt we had the affection of the city.

André's charming command while carrying off priceless furnishings from the best families—temporarily obviously—convinced me there would be no limit to what the man could achieve in peace. He was so guileless, so liked, whether laughing with a city grandee or sitting with army engineers calculating the capacity of the weight-bearing wall they would need to avoid a crashing calamity.

Careful to keep my voice light and timeline vague, I asked him about returning to England. "Do you miss it?"

"I miss my mother and sisters. I miss the proximity to France. The whole of Europe."

"England feels too small for you?" I teased.

"For my limitless ambition? No. I love it. But you have to see Paris!"

I looked out the window. The frustration was unbearable. With the war won we could begin a real adventure.

Back at Walnut Grove, André unloaded the mirrors, while I took inventory of provisions.

"André come and see! The cakes are higher than my hair!"

He laughed, and tugged lightly at a pin in my hair, sending my stomach plummeting with lust. "I think the ladies should wear their hair loose and soft, in keeping with the theme—"

I arranged dishes of candied fruits and ginger, marshaled candlesticks and cutlery, sent endless cases of wine and champagne to the cellars to chill, and when at last everything was perfect, I returned to the carriage, leaning against it and dabbing my neck from the heat.

Esther Reed loomed into view, and I felt my spirit drop like a plumb line. She was escorted by a young woman radiant with the confidence of wealth beyond worry.

"Peggy," Esther cooed, gripping my shoulders with bony fingers as she kissed me. "Meet my friend Eliza Schuyler—"

Eliza bristled slightly at Esther's proprietary pride.

"How do you do, Miss Shippen?"

She took my hand with a warm, frank touch and pretty smile. I was guilty of surprise to realize these two were friends. I had a low tendency to underestimate Esther, with no justification I could identify beyond her slightly lank hair and ratty aspect. Eliza and Esther had in fact very similar figures, but Eliza was vivid, her skin and hair glossy with health and her eyes shining with intelligent good nature, where the impression Esther made was pale and aggressive.

"As well as any American woman can be, I suspect, when our soldiers are enduring what they do," Esther said.

"Are they still suffering very terribly?" I asked her.

"They are reduced to eating their own shoes, Peggy, leather and shoe bark."

I looked at her, appalled. And thinking: *If only they could go home.*

"I have means in mind of alleviating that suffering, Peggy. If I might call on you and your sister one afternoon soon—"

"Yes," I said vaguely, my eyes darting to find André. "Perhaps next week, after the party?"

I saw too late my tepid response had given irretrievable offense.

"Indeed, if one might ever catch you in. You are by all accounts a busy bee, out all hours with Captain André."

"In service of our little celebration—" I began.

"Of what? The triumph of failing to conquer America?"

She clicked her crudely nailed heels as if the ugly, uncomfortable footwear was a point of pride.

"It's meant to signal unity," I said.

She guffawed.

"What is it you hope to achieve?" Eliza asked, with what seemed charming curiosity, though enough of a suggestion of derision to make Esther smirk.

"To see the suffering end. Make life fun again."

"The Quakers are set against it," Eliza said frankly.

"Well, yes, it involves music," I said, "and dancing. But forbidden pleasures aside, I'm sure they appreciate it's a peaceful initiative—no violence in it—"

André had seen us. He froze momentarily, weighing our visitors as predator or prey, while his expression stayed mellow.

Handing a basket of bread and a bottle of wine to his helpers, he walked over, full of joviality and respect.

"Eliza Schuyler!" he exclaimed, with a comforting absence of flirtation. "How good to see you again."

"Captain André." She blushed, whether from his attention or the beady fury of Esther beside her wasn't clear.

André explained he had stayed with the family at their home upstate on a number of occasions.

Esther stared at him absurdly while Eliza looked as if she'd rather be anywhere else.

Still, for now, the paperwork was in order and the money, it seemed, with the British. If the mirrors were any indication, André had more of the city's goodwill than Esther felt wise to mess with. She could only give a last look of theatrical menace and retreat in peevish defeat.

"Joseph Reed is a zealot," André said, watching them go.

"Esther's fairly fanatical herself. Talks of flinging herself into the flames for liberty—"

He laughed, which encouraged me.

"And she's barely out of England! She must be struggling with some of the divided affection and internal conflict we all are, but you'd never know. Whereas Eliza is so likable. She's very attractive—"

"Peggy," he said, dismissing any sense of competition so straightforwardly my worry vanished. "They always say her beauty is underrated—"

"That seems a very British way of being offensive! And not fair—"

He laughed. "No. I think she suffers only in comparison with her sister Angelica."

"She's very respectable, I find myself wanting to please her. But a little bit literal?"

André smiled. "I knew you'd be good at this—"

"Party planning?"

"Assessing threats, gathering intelligence, winning influence."

Pride shot up my spine.

"Reed is close to Washington," he went on, "but he conspired to oust him this winter."

"Reed did?"

"Washington intercepted the very letter in which Reed cast aspersions on his leadership—"

"How excruciating for both of them," I said, wondering how letters of such sensitivity and significance were being read by the British. "But hopefully that internal conflict might make them more receptive to the approaching bid of peace?"

"There are elements who won't accept anything short of complete independence now, others so inured to fighting they don't want an end to war however dire conditions get. But we will win, one mind at a time. The peace commission should give men like Reed, and his fellow disaffected, their particular attention."

"It's not really possible Washington will be replaced?"

"He won't go easily. For all his affability, he hates to be slighted. He's been urging his supporters to take on doubters in duels."

"He's calling for Esther's husband to be killed?" I asked in alarm.

"No, Reed he seems to indulge. He's a good administrator, and communicator, with a flexible approach to facts. And Reed understands the power of the newspapers in moving opinion like nobody else alive. You've read the Militia Man's toxic contributions in *The Gazette*?"

"Yes, I've seen those letters. His hatred for Tories. Scorn of Congress. A very persecuting energy. Less about making a case than designating enemies—"

"We believe the Militia Man is a pseudonym for Reed."

"I'm surprised Washington wants anything to do with him."

"Washington must judge that Reed's mortification at having his disloyalty discovered will make him useful."

"A pet thug?"

"The fear Reed incites isn't unproductive. And perhaps it flatters General Washington to see a doubter who's learned to bend the knee. Certainly he knows it's propaganda and spy rings which will give the King a run for his money, absent a more serious commitment from the French—"

I sighed, so tired of all the cynicism and scheming.

"Something must win this, Peggy. Ideals can't prevail without practical help."

We made a final stop at Mount Pleasant. Sitting high above the Schuylkill, approached by an avenue of limes, it was, André told me, the most handsome example of Georgian architecture in America, and currently home to the Spanish ambassador. The main house was flanked by a pair of symmetrical outbuildings sharing the same beautiful windows and brickwork and trim. I thought it was the prettiest house in Philadelphia. Nobody seemed to be home, and we circled the house, allowing a peek at the lawns, lined with classical statues, and the tree-lined path running down to the wide river's edge. There were two front doors, of identical grandeur, one facing the park, the other the river. Uncertain which to approach, André suggested we take a third way, the side door, since we weren't known to the owner.

I had a disconcerting feeling of déjà vu as I looked at the iron crescent of the boot scraper while we waited for the housekeeper, as if I were recognizing the moment, not living it for the first time.

I shook that ghost off as we were welcomed into a beautiful modern kitchen, through which we glimpsed the light-flooded, soaring-ceilinged hallway, with parquet flooring, classical moldings, marble mantels, and a spectacular curving staircase with a polished mahogany banister.

The ambassador was not at home, and the housekeeper didn't feel able to contribute mirrors without his permission, but she gave us ice, and with that safely installed in hay for transportation back to Walnut Grove, André insisted we have lunch.

"Do you think all those families would have surrendered their mirrors without you? You must at least let me feed you before returning you to your father. I'll have the engineers join us there."

As he helped me into the carriage, I caught the good smell of him, tangy from lifting, and again all my nerves frayed.

We'd rolled on only five minutes, acutely conscious of being finally alone, when André called to the driver to stop in front of a little stone church. He climbed out, looked back at me in mischievous delight, and took my hand to help me down. I didn't trust myself to speak. The musty stone interior was a welcome relief. The nave was empty, but I heard an orchestra warming up beneath our feet. I don't think anything stirs anticipation like that muted cacophony before a performance.

As we reached the basement rehearsal, the celloists embarked on Bach, their gleaming instruments and crisp shirtsleeves moving in unison. We leaned together against a cool back pillar as the music quickened and stirred my vast, inarticulate wish. All the pity and the beauty coursed through my body as André smiled at me. It felt the music had been laid on just for us.

The horses carried us on from there along a dense tree-lined lane which shone like an emerald tunnel pulsing with sunlight and chattering birds. We flew faster through the green until the canopy cleared and we reached a sunny, low-slung inn.

It wasn't only that he was gorgeous—though he was—it was the feeling he was the best thing that would ever happen to me. The high-water mark in a life that would mock every other effort at happiness. I felt every moment with him like an ultimatum and frightened myself with the force of my feelings. If

I couldn't have him, I wouldn't want life beyond. At the same time, I knew he was an army man who must be moving on. I knew it and refused it. Our party, our peace, would stop time.

The inn had a dim, timbered public bar, and booths in sight of the fire. André ducked beneath the beams and, greeting the host warmly, established his men with drinks while he and I slid into a high-backed booth.

He poured us each a glass of sweet cold water, another of wine.

"I couldn't have put on this thing without you, Peggy. You and your imagination, and courage—"

"I've done nothing brave—"

"You weren't fazed by efforts to intimidate us. And I've come to rely on that generative, book-lined mind."

"Please. You could fill the Pennsylvania Statehouse with all I don't know."

"I can't wait till you see the size of Westminster. That building gives a new estimation of what humans can do."

"There you are. Another thing I don't know."

"When you read and think as much as you do, I believe you can trust the right idea will find you at the right time. It's when you encounter a gap in knowledge, when you're forced to think—that's when imagination kicks in. Anyway, it's when conversation gets interesting."

He took a sip of wine and ordered for us both. It was all I could do not to take his hands in mine across the booth. Everything under my skin felt liquid.

"I don't think there is anything you couldn't do if you put your mind to it," he said, looking at me seriously.

"I would say the same to you."

"No. I'm a good number two. Useful to those who lead. To reach any sort of parity I'd have to marry cleverly, follow Washington in finding some rich widow who would eliminate all financial concerns. Someone so fierce she obliterates by force of personality every unconventional element in me. Or overlooks it." He looked up from under his lashes.

That was too much to process with composure, and I blushed deeper to find André looking steadily at me.

I wanted him to kiss me, seize me, obliterate all thinking.

André sat back, taking out his notebook and returning the conversation to the safer ground of the plan. There were still flowers to finalize. The tiny hairs on my fingers touched his as he swiveled the notebook my way to share work on the design.

When he excused himself to settle up, I thought desperately about what else I could say which might persuade him what he needed was me. Perhaps it had been the wine, but the scene before me, the sketches in the foreground, the booth, the array of sun-dappled bottles and glasses above the bar were so perfect I felt I might cry. As he slid back across from me, I was quick to smile.

"I hope the King knows how lucky he is in you."

André dashed that away.

"I doubt it's lucky the King is feeling. Think how heavily this weighs on us, and imagine the diving bell in his chest. Everything his ancestors achieved now his to lose. The French nemesis back in the fight. His father's war here again to haunt him. And then the infighting. The feuding in Parliament is brutal—"

"Think of the creative freedom you'll have after the war. Head of a company of players—"

He shook his head. "I've had a captive audience. I couldn't compete in a London theater. Mine are entertainments, advertisements for the King."

"That doesn't make you any less of a genius."

"It very much does! Real art makes the audience feel it sees them. I'm afraid my own attempts would only allow the audience to see me. It doesn't matter. It would be sadder if I were talented, working in these circumstances. Honestly, I've come to slightly despise this role, I have my eye on a position where I can make a bigger difference—"

"Not fighting?" I said, unable to bear that.

He looked into my eyes, seemed on the brink of an admission, before retreating.

I was brimming with rebellious insistence the horror finally stop.

"You know I'd gladly help you again. What else could we try? With spectacle, and art? Just in the spirit of 'what if'? When thinking of that music, I can't understand anyone hearing it ever entertaining the thought of violence—"

"We can't play it continuously, Peggy. Incessantly? By imperial command."

"No, that does sound a bit Nero, but I don't know, can't engaging people's senses harness their thinking? Bach feels stronger than a committee telling us what to think."

He bit his lip, and I worried I'd been too sincere.

"Talking to you lowers my guard, makes me want to believe. But the truth is I can hardly stand the word *Mischianza* any longer. I'm trotting about, the King's performing monkey, while all I can think is *We are finished. Utterly done.*"

"I know the bleak feelings, André. The panic."

There was comfort and sadness in his smile.

"You can't give up before the party's started—"

"We need more than a party, Peggy."

"What would it take to end it, once and for all?"

"I'd say the surest way to stop a war is lose it."

"And that's unthinkable?"

He gave a sad tilt of the head.

"We need unambiguous victory."

"But without further casualties."

"Ideally." André dropped his head, and then rallied, "Beautiful unity, in one shining stroke."

I sighed. He smiled shyly, glanced up at the servers' station, and satisfied we could not be seen, put one hand in my hair, the other on my chin. Pressing his soft lips to mine, he took my lower lip in his, and kissed me expertly, deeply, until a discreet cough from the approaching server brought the world hurtling back in.

He handed me into the carriage, and during the whole ride home it was all I could do not to climb into his lap.

Outside the house, he put his coat around me. When I felt his hand at the base of my back, my legs almost gave way. One thought kept beating in my head. *He must mean marriage.*

Inside the door, André gently reclaimed his jacket and said he would come in to see my parents for a quick cup of tea. This was the moment he would ask my father for his blessing, permission to propose. I had been silly and impatient to expect it when he'd come before—only the first time in our home. Now we were ready. I had as good as told him there was nothing he could do I wouldn't love. I was sure our commitment must be visible to my mother, but she seemed not to notice, pouring milk, topping up the water, inquiring about the weather expected for the party, while André sketched me in pencil in the notebook on his knee, his thoughts impossible to guess.

It was suffocating: the stopped clock, close air, excitement I couldn't yet own. It did occur to me to wrench the clothes from my body, but I limited myself to opening the window. André's pencil continued scratching on the page. After what felt an unbearable interval, he stood, gave me that sweet, lopsided smile, no more particular than the one he gave Betsy, handed the sketch to my parents as a token of his thanks, and left.

My father conceded it was an accomplished likeness. I barely glanced at it. My hair looked ludicrous, and anyway it wasn't what I wanted. Nothing but a full declaration would have done to end the evening.

I excused myself so that I could stew unobserved in every detail of our day. A perfect day, except for all that hadn't happened. I could not stop thinking about the feeling of his lips and let out a new sigh at every memory of the kiss. The awkwardness at tea, the deadening pleasantries, only made me more impatient to be taken away.

What had he meant I'd be good at this—if not by his side? Even if it weren't in our immediate power to end the conflict, we could be together, loved by friends. We might set trends, shape agendas, visit with Benjamin Franklin and the King, live, like William, here and there.

Suddenly humble, I wanted to be grateful. I had Stansbury and Odell to thank for my confidence in talking to him at all. Theodosia to thank for introducing me to them. My parents for having me and bringing me this far. Oh, I hoped I had shown him how I could help him, the wife I could be. With that kiss we were surely agreed. I knew my parents had doubts; I would show them worry was unnecessary. I agonized over how it could be he had not proposed. Perhaps he'd mistaken how much money we had, perhaps I'd done something wrong with the kiss— When it landed like an epiphany: of course, the right time was ahead! If he was going to ask to marry me, the moment would be at the ultimate gesture itself, the Mischianza.

I was drifting happily off when I heard Father's voice on the stairs. "I share your reservations, my dear, and support you in all, as you know, but I see no great harm—"

And Betsy cutting in: "Having permitted her to assist with the requisitioning of mirrors, I feel— She's very fond of him—"

"Inordinately fond—"

"Women as well as men seem these days to be alike infatuated," my father marveled.

"We have position," Mother said grimly. "And there is a responsibility that comes with that influence."

Light guillotined the bed. She stood in the doorway, Father behind her.

"It is indecent," she said, alive with purpose to find herself in crisis mode. "This party Captain André's planning. Every detail which reaches me, thanks to Mrs. Frankie, suggests depravity"—she took her volume down a notch—"even were the city not as tense as it is." Her hand was trembling, but her voice was firm as she raised it: "You will not attend. We forbid it."

Chapter Nine

For a moment, I let myself believe she was joking. I glanced between my parents. My mother played Father so effectively, without needing to touch a string. She gave a flash of unimaginable suffering before assuming an expression of such courage and composure he'd never consider resisting her.

"I can't allow it."

"Please, Father! I've worked so hard— Perhaps the costumes are a little bold but it's a theme, and every girl going will be wearing the same. May will."

"Oh well, if it's good enough for Miss Chew."

"Mamma. What of the trouble and expense the army have been to? Our absence will throw off the placement, the tournament, and all."

"He will manage," Betsy said. "Thanks to all you've done to set it up in advance."

My sister's instincts were only conciliatory, but still I felt betrayed.

"He'll know to give credit. And Peggy, Neddy does say the wind is changing—"

"Please, no—" I sank onto the bed.

Mother saw the flash of defeat in my eyes and sat beside me, her voice tender now.

"Peggy. You're not still telling yourself he's a serious prospect?"

I felt my cheeks burning with rage and shame. My mother pulled my head against her shoulder and stroked my hair. I sobbed.

"You will not marry him. He will never marry you."

The dishonest honesty of frankness meant to hurt! I had no defense, not when she was voicing my deepest fear.

Scraped like that, I regretted every unguarded moment I had ever shared with her. It was my own fault. I had boasted of my hopes by showing my happiness in André's company. Paraded my role in the party as if they'd be grateful.

I still longed for her closeness and her approval. I still felt sympathy. I knew how much she missed the boys. I had dared think my marriage might help her happiness. That vanity again. I sobbed harder. I desperately needed air.

"Peggy, this is excessive. He's as fond of May Chew as he is you!"

When I tried to step past her, she took a nasty turn.

"Margaret Shippen, don't you dare—"

"Mamma, please. Let me past—I can't breathe!"

She stepped aside but then followed me out of the room. "What about me?" she called, following as I fled down the stairs, hemmed in by the house, respectability, the suffocating impossibility of running into the street. "What about my needs? Do you ever have a care for me? What people will think of me, while you're flinging yourself at that penniless connection?"

"Mamma!" Betsy pleaded. "You're being too harsh."

"My friends can't believe how little love she shows me."

"Mamma," I tried, my back to the front door. "I do love you—"

She jerked her head back as if physically hit. "You don't love me. Oh, it's easy to say. But I've known love. This is not love. Don't walk out now. Come back here!"

She was close to exhausting every compassionate response in me, and I didn't want her to see it. I shut myself in the library, my heart pumping in my stomach. I was frightened of my own mother, how unbelievably feeble, but grief had created an appetite for anger in her it felt I'd never sate.

And I hated to think what might happen if I weren't to attend—everything which would humiliate me and prove my mother right. André needed a queen for his fête, and I was to have played the part. Together, we had designed every dance and performance, paired every knight with a maiden. Not being there would be so humiliating. And with me off the scene, it would be May who was honored as his consort. I had been robbed of the only man I loved, and the only useful thing I'd ever done. And what if our not going encouraged others to stay away—what if my mother's boycott undermined the success of the entire evening, of André's career, of peace? Instead of helping, I had set the whole plan back.

I couldn't understand. Had Esther Reed somehow engineered this? No, I'd have known it. Perhaps some message from the grave insisted my mother keep me home? Mrs. Frankie might have tried it, but that only proved her a charlatan. Nobody in heaven would get in a lather over an outfit. The Quakers disapproved of course, but my family hadn't been seriously swayed by Quaker beliefs for two generations. It couldn't be that she had seen me happy and wanted to hurt me?

It was hard not to see malice in the decision, and weakness in my father's capitulation. I hated the way he could allow himself to be buffeted by opinion, listening to everyone, but never taking a stand of his own. I was tortured all over again by the unbearable ambiguity of our family's place in the war. It had been a relief over these weeks, whatever Stansbury and Odell's flexibility, whatever André's supple positions, to have taken a side. Part of what made marrying so appealing was the relief of allegiance. Without distraction from the conflict, the relief of helping do something to decide it, there was no end to the dread.

My father sent Atty to return the costumes. It killed me to think of General Clinton bearing witness to my embarrassment.

He might think the motive was political, as well as puritanical. Or that our withdrawal was intended as snub. A prominent family casting aspersions on his administration's efforts before the party had even begun. It would make him angry, after all their hospitality.

And André would take it personally.

He might think I regretted having kissed him. He might regret kissing me. I couldn't be sorry. The moment had insisted on it, and in a life with any luck, a kiss like that was meant to be. What if he thought my parents were saying he wasn't worthy to marry me? How wrong that would be. What if he felt I'd misled him? What if he'd misled me? But he hadn't. I would never stop thinking the best or wishing him well.

Father seemed disconcerted to find me in his library. He looked at me with pale eyes. If he remembered the turbulence of first love, it wasn't evident.

"I thought we supported the British—" I whispered.

"We can't pin our hopes to them now, Peggy. They have the French to contend with."

"We could resettle in Canada! I hear of families moving north of the border, rebuilding their whole homes up there— Move to England, even—"

"Do you mean to taunt me? Speaking as if we're made of money."

"No!" I cried, though in truth I longed to know what it was we were working with.

"What do you imagine we would we get for the property in this climate?"

"I don't know. Help me understand—" I begged.

"We have no choice but to stay and convince the Patriots we are the complete Americans we need to be."

The night of the party was warm, and from my bed I could hear the orchestra and female laughter wafting through the city. I could imagine myself walking down the lawn at Walnut Grove, champagne glass in hand, the hem of my sheer dress stirred by the warm wind off the river. I knew the order of events by heart, and I tormented myself with a horrible carousel of scenes, including every imagined embrace between André and May.

I knew I'd never have another moment so close to him—and that I'd never see a night to rival that one in my life. That near miss, all the pent-up hope of securing safety for me, my family, my city, two countries, all of it had come to nothing.

I tried to find a silver lining. The pressure to submit to my desire would have been overwhelming given the threat of his impending departure and the high of seeing our designs for the night realized—and the chances of being undiscovered were hardly on our side. If I had wanted to succumb, would he have let me?

Oh, but he might have proposed! Married, we'd have found the formula to win the war and secure his glory. We would have lived the big unconventional life he wanted, whatever that meant. It was him I needed.

As it was, I'd been left another year older, and a lot more in danger, than when the British arrived. Was either side even any nearer winning after all this time? I felt wretched as a smeared insect, and ready for death.

I lay wallowing in misery until I heard the first vivid crackle of fireworks.

I ran to the back window and watched the rockets race and sparks shower. It was impossible not to smile at the sounds like scattering seed, chains pooling on tables, and at the pop and flare and wonder of the light.

The symbolism was not subtle. I almost laughed through my tears. The British were going out with a bang. Showing America they had money, resources, and gunpowder to burn—aweing the undecided into submission.

The choreographed boom and flare of the fireworks was answered unexpectedly by a genuine explosion coming from Germantown, and the tat-a-tat volley of Patriot artillery. I stepped back: This was not scripted.

The shots were the Patriots' insistence they were still in the fight. After all the care and expense, the commitment to more killing had the last word.

I woke late morning to Atty's irrepressible voice greeting a messenger, detailing her family's latest bout of difficulties—a grandmother dead in her chair, though at a good age—before finally taking whatever the letter and climbing the stairs toward my room. I was gripped by a sudden conviction the letter would bring word of André's engagement to May. I knew my jealousy was ugly, and unworthy of him, but to lose him to her felt it would risk breeding despair.

Atty gave the letter a little shake, the poor girl had a hundred things to do, and I took it sheepishly, noticing the envelope contained more than paper.

Looking at the outstretched letter—my fate suspended as long as it stayed unread—I wanted every clock to stop.

"I'm sorry about your grandmother, Atty," I said. "I heard you downstairs—"

She nodded kindly and stayed while I read. It was from André and contained a lock of his hair. My eyes raced back and forth across the page, frantically reading fragments that fractured in my hurry. Was it a declaration? No. I breathed, began again, and read as he told me how much he had missed me, how dim and silly the evening's glitter had seemed without my company. He assured me that every detail we had conceived together had been perfect and there hadn't been a minute I wasn't missed. One detail alone had deviated from our plan: in my absence, he had given me honorable mention and every British officer present had knelt at my name.

Then he confirmed what fear had already announced: He was leaving Philadelphia, along with any Loyalists who wanted safe passage to New York, his life in the city complete.

I hadn't realized how much hope I'd held on to through the stupor of despair all that last night. Instead of the proposal I had imagined, instead of a ring sliding to the hilt of my finger, he was leaving me with a lock of his hair. It was good hair, springy and silky, but like a cut flower, for all its beauty, it felt dead already.

I felt massive twisting weather in my chest. I was angry as well as heartbroken—the anger taking longer to own. We had shared such intimacy, admitted all secrets, and all the while he was encouraging me to sketch and plan his party, even to believe it might prevail, he must have known the British had been preparing to concede the city. It felt an unthinkable betrayal: They hadn't been fought out of town, they had abandoned us to their enemies. All the talk of protecting us from the rebel menace, only to voluntarily leave us stranded. And, I realized with a sudden sob, I'd never returned Franklin's book.

I fell back and pulled the covers over my head. Atty gave my shoulder a squeeze through the sheets and, muttering something sensible, left me.

Nine thousand British soldiers massed that June, along with three thousand Loyalists taking Clinton up on his offer of safe passage to New York. There was a different quality to the soldiers' stride as they left town from when they'd arrived. Instead of the liberators they'd believed themselves to be, they were conceding defeat, resigned to more war. The officers were mounted on frisky horses turning brisk circles, the British elite effecting familiar insouciance as they oversaw the massive exodus—even before the vaunted peace commission had arrived.

Twenty minutes after the British boats departed, the American light horse entered the city with swords drawn, galloping around the streets with a lot of unnecessary shouting given nobody was getting in their way. Officers were billeted in the houses and public buildings the British had just departed, and the city was put on blackout. A bellmen going door to door told us to stay inside. The order might have stopped looting, but we could hear the carousing of the Patriot soldiers who now controlled our fate. Into the early hours, Bluecoats spilled out of taverns, kicking the rubbish and waste the British had left through our streets.

By morning, we learned General Benedict Arnold had taken command of the city. My father slowly lifted down the portrait of the King, leaving a dark rectangle of wallpaper which he partially concealed with a clock.

Aside from the pain, my failure was mortifying.

I had fallen far too hard and fast. André had made me want to stand up every time he came into the room. I hadn't, thankfully—but I had felt like it—he just had that effect. It was as if he understood everything and still knew what to do.

I had overexposed my hopes. With him gone, I couldn't think of anything about our time together without crying in humiliation. I was a fool for suspending disbelief all those weeks when there were signs it couldn't last.

Even as Theodosia's kind and patient voice was telling me, "Peggy. There's better yet ahead," a much more calm and charming voice was needling, *Something is wrong with you, Peggy Shippen. For a while you might seem viable, but underneath you're fundamentally deficient. Your mother sees.*

I thought ending my life was the best thing for everyone. The idea was an insistent snake in my inner ear, clearer and closer than any voice in the real world I could hear. I practiced knots with the drapery ties, eyed the ornamental sword above the fireplace, and coveted soldiers' muskets. I chastised myself with the life I needed to live for my brothers' sake, but contempt for my own selfishness only made me want oblivion more. *Wait for Theodosia*, something told me. *Hold on for her.* In desperation I wrote to her, begging her to find a way through the lines to Philadelphia.

I would pretend to swallow food and stash it under my pillow, later throwing it from the window. Atty shooed dogs enjoying the scraps from our step and persevered, bringing me small portions of the most enticing elements from any of the family's meals, keeping up a constant natter about the latest family drama, her younger sister's interrupted elopement, and spelling *yes* in the frosting on a tiny cupcake, so I couldn't not take a bite.

Theodosia wrote to tell me she was on her way. There were strings she could pull in New Jersey, and Abraham was still on the gate. I took that good fortune to mean the authorities knew, war or not, they had to let bonds between women hold strong. Even thinking of seeing her again, I felt better, and became stern with my self-pity. I would not collapse in madness over a man. I would not give up. It was hardly as if peace should be easy. One way or another, I would find my spine and a new way to contribute.

The better I felt, the more ashamed I became to think of my pathetic self-indulgence in front of my family and Atty. Atty, who was always contending with some terrible difficulty and staying relentlessly cheerful. I washed and dressed and said a frank "sorry" to her. She made nothing of the bother, saying she was glad to see my appetite back and trusted there'd be less mess on the doorstep.

After a small breakfast, I went down to the garden, the farthest I'd felt able to venture in days. It was good to feel the sunlight on my face and, stooping, to run my fingers along the same yew hedges I had run through as a child.

My mother had planted and tended those gardens. I'd never given her vision its due, when what she'd created here was beautiful, and useful too. I'd always overlooked her inspiration and effort, given the digging was done by Henry, the man my grandfather had gifted my father, and I never could feel right about his life. I thought of him now, the hope he must have had of the British liberating more and more slaves as they prevailed, and I was newly ashamed of my selfish preoccupations.

In the compost pile, I saw a single improbable bluebell sprouting from the mulch, and that seemed as good a sign as any I should pull myself together.

Theo saw immediately I was low on spirit, and after a brisk hug she insisted we take a walk. We settled on a bench in the shade of Christ Church, and she asked after the last days with André.

"Oh, Theo, I let myself hope—"

"I know."

I shook my head, banishing the threat of tears. "Disappointing he's gone. *Godawful* to think of more war. And the waste, Theodosia, my parents spent a small fortune, and I failed at the one thing they wanted me for. I am so sick of feeling this fear. The dread of every day's developments. I want it over!"

"There is a difference between wanting out and wanting peace," Theodosia said.

"I want peace," I said. "I want it for my sake, and I want it for all. At least I can remember life before. I refuse to accept a generation knowing nothing but this misery. I told André, and before God, there is no way I'm bringing a child into a world at war. It must stop if I'm ever to be a mother."

Aware I must sound irritating to Theodosia, who had children of her own, I said I was sorry. I was tired of saying sorry, which must have meant I was ready to be better.

"Besides, it's not as if any prospect of children is apparent—"

She laughed. "Peggy, you're not yet eighteen! Though I know how you're feeling. Not knowing how much longer it will go on is exhausting. But we feel our way slowly forward, striving for calm, alert for opportunities to do good. I think if you know that is what you want, and prepare best you can, sometimes a window will open and you can move very quickly to your goal. Almost effortlessly, when the time is right, carried by the energy of good intention—"

"I knew you'd be important to me the minute we first met."

"I loved you at once, but I worried, I think." She rapidly rubbed my back. "Saw something needing encouraging, if you weren't going to be vulnerable to despair."

"And here you are steering me from the abyss."

"Feel sad, Peggy, but don't feel fear and shame about it. André, clearly, has shown you what rapport with a man can be. He's elevated your aesthetic—and shown you a more exciting life. Your disappointment is natural. And it's survivable! Let it drive you. Look for a man even better. Perhaps, with a little time for reflection, and more of my maddening prompting, you might see André was something of your twin?"

"I did love the mirror he held up to me, his generous take on everything I did."

"I don't doubt the importance he will have in your life. You'll remain friends, Peggy. No need to lose all that pleasure and benefit. You should begin a correspondence. But perhaps his real gift is in pointing the way to what's next? Think of André as Romeo's Rosaline, preparing you for the true love ahead—"

"Without the tragedy," we said in unison, and I laughed. Enough.

Part Two

Chapter Ten

It was a few weeks still before I had the front to visit Stansbury and Odell. Nobody knew better the store I'd put in André, and I risked more tears even thinking of their sympathy for my defeat. In the privacy of my bedroom, I tried out the wry, resigned line I wanted to take on the British departure, without my voice wavering and betraying my feebleness—"Ah well, the end of an era."

But I couldn't linger in self-pity forever. I'd come to need the news filtered by my friends' wit and lightly delivered dish. Perhaps I was addicted to their insider perspective. Proximity to power had given an illusion of control so comforting it had stopped my Dread Index from rocketing, and I wanted more of it, however unreliable it had proved to be. I splashed my eyes with cold water, slapped my cheeks, and set out.

There was tense but irrepressible energy about the Colonial forces in the city. The Bluecoats had visibly raised their game. Well-made men marched in impressive configuration, proud and intimidating with their gains.

Stansbury's store was shuttered, which frightened me, but when I knocked, a curtain twitched aside, and he let me in. Even by candlelight it was clear the floors were unswept and the cubbies empty.

"You're not rich enough to be this thin," Odie teased me.

"His Excellency will smell weakness, and that helps nobody here."

I looked at Stansbury sharply.

"Joseph Reed. Now our highest civilian authority: president of the newly reinstated Supreme Executive Council."

Making Esther first lady of the state. What would I have to call her? It was an endless dilemma, when to move from title to first name to nickname or not.

"His first action was to persuade Congress to shut the shops and seize our stores—"

"What does that achieve?" I asked, staring at the dusty cubbies.

"The idea is the army gets the use of all goods, but you can bet you'll see our silks appear for resale on the black market—"

"What of your income?" I asked.

"We have enough to tide us over a couple of months, thanks to the party of parties, but the worry is how our role in it will come back to bite us now. Reed talks of fining everyone who attended the Mischianza one hundred thousand dollars—"

"That's an insane amount of money. There's nobody it wouldn't ruin. It cannot be. The peace commission might still prevail?" I said desperately. "They can barely have started."

"Imagine their anger on landing to find Clinton had given up the city. Surrendering the seat of government hardly helped their chances of negotiating peace."

"I think we need to accept the commission is dead on arrival," Odie said.

I felt my eyes fill. I turned away and tipped my face to the ceiling. It took everything I had to steady my breathing. Stansbury tactfully faffed about folding clothes until he gathered I was ready.

"What do we do?" I asked.

"I'll swear the oath of allegiance if it gets us back in business," Stansbury said, and then, acknowledging my surprise, "I've become rather attached to staying alive. And I want to see you safely settled."

"I'm afraid your marriage has become Joseph's special project—" Odie said.

"André did write me a nice letter after the Mischianza," I said pathetically.

"We miss him too, Peggy. But clearly André wasn't the one."

"The 'one'?" Odell scoffed.

"Yes! Whoever he is, he's out there," Stansbury insisted, "getting ready for Peggy."

"Will you listen to yourself?" Odie said, "That's like looking to a horoscope for hope."

But I was a little comforted, as a person can be by timely astrology.

"What you need, Peggy Shippen, is a man of power, with the freedom to commit to you. Romantically unequivocal, but with the skill to navigate this city's lethal currents."

"Decisive, but amenable to influence," Odie chipped in, and they laughed.

"Not too biddable," I said. "I don't like the glimpses I've seen of wives using tears and guilt and threats of withholding heaven knows what to get their way—"

Stansbury laughed. "Not excessively uxorious then, but indulgent enough that we can keep dressing you."

"Belle of the ball will take more investment after eighteen—" Odie said.

"Cheek!" I flicked his sleeve. "How lethal are these currents? Really?"

"If we were entirely at the mercy of Reed's civilian authority, I'd be halfway to New York already, but Washington has given military command of the city to Arnold while he recovers from another battle injury."

"And you trust him?"

"He's tasked explicitly with preserving security for all city residents. Should prove some check on Reed's retaliatory instincts."

"Which has more power of the two?"

"That remains to be seen," Odie said.

I gave a jagged breath.

"You worked so hard on the party, Peggy, only to have the British pull out of town. Given the line Reed's taking, I'm not sorry you weren't in attendance, but it's hard to have received no credit."

"I don't mind that. I liked working behind the scenes. I am sad it didn't succeed."

"Success? Failure? Who can say without the benefit of a long view? A creative contribution might not be recognized within one lifetime," Odie said.

"Poor unappreciated poet," Stansbury teased.

"There's all sorts of good work to be done in the wings," Odie said pointedly. And then, as if apropos of nothing, he added, "If you did wish to write a reply to André's letter, we'd be happy to relay it. Safer that way, with the Committee for Observation eager to make an example of anyone implicated with the British. I'll see the captain in Manhattan and can bring his letters by return."

It was tempting. I craved him, and missed the sense of safety he'd lent me, but I needed time before I was ready to take any line except the childish whys still bleating round my mind.

I was more worried about being interesting to him than the risks in writing.

I turned eighteen that July, which felt nothing to celebrate given we were entering the fourth year of war. I spent the morning bleakly reading details about the failed peace commission. I was touched by the effort with which the British delegation had been put together, even as I saw why Patriots would find it condescending. In the Militia Man's printed opinion the whole endeavor was reason for rage. *The Pennsylvania Packet* reported that any man or group who came to terms with Lord Carlisle would be declared an enemy of America. How could peace ever be achieved if even entertaining it was criminal? I hated to imagine André's dejection, and the escalation in Patriot rhetoric made me feel the sharp stakes of our failure all over again.

Just as my birthday was feeling as far from fun as it could be, Betsy opened the door to a visibly pregnant Esther and, in her nervous attempt to deflect the visit, needlessly let slip the occasion and the fact we had nothing planned.

Esther insisted on lifting my spirits with a little visit and, powerless apparently to stop her, Betsy showed her in. I was irritated with both of them. Clearly, I'd wished to make a nothing of the day or I wouldn't have been spending it like this, and Esther was the last person I wanted as a witness.

Her eyes appraised the furniture as she wished me "the happiest of birthdays."

I congratulated her on her pregnancy and her husband's new position, and she talked of her "gracious wish as first lady to turn the women of the city's barren wishes for revolutionary success into useful action." Was that a twin dig at my failures? No, I would not spend my life recoiling from slights, real or perceived, while looking for my own chance to strike. Even if I was a barren failure of a spinster sister, I refused to be a drag on anyone else's happiness.

I thought of my delight on earlier birthdays, turning seven in a smocked dress, my brothers' faces lit up by wonder at the cake and the candles. I remembered my weight on my hands as I leaned in and blew. What was it I'd wished so hard for? To be shown what I was good for, what it was I was meant to do.

That longing wasn't so different from Esther's probably. I sat straighter in my chair, resolving to appreciate the things in Esther that Eliza liked. I looked at our visitor with what I hoped was warmer curiosity and asked what it was she had in mind.

Esther told me her first scheme was assisting her husband in staging a rally to celebrate the failure of Carlisle's peace commission. My heart sank to imagine a gathering glad of more war, but I'd heard enough to know the danger in refusing. I was curious, too, to see how her husband presented, now that I knew so much about him: a Washington favorite and the Council president, a foiled conspirator, and a pseudonymous newspaper contributor, a man who'd risen as close to the Patriot pinnacle as André was to the British.

He made us wait, but the crowd seemed patient. Esther had organized a band to play a few Revolutionary staples on repeat. When at last Reed did appear, he was immaculately shaved, with hair that showed the comb tracks and a long, prominent nose. The crowd roared their approval as he took center stage. It was a while before he could be heard over the cheering and when his voice did rise above the din, I shrank from it like an allergy. He announced the formation of "the Patriotic Society, to support each other in disclosing and bringing to justice all Tories within our knowledge" while men shouldered through the malodorous crowd collecting money and doling out patriotic pins.

As donations slowed, Reed ramped up the invective, talking of Loyalists as "vermin emerging from obscurity, like insects after a storm." He urged citizens to gather evidence on neighbors they suspected had been collaborators. Two witnesses would be sufficient to convict.

Did I hate all this as viscerally as I did only because we were at risk? There was self-interest in my fear, but it was true too that contempt for neighbors and relish for political violence felt objectively repellent.

The crowd jeered their obedience, men and women—and children—straining at the leash to please him. Esther joined him on stage to take his hand, looking from the sea of loyal followers to her husband, object of their devotion, with a smile of delighted surprise and pride. She looked radiant, while he called for war on all internal enemies.

They came for Mrs. Galloway again that night. I sat with my back to the window as she declared her right to possession of her property, her voice quavering only slightly. A man retorted her husband had forfeited her all protection of the state when he left for New York with General Howe, and then servants were crying, a horse was rearing, and I had to turn and look as she was pulled from her own home, yanked by the hips in unthinkable indignity, the tips of her fingers prized one by one from the doorframe while her young maid, restrained, whimpered like a trapped animal.

All the sleepless night, I could hear the creak of my parents' rope bed in the room beneath me. My own guilty breathing. The sounds of nothing being done.

By sunup, a couple of men were looking on from horseback, reins relaxed in their laps, appraising the property, Mrs. Galloway reduced to a nuisance removed.

I didn't know who to mind more: the man who could pull a woman from her home and profit from its auction, or the one who could leave his wife alone to face violent eviction and the loss of everything they owned. I was haunted by wondering where she had gone, where I'd go if thrown out of our house.

Newspapers printed more names of those considered guilty, as if endorsing the resulting harassment and physical attacks. I watched my father scanning the lists each evening, gathering from his forehead if our own names were there yet.

"There's going to be a great deal of suffering," my father remarked one night, folding the newspaper crisply.

"Well, yes," mother agreed, sewing impassively. "A great deal."

Confounded by their complacency, my Index soaring, I claimed the paper and retreated with it to bed. I scanned the words too rapidly to read them. I slowed and tried again, stomach tilting with fear. My heart stopped to see the name of Abraham Carlisle among those suspected of British sympathies.

My father invited Joseph and Esther Reed to tea.

"Why would you do that?" I objected. "André called him a zealot."

"André." My mother shrugged, consigning him to irrelevance.

"Joseph Reed is a respected man of the law, Peggy. Comes from jolly good stock. A lawyer's livelihood depends on seeing both sides. I thought you were friendly with his wife."

"I believe he takes provocative positions to satisfy his followers," Neddy said. "Keep them appeased and distracted so they don't notice he doesn't act on them."

It was a curious and unnerving thing to witness a new political atmosphere establishing itself inside the house, to feel affinities shifting in real time. Reed, a man whom the men I trusted—along with my own nerves and senses—warned me against, was suddenly not only tolerated but grudgingly respected and then, apparently, plain admired.

My father, who had deplored the overweening ambition of radicals—despised the progressive vision of Paine—now listened respectfully to Neddy while he talked excitedly of the Declaration of Independence settling into history, giving him a scale for understanding how the Gospels had coalesced and come to mean to us what they did.

Sporting a big, conspicuously expensive watch and buttons embroidered with *USA*, Reed took evident satisfaction in recounting that Abraham Carlisle had been seen to cry as he was pursued from the gate to his door.

"Who chased him?" I asked.

"Civilians, and fine citizens among them. They're nothing if not committed," he chuckled, and sighed. "God only knows what becomes of his family without his protection. You know the man has granddaughters not much older than your girls—"

He was practically gleeful, willing the pillaging to begin.

My mother asked Esther the conventional questions about her pregnancy.

"You'll have grandchildren of your own soon, I gather." Esther smiled, acknowledging Betsy and Neddy's impending wedding. Betsy blushed scarlet.

"I'm sure you're looking forward to seeing both your daughters settled, Edward." Reed flashed his outsize teeth at me. My father didn't contradict him, which made me feel I was being tipped from the nest.

"The choice of husband will be of more than material interest at this time of inflamed sentiment." Reed leaned back, one arm slung awkwardly over the chair back, parading his narrow chest. "Will the young ladies resist, or submit?"

He really was intolerably on the nose. I stood abruptly and walked to the window, feeling his eyes follow.

"A pity to compound an already dangerous suspicion of ambivalence, Edward—"

"Perhaps we make a different assessment of risk," Father said.

"Apparently so."

Reed stood. "One precaution, you know, on which I'm sure we can all agree, is the loyalty oath."

"I keep my own counsel, Joseph."

Reed smiled unpleasantly. "Purely a courteous suggestion, at this time—"

He tipped his hat as he and Esther left.

"Father, please tell me you won't expect me to marry to please him and his regime—"

"Try not to think only of yourself, Peggy."

"He feels like an enemy to the whole family—our entire city—civilization itself!"

"Shh, Peggy. He wouldn't dare come for me."

"How do you know? I'd say we're exactly the kind of prize he'd like to claim!"

"Watch your tone. Reed holds me in too much esteem."

"Mr. Galloway was the former speaker of the Assembly and that's been no protection. And Abraham Carlisle everyone likes—"

"Is rebellion encouraging your insubordination, Peggy?" Mother asked. "I will not have such insolence."

"I didn't mean disrespect, only to understand the extent of the threat!"

"Remember who it is you address. Elders and betters, Peggy! Enough!"

I was sent to my room, where the feeling of powerlessness and anxiety threatened to slay me.

Chapter Eleven

Headquarters, New York City, August 16, 1779

Madam, our friend is so good as to take charge of this letter, which is meant to solicit your remembrance, and to assure you that my respect for you, and the fair circle in which I had the honor of becoming acquainted with you, remains unimpaired by distance or political broils. It would make me very happy to become useful to you here. You know the Mischianza made me a complete milliner. Should you not have received supplies for your fullest equipment from that department, I shall be glad to enter into the whole detail of wire, needles, gauze, etc., and, to the best of my abilities, render you in these trifles services from which I hope you would infer a zeal to be further employed.

I beg you would present my best respects to your sister, to Miss Chew, and to Mrs. Shippen and Mrs. Chew.

With the greatest regard, I have the honor to be, Madam, your most obedient and most humble servant, John André.

* * *

I looked happily from the precious letter to Odell, who'd delivered it while Stansbury pinned me into the dress he was making me for the first of General Arnold's impending gatherings.

I felt I'd be attending only under duress, and when it came to what to wear, I couldn't care, but my mother sensibly insisted my outfits must not risk reminding anyone present of dances with the British. And when Stansbury told me he'd had to buy back his own fabric on the black market, I was determined to make the money he'd spent pay.

I read the letter a second time, only then wondering about his "zeal to be further employed." Did he see I might need him? Consider me in immediate danger under Reed?

"I should respond?"

"Certainly, you should." Stansbury smiled. "You never did get back to him after the Mischianza."

"I was waiting to have something worth telling him."

"Meeting his former captor should be interesting."

Perhaps I could come to tease him about that, the veteran who'd got his better.

"What you write is immaterial. The point is only to keep the channel open. For all of us to feel we can still reach each other, should things deteriorate further—"

André in New York, Theo in New Jersey, all of us apart was too much already. I couldn't be without Odell and Stansbury and was scared to think what new extremes their needing to leave would mean for me.

Odie said what worried him was it becoming impossible to get word in and out of New York, full stop.

I had been aware all my life of the risk and irritation of letters miscarrying, and the need to choose men and methods of conveyance carefully. My father often referred to trusted channels of his own, and to the dangers in saying anything of public interest in writing, but if they could take away the freedom of friends to write at all, I'd have nothing to read but stifling political pieties and competing propaganda.

"I'd rather die than lose touch with all of you."

"That we cannot have," Stansbury said.

Odie said there was something they had wondered about discussing with me. He hesitated.

"Please," I said. "Didn't we agree to speak freely here?"

"It's an interest André and I share, as it happens. An informed curiosity about the arts of intelligence. While there's nothing clandestine expected of you, it might not be a bad idea—given letters are increasingly being intercepted—and perhaps even a helpful distraction from unwelcome developments to experiment with learning new skills—say communications in code and invisible ink?"

"That way we'd always have a path to each other," Stansbury said, squeezing my hand. "Come what may."

They could teach me, Odell went on, how to interline a letter with hidden messages, and though we would only ever, God willing, need to exchange personal news and stories, we could take comfort that if some suspicious official did rip open our letters, our privacy would be protected. Our right—as fundamental a right as I could imagine—to correspond without interference would remain.

I was intrigued, and a little excited, but Stansbury was stern. While he would never intentionally endanger me, not for anything, there were risks I ought to understand in attempting secret communications, even if the letters themselves were of no consequence.

He spoke of a woman caught carrying messages to and from the invading royal forces in the summer of 1776. Denounced as "the damned Tory penny post," she had been stripped naked and exposed to the mob, leaving her with a permanent "horror of the mind".

I felt a stubborn defiance, a child's assertion of what was fair. To have had word from André—him reaching for me—only to be threatened with his removal forever was unacceptable. Learning to circumvent the scrutiny of a crude and cruel regime like Reed's felt justified, a matter of pride. And I knew there was nothing like activity to relieve my anxiety.

The threat of madness felt safely theoretical then.

* * *

It was a game, initially, a fun puzzle with paper and ink, played in the warm beam of my friends' attention.

Each fitting I attended, the lessons became more serious. Stansbury would set ever more exacting challenges to occupy me while he did the dressmaking that remained our alibi for my time.

They had me practice delicately stroking a brush dipped in counter liquor over a piece of apparently innocent paper until script started to appear as if by magic. Initially, my touch was too heavy, and the reagent instantly smeared the message into illegibility. I tried again, my hand shaking to keep a featherlight touch, slowly using ink and acid to summon faint green script from somewhere within the paper. I laughed in relief to see the message Odell had prepared for me was "Boo."

Next, Joseph lifted the lid from another pot with a flourish. The solution was made with lemons, pungent but not unpleasant. As we graduated to leeks, vinegar, and piss, my enthusiasm faltered. The so-called stain was smelly and, I worried, ridiculously suspicious. "Anyone coming upon a letter that stank to high heaven would know they had intercepted something secret! Wouldn't they apply heat just to see?"

"Trial and error, Peggy. There's no manual for this."

And there were hazards, we discovered, in the application of heat. The iron—always at hand to press my dresses—would slowly, gradually, bring hidden lines to life, but too much heat and the pages burned, obscuring what might have been a vital secret forever. Several of our test communications caught fire before even a hint of their contents could be gleaned. Stansbury and I started to giggle. Odell's crossness only made us laugh harder. But with evidence of escalating conflict in every edition of both newspapers, we were soon trying seriously again.

Stansbury covered me in a vast apron and gloves. The men laid out various solutions in lidded pots, along with brushes and an assortment of parchments. It was fun, and interesting, and I loved the chance to make a mess, all while feeling this was the most useful thing I could be doing. I believed I was getting ready to be where I needed to be.

"You're a quick study," Stansbury noted, and I felt my back straighten.

Unlocking an initially inscrutable message was as amazing to me as the ability to read. I could still remember the satisfaction of cracking that key. The delight in realizing, at five, that there was now no word in English I couldn't decipher and nothing, by that logic, I couldn't find out. I thought the whole world was legible to me then. No more mystery and hidden intentions. I'd been so excited to teach my brothers, I set up a schoolroom before they were walking, propping them on pillows in front of my blackboard years before my lessons would ever have meant a thing.

I was proud now to master the new, harder-won access of code, and doubly so when Stansbury presented me with my first secret letter from André, a test of my proficiency.

Though it was addressed to the store, and looked every inch an order for braid trimming, Odie showed how discreet flourishes in the *p* of *Joseph* and *S* of *Stansbury* designated the letter for me. Under the optimum heat, André's elegant handwriting came slowly swimming to the surface. I was spellbound.

"Are you frightened?" Stansbury asked. "It would be natural."

"I think it's guilt, not fear I'm feeling, just because it's secret."

"Secrecy is only sensible at a time like this. And besides, nothing material's being said."

It was true: André was simply repeating his wish to be of service to me, and venturing a suggestion that rather than run a single unnecessary risk, I should write to him of nonsense and shopping while interlining in invisible ink anything needing discretion.

I lay the letter in my lap, feeling the familiar exhilaration in sailing close to the wind in conversation with him.

The danger still felt safer than despair.

Chapter Twelve

The night of General Arnold's party arrived, and Stansbury had gone all out. He needed the Patriots' business, and I was to be a walking advertisement for his work.

"You're trembling like a thoroughbred longing to bolt." Stansbury smiled, smoothing the fabric over my back.

A fair analogy for the amount of agency I felt over my fate.

"Is it irrational to fear the party might be a trap, a lure to round up anyone still feeling the smallest misgiving about Patriot tactics? It wouldn't be difficult to eliminate us all in one place—and would only be in line with Reed's rhetoric about routing every last neutral and Tory from the continent."

"Don't confuse Arnold's Patriotism with Reed's brand of it."

Even if not immediately dangerous, was it sickening that the city seemed in such a hurry to kiss the ring of the new regime?

As Stansbury made the final adjustments, he tried to calm me by making me laugh with impressions in a dozen regional accents of accounts he'd heard about the disabled general from veterans in the tavern:

"He was our fighting general, and a bloody fellow he was. He didn't care for nothing; he'd ride right in. It was 'Come on, boys'—never 'Go, boys.' He's as brave a man as ever lived."

"He was active as lightning, he was, and with a ready wit always at command."

"The excitement of danger has for him an irresistible charm."

I laughed. "He sounds a proper old Hotspur."

"America's Hannibal, they call him. And on water? He's unmatched as a sailor—"

"Reed can't welcome such a star as his counterpart. How do the two of them get on?"

"Reed will see this party as a provocation," Odell warned. "Lavishing Patriot funds on Philadelphia high society. Known Loyalists among them. He's calling it 'extraordinary,' and you know he won't let it go."

"I call it consoling," Stansbury said. "We're all residents of the same city." I noticed how much older he looked, the worry of recent weeks taking its toll.

Uncle William was in town, now chief medic to the entire Continental Army, and he and my father, along with Neddy, were to join us at the party. My mother's rheumatism was troubling her, and Betsy stayed home to keep her company.

I was grateful for Stansbury's finery when it came to seeing my uncle again. "My dear Peggy." He bowed and took my arm. "Shall we? I'm curious to see how the general's leg's healed up."

"Was the injury very terrible?"

"Hessians shot his horse from under him, piercing his leg with a musket ball, and as the horse fell, it landed on the wounded leg and splintered his thigh bone. Tried to wrestle me from his bed to not amputate. It was months before he could even sit up without splitting the stitches."

He glanced at my expression. "Too many specifics?"

I laughed. "I am curious to meet him."

"I was glad to see you invited. Maybe my brother knows what he's doing after all, tacking this way and that across the water."

I smiled back at my father, proud of him, and grateful. Perhaps asking me to sacrifice the Meschianza had been a wise strategy—it wasn't a bad calculation, as it happened—and I did love to trust him.

"Where's Mrs Shippen?" William asked him.

"Home with swollen joints. Been creeping about the chamber on her crutches all winter."

"You should let me see what I can do—"

"A disciplined diet should see to it. That's the best medicine."

William looked at me, tongue between his teeth.

"How are conditions in camp?" I asked.

"Better since General Arnold's arrival. Farmers are making deliveries again. Our young warriors look sturdier every day."

"I'm happy to hear it."

I lifted my skirts to avoid tripping and smiled at the barely restrained excitement with which William and Neddy looked out for our host. I scanned the small crowd at the top of the stairs, expecting an old duffer with a powdered wig, high color, and a peg leg.

As the new military governor of the city came into view, I almost laughed. My friends had made the man sound an ancient mariner, an invalid widower, near dead from a lurid litany of injuries. Instead, an elegant crutch was the only hint he wasn't at full force.

"Note the epaulettes, a gift from Washington," Neddy muttered.

I nodded, more interested in the chiseled muscle definition than his shoulder ornaments. He projected a great, lean strength. My glance reached his face. His smiling eyes beneath dark winged eyebrows were an unusual sapphire blue. Why had nobody mentioned the man was Greek-god handsome?

His hair was thick and dark, drawn in a good, clean ponytail back from his face. His skin was the sort to age well, and the line of his jaw highly inviting. When my turn came, and he took my hand in his, I felt enjoyably small.

He murmured his compliments to the "legendary Miss Shippen"—extravagant gallantry, given his own earned celebrity. His voice conjured cannons and sea shanties. He was greeting me a little as if I was his captive Queen—his manner acknowledging I had known more power and freedom, but that fate had seen fit to deliver me here. His deep blue eyes told me I was welcome and had nothing to fear.

He turned to William and slapped his back.

"This man's pieced me back together more than once."

"Oh, we've seen a thing or two," William said, bashful and happy.

"I'm afraid your uncle could tell many tales which wouldn't speak well of me, Miss Shippen. I am not the most patient patient."

He was welcoming my father and Neddy now, directing them to his personal supply of good whiskey.

He gave me one last smile, eyes like warm inviting water, before gently pressing me into the party, my whole body abuzz.

He was so entirely a general, but much younger than a man twenty years my senior had any right to seem.

All evening I willed him to come to me, but he had the entire city's who's who to meet. Nobody talked of anything but him—his magnificent exploits and irresistible wit. He couldn't have set it up better if it had been his intention to seduce every woman in Philadelphia.

Effusive with champagne, Uncle William testified at increasing volume to "his noble and Christian command and useful knowledge of apothecary."

"He thought nothing of abandoning prosperous business interests—a successful store, ships, and stables—the minute soldiers were wanted," he continued. "And he paid his own soldiers for months on end when Congress failed to furnish funds."

"I heard he forbade inoculation on penalty of death," my father said.

"Only to prevent devastating spread. Soldiers were self-inoculating without quarantine—which led to rampant rates of infection. You could never accuse Arnold of not having his men's best interests at heart, Edward. He's the men's favorite of all the great generals. And Washington loves him like none other—like a brother." My uncle seemed in danger of moving himself to tears. My father clapped his shoulder. I turned away to hide my delight. If Arnold had the power to unite these two, he was already a hero to me.

Later, I sat beside my father watching the dancing and feeling full of goodwill.

"If my going to the Mischianza would have prevented this—our safety—I'm glad you stopped me, Papa. I'm sorry I worried you."

He nodded, taking my apology as overdue.

"I was hurt at the time that you didn't trust me."

"We never said that."

* * *

"Well?" Neddy asked, as we watched Arnold surrounded by women vying to show him more cleavage. I watched him share a moment with May—who was flirting up at him from layers of unapologetic taffeta, his on a silver platter. Not again, surely. She could have anyone!

A mild-mannered young man with a great head of hair, Major Franks, came to refill my glass and talk of Arnold. He described crazy experiments with gunpowder, adventures with pistols, barrels, constables, and criminals. The drinks were liberal and with a small audience egging him on, Franks acted out Arnold keeping his feet on a waterwheel while it was turning full circle! Even as a small child the general had been a baby Hercules, with "few, if any, superiors as a marksman." By Franks's account, the man was never not running, fencing, boxing, or leaping.

"Even after he recovered from his wound received at Quebec, at Fort Stanwix, he'd vaulted over a loaded ammunition wagon without touching hand or foot.

"He ran away twice from home, the first at fifteen to enlist as a soldier in the 1755 war between France and Great Britain, and soon after being returned safely home, left again to join the provincial troops in Albany and Lake George."

If he hadn't been in the room, I'd have dismissed all the talk of his preternatural abilities as propaganda. Looking at him though, I dared hope God had produced the man to win peace. And if he was to lead us, it was a relief his spirit felt the furthest thing from Reed's.

I found myself meeting, just fleetingly, Arnold's vivid blue gaze as he passed. It was almost unfair, the advantage those eyes gave him. The attraction I felt was so insistently physical—primal—it carried me faster than floodwater. I was ready to be flung over his shoulder while he waded to Quebec, to let him build me a shelter and stare at me across a campfire before taking me to bed.

Neddy brought me a drink. "I swear I counted nine admirers using tales of the general to woo you."

"He has the city eating out of his hand," I observed, watching him deflect all the flatterers with affable modesty. Though sorry to think of him suffering,

I liked the fact of his injury. He had given everything a man could, and lived. That put him beyond contest, and the way he shrugged off the heroism, and welcomed citizens that others—the Militia Man—would swear were enemies, made him as reassuring a presence as I'd met.

"Peggy, do I see old attachments loosening?" Neddy teased.

I was never such a Loyalist I had trouble seeing the merit in a Patriot. Uncle William had been nearly as dear to me as my father, all my life. But looking at the general, and thinking of André, a hot lightning fork ran through me, the burning enormity of all I wanted reconciled impossible to escape. I laid a grateful hand on Neddy's steady arm.

"Let's get home."

I didn't write to tease André about his old captor. I couldn't find the tone.

The next time the general and I met, the gathering was more intimate, a lunch party for twenty: Neddy and Betsy; my father and me; the affable narrator from the party, aide-de-camp Major Franks; and a few other senior officers, along with the Reeds.

"I remember that dress, Peggy," Esther said. "Pretty."

Her own wardrobe, I noticed, was becoming more expensive. Joseph, sporting his signature USA pin, was accusing Major Franks of having asked a guardsman to fetch a barber.

"Freeman will not submit to such indignities—" Reed fumed. I glanced at our host. Reed's seemed an unnecessary scene to make as a guest.

"What's all this?" Benedict's voice was friendly, but with an edge. "We're not worrying about a short back and sides, are we, Reed? I'm sorry the young guardsman's pride was offended to be asked to summon a barber, or that he came to find he felt it was when he later spoke with his father—Matlack, a friend of yours, I think?—but as an orderly sergeant, it was the guardsman's duty to obey every order of my aide Major Franks, as of mine, without judging its propriety. Now. Shall we eat?"

I was seated next to the general, but his ongoing habit of hardly looking at me wasn't encouraging. Though I thought he'd handled himself well with

Reed, the confrontation had clearly cost him, and he remained uneasy. Reed, unscathed, was addressing the table:

"Yes, I very much look forward to working with the general, sharing as we do a mutual friend, General Washington, you know. I flatter myself I might help him with any difficulties with the city administration. Politics will be an adjustment, after the brute force of battle."

Arnold ignored him. He was like a great snared bear, Reed prodding him through the bars.

We were served the best of colony produce: buttered new potatoes, salads, and chicken in delicious dill dressing. Only the wine was un-American—a gift, Arnold admitted ruefully, from the French King.

The meal was something of a guilty miracle given the difficulty Atty had finding anything in stores. We'd continued to go together to the market and sigh at the shortages—the eye-widening price of eggs and lack of variety. Some days there was nothing in the market but tinned pilchards—and it was touching to see the care with which store owners attempted to arrange their dismal, identical wares.

People were already tending to blame the new regime for shortages, and rising costs, though I imagined the truth was complicated, given the chaos and unpaid debts the British had left in their wake. Whatever the injustices, that lunch made clear Washington's governor general could procure a feast.

When I praised the changes he had made to the house since Howe left, Arnold said, "I'm pleased you like it. After all those nights in freezing encampments, creature comforts feel a little unreal. And I admit, the improvements are limited. You wouldn't find much furniture if you strayed upstairs—"

He turned away. I was forced to watch Reed as he lectured poor Franks again.

"Our noisy sons of liberty often prove the quietest in the field . . . An engagement, or even the expectation of one, gives extraordinary insight, you know, into character. The brave-talking bombasts can be first to flinch." He stared at Arnold. "While a man celebrated for bravery quickly becomes vainglorious and complacent about the enemy—"

Major Franks was longing to defend Arnold, I could see, but it was not in his nature to contradict a superior.

"Your feats are legendary," I said to the general.

"With the benefit of age—and injury." He nodded to his leg. "I can't hear the word *brave* without suspecting what's meant is *foolish.* I was never brave so much as guilty of feeling invincible. That and proud. My father had been disgraced"—he gave me a quick testing look—"arrested for public drunkenness. I was defensive—sensitive to slights. Submerging in a collective effort, purpose, was just the thing."

"I can see that would be a relief," I said.

"Men rush to it."

"To find they regret it?"

"The initial euphoria does not endure," he conceded.

"Then the priority must be making an end of it—"

"Yes. With victory and honor intact."

"You were a shopkeeper, I understand, General Arnold, before the war?" Esther asked in her high, clear voice.

"A general store," Reed smirked.

"Yes," Benedict said straightforwardly. I was briefly embarrassed for the Reeds, Benedict being so much the bigger man. "Thanks to my uncle. He gave me a little capital and I was lucky with it. Built and sailed a few ships. Sourced goods for the store. In New Haven." He glanced at me before looking sharply away. I was beginning to feel offended. He asked tightly, "Have you been?"

"Not yet."

"You fought for the British initially, I think," Reed said.

"As did General Washington," Franks said crisply. "I think we all felt a debt of allegiance at some time—"

"Rather than blaming Loyalists for being slow to adopt our thinking, better to illustrate the merits in our cause," Arnold said. "It wasn't unreasonable some men hoped for a time the rot could be repaired without destroying the entire edifice. As it is, the colonies have come of age and stand ready to hold their own, and now the world must acknowledge there can only be one outcome—"

He looked at me.

"Which is the better story, after all?"

I conceded his case with a tilt of the chin.

"What do you make, Miss Shippen," Reed asked unctuously, "of the motto General Arnold had installed above his shop: *Sibi totique*, 'For himself and for all'?"

"I think *Sibi totique* makes a fitting motto for a man selling remedies. Isn't that the reassuring promise of the self-inoculating doctor? I trust this myself—and recommend it?"

Arnold smiled. "An apothecary certainly should take his own medicine."

"I doubt you'd have been eager to sit beside the general if he'd still been a shopkeeper, Peggy." Esther laughed, and Reed looked eagerly to see if she'd offended me. I shrugged. It wasn't as if she were wrong, not in war. But back on a peaceful planet, an apothecary and bookseller, sourcing the best remedies and stories and imported luxuries, a handsome, strong man who could sail and ride, inspire and be trusted, would be all I'd want and more.

"Will you return to New Haven after the war?" I asked.

"Until the war is won, victory is my only horizon." I could see why men loved him.

"We'll annihilate every last enemy," Reed declared. A goal close to Arnold's and yet so far.

The general's voice dropped to a growl as he addressed himself to me alone: "We'll prevail, but how soon is harder to answer."

I couldn't help making comparisons. He didn't have André's ready elegance, but his unmannered way of speaking was appealing, and he was exciting in being so completely different from me. I liked the feeling he was making life up as he went along rather than taking a designated role, as so many seemed compelled to do. And the contrast with Reed made him feel not just necessary, but elemental.

"Miss Shippen was a great favorite of the British before their retreat," Esther said silkily.

"Were you sorry not to attend the Mischianza?" Arnold asked.

"I was abject."

He laughed.

"*Then*," I said.

"How is Captain André?" Reed smiled.

"Your former prisoner, I gather," I batted to Benedict.

"I remember. Appealing fellow. Widely beloved—"

"I hear nothing but affection for you—" I said.

"Stick around a while," he said, with a barely perceptible nod across the table.

"Who would criticize you now?" I asked. I meant given his victories, and hoped it wouldn't seem I'd made too much of his injury.

"Reputation is a perishable commodity." He smiled.

"As any lady is aware."

He glanced again at Reed.

"I was not always assiduous in keeping accounts of my contributions. Somehow, forging north to Quebec, I had a devil of a time keeping receipts."

"I imagine anyone capable of greatness in one arena must suffer a little deficit in another. It would hardly be fair to the rest of us if not. And who would want a stickler"—I glanced at Reed—"at a time like this?"

"In politics, I am learning," he said, "a man must be beyond reproach."

"Is reproach ever out of reach for those determined to find fault?" I asked, then worried I'd sounded sour.

"The trick is deterring underminers, without repressing dissent. A tricky needle to thread, even if we weren't at war—"

Esther was telling Franks she would plead no special treatment for females. "Nobody should be spared, whether mother or child, if an impediment in throwing off the odious yoke of the British."

"We'll see if I can find the balance—and stand it," Arnold muttered.

"Relations between the Council and Congress sound testing," I said.

"Don't they? A source of shame. And a great disappointment to our Commander in chief."

"Do you think a new government of the United States could avoid the opposition and antagonism of British political parties? Questions put to ministers of the Crown can sound so aggressively rude. Any squabbling makes me want to pay no attention, except that's not acceptable when such terribly consequential things are happening." I dropped my voice. "Arrests of friends—wives abandoned, cast out of their houses."

"I intend to ensure fair trials for all."

"That's a great relief."

I realized I'd been holding my breath and made a deliberate effort to release it.

"Is it reassuring, having the best information? Or more alarming, being privy to things far worse than the rest of us know?"

He considered. "The picture is always incomplete. Hardest to see are enemies on one's own side. And where there aren't hostility and intrigue, there's often incompetence. Contradiction, conjecture, falsehood. Most of the information which reaches us can't be trusted."

He was too honest to be a political animal, it seemed to me, which made me feel protective.

He fell in step as we walked through to coffee, and I felt his nearness in every cell of me. Esther laughed loudly and we both stiffened.

"Why did you invite them?" I asked quietly.

"Apart from the fact we have to work together? They're my neighbors, Miss Shippen."

"That's very Christian of you, General."

"Please call me Benedict."

"I'm not sure I don't like saying *General.*"

"Literally my neighbors, Miss Shippen. The Council appropriated the house from Loyalist heirs, and they moved in."

My mouth fell open. "Did they really?"

"They really did."

The next day a letter was printed in *The Pennsylvania Packet* from the "Militia Man":

> *To stand at the door of any man, be he ever so great, and when there be liable at the whim and caprice of any of his suite to be*

ordered on the most menial services, piques my pride and hurts my feelings most sensibly. I cannot think that the commanding officer of Philadelphia views himself exposed to any real danger in this city. From a public enemy there can be none; from Tories, if any such there be amongst us, he has nothing to fear, they are all remarkably fond of him; the Whigs, to a man, are sensible of his great merit and former services, and would risk their lives in his defense.

I was repelled and fascinated by its insinuating tone, the palpable feeling of threat coated in treacly flattery. It had the ring of a scandal sheet, and I might have suspected a woman was behind it, if I hadn't been told Reed was the writer. Perhaps he and Esther collaborated. That would be fun for them, I could see.

I still couldn't believe that Major Franks having asked a junior officer to call a barber would be a problem for long. Not given the real injuries and issues to worry about. And not given the general's record, and strength.

Chapter Thirteen

I DREAMED I WAS APPROACHING A PALACE, CLIMBING WIDE MARBLE steps to a building resembling the splendid ruins of Rome. Just as I realized Benedict was beside me I sensed André at my other shoulder, bringing up the rear. "*Complimenti*," he murmured appreciatively, and I woke aglow.

I told Stansbury and Odell I'd dreamed about the general when I saw them next.

"Some say we dream about significant people coming into our lives," Stansbury said.

That was all my besotted body needed to hear.

Odell teased me for being busy since the British left town, but they were happy, I could tell, to see me animated again, and probably cheered to think of the possible protection a friendship with Benedict might mean.

I said I liked how he felt my opposite.

"Not really. You're both resourceful. Brave."

"Don't say that. Can I ask the obvious?" I ventured.

"He is a lot older," Odell said, and Stansbury narrowed his eyes theatrically. There wasn't any bigger a difference in age between the two of them.

"The question of allegiance."

"There will never be a single certainty about the fate of war," Stansbury said. "Not until it's over and historians become know-it-alls. All we want is a world right side up where we can think freely without fear."

"Perhaps being his bride, you could unite the two tribes." Odie smiled.

"Psshh." Already I was frightened of jinxing things. And lit with excitement to consider new possibilities for reconciliation. I didn't admit in the dream I'd been with both Arnold and André.

The Packet reported five hundred suspected Loyalists were to be tried for treason. Arnold's appeals for leniency seemed to prevail over the coming days, but after weeks of disputes and quarrels and anonymous letters of dissent, it was confirmed that thirty charges of treason against Abraham Carlisle and another wealthy Quaker, John Roberts, would stand. Reed himself was temporarily resigning in order to personally direct the trial.

In Christ Church that Sunday, I tried to take comfort in the familiar choreography of priests and attendants, gleaming silver chalices, red velvet and gold. Christ Church had always felt an extension of all I imagined in England. It seemed the Patriots had now made another Philadelphia palimpsest their own.

To a heavily blue-coated crowd the reverend cited the thirty-fifth Psalm: *Plead my Cause, O Lord, with them that strive with me: fight against them that fight against me . . .*

A prayer that called for an end to all enmity would have felt more helpful.

I spotted Benedict sitting in what had been General Howe's pew as I returned from taking the Eucharist. I was always a little self-conscious passing the sea of faces as I returned to my place, and under his gaze I burned.

Benedict stepped forward as I left the church. He'd been watching me since the opening hymn, he told me.

"I hope you weren't close enough to hear me."

"You look like you could hold a tune."

"I'm afraid not. I love to sing when the organ's loud enough to drown me out. Sometimes I imagine if I wish hard enough, think with a pure enough heart, I'll suddenly find I can. As it is—"

He laughed at my expression.

"I was sorry to see the Militia Man in your ear," I said.

"That mosquito—" he dismissed, and asked if he'd be welcome if he called on me for tea.

* * *

I was consumed all week with the painful pleasure of acute anticipation. I spent my days reading William's copy of Thomas Paine, ashamed of how slow I'd been to get to it, amazed something as explosive could have sat dormant in the house waiting for me. The irreverent intelligence in those pages was so exciting there were moments, reading, I had to get to my feet and just breathe.

A French bastard landing with an armed banditti and establishing himself king of England against the consent of the natives, is in plain terms a very paltry rascally original . . . the truth is that the antiquity of the English monarchy will not bear looking into . . .

The King himself Paine called "the royal brute of England."

The absurdity of a continent governed by an island! The misery and indefensibility of war, corruption, excessive taxation, and vast disparities in wealth! The qualities wanted in citizenry: virtue, equality, and independence! All good ideas and utterly accessible.

I gave guilty glances at the shadow where the King's portrait had hung as I read what felt like American heresy. If the King was a tyrant, how much longer would he let me read this? Had he lost his power to stop me?

I longed to discuss Paine's ideas with Benedict. My heart sank each dusk when it was clearly too late for tea and still he hadn't come. I tormented myself imagining all the things and women which might have kept him away.

On Friday, his monogrammed carriage finally drew up outside the house. I turned from the window and clutched Atty's hand in excitement.

My mother greeted him with surprise, touching her hair repeatedly in a way I hadn't seen her do. They were close to the same age, which might explain it, but she was deferential and a little girlish in a way she'd never been with André.

Benedict had brought a basket of treats: quails' eggs, French cheese, pears, peaches, and cut flowers. Mother was charmed and retreated to find a vase, leaving me and Betsy alone with him. My sister tactfully absorbed herself in embroidery.

Tied up with my desire for this man—I had to be careful my lips didn't part as I looked at his hair or the line of muscle visible along his thigh—was a longing to learn from him. I was late to the ideas which had fired him, but found I wasn't afraid to sound uninformed. Given the discrepancy in our experience, any pose I made of being knowing would have been even sillier than ignorance. I had an idea the relationship would be serious, from the very beginning, and I didn't want to be misleading or miss any chance to understand a thing about him. There are some questions more easily asked early in any relationship.

After I'd expressed my excitement at Paine—"He rips dust cloths off things I hadn't dared think! Who could now doubt a colony's destiny is to be a sovereign nation?"—I picked up the conversation about victory we'd begun at lunch.

"I have been thinking on what you said, General, about the need to wait to end a war until that can be done with honor and victory intact. Since obviously such a goal cannot be achieved for everyone involved, how to grapple with that? I don't want to live with unnecessary war, and I worry how we have all adapted. Wouldn't it be a very wicked thing, given nothing makes us more miserable than war, if we were to get used to fighting, to find all the loss normal, and to delay resolution for, say, a stickler's list of conditions—"

He looked steadily at me and said, "We must trust the process, Peggy. Forests need forest fires. The war will clear a path for a better future."

"The seeking of peace with a sword. Doesn't any violence always prompt worse?"

"At a certain point, history suggests, hostility dissolves."

"If someone's prepared to surrender?"

"Perhaps true victory—real peace, in the minds of both sides—is like the marriage which follows the certainty of having found one's companion. Love strikes, and sometimes, with luck, and time, happiness and satisfaction are realized."

"Some would steal that satisfaction."

He laughed. "Not and achieve happy marriage. But we were talking about warfare."

"Reed talks of vermin, swarming insects, when conjuring the enemy."

"Indefensible—" he said.

"It shocked me at his rally to see how well the rhetoric was received, and it frightens me to think how that appetite, once excited, will have to be constantly fed with ever-new enemies, those inside and out. As a suggestive metaphor it's probably horribly effective. We know how it is in the house. One mouse appears—sweet—we let it go. Two, we become uneasy. Five, and who's not inclined to set traps and fetch a cat?"

"One side might exert disproportionate force, on finding they had the opportunity and means, hoping by 'annihilating opposition' to win beyond question, but genocidal excess will inevitably engender resentment—even a very few surviving witnesses may bide their time to exact revenge. And the moral cost of unanswerable slaughter could not be expected to give peace to the victor."

"Why in war is it considered acceptable to claim God is on your side, when in any other context, a business transaction, say, such a claim would be in bad taste?"

He looked at me in a way which encouraged me to go on.

"How does anyone dare state what God wants? Or to imagine He's rooting for red or blue? Both colors we'd have to imagine he's fairly fond of. We're all important. And also utterly insignificant."

"No more than an oyster," he said.

"I'm sorry?"

"Something I think Hume said about a man's life having no more value than an oyster's."

"Oh, I've read—been meaning to read him. One oyster's not a lot."

"No." He laughed again. "And people do like eating them."

"Have you felt God taking a side in any fight?"

"That capacity to see, and judge, everything that's happening in battle in any one second—well, it beggars belief. Accidents happen in busy places: eventualities—casualties on both sides—that I can't believe any good god would *will*."

"It's a mystery—"

He smiled at his feet. "If we stop short of claiming any divine favor, or right, perhaps we can acknowledge there are times we feel blessed, in the presence of benevolence, whether Fate or Chance?"

"Chance feels less moral than God. And more chaotic. Aren't there enough unpredictables, without wanting more? And Fate can be terribly unfair!"

"Whimsical, certainly. Less judicious than we might wish God to be—"

"I do believe God wishes me well, even if He can't intervene. Whether Fate has good intentions, it's harder to say."

We smiled at each other.

Who could mind cosmic irrelevance when being stimulated by this man?

"I have felt something like a higher power at times," he considered. "In the thick of the fight. A fleeting intimation of being an instrument, guided to do what's needed or right. And then perhaps you spend the rest of your life trying to recover that sense of elevation and clarity. The point of faith I suppose is to keep you steady while you wait again for the sense God wants you where you are."

He heard my breath of recognition.

"Have you felt it?"

"Yes," I said. I felt like shouting, *I'm feeling it now!*

After a long smiling silence, in which Betsy's needle steadily went on, along with the clock, I continued.

"This airborne feeling, of being carried by a greater force—how is one to know whether to surrender to a current, and when to resist? Heading for a waterfall might feel much the same—"

"An undertow does not feel like flow, Peggy—and being tossed by a wave brings no feeling of divine favor—"

"I'll have to believe you. I'm yet to learn to swim."

"We'll have to see you shall."

"What of those in the sway of baser temptation?" I couldn't take my eyes off his.

"We pity the poor sinners? I believe the course of a life is decided by those moments when you know without doubt what's right and true."

I glanced at Betsy, still giving us the gift of appearing deaf. I was longing for Benedict to kiss me and wondered for a second what my sister would do if he did. I could recover only by resuming my interview.

"What would it take, General, to secure a convincing win, without resorting to unanswerable atrocities? The British, having recently tried, quite hard, with Lord Carlisle, I imagine will need some time to wind down from that push. Is it for the Patriot side now to make some gesture in the interest of America, and all?"

He leaned back, and I tried to keep my eyes on his face.

"It's only when war is exhausted that the peace process can begin."

"But how do you know when it's properly exhausted? Everyone seems quite worn out as it is! I have been heartily sick of it from the beginning. Is there some number of victims that's considered sufficient?"

"British losses are encouraging many in Parliament to make peace. I hope we find the key to persuading them completely to concede—the one shining stroke that ends things."

André had used that same phrase. I felt the air suddenly still.

"I didn't know that was a notion in circulation: the one shining stroke."

"I'm not sure it is. But good news if so, it's an idea which needs spreading. If God is attending to us, I believe he'd sow a good idea in a variety of fertile minds and see which comes to crop."

"Will you miss it, General, the cut and thrust of battle, on the other side of peace? After all that adventure, could you be happy in a quiet life? The domestic realm has its dramas, but it's hard to believe they'd be worth a general's attention—"

"With the right woman"—he smiled—"a little domestic drama sounds delightful."

I glanced again at Betsy, who sewed blithely on, God bless her.

"It's incredible what soldiers do. Unthinkable. And I'm grateful. But what I'm wondering is, where does that capacity for violence go? It can't be spent in everyone the minute victory is declared."

We were interrupted by mother bringing back the arranged flowers. Benedict chatted pleasantly with her, and I felt my old childish impatience at convention getting in the way of conversation.

We both had time to consider what answer could satisfy me before Mother left us again.

"Once this leg's mended, I'll fight for as long as there's fighting to be done, but I'm not thirsty for it, as some men are, or so sensitive as to be broken by it. A lack of imagination, maybe, but that might be a mercy.

"The drive finds other outlets. Riding, sailing, business, building, farming. I'd love to build a settlement with soldiers who fought alongside me, create a real community. There'd be flexing of the better muscles built in combat in all that. So no, I don't worry I'll miss it."

I couldn't imagine him roused to private violence, though I could believe he had a temper—Reed had been able to needle him, but then Reed could rile a saint. Still, I thought—already contemplating an entire life with him—it would be wise to meet his sons and sister and see the way he was with them.

I grilled Betsy after he'd gone. "Did you find him sincere?"

"I did. It was fun to hear you talking with someone who likes to explore ideas the way you do."

"Was he a little guarded though?"

"He might be worried he's too old for you. He can't afford to look a fool, Peggy. The whole city's watching."

"He'd be risking humiliation only if I didn't return the feeling! But perhaps he needs to marry money, find a rich widow who knows something about mothering—"

"That might satisfy conventional wisdom," Betsy said. "But not a pair of romantics like you. Though you're right: As a father he needs to be more careful than a bachelor. And what his own financial situation is, I've no idea—"

"There is something very romantic about a handsome widower, don't you think? Those poor motherless children."

Betsy laughed, a little outraged, but conceding. "There is."

"What are you giggling about?" Mother came in.

"Nothing," Betsy said. "Did we disturb you?"

"What's this about children?"

"The general has two sons," I said gently, "eleven and thirteen."

She looked at me as if I was being deliberately disagreeable.

"Perhaps we'll meet them," Betsy said.

"Why would I meet them? What are they to me?"

"Peggy and the general—"

I liked the sound of that.

"What does Peggy know about generals?"

I laughed, which wasn't helpful. "Sorry. Nothing, you're right."

"And now you think you're a match? You don't know the first thing about battle."

"No," I said. (Would she have me know more?) "Except this war's been the weather we live in for nearly five years and that fear contributes to everything. Abraham—"

"I don't need to hear any more about your concern for Abraham Carlisle. I've lost plenty of people closer to me. He manned that gate for all to see. There are consequences. How dare you think you can console me with a general's children?"

It went on. The implacable anger, non sequiturs, a thicket so defeating that surrender seemed easier. My father, summoned by raised voices, tried to intervene—"My dear, what can you mean?"—and took her aside to speak with her.

When he emerged, he shook his head.

"You need to apologize. No protest. She's the staff of my age."

We went to her together then and reached for all the loving sorries anyone could mean.

Nothing softened her when it came to me.

Chapter Fourteen

Benedict wrote me a letter, which I read and reread between lying down to fantasize. The power he suggested I had over him, his ardor, was headier than anything I'd ever encountered. He insisted he see me again. And then admitted his fear I might refuse him. His diction was more formal than in person, and the compliments, I suspected, were rehearsed or recommended by a friend, but I wasn't put off. I was touched a man who had done so much would feel he had to work to charm me.

I wrote to Theodosia. What could her hive mind fill in of his life since his wife's death?

She'd heard there had been one attachment, last year, during which Lucy, the wife of Brigadier General Henry Knox, had acted as his go-between, but something or other had foundered, and as far as she knew there'd been nothing since.

He was almost forty; I could hardly mind a history. I found it quite exciting, thinking of the women who had come before, and only hoped I'd stand comparison.

I was glad earlier stars hadn't aligned, that fate had waited for us to meet when he was free. And me. He and André were often together, a diptych, in my mind. Before and after, I supposed.

I saw nothing in our age difference to bother me. I had always been drawn to the conversation of those older, and Benedict had a good childish defiance alive in him too, an honest boyish rebellion inseparable from the most admirable Patriot energy—its invention, independence, courage, and strength. The whole idea of enemies needed defeating now. We needed to see the best a former colony and the nation which had helped foster it could be. I wanted Benedict's sense of justice to define a new, peaceful homegrown administration. I wanted him to heal completely, be fit for everything, without that meaning he'd ever need to fight again.

Stansbury said he had it on good authority the general was smitten. "His men say it's taken years off him."

"According to my sources," Odie chimed in, "he asks everybody for clues to the happiness of Miss Shippen. In your presence, he's so enthralled, he doesn't worry. When he leaves, he's plagued by doubt you'll ever be his. He's fascinated by your changing moods—frightened of them too—"

"I must take care to seem more stable," I said.

"I think you're sturdier than you know," Stansbury assured me.

"I don't think *sturdy* is something you say of a lady, Stansbury."

"He's interesting enough?" Odie asked.

"Yes! All the stories! His childhood antics!"

"Those more than the military achievements?"

Was it wrong, that focus? My mother was right that I didn't know about the reality of battle.

"I haven't asked him for blow-by-blows of those," I admitted. "I don't like picturing violent scenes, though of course I know the outcomes are important. I prefer a quick description from a trusted intermediary: the winner; number killed and taken prisoner; who was underhanded; who was valiant. It's squeamish of me to look away from the details, evidence I'm unserious probably, but I don't feel able to judge a situation I could never enter myself. I vaguely imagine a lot of noise and unpleasantness. Hard for anyone to come out well? Which makes it all the more impressive the uniformly wonderful way his soldiers talk about him."

"Unprecedented." Stansbury clapped his hands.

Odell cocked his head. "Have we *never* seen her so enthusiastic?"

"Not like this," Stansbury insisted. "Your parents must be very proud," he said, as he saw me to the door.

"I can't seem to make myself understood."

"Perhaps they don't want to understand. Don't let it strike at your sense of yourself, Peggy. We think the world of you—as does your friend in New York."

I owed André a letter, I knew, but I didn't want to write of Benedict, not yet. I wanted the story settled before I told it. I wanted the general to propose.

Abraham Carlisle and John Roberts were convicted by Reed, but consensus in the papers, and every word heard, insisted the trial had been unfair. Dozens of petitions requesting the two men be pardoned sprang up around the city. Thousands protested. It gave me hope, hearing the good-hearted, rhythmic chants to *Set them free*, but until they were released, I was anxious.

I asked Benedict as we walked between the pretty pleached trees in his garden if he was sure Abraham and Roberts would be acquitted.

"Reed hasn't gone ahead with the Mischianza fine he threatened, has he?"

"No."

"There's an element of performance. Swagger, for his more belligerent followers."

Franks interrupted, needing several signatures from the general. Benedict's administration was gunning out letters, putting out fires, and I liked to hear the men's busy repartee—loved that he still made time for me.

"Was I wrong to take part in the Mischianza planning, do you think? The intention wasn't harmful, but I took pride in the idea it might help end the conflict. As much as dreaming of peace, it was being useful that I loved, the whole creative endeavor. Lately I worry self-satisfaction about that contribution made me blind to the fact it's wrong to put beauty in service of an army. Doesn't that only glorify war? What if artists refused to design uniforms or flags or write military marches at all?"

"Such organized resistance would lead to oppressive oversight, the sort of councils and enforcement you wouldn't like. And there are moments of honor and glory we ought to remember. Pivotal history should be illustrated, for posterity. I don't think an artist moved to capture a victory—or a person who likes that art—should feel ashamed. There will always be the risk of strangers at the gate. We need fair fighters, and we need them inspired by earlier heroics, well-depicted—"

"We could do without pictures of battleships on stormy seas if that meant saving lives."

"You are friendly with artists," he said. "I gather. Odell. Stansbury. Would you have their freedom to express themselves curtailed?"

"No, but I'd like to see what they'd create if they were free not to think about war."

"How do they manage for money?"

"Stansbury takes commissions. Odell, I can't say. He's a poet, and I think quite prolific, but I admit I don't like the little verse of his I've read, not as much as the man as I've come to know. His parents founded Princeton, and I believe he's independently wealthy. He gives the impression he's not beholden to anybody."

"Perhaps the work would be better if he did need to please?"

"I'm not saying it's bad!"

He laughed.

"But I would hope it's possible to take funding from a patron, and accept their creative steer, without selling out entirely?"

"Money doesn't corrupt art?"

"It would be lovely if it weren't necessary! But even in the sincerest religious art, those gorgeous Sienese Madonnas, someone's paying for time and gold leaf."

"Perhaps I'll give Stansbury some business," he said. "I wouldn't want anyone thinking I'd missed a trick."

We were interrupted by an officer bringing back a purse of money.

"The waggoneer would not accept payment, sir."

"Didn't you insist?"

"Repeatedly. He wouldn't have it. Insists in turn the service was his pleasure."

The officer was still holding out the purse. Benedict hesitated, pocketed it, and shrugged. "That's very generous. Thank him for me."

I ran my fingers along the leaves as we passed. "You make governing look easy."

"You find me at rest." He laughed. "And I should get back to work. We are a long way from the universal security and well-oiled clockwork I mean to see before I leave. Washington came to me for military assistance, and Congress delayed two weeks in granting permission, blowing the best chance at taking Manhattan we've had."

I'd have whistled if I could.

"Could you see governing the entire country, if and when?"

"I wouldn't seek it."

"You'd be a contender," I said. "Even if the British win, you could be viceroy, or president general, whatever they'd call it."

He laughed. "I don't believe I'd be the first choice."

"Men trust you."

"On the battlefield," he said. "Not in Council. Not in Congress."

"So not supreme ruler. Elder statesman maybe."

"That is wish-list stuff."

"Can't we give a little time to wish lists, even in war?"

We watched possibilities dawn in each other's eyes.

"Do you feel like kissing me at all?" I asked.

Benedict made a sound around a groan, leaned toward me, and met my lips in a firm, perfect, lingering kiss.

We were moments from discovery. He pulled me to him, pressed his mouth hungrily to the nape of my neck, and released me, my stomach in knots.

The eve of Carlisle's scheduled execution, Benedict threw a party to reassure the city.

He sent Stansbury with the dress he'd commissioned for me.

"He is very easy to like," Stansbury observed. "And he's confident the appeals and protests will prevail in saving Abraham."

"Thank God. You didn't scare him off?"

"Peggy Shippen. A man who has spent so long in the military knows a thing or two about human variety. And in case you weren't clear, he is a man very much in love. I don't think there's any friend or choice of yours he wouldn't approve of."

It was a new sensory pleasure dressing in clothes he'd chosen. Tightening the bodice and turning so that the deep blue-black feathers of the skirt fanned and settled with a tiny sigh, I felt the delicious anticipation of another kiss.

When my mother saw the new dress, she asked, "General Arnold? Really?" a corrosive droplet of surprise.

Betsy saw my hurt and reminded her, "You quite liked him when you met him, Mamma."

One of a hundred guests he was greeting that evening, I savored the anticipation as we filed forward to meet him. My stomach dropped along with the sweep of his gaze from my bodice to my skirt. He'd assembled the best musicians, men familiar from the British era, and lit the room with a thousand tall beeswax tapers on tablescapes of trailing vines. I tried to keep my eyes off him, while my body tracked his position in the room like an animal. I needed him near me. I'd hear the irresistible rhythm of his limp and melt in expectation as he came my way. I danced with one man after another, only wanting Benedict close. He saw my surprise when he set aside his crutch with a flourish and asked me to dance. I was smiling more than could be seemly as he took me in his arms.

"You're looking very limber," I said, my head barely an inch from his white shirt and the paneled flatness of his chest. "Have you been exercising?"

"I've found new incentive."

He inclined his head as the first familiar chords of the dance began.

"You look beautiful," he murmured.

"Thanks to you. You approve?" I asked, turning slightly, so the feathers could rustle and resettle.

"I do," he said.

"And you liked Stansbury?"

"I did. I see why you do." We turned and found each other's hands in step again. "Tell me a secret you shouldn't keep," he said, and my heart hammered.

"I can't wink," I said as we crossed paths and turned again. "Or whistle."

"Or sing," he shook his head in mock despair.

"Now your confession."

"My scars are disfiguring. Occasionally gout gets in."

I worried he'd think he'd repelled me as the dance took an age to bring us back full circle.

"Is that very painful?"

"Hurts like hell."

"We'd better look after it."

We turned and found each other's eyes and hands again.

"Your turn," he said in that lovely low growl.

"I hope there will be no opportunity for further injury."

"That would indeed be humiliating."

"We need you in the city. Couldn't you come to like civilian life?"

"I've been a soldier since I fled home at fourteen," he said. "And politics are not for me."

The music stopped and we stood breathing in sync. I loved the clean spice smell of him.

"Encore!" he called to the orchestra, and they restarted the dance. I laughed and took his hands.

"I ran away at seven," I confessed. "Some injustice I couldn't stomach." Again we turned and found each other's hands. "I got half a mile before my mother's carriage pulled up. Back at the house, she made me sit beside her while she wrote a letter to the orphanage asking them to come to collect her ungovernable daughter. Sealed it and sent it by messenger."

"Was she in earnest?" He looked horrified.

"I don't know." I said, though I had believed so at the time, and felt the infestation of the black beating wings I'd come to know as panic, the cold that no shivering would stop. "She told me she would help me pack a bag. When it was ready I broke down and begged to stay."

"What did she do?"

"Left me to unpack." I felt sad suddenly. That scene had branded me in the family. The juddering great breaths, gasping for air like a drowning girl. I'd been forever after considered too much. I tried to brighten by the time his face next met mine.

"Sometimes I wish I were a man," I confided. "To be able to live independently and make a useful difference."

"The right man might make you very glad to be a woman."

The music ended and he gave a deep bow.

After two dances in succession, we couldn't not move on to other partners, though every second away from him by then felt wrong.

Taking air on the terrace, I could see Esther in her garden, watching the party while conferring intently with Reed.

"Did the general invite them?" It was Neddy, at my side.

"He says yes."

"They're telling everyone no."

"They'd have found fault if he did or if he didn't."

"It has to help, that they can see there's no appetite for vengeance from him, and with so many in attendance, only broad support."

"Yes."

I was tired—one occupying force replacing another, the Reeds right there, new neighbors in the Galloways' house—but defiant. Good surely would prevail.

Let them whisper, I thought, *let them scheme*. Benedict was showing what benevolent strength could be.

I fell asleep believing the prisoners would be freed.

Abraham was killed on the common the next day. The execution played in slow motion. The formality of the proceedings, the pantomime of legitimacy, was surreal. With his last look before they tied the blindfold, he assessed the angle of the gallows.

I held on to Betsy, our faces covered in tears, shutting my eyes against the sound of the creaking rope, a handkerchief over my mouth. I heard the sickening jolt of his drop, before the crowd cheered, and I opened my eyes to see the shock of his familiar hair above his blindfold. The feet always hurrying to help, the hands gesturing to illustrate and build, were now slack and slowly swaying. Vomit rose in my throat. I looked up from wiping my mouth and saw men gloating.

The crowd was energized by the killing, Reed exultant. He climbed on the platform to warn remaining Loyalists they were a cancer in the city and would soon enough now be cut out. Women moaned in excitement, men roared their approval, their blood up as he talked of roundups, deportations, imprisonment, and execution.

I was disgusted, and ever more exhausted. Entirely persuaded now, by Paine, by Benedict, of the freedom and dignity America deserved, of the essential distortion in any ongoing submission to Britain, I wanted to feel proud of us. I wanted to see moderation and tact in our self-management, feel we were an impressive body politic, obviously managing very nicely, so that the King, an honored if tricky parent, could glide into retirement.

We were here to improve on British rule, and instead were descending to rabid invective, retaliation, and political killing. Reed was raising a monster toddler ready to run amok.

Chapter Fifteen

The morning after Abraham's killing, Atty let Esther in.

Thrumming with self-importance, she joined us in the sitting room.

"Good morning, ladies! Ah, Mrs. Shippen. I hope I find your family well. Girls—"

I caught my mother's eye and fought to keep my face impassive.

"I come now with a ladies subscription scheme of my own devising to raise money for the Patriot cause. The scheme is already underway in several colonies—and every penny we raise will be carefully tallied and relayed directly to General Washington for soldiers to spend as they think best. Any contribution is helpful, relative to one's means—"

Esther fingered the crimson silk curtains.

"And those families who can join to their patriotism a great capacity to contribute have all the more happiness—"

Mother looked at us. In a rare moment of easy consensus, it was clear that however much we resented this charmless, coercive invasion, we'd capitulate. Mamma handed over her entire week's housekeeping, which seemed to satisfy Esther for now, and we sank back into silence.

The feeling Reed was winning was sapping my strength like a virus.

André's next letter was nothing but numbers.

I held it up to Stansbury and Odell in stupefaction.

"André, clearly, is taking covert communication increasingly seriously."

"Give each letter of the alphabet its number," Odell suggested, and called out the numbers to see if there was any sense to be had by that. We got only nonsense and stared at each other in defeat.

Stansbury said he'd heard of one cipher so brilliant—yet so confusing—it was literally impossible to unlock. Rumor had it that Patriots had for years been receiving secret missives from a spy who insisted on using his custom cryptography in letter after letter, not one of which the recipients had been able to decipher—a problem they wouldn't admit.

I laughed, though I knew I shouldn't.

The next week Odell brought a heavy bundle wrapped in hessian. Stansbury pulled the interior shutters closed as I unwrapped it.

Inside was a book: William Blackstone's *Legal Commentaries*. No note.

I looked up from the dense text in confoundment. What did he imagine I could make of this?

Odell retrieved André's last letter from a tube in a roll of fabric and pulled chairs around the table.

"Here. Let's take it slowly. Sit with uncertainty. Give me a sequence—"

"Thirty-five. Twelve. Eight."

Laboriously, we made the alphanumeric substitutions and pieced together the system. Three numbers were needed. The first number corresponded with the page, the second the line, the third the word.

"It says 'General'! 'My regards to the General.'"

The discovery was energizing. I forgot my anxiety. The deliberate work of deciphering each word was a chance to convene with André, imagine a little more of his responsibilities, and consider what would please him and rescue me, if needed. With that one line he was acknowledging I was attached to Benedict and suggesting he thought well of him and that in the three points of our connection there was strength.

So André wasn't my love story, but we could work together, and maybe later do more. I couldn't articulate it, but I knew I wanted him in my life, as well as Benedict. The two of them represented the best in humanity, the best bet for happiness, mine and the colonies', that I could conceive. I wanted to be the hinge between them.

Betsy and Neddy were finally ready to marry after eighteen months' official engagement and saving.

I tried to make the most of sleepless hours dreading my sister's departure by deciding on the right gift and spent days scouring the city for what I had in mind. I found it at last, a delicate jade-and-gold cross and a tea set so pretty it would make a little ritual treat of every use.

December was a beautiful time for a wedding, and I launched gladly into the distraction of party planning again. Atty and I decorated the mirrors and mantlepieces, draping door mantels and windowsills with evergreens and berries, setting the best beeswax candles in polished silver sticks and gold-rimmed crystal bowls of oranges and pomegranates on top of cream antique linen cloths. We had fires burning in every grate, and profiteroles, delivered by Major Franks on Benedict's behalf since the general had gone to Connecticut to see his sons and sell a house and couldn't join us.

Betsy and Neddy exchanged their vows with merry reverence, my sister's twenty-five bridesmaids—she hadn't been able to decide—fanned at her sides.

Mother rested her head on Father's shoulder, and he kissed the crown.

After the feast, I helped Betsy change. "It's only the other side of the city." She smiled, seeing the tears that threatened to spill.

I gave her the gifts but said to open them once she was in her new home.

"I'm sorry I've been a lot."

Betsy brandished the familiar spoons.

"Oh, don't go!" I laughed. "Who will help me next time I need them?"

"We could take you with us."

"No, I couldn't abandon the parents. And what would you want with a sister cramping your style?"

"I'm a little nervous of being alone with him," she admitted. "No idea what that side of things will be like—"

"People seem to manage?" I said. "And you do have the assistance of attraction. I can't think of a man more likely to make you happy, Betsy. Next time I see you, you'll be glowing with new information, and I hope very reassuring to me! I'm going to miss you so much though. Our poor parents. Their least favorite the last to go. I will try to emulate your tact and kindness. Do more of your soothing sort of good."

"You be you, Peggy Shippen."

"When did that ever help?"

"They came round to Neddy," Betsy said. "Mother's besotted with him now. When you remember she could hardly look at him!"

She held my face and kissed my head.

"Neddy thinks that general of yours will make you very happy. Everyone with a liberal way of thinking loves him."

"I love you, Betsy!"

We waved Neddy and Betsy's carriage out of sight, just as it started to snow. Uncle William congratulated his brother on having only my expenses to answer now. My father replied it likely wouldn't be long there either.

"Oh? Are you in love, Peggy?" William asked.

"She's only in love with his height," my mother said.

William widened his eyes at me, and I was grateful to him yet again.

Benedict and I were at a concert—a glorious orchestra, moving like wind on water, the sound filling us with love and light—when the officer who'd returned the unwanted payment from the waggoneer came to report he'd been questioned by Reed over the incident.

"He's investigating the appropriation of government wagons for private profit."

"I offered to pay," Benedict pointed out.

"You did," I said, and turned to the officer. "I heard him."

"Me too," the officer said. "He wouldn't listen—"

"It's not about the money," Benedict said, as the officer left. "It's punishment for what he considers my leniency to Loyalists. I wouldn't forgive a conspiracy. I know my enemy, but I can't punish citizens who were only trying to read the wind. If we're to win trust and show strength, surely what's wanted is a commitment to tolerance."

"I'm afraid I might be making your life more difficult, when all I want to do is help."

"There's no reason to Reed; he's all vicious instinct."

"Does that track with what you know of Washington?"

"He must calculate it's useful to him."

"Does it test your commitment to the cause at all? An act like that against Abraham by one of Washington's closest advisors?"

He shook his head. "Not to winning. We cannot continue a colony. Resisting unwelcome authority is my natural inclination, my disposition, perpetual adolescent though that might make me. First chance I got, at fourteen, to run away from home—well, that chance was given me by the King. My first rebellion was to fight for him. But then to see Colonial soldiers paid less than the British in the very same role? Men risking their lives, giving everything, and that contribution considered second-class? Once you've seen it's rigged, felt yourself in the shadow of that overreach, then you begin to feel oppression like a boot on your neck and can't stop kicking 'til you're free."

I held his head in both hands and kissed him, refusing to believe a man with such strength of conviction could be the object of suspicion by his own side for long. In a fit of optimism, I suggested he try talking to Reed, mend relations without the need of formal charges.

"I won't meddle," I said. "But Esther and I being present might just keep it civil, and the fact he's been my father's guest could help? If I can begin to try to overlook what he did to Abraham Carlisle, for the sake of the greater cause, he can surely forgive your tiny oversight. At the least, I can be a second pair of eyes, catch anything unsaid you might miss."

Benedict was so tense I worried he wouldn't be able to listen. I helped him into his jacket and smoothed the fabric between the span of his shoulder blades, loving him for letting me feel a little like a wife.

"We have a minute before he gets here. Let's think this through," I urged. "He campaigned on unity, so he knows there's value in that. And he knows the power of your reputation—the love every Patriot soldier bears you. Your entire strategy in the city has been about winning last holdouts to the Patriot side. There must be room for alliance—"

"Not while he kills men and deprives their wives of rightful inheritance. His politics mask a jealous class agenda. The irony is he was born to plenty but has harnessed the anger of the have-nots. I came of age with nothing, and he manages to depict me as the creature of elites. I consider it my job to govern the entire city, not half of it. He thinks that's evidence I shouldn't be trusted. It isn't as if I don't know he has it in for me. The trick to governing, I thought, was ensuring every decision could survive hostile scrutiny. To be careful, in a way I wasn't on campaign. But with a thousand decisions each day, there was sure to be a slip."

"The business with the wagons wasn't a serious mistake, Benedict. You tried to pay, but in a distracted moment, you didn't sufficiently insist. Reed must understand there was nothing underhand."

"He won't rest until he wins—"

"But must that be at your expense? If he came to feel he was your champion, perhaps that could excite his pride? He'd have the love of your men by extension. Can you find some concession for which he can claim credit? Something for the good of the city? Band together in banishing slavery? He can't want to be remembered only as the Loyalists' hangman."

Reed was announced.

"No Esther?" I said, as I greeted him.

"She's in early labor," he said.

"I hope the child will soon be safely delivered."

"They'll send word," he said.

Benedict welcomed Reed with every courtesy short of friendship, but all my hopes were quickly made to seem stupid. Their mutual dislike was too obvious. Neither, it seemed, could resist trying to puncture the other.

"I believe you know what it is to stumble," Benedict began. "I heard your letter recommending Washington's replacement was intercepted by the great General himself? Of all the bad luck—"

"Not optimum," Reed said tightly. "But now history."

"Gates was your preference, I think?"

"For that brief period—"

"The greatest poltroon in the world!"

I twisted in my seat, hating the tension and dismayed to hear the pomposity in Benedict that came out when he was tense.

"It's a credit to General Washington he doesn't feel the need to punish every suggestion of disloyalty," Benedict said. "As a weaker man might."

Too pointed.

"He knows when force is warranted—"

"As anyone does who's seen active service. But we encourage the best by thinking the best. If we're to build this nation on the principles which inspired it, we can't indulge in the worst excesses of a despot—"

"It would be stupid, you know, to trust a man where there's evidence of wrongdoing."

"Crime must be punished, but as I say, a man can make a mistake. The bigger man forgives."

"Self-serving words for a man prone to error."

"An innocent mistake is preferable to conspiracy," Benedict said.

"There is no question mark over my loyalty. The King's envoys offered me ten thousand pounds to defect."

Benedict raised an eyebrow.

"Did they, Reed? That's quite an admission—"

"Has nobody offered you such enticement?"

"They have not. My reputation clearly precedes me."

"It does, sir. Hence my question."

Their rivalry would never end! Only complete defeat of one or the other would settle it. I had seen tiredness in Benedict, while Reed seemed to draw strength from conflict. I caught Benedict's eye and smiled fresh encouragement. He sighed.

"How long since you fought in this war, Reed? Tackled a man with your own hands? I don't speak of arrests or executions you've ordered—"

"Loyalists are traitors, Arnold." He stared at me. "There is no offense more grave."

I fought the urge to shout *Murder is more grave!*

"You're a good enough lawyer to know the charges against Roberts and Carlisle were a sham, Reed. We must give due process. Honor the best of our inheritance. Habeus corpus! Do as you'd be done by! It will help our side—"

"Your notion of our side is called to question by present company—"

"I need no schooling in the enemy, Reed. I've run forty men through with my sword."

I made an instinctive start backward and had to pretend the fire was too hot. Forty?

"What is not legitimate is the persecution of women and children for their husbands' and fathers' missteps. It's barbaric. And the subsequent redistribution of those assets to Patriot leaders cannot help our reputation—"

"Would you accuse me of financial impropriety, Arnold?"

Benedict had no evidence, only very reasonable suspicion. Loyalist property was finding its way onto the black market. Reed was living in it. Esther, lately, looked unaccountably rich. I saw it had not occurred to Benedict to investigate, and a counter-investigation now could only look like petty political tit for tat.

"It is only with victory that we can afford lenience. We must first convince the inbreeds we mean business."

"Does your wife object to your characterization of her countrymen?"

"My wife is a complete American, sir."

"We are all Americans here. Let's work together, Reed. Let it go. I offered to pay for the infernal wagons—"

"In such a way as nobody took you seriously."

"I'll pay now! Would that end this amicably?"

"You'd bribe me?" Reed sneered.

"No! Oh, for God's sake. Get out."

There was no pretending it had gone well.

In a move which marked a new political low, Reed had the charges against Arnold printed and distributed before the case was even heard. Reed wanted the city's opinion on his side, and a court predisposed to convict, and he got it.

My mother hummed quietly as she read the charges while I pushed my breakfast around my plate, imagining André in New York and Theodosia in New Jersey reading about Benedict's humiliation.

"The first charge," she began, as if I were the one on trial, "concerns the vessel named *Charming Nancy*." She looked over the paper. "Wasn't that a boat Captain André raided?"

"I believe so. Coincidence—"

"Second charge," she interrupted. "It is claimed that your general granted persons of disaffected character passes which enabled them to transport this ship out of British-occupied Philadelphia, permitting illegal profit."

"He helped them deprive the British of the profit. That cannot in this moment be a crime?"

"If he himself had interest in the *Charming Nancy*, such a pass would have been granted for personal gain."

"There is no proof of that!"

"Third charge," she continued, licking some jam off her finger. "He illegally closed city stores—"

"Reed too closed stores!" I objected "On direct orders from Washington!"

"And continued to personally trade the goods of shops he had closed under martial law."

"We are at war. The black market is active. I think every enterprising gentleman alive has sought goods not otherwise available for his family, and likely shared or sold on any excess?"

She glared at me.

"Profiteering is a crime now carrying penalty of death. Fourth charge! He commandeered public wagons for personal gain."

"This is true," I said, "but I was there. He offered to pay!"

"How hotly you defend him," she said, biting a corner of toast.

Chapter Sixteen

One week later, Benedict was cleared in a regional hearing, but Reed immediately began pressing for a court martial.

Benedict came by carriage that afternoon with a bottle of champagne for my parents, "a small consolation" for Betsy leaving home, and asked my mother for all the details of the wedding he'd been sorry to miss.

After giving a proud account, she saw him into the little sitting room and left us to it.

He threw himself into the armchair, his leg elevated and face shadowed.

The injury was playing up. It had knocked him sideways, being confronted by Reed's image of him as a crook.

He admitted he'd tended to take a self-forgiving approach to his own shortcomings, welcoming the chance to learn from old errors, but believing himself fundamentally good. "Perhaps I have become too attached to the Benedict Arnold my fellow soldiers celebrate and forgotten to worry about the damnation my mother always warned me was so near."

Seeing his mistakes paraded in print, for all the colonies to see, was making him question everything.

He talked of his siblings' deaths; the disease that seemed to stalk his childhood; the slide into poverty; humiliation at his father's inebriated scenes in the street; his worry for his mother; guilty relief being away at school, before the mortification of being called before the boys to the headmaster and forced to abandon his studies and find work.

"It's driven you," I said, incapable of listening to the misery without salvaging some hope from it.

Elbows on the table, he raked his hands through his hair and looked up at me with that brilliant deep blue.

"I could have been more careful."

"You cut a corner. Don't fall into believing Reed."

He looked desolate. Outraged on his behalf, I exclaimed, "Why would Reed want to demolish one of the few great heroes his cause has? Is it jealousy? And why the incessant attacks on the authority and integrity of Congress under the vile cover of the Militia Man? Is it that he wants more power? President of the Supreme Executive Council of the leading city in the colonies is not enough? Or is it all deflection, incessant aggression veiling his own wealth and power from a following that mistrusts formal authority and the rich? Whatever his reasons, he's spreading hate like contagion, and undermining trust in a government that needs faith at this stage. I could almost suspect he's an agent of the British—revealing the attempted bribe being only more misdirection. Would the British be low enough to undermine the rebellion from within with a tool like Reed? Even if they could control him, I don't believe anyone at British Headquarters could stand him!"

Benedict laughed and then groaned in pain. He asked me to pour him a whiskey. I had never felt so grown up, unstopping my father's crystal and pouring him a generous glug. I wanted to sit on the arm of his chair and scratch the back of his head as he drank. I wanted to be his wife.

"Reed's flunkies are tampering with the evidence, ineptly altering entries to make it seem the waggoneers received their orders only from me."

"That's outrageous," I said. "What's your redress?"

"The witness confessed. For what good that does me. The rapt readers of the Militia Man already think me guilty as sin. What can you do?"

"Perhaps a little more?" I suggested gently.

"I refuse to be intimidated by a newspaper."

"I hate the tone the slander's written in," I said, "but I wonder if not engaging is becoming a mistake, when Reed seems to be wielding the paper's pages like a weapon?"

Benedict agreed to submit to *The Pennsylvania Packet* a transcript of the witness's original, undoctored testimony and was promptly exonerated from any wrongdoing in a special edition of the paper dedicated to him.

Four days later *The Packet* reversed without any acknowledgment of its previous stance. Now it was the father of Matlack, the soldier who had resented being asked to call Major Franks a barber, raking over charges of which Arnold had been completely cleared two years earlier—including the ludicrous assertion he bore personal responsibility for the spread of smallpox in the northern army.

My father ducked his head into the sitting room to sympathize.

"I have weathered scurrilous slights in print myself, General, from Peggy's favorite, Franklin, no less. Criticism is inescapable for a man of wide acquaintance, especially one generous in entertaining requests for help and advice. Best though to nip this slander in the bud."

Benedict wrote again to the paper, protesting his innocence:

"Envy and malice are indefatigable. Where they have not invention enough to frame new slanders, they will call in the feeble aid of old calumnies."

Back *The Packet* came with another pseudonymous attack. Benedict tried to make light of the piece, jokingly reading it aloud to me, but the poison and shamelessly changeable positions in the paper were getting to him, and there was vinegar in his laughter.

I had been wrong to persuade him to engage with the papers. *God, let me be a better help to him*, I thought, and just then, an article in *The Gazette* rose to my attention.

"Benedict, will you credit it? The very same day *The Packet* tries to demolish you, *The Gazette* is hailing you as '*an officer more distinguished for valor and perseverance than any commander in the Continental service . . . General Arnold is now in the unmerciful fangs of the Executive Council of Pennsylvania, Mr. Joseph Reed, President.*'"

He reached for the paper, shame and fascination mingled in his eyes. "The British see?"

"And if *they* do, General Washington must too! Go to him, Benedict. Talk it through at the top. Surely, he needs no reminding of the principles inspiring independence. The fact he hasn't intervened before can only mean that he's been distracted. Once he sees what Reed is putting you through, he'll recognize persecution for what it is and put a stop to it—"

He wrote from the road:

> *My Dearest Life. Never did I so ardently long to see or hear from you as at this instant . . . I am heartily tired with my journey, and almost so with human nature. I daily discover so much baseness and ingratitude among mankind that I almost blush at being of the same species, and could quit the stage without regret was it not for some few gentle, generous souls like my dear Peggy, who still retain the lovely impression of their Maker's image . . . Let me beg of you not to suffer the rude attacks on me to give you a moment's uneasiness; they can do me no injury . . . Til we meet again all nature smiles in vain, for you alone, heart, felt and seen, possess my every thought, fill every sense, and pant in every vein.*

After weeks of oscillating between enjoyable yearning and agonized imagining, I watched at the window as Benedict arrived through the snow. I searched his face as he took off his cloak, heartened to see a wide smile.

"It went well then? Washington understood?"

"He was sympathetic. Told me Generals Schuyler, Lee, Knox, all sorts of others have written expressing support for me. He acknowledged how much of my own money I've contributed to the campaigns, how long overdue repayment's been, and he sees the toxicity in this city."

I exhaled in relief.

"I told him I wanted to resign as military governor, get out of Reed's sights. He understands, and won't stand in my way, but we agreed I should endure the court martial, see off these charges formally, before stepping down. Anything else would be premature, suggest my enemies are privy to real guilt. I'll keep my head down, wait out the legal proceedings, use the interval to get this leg as strong as it should be."

"Good. I've missed you," I admitted, kissing him.

"Let's take a ride?"

I ran upstairs to change into thicker stockings for the winter air, leaving the door ajar as my father began peppering him with questions about his upcoming trial. I was relieved to hear Benedict sounding calm and confident, telling my father, with no disrespect to an eminent profession, he'd be defending himself.

"Is that wise?"

"Well, sir, I'm hoping so." Benedict laughed, walking a nice line of deference without submission. "Since I'm innocent, I see no sense going to unnecessary expense. No offense to your profession—"

"None taken." My father chortled. "Certainly, for my part, I rarely see the merit in professional medicine. There's little a doctor can do that a sensible diet cannot."

I tugged the stockings up, hooked them, and grabbed my warmest gloves.

Benedict was stomping off snow after having retrieved two packages from the carriage, a pair of fur-lined boots and a cape with a matching hood.

Bundled up in that luxury, we glided on gleaming carriage blades through the snowy streets of the city, tack jingling, up through Fairmount Park, where bare, gray branches of oaks were trimmed with brilliant white, and deep green pine needles sparkled under the snow's weight.

When the drifts did begin to slow the horses, Benedict said we'd move faster and warm ourselves up by walking and could lead them the last way on foot.

"The last way where?"

"I'll show you."

Walking through that snow was like climbing an unreliable staircase. I tried to stay on the crust, treading soft as a tracker as Benedict mock sternly instructed, but every few minutes my boots would plunge inches deep. When the ice stung the skin of my thighs above my stockings, I followed in Benedict's footprints. It felt good slotting my feet into the packed prints his boots left behind, dodging the shutes of snow that slid from the pines, and I saw he'd been right. I could come to like being a woman in a life with him.

A sudden breeze lifted a shower of flakes, and the air was alive with twirling motes of light. Benedict pointed to the top of the hill, where the gorgeous Georgian masterpiece Mount Pleasant crowned the view, its immaculate brick and paintwork set off by the snow.

"Like it?" he asked me.

"It's the handsomest house in America. Prettier even than Cliveden!"

He lifted me off my feet, his mouth on my neck.

"When this is all over—" he began and lifted my chin so I was looking into the brilliant eyes beneath those dark eyelashes.

"Yes?" I said happily

He kissed me again.

"No, it's too soon to say."

The suspense was delicious torment.

Warming my toes later at home, I supposed it might have been too soon after Betsy's wedding.

In love as I was, I could wait.

Esther had used the funds from her subscription scheme to buy linen for soldiers' shirts and now offered a third test, giving "some of our female citizens an opportunity of relinquishing former errors and of avowing a change of sentiments by their contributions to the general cause of liberty and their country."

It felt more a summons than a suggestion, but insulated by the belief Washington would deliver Benedict from Reed, and that good again had the upper hand, I felt less threatened by whatever list of former collaborators the couple had me on.

Between the two of them the Reeds had claimed so much of my attention it was beginning to feel like theft. I was looking to be a general's wife and mustn't be pathetic. I would focus instead on the comfort a new shirt would give a boy at Valley Forge.

Sewing wasn't a contribution which would impress an exacting observer—I always pictured Clinton's froideur when considering the point of me—but it was a little way to be useful. I admired the women who manned the charity kitchen at Christ Church, good, stout sorts reliably feeding anyone needy, and I had enjoyed a pleasant sense of virtue myself by baking cookies for a Quaker fundraiser. The least I could do was sew a perfect shirt.

I was signed in and given a work basket by a woman at the door. Esther was there, her baby in a cradle at her feet, and who could resist that new little face? Straightening, I exclaimed in genuine admiration at the snowy stock of linen she'd secured.

Grateful to find friends there, I joined May Chew and Mrs. Cartwright and half a dozen of Betsy's bridesmaids at a table against the wall.

"Have we been assigned a deliberately drafty table out of spite?" May asked. "I know what we did. The blasted Mischianza. What about the rest of you?"

Esther glided around like a bountiful headmistress, checking stitches and suggesting fixes, between reading from a new tract she'd written, "The Sentiments of an American Woman."

"The situation of our soldiery has been represented to me, the evils inseparable from war . . ."

"I wish we could metal plate the shirts we're sending them," I said. "Whatever happened to chain mail anyway?"

"Heavy and expensive," Mrs. Cartwright murmured.

May whispered that Washington had sent back all the money Esther had raised in her last scheme, with a letter regretting the soldiers would waste it on alcohol—hence the linen we worked with now.

I tried to squash the dismay I felt at the fact the Reeds were clearly closely in touch with Washington too, and share May's amusement that Esther's original intention had been over-ruled.

"I bet they could have used a drink—" Mrs. Cartwright said.

"This is the offering of the ladies!" Esther cried, lifting each completed shirt as if to an altar.

She did look a little hysterical—*crazed,* May mouthed—but if we could be friends, it might help Benedict.

We talked of Betsy's wedding and her bridesmaids' various beaus.

"How's your general, Peggy?" Mrs. Cartwright teased.

It was startling to think how many at that table might be married within the year. I had an uneasy image of us as seasonal produce.

"He's well. Given a challenging climate in trade and public life—"

"He should work with my husband, innovate some new model of rifle—the Benedict Arnold—people would buy it in droves," Mrs. Cartwright said.

"No," I said. "No, I don't think so."

"I'll miss being able to talk freely to you all," May pouted.

"Married ladies can still talk, May!" Mrs. Cartwright said with nervous mirth.

"Of course, but it's not quite the same, is it? There's that obligation for discretion—a greater intimacy within the marriage than anything outside it, or else a risk of disloyalty."

"We do become who we marry, in many ways," Mrs. Cartwright admitted.

"My mother always said there should be only one door in a marriage house, open always to the husband. Doors to the outside should be firmly closed," May said. I didn't like the sound of that.

"How did you *know*?" I asked another girl recently engaged.

She considered.

"He was the only man I'd met I was sure would never bore me."

"How did you know, Esther?" May asked her as she passed. "That his Excellency was your one and only?"

"He was the most impressive specimen I'd ever seen."

"Reed? Really?" May asked.

My laugh was involuntary, but that didn't make the insult any less.

"Who does she think she is, Queen of the colonies?" May said as she walked away.

"It's a halo she wants, not a crown," Mrs. Cartwright said. "Goodie Reed."

There was a prim orthodoxy about her which was annoying, and oddly hypocritical given how unmercifully her husband behaved, but perhaps she was in her own way trying to launder his stains.

Again, I focused on the shirt, and the small pleasure it could give a boy who'd been months without the comfort of home.

"Look at her," May muttered, as Esther held another shirt aloft in fervor. "Any minute now she'll be sacrificing a lamb."

I was grateful for the valve of May's humor, but frightened too. "Don't let her hear. You'll make her more of a monster. Humiliation is very dangerous."

"We can't let her think we're scared of her," May insisted.

"But we are," Mrs. Cartwright admitted. I looked at her in solidarity and saw how unhappy she had become.

When the shirt was done, I embroidered my name as instructed, severed the last thread, and thanked Esther for including me.

"We wouldn't have been without you," she said.

"It helps to help—"

"I'm so glad we made you feel better, Peggy. That's what it's all about, of course."

Esther's sidekicks were still tittering when May swept by and took my arm.

"Carry on," May said to Esther over her shoulder, sounding uncannily like a supercilious British officer.

"Every lady shall be at liberty to adopt a different plan," Esther called after us.

"Thank you. Perhaps I will!" I replied.

Chapter Seventeen

It snowed all month, which at least seemed to freeze Reed's persecution. By February the world had been white so long I dreamed of hyacinths, and swore on waking I could smell them.

I missed Stansbury and Odell and longed for news of André and Theodosia.

I decided to use the time cooped up to improve my French, since Benedict said one way or another France was part of America's fate, and reciting verbs was a good excuse for seclusion in my room.

When the world finally thawed, Benedict's sons and sister visited from Connecticut, and I was invited to meet them. Excitement at what that meant mingled with worry about what they'd think.

I arrived at Benedict's house before the boys did and was touched to see his concern at their delay, followed by his all-out joy when the carriage came into sight. The boys had the door open before the wheels had stopped and leaped onto the drive and into their laughing father's arms, followed by a bounding wolfhound introduced as Manitou, a shaggy grey soulful creature Benedict clearly adored. The boys, Benedict—Bean—and Henry, were lanky and handsome, and, with only a year between them, hard to tell apart, especially with an excitedly barking dog creating more confusion. Having shaken my hand very charmingly in their soft young grips, they helped down Hannah, who gave a wince I think we were meant to notice.

"You must be tired—let's get you settled," I said, and got a look which told me I wasn't her host just yet.

While I tried to move past that little difficulty with respectful questions about the distance and the weather in Connecticut, Benedict wrestled and mock boxed with Bean and Henry, giving me a good glimpse of the child he'd himself been, and sending Manitou into an arcing frenzy.

Herding us all inside, Benedict poured his sister a large glass of wine and peppered his family with questions, beaming with pride at the height of the hurdles they'd cleared and personal best speeds they'd beat.

Hannah unsuccessfully suppressed a proud smile, and it was lovely to feel her ally in the family's happiness.

When the boys did stand still, it was easier to tell the difference. Bean was darker, heavier set, with sensitive eyes and an open face. Henry was a slightly less finished version of his brother, paler, and with more defenses.

Bean was talking of his impatience to enlist.

"Not until you're fourteen," Benedict said.

"That's only a year away."

"There must be other adventures," I said. "Sailing? Or what about a trade?"

"You can't get in the way of the fighting drive," Hannah said. "Wouldn't want to, not in war. You'll see."

"Let's pray the war will be over before Bean is old enough to go," I said.

"I doubt it," she said bluntly. "Both sides seem to be waiting for the other to admit they're wrong, and I can't see that happening. And now the French butting in."

I couldn't write off another year to fighting. And I refused to consign these sweet boys to blades and chain shot. To think of their narrow backs and bony wrists, the soft hands too big for their arms still, their curious features and shambling gait pressed into formation and marching into the mouths of cannons—worst, never to come home—I wouldn't have it. I could see myself suddenly at Hannah's age, worn out with worrying, even if not grief, trying to put a pleasant smile on tired, defeated features, never shaking the guilt and failure for not having done more to secure the boys the life they should have enjoyed. I looked at Bean and Henry with a surge of protective affection and pig-headed ambition. It could not come to their having to go.

I fell back from conversation and let the four of them catch up. Benedict was a little impatient with Hannah already, chafing at the ways she contradicted him, visibly irritated by malapropisms and the sarcasm with which she conceded to his opinion. She did tend to pronounce commonplace phrases as if they were an original revelation, but then again, clichés bear repeating for a reason.

How would it be though, I wondered, to share a table at every meal? How would it be to parent a boy only four years my junior, especially if more war meant I wouldn't have children of my own? Hannah was old enough to be my mother, a fact I didn't feel either of us would easily forget. When Benedict asked proudly, *Do you like the house*?" she picked something from her teeth, winked at the boys, and said, "I told you it'd be fancy."

After lunch, Hannah told me she had known the two of us were for keeps after Benedict kept her up after a party.

"That time you traded truths while dancing? He wouldn't give away your secrets—though I tried, didn't I?—but he was far gone, no mistaking. He wanted help finding a line of poetry that did you justice. Had every book off the shelf and took an entire night deciding—"

Benedict swatted his sister with a napkin, feeling a little more sentimental after the wine at lunch.

"I can't begin to tell you how much Hannah's done for me. She looked after the boys' mother to the end. Buried her, while I was in Quebec. And she's raised these two scamps since they were babies."

"I didn't want them following their father pillar to post. They needed a fixed home."

"I think you'd like Philadelphia—" Benedict said.

"Let's see if you're staying, before we change everything. We like living in Connecticut, don't we boys?"

"Will you fight again, Daddy?" Bean asked.

"We'll see," Benedict said. "More me than governing."

When Hannah and I were alone by the fire, the boys playing billiards with their father behind the sofa, I said, "You've done a wonderful job."

"Oh, I don't know." She smiled though.

There was a pause as we looked at the flames and sipped our coffee.

"I am glad," she said, jerking her head over her shoulder toward her brother. She didn't meet my eye, but I gathered that was her blessing.

By the end of the visit, I said goodbye to the three of them with real affection and marveled that life had been kind enough to supply new family just as I'd see Betsy less.

Benedict said he'd drop me home.

"That was so nice! Hannah never married?"

"Not yet," he said. "Perhaps she'll feel more freedom now."

"Oh?"

We smiled at each other.

"I'd like to think I hadn't hijacked her whole life. She's a good-looking woman still?"

"Very much so."

"She may yet have that happiness. Some late-stage bachelor—"

"Or handsome widower—"

Abruptly he called for the carriage to halt. I felt I'd drawn the question out like a stubborn splinter.

"Peggy"—he winced briefly, kneeling in front of me.

I searched his face.

"I was beginning to think you weren't sure," I said.

"I was sure from our first meeting. I needed time to believe you loved me. Deeply enough for a lifetime. Take on all these flaws and faults—love my boys—be my wife. Peggy Shippen. I am asking you to marry me."

The next morning Atty answered the door to a beaming Benedict. I watched through the banisters as Mother said he'd better speak to her husband. As the door closed, I heard, "The most marvelous thing, sir, your daughter is willing to have me."

My mother and I sat in silence, me straining to hear, she appearing not to listen. All the questions I was tempted to ask—how my mother had known that my father was the one for her, what advice she might give as I embarked—

somehow stalled in me beneath the oppressive tick of the clock. Partly, it was nerves. What could they be discussing so long? It wasn't possible my father might say no. If he refused, I would elope, spare them the cost of a wedding and reconcile from the other side, but it would be a shame to let the world know, for Benedict to feel, we didn't have their blessing. He could do with some parental approval, and I wanted their goodwill—longed for it. I hoped a wedding, me being less of a burden, off and secure in a general's care, might help set some of our fractures. Benedict could be as Neddy was, a bonding agent. I would ask him to continue delivering flowers and little treats out of season for my mother when I was gone.

Beside Mamma was my brothers' rocker, which had never been put away. My eyes filled with tears suddenly, for all the family sadness, and I reached for her, but she was far removed behind her caul of grief, and the door was opening now, the men emerging, and she missed the gesture.

"Let's relieve Peggy of any suspense—and share the news with my wife."

My father poured us all a glass of sherry and seemed to feel there were aspects of the deal he should clarify while he had time.

"She has great sensibility, General, and can suffer from anxiety—"

"She has spoken of it." Benedict smiled at me. "We all have our Achilles' heel," Benedict said, tapping his bad leg wryly with his sword.

"She's stubborn," my mother said.

"I find her delightfully decided." He smiled.

Chapter Eighteen

The next day Benedict came back to take me riding. I was so occupied watching how he handled the horse and moved in the saddle, I barely noticed the way we were going.

When I looked up, I was surprised to find he'd taken me back to Mount Pleasant.

"You like it?"

"I do," I said mildly, only then noticing the intentness of his question.

"I've bought it, settling it after my death on my wife and children."

For a second, I thought he spoke of his first wife.

He took my hand. "We'll have a home of our own, Peggy. A place to raise a family and grow old together after the war."

I felt joy like a rush to the head. I had thought no further than marrying him, never even peeked beyond that happiness, and to have such a massive and unexpected gift, to think we could be equal to this, felt like unimaginable security.

He told me it would be some months before we could move in, but the Spanish ambassador's rent would supply helpful income until then.

I nodded rapidly, recalibrating.

"Are you very disappointed?"

"Disappointed? Benedict, no! It's unbelievably romantic, and the thought of moving in with you is already heaven."

My eyes fell on the iron boot scraper I remembered from visiting with André, the strange presentiment I'd felt, and hoped it meant life was unfolding as it should.

"Shall we hold on to that?" Benedict asked. "A reminder every time we cross our threshold of the future coming our way."

"I'd like that," I said.

"Then I'll see to it."

We kissed all the way down the long avenue of limes, feeling his excitement and mine.

"Don't drop me off," I said. "Not yet."

"I'll take you home." He smiled.

Back at his house, Benedict lifted me down from the horse and carried me, turning sideways through the door. I worried Benedict's bad leg might buckle under my weight and held my breath to be light as could be as he swept me in. Major Franks stepped back from the entrance in surprise before ducking his head discreetly and darting out the door.

Benedict kicked the door shut behind us and laid me out onto the chaise longue. I used my toes to kick off my heels and lay back in happy anticipation.

He built up the fire burning in the grate. Watching his broad back bent over the work, the ease with which he had it roaring, I had never felt so luxuriant and safe.

"What is that smell?" I asked.

"I think it's the blend—oak and pine."

"It's an amazing combination," I said. "Home."

He made love to me then for the very first time, gently, until I was trembling beyond embarrassment with wanting. It was everything it ought to be. The most extravagant fantasy and the most natural thing going.

Soon, we'd christened most surfaces, and I was making love to him.

Later, we raced around the house—I had license now to explore—flinging doors open like an advent calendar's. There was a large, light-filled room adjoining Benedict's own which I pegged as mine, and in his, a massive, canopied bed too large to leave (or arrive, Benedict said wryly, by any visible scientific principle). It was the sort of bed I thought I'd happily conceive, give birth, and die in, with lots of lovely new linen.

It was true there was little furniture beyond that on display downstairs, and one too many dust bunnies. The bathroom was definitely that of a bachelor, a little grubby around the sink, with a sad sliver of soap and a towel gray with use. I looked around happily while drying my hands gingerly. There was work for me here.

After we'd made love one more time, Benedict delivered me back to my parents, and for all the laughing care we'd both taken trying to restore order to my hair, my mother's glance left me certain there was nothing she missed.

Atty ran the bath for me and teased me for being so dazed and sated, dozy with love, above the steaming water.

As she patiently redressed my hair, I asked impulsively, "Will you come with me? Atty? Be my maid when I marry the general?"

"Gladly," Atty said. "Thank you, Miss Peggy. Now, get down to dinner. You're late again."

My parents were already at the table. I pulled in my chair and said sorry to keep them waiting.

"I invited Atty to come with me. I hope that wasn't wrong?"

"You should have asked us."

"I should. I'm sorry. It just popped out. I love her, and she's always done so much for Betsy and me. I hoped it might be helpful to you, one less expense. I am so grateful for all you've spent on my education, the endless dresses. I hope to be able to look after you a bit now, should you need it, in time—"

They looked skeptical. Hurt by that, I told them Benedict had bought Mount Pleasant for me—and our future children.

"Has he got that kind of money?" my mother asked.

Father glanced at her.

"You said yourself, Edward, he's living beyond his means."

"Mount Pleasant is an exceptional expense," my father said. "Exceptional. Well, we'll see."

I clasped my hands to keep back tears.

"This is all very hasty, Peggy, when you think of Betsy and Neddy—" my father said.

I felt my frustration surging. "You gave your permission only yesterday. We've had plenty of time. I know my own mind—and Benedict's."

"This is nothing personal about the general."

"Please then," I begged, "only wish us well."

I wanted to buy him a gift, after all he'd given me. Browsing on my way to Stanbury's, I spotted a leather case containing a pair of pewter flasks, each with a cup embedded in the front face. The symmetry was appealing, and the present felt meant to be. I spent the last of my own small savings on the gift, astounded to think I'd be marrying him without a penny.

"Peggy! Look at you shine. I hope you've been awash with champagne!" Odie embraced me.

"Now for the wedding dress—" Stansbury drumrolled on his workbench. "The general already sent word he's assuming responsibility for your account."

Together we settled on something very simple, in the medieval style I loved. We paired the dress with low-heeled lace shoes, to which Stansbury said he would add a sparkling sprinkle of stones.

"Peggy," he said as I was leaving, with my usual reluctance. "Don't let anything shadow this? This war has meant enough muted and missed celebrations. Enjoy every minute."

"You're right." I shook my head. "I am happy. I know I'm lucky. And when the war is over, I swear, I will never worry again."

I turned. "You'll share the news with the captain?"

"Major now." Odie nodded.

"Major! Well then, add my congratulations." I smiled. "Major André. Has the ring of history."

"Benedict," I said, when I saw him to thank him for taking on my account at Stansbury's. "This isn't all too great a stretch? Mount Pleasant? The clothes? Forgive me asking. It's only you've said you're still owed by Congress and hardly able to do business while Reed's policing every transaction. I know nothing about money. I know how well you've done. Only, I find the idea of borrowing frightening. The idea of being beholden to anyone— My father was always avoiding being paid in Continental currency, and so unaccustomed to debt he discharged the smallest obligations at first opportunity."

"Debt can be very productive," he assured me, pulling me closer on his lap, while I kept one leg on the ground taking my weight.

"Wealth can't grow without credit—you don't need to worry about money, Peggy. Leave the providing to me."

And I did. It was seductive, relief I wanted, just as much as I wanted responsibility.

The night before my wedding, I laid out the shoes and smoothed the dress and, flushed with anticipation, had an early dinner with my parents. Conversation centered on arrangements for the next day. The hairdresser could come only an hour before the ceremony, which might make me late for the service at Christ Church.

"It wouldn't be the end of the world if I was a few minutes late," I tried. "Isn't a little delay expected from the bride?"

"Who does she think she is?"

I was startled by my mother's fury. Father reached to still her hand. She pulled it away.

"No, it's typical Peggy not to think of the vicar, or those who might need the church after her."

Who did I think I was? I was so close to being Benedict's, the question caused less confusion than it had the first time, though it still made me cry.

I applied the spoons to my own eyes. My life would make sense, it would, because it would be spent by his side. I could barely wait for morning.

An hour or so after I had blown out my candle, I was woken by my mother peering over her own flame.

"I have taken advice: Your brothers tell me initially your attraction to Arnold was only nervous excitement, but now it seems the energy is settling and he may yet be the right choice."

"Please leave," I said, my tight voice masking my fear.

I did find it frightening. Entertaining what the dead felt about my wedding felt too like letting madness in.

The morning of the wedding was oddly foggy and the atmosphere in the house very somber. I was relieved when Betsy came to help Atty get me ready. Atty's chatter about the dreadful goings-on in her own family distracted me from the weird gloom in mine. We assembled in the hall, my mother elegant in white lace, my father handsome and impeccably dressed.

By the time we reached the church, the fog had burned off to give a beautiful April day. Benedict had arranged a male choir of his former soldiers—a surprise which I loved. I felt so happy hearing his strong tenor beside me—and with that loud choir around us, free to sing my heart out myself.

"Do you, Margaret Shippen?"

I smiled from the priest to Benedict, delighted to feel the power of those timeless vows as ours.

"I do."

Clasping hands at the altar, we turned to face our friends with shy excitement.

In the burial ground, I put my flowers on the boys' graves, Bean and Henry beside me, sweetly serious to read those sad, short dates.

My parents sat unhappily throughout the brief speech in which Benedict thanked them, and it hurt to see the fleeting confusion in his eyes when he caught that. Major Franks, Benedict's best man, gave the warmest of toasts to us both, and read messages sent by Theodosia, George Washington, General Schuyler, Alexander Hamilton, General Knox, and the Marquis de Lafayette.

Atty packed all my beautiful new clothes—allowing herself a raised eyebrow at the nightdresses. I let her go on ahead, taking one last look around the room.

Uncle William shook Benedict's hand and kissed me.

"I'll inoculate all your children when it comes to it."

"That sounds the best wedding gift."

Atty was ensconced on the back of the waiting carriage in happy if tactless anticipation.

I kissed and thanked my mother. My father embraced me and wished us luck. Neddy and Betsy hugged me tightly.

"Don't forget us," Odell hammed.

"I'll see you next week." I laughed.

Hannah had finally rounded up the boys to say goodbye, and I loved that their easy family teasing now extended to me. Henry called me Mama! I looked rapidly at Hannah to be sure that wouldn't put her out, but she looked pleased as punch.

Finally, we were alone, the plan to spend an entire week with nothing to do before Benedict resumed his duties.

We drove as dark fell to what was now our house. On arrival, Benedict introduced me to Mrs. Green, the new housekeeper he'd hired, and asked her to make Atty as welcome as could be.

Mrs. Green said she'd prepared a simple supper to be had in our room, imagining how tired we must be, and that it could be ready shortly. Atty would help me unpack, while Benedict had a whiskey by the library fire.

Leading Atty up the curving staircase, I was almost embarrassed by the number of rooms.

"It's magnificent, Mrs. Arnold." She was enjoying every arbitrary opportunity to call me by my new name.

"A lot to be done."

"That's a good thing. You can make it your own."

She unfastened the wedding dress and let me step from it. Underneath I wore lace-topped stockings tied with rose ribbon, a bodice, and the softest silk short knickers. Atty considered the new purchases, pulled out a soft robe in the same pale pink, and settled it on me, loose to the waist, then released my hair so it fell around my face.

There was a knock as Mrs. Green brought a tray laden with chilled wine, a large jug of water, and dishes covered in silver domes.

Atty followed her out, with a last warm wink, and I was alone, a married woman, the luckiest alive, in an outfit even I found exciting. I poured myself a glass of white wine and inspected the dishes. A plate of finely sliced Spanish ham, mushroom risotto, salad, and a tiny pear tart with crème fraiche.

Tearing off a small piece of the serrano, I took the glass to the big blue bed and set it alongside me. The sheets were good, soft and just the right bit of rough. Reconsidering, I took everything I was wearing off.

There was a quick authoritative knock, Benedict's voice saying, "It's only me"—I'd come to know and love that little routine—and the general joined me there.

* * *

Later that night, when more patient, Benedict fully undressed for the first time. I was moved to see him lying in the firelight: one long leg flung across the bed in the casual athletic abandon of the magnificently fit—the other mangled and swollen, his skin taut with wide stretches of scarring. It was amazing he had made it out alive from that wound, that he had made it all the way to here.

"I was guilty of pride in my younger years," Benedict said. "Vain about the strength in my legs. Now I'm sorry you couldn't see me then."

I kissed him.

"I wouldn't have you any other way."

"Nor I you."

"I'm sorry my mother's not warmer with you," I said. "I think she tries to rally her old self, and for a few minutes she can manage, but then the sadness catches up."

He kissed me. "My mother became stern after losing my siblings, all thought trained on sin and death. My damnation felt a real and present risk—"

"We both looked for more love and trust than our poor bereaved parents could give—"

He turned his good side toward me, though that meant weight on his injury.

"We'll have to trust each other—"

"Can you believe," I said, "there's no sin in this?"

We had breakfast the next day in bed, deciding we'd do nothing all week but build his strength and banish all thoughts of politics. He'd sign off from official duties and I'd take a break from reading the papers, and we'd wash the poison of it all away. We took a morning ride across the park past Mount Pleasant, sharing happy anticipation of our future there. We walked down to the river, dreaming of the picnics we'd have and how he'd teach me to swim that summer. And after lunch, we went back to bed. For the first time in years, I was conscious of not worrying about a thing.

The next night I was woken by Benedict crying out in his sleep, thrashing and sweaty.

I soothed him while he cried, a little frightened by the unfamiliar sight of his great frame heaving with tears. Flooded with love and worry, I held his head to my breast, soothing him slowly until he was ready to sleep.

In the morning, I asked if he'd been thinking of the moment he was injured.

"No," he said. "It's the dead I try to forget during the day. The men I killed. The friends I didn't save."

I let him describe the worst of it, things he hadn't admitted to anyone. That epic journey, through the winter months, to Canada, undersupplied and exhausted, keeping his men believing despite impossible odds and appalling conditions, the smallpox more terrible than the British and Indians combined, and then, after months of holding it all together, paying the men himself so they wouldn't starve, he was confronted by hundreds of soldiers threatening to desert because of disease. He and Montgomery had been forced to attack the city of Quebec sooner than they knew would work, with too few men, and his old friend had died before his eyes, along with hundreds of others.

He took a drink.

"Where is the sense in it?"

"You mustn't be haunted, Benedict. Live bigger for all those that died. I try to."

I read to him from Franklin's Cotton Mather, which he loved, until he'd had enough and took the book from me.

We spent the remainder of our honeymoon never far from bed: one heavenly week of just us.

He had so many creative ideas—for imports and exports, for innovative schemes and the promise of investment capital from friends. "I've built a business from scratch before, Peggy, and when peace comes, I'll do the same again. I don't want you ever worrying on account of money. The harder I work, the luckier we'll be—"

Lying beside him, I felt sure if he followed his instincts, he couldn't go wrong.

"Would it be a good idea for me to decorate?" I asked over breakfast. "The house is beautiful, but it does feel just a little too like a rental? Too easy to remember Howe's tenure, looking at all the Chippendale furniture and English silver. I think we should make the governor general's house a symbol of American style and reassuring permanence—a beacon of our values. If we furnish the public rooms with well-made local pieces, the clean lines of our best Shaker furniture and New England pewter, it will be a reassuring indicator the Patriots are here to stay, the good ones, committed to Jefferson's vision. By supporting local business, celebrating our own aesthetic, the trade and invention which make us well-set to make a stylish success of our liberty, we'll show them stability, so that gradually any lingering uncertainty will lift. Let's help them see what to think, not tell them."

He gave me a generous budget to do just that.

Chapter Nineteen

I knew Benedict's return to governing would be hard work after the week's retreat from reality we'd had, and I was determined to match his efforts. I teamed with Atty and Mrs. Green on a deep spring clean of every room, and then after a quick bath went off to choose paint. The bones of the house were so good, I could hardly go wrong, but I wanted to do justice to all that order and proportion, providing the money would stretch. I made a study of the changing aspects of each room as the sun moved west, having fun with paint samples, swatches of silk, and worsted damask. I loved beetling around in my own little carriage on errands, giving Stansbury business, garnering antiques and recent American pieces. My new life made even picking up provisions feel like traveling. I learned to drive a decent bargain and delighted in giving craftsmen commissions. Soon the house was fragrant with fresh paint and new upholstery and the blissful Schuylkill breeze, and I was happy, busy bringing design ideas to life.

I had a letter from my parents, in response, I imagined, to my thanks for the wedding. Happily slicing it open, eager already for news of home, I found myself in a mirrored maze. They told me I had not done enough to make them feel special on my wedding day. Spoke again of my selfishness in taking Atty. And of my insensitivity over money to have suggested we move to Canada when I did. They told me they wouldn't be visiting because they couldn't see circumstances in which that would be successful and closed with conventional expressions of love. I didn't tell Benedict, didn't want to set back his feeling about me or my family, or bring up what felt petty and unnecessary given the order of worries he had.

I felt I had a knife lodged in my back though, a wound between my shoulder blades sending pain shooting up my neck. I went through every motion I was meant to, careful to be pleasant with everyone, but lost days of real presence in relentless rumination over how to answer each facet of the letter and reach the parents I remembered. I was too ashamed even to tell Theo, but I did write thanking her for her wedding gift and begging her to visit.

I felt a little infected after those letters, superstitious, an extra dread at what bad things were getting in and what harm might come, lonely too from the barrier between me and Benedict, just as I was ever more exclusively dependent on him. I tried not to do anything to inflame his worries, or to make him regret choosing me. The news in the paper was never good, and more often than not the Militia Man was maligning him. He returned from sessions with the Council battered and out of sorts and all evening the doorbell would ring with poor soldiers, men he'd fought with, in a pitiful state of need.

Benedict gave every man an audience, and took care with their dignity, reminiscing with gentle flattery about their contributions to the fight. He never let one leave without money in their pocket and the promise of a letter to Congress to get redress. They shared terrible stories, every variety of sacrifice and senseless answering parsimony—one orphan paid for, three others in the same family left wanting—so many of them facing absolute ruin. I took Benedict's dictation in bed, so the letters were ready to send each morning before he embarked on another round with the Council. After seeing him off to sleep, I'd lie awake worrying what was coming our way.

There were vulnerable women that sought his help too, the wives of injured soldiers, widows needing money. I was sympathetic, and threatened by the more gorgeous ones. It was daunting, to see the temptation faced every day by a powerful, attractive man. Benedict always reassured me, but when we weren't in bed, those visits, the weight of all that need, and the cold, implacable realities of money, made my anxiety run rampant as well as doubts about my judgment. With my Dread Index climbing I kept checking the expanding budget for decorating with Benedict. He shrugged off my worry, saying he'd heard my charming bargaining and knew I wouldn't be overcharged.

* * *

In May, Stansbury came to see me along with two shopboys bearing a towering stack of packages: all the curtains and bedlinens I'd commissioned as well, he winked, as my wedding present.

I showed him around the house, and he admired the choices, chattering about the wedding.

"How are your parents?"

I shook my head.

"The mother of the bride's demeanor did occasion some comment," he said waspishly.

As I settled him in the small sitting room, he asked after Benedict, and the length of days he was working, and how he was managing. I told him I hoped he could hang on just a little longer, as he had Washington's blessing to resign as governor as soon as the trial was behind him.

"Have they set a trial date?"

"Not yet."

"Ingrates."

He admitted he was feeling a little adrift with Odell spending more and more time in New York.

"He's ready to settle there, but I'm not ready to leave. Makes me feel our age difference."

"You always seem a perfect pair."

"Sometimes I wonder if jealousy's inevitable."

I felt jittery with reflexive fear. What would I do, trapped with a husband I couldn't trust? There was no going home.

"Stansbury, there are the same years between me and Benedict, and you wouldn't have him worry—or worry about him! Odell is devoted. What is it you're imagining?"

"That he strays," he said quietly.

I was flustered to think of specifics, but flattered he was confiding in me.

"Who with?"

He looked at me steadily, as if considering how much to share.

"Not André?"

"No. I mean Odie's half in love with him. Who's not? Poor Clinton, I think, is smitten but doesn't understand it."

I thought of the possessive, competitive way he had observed me talking to André.

"I don't think our major feels he can risk succumbing to anyone. He needs to keep rising. Achieve a feat so dazzling he has the power to win his privacy."

"Here's to that then. What about you?" I asked. "What would help?"

"More business," he said.

"I'll be doing my best," I said, uneasy with guilt that I'd spent all I would for a while. "Could you forgive Odie, if there was someone else?"

"I might. If it meant otherwise being without him at all. I don't think I need to be his answer to everything. And it isn't as if I don't enjoy my time alone. Or find novelty appealing. A triangle is the most intriguing and satisfying shape in geometry, don't you think?"

Mrs. Green laid out tea while my mind reeled. I was glad to be hosting him after all the comfort and company he'd given me, and enthralled as ever by his mind-expanding ideas. Such freedom a man had—such possibilities.

"What news of our major?" I asked, pulse quickening, as Mrs. Green closed the door behind her.

Stansbury pulled the wedding present package from the stack and set it in my lap. Beneath the beautiful wrapping: the copy of Blackstone's *Legal Commentaries* that had been our key. Tucked inside, a letter.

Stansbury drained his tea and started to hang the curtains, while I slowly decoded the note.

André offered sincere congratulations on my marriage and expressed his respect for Benedict's era-defining achievements, adding the wish such sacrifice would be given the recognition it deserved. He closed by stating once again his earnest desire to help me and signed off *your devoted friend, JA*.

I was a little affronted by his feeling sympathy was necessary for Benedict, and worried I'd been naive to believe legal resolution and freedom were in sight. It was reassuring though, knowing my marriage hadn't proved an impediment to our friendship. If anything, I felt our frankness—our closeness—could now progress. The awkward imbalance between a woman in want of a husband and a man who might marry her or not was no longer relevant.

"Elegant as ever," Stansbury sighed, reading it over my shoulder. "He and Benedict would get on, in other circumstances."

"They would," I said. *They will*, I wanted to add.

I held the letter above the embers in the grate, frustration rising with the flames.

When Benedict returned from work, I received a powerful whiff of whiskey along with my kiss.

I poured myself one, so the smell of his wouldn't be hard to take.

"How was your day?"

"Hell as ever. How was yours?" He was slurring slightly.

"I saw Stansbury. He hung the curtains—"

He barely glanced at them, instead zeroing in on the new book.

"What's this?"

"A gift from Stansbury."

He refilled his drink. "*Legal Commentaries* for the lawyer's daughter?"

"I had a letter from Major André. Congratulating us on our marriage. Sending his particular good wishes to you. He thinks of you very highly—sees and sympathizes with your plight."

"Where's the letter?"

"I burned it," I said.

"You did what?" he said, his features contorted with disgust. "You sly little bit—"

"No! Benedict. There was nothing in it you couldn't have seen. Only, it's a precaution. His friendship is important to me. He let me help him, contribute ideas, got me ready for the conversations I so love having with you. He isn't looking for trouble. He wants the war behind us. Destroying the letters is only practice, in case there ever comes a need for secrets—"

He threw his glass—a wedding present from Neddy and Betsy—into the fire. The alcohol flared.

I felt my eyes fill with tears. This was not a Benedict I had seen before. This was not an island I wanted to be on.

"Not secrets from you!"

"I'm sorry," he mumbled, pulling me onto his lap. "Come here."

"I'm sorry too," I said. "I didn't mean to upset you. You do trust me? I needn't have told you about the letter if I hadn't felt you could know. I want us to share everything."

He said he did trust me, he was sorry, only tired. He didn't think he could hold on as governor much longer: If he didn't step down first, Reed would drive him out, but they still hadn't set a date for the trial, and though he was longing to be vindicated and free to resign, he had no idea what he'd be in position to do on the other side. And the prospect of fighting again filled him with dread in a way it never had. He had been beaten up too badly, for too long. He couldn't imagine leaving me and was dogged by the feeling he'd exhausted his luck—superstitious that if he did try to fight again, he'd die this time, or worse, let down his men.

I listened, murmuring support, stroking his hair. Occasionally he'd fling me from him to pace or grab another drink, only to snatch me back. He had ignored so many worries since the wedding and drunk to dull the threat of all he'd neglected. He could get morbid after drinking, he admitted, and now that we were living together, he was sure to become contemptible to me. Everywhere he looked was misery.

Out of my depth, I begged him not to say those things. I loved him, adored him, and could never think less of him.

I left briefly to tell Mrs. Green we'd have a cold supper and eat by the fire and rapidly assembled a tray without meeting her or Atty's eyes. I would never be a natural aristocrat, I realized, never feel grand enough not to mind the servants seeing Benedict compromised, or me embarrassed. I said I'd bring back the dirty dishes myself, and ring if there was anything we needed.

Returning with the tray, I found Benedict much worse. He stared glassily, his head swaying like a drugged bull's. He spoke deliberately and thickly, jabbing the air with his finger.

"Washington is never going to give me my due. Even if he wanted to, Congress won't let him. I'm not popular with the politicians. I can't play their games. They'd do nothing rather than risk a decision and face recrimination. All the energy's in opposition, their only satisfaction defeating a bill or doing a man down. You have to make them frightened of you. Nobody's scared of me—I've got it all wrong."

I glanced nervously at the bottle beside him, calculating how I could hide it before he saw.

Everywhere his eye lurched, he saw evidence of the spending he'd encouraged. And with each sign he'd overextended to please me, he was newly enraged.

He told me my father had insisted on his settling property on me before we could marry, and how was he to manage between this house and that and the house and school fees in Connecticut? The purchase of Mount Pleasant had some saying Benedict was dipping into government funds. They were jealous nonentities who'd never neared a battlefield, but a man could be hanged without evidence these days.

He talked of a labyrinth of trade transactions, all of them impeded or undermined, and I tried to keep the details straight, to soothe and defuse, or venture distraction. As the hours went by, I also desperately wanted the night to end. I did try hiding the bottle, but losing it confused him, which made him angrier still. I had not seen anyone drinking whiskey to such excess, and clearly the effect was very different from wine's. It felt literally as if an unhelpful spirit had got in.

A couple of times I thought I had settled him down into a doze and started tidying the room, but he'd rear up again, animated by some freshly remembered outrage, the despicable Reed, pandering Washington.

It was André his conversation circled like a drain. "How dare he condescend to feel pity for me? What kind of wife welcomes letters from a former admirer, what kind of liar burns them? How would you feel, if I was doing the same?"

He began reeling off the names of women in his past, chanting them grotesquely. Did I want the sort of man who had a woman at every stop on the road? A mistress discreetly installed in some convenient apartment in town?

I scanned his chest, his face, wanting to appreciate him, and to find the most sincere and efficient way to convey the essence of André without threatening or offending him.

"Listen to me. André is intelligent and artistic, connected and adept. He was the British social secretary, expert at entertaining. Lots of affinities with Odie and Stansbury and with the ladies, but he's not a soldier, or a leader, certainly no general, Benedict—"

"General," he said with contempt. "Firing men up with easy rhetoric, persuading them to risk everything, steel them to kill, live in violence and fear, for what? Uncertain ends. The hubris of it. I punished men for self-inoculation—when they were only desperate."

"You were looking for the greater good—the health of the regiment—the forest not the trees? What would have been the alternative?"

"I punished them for desertion!"

"Haven't armies had to, from time immemorial?"

"They were facing death by staying with me!"

Nothing I said made a difference. On and on he ranted. Holding me close, barring my way. Veering between mistrust and belief in me, venting about the relations between the Patriots and France; Washington's derisive record in battle; the pretentious accent at the end of André's name. A fey insistence on his Frenchness! Wasn't everyone too busy for such an affectation?

I felt a surge of frustration. "We don't have time for unnecessary jealousy!"

"If I knew it to be unnecessary, it wouldn't exist. Why would I believe you?"

"Because I love you and I'm very well looked after at home. Of all the dangers we face, André is not one!"

Benedict's swaying was slowing. He lay back on the sofa and looked at me. The cloud over his eyes had cleared enough that for a second, I thought I could reach him.

I sat on the floor beside him, my back to him, his hand over my shoulder in mine. "I'm devoted to you, Benedict. Don't I show it, over and over? But my loyalty to my few true friends is real and that includes André. What I owe those I love will always be greater than my debt to a war I don't want. I worry what becomes of André if we win. I'd want his help if we didn't! He's on your side, because on mine—"

A shuddering snore. He'd fallen asleep. Deeply, finally. He wouldn't be rearing up again tonight.

I laid a blanket over him. I needed movement, time to think. I grabbed my cloak and let myself into the garden, grateful for the cool night air.

Benedict hadn't turned his anger against me, but he might in time, I could see. He was alarmingly past controlling what impression he made and his strength in that state was, if anything, greater than when he was sober.

I glanced up at the Reeds' house, already in darkness. Something needed to be done to relieve the bitterness, or it would finish us.

I had known he liked to drink; I'd been excited to pour him wine. I had known he suffered from gout; I'd been proud to nurse him through it. I had gathered he worried about money and still accepted his gifts. I could not claim I had not signed up for this. I would not shrink from it now.

Evidently, I had not married a man with the moderate instincts and temperament of my father. I had been too busy looking for adventure to value that. Benedict was a big, bold dreamer, but he had a daunting capacity for anger. If a tendency toward tirades was the cost of his passion and bravery, then I must manage it. I had smiled far too broadly on my wedding day to admit defeat now. I needed him happy and satisfied when with me, active and valued when not. The alternative—a frustrated and humiliated husband—would be a lifelong nightmare.

I waded into the little neglected grove at the bottom of the garden, ferns dense at my feet, and started thwacking with a stick at the tangle of branches to widen a path.

There were some things, of course, I couldn't have known before marriage. The extent of his snoring, or drinking when not in company during the day, other regrettable little habits which meant I had to remember the generosity with which Benedict had overlooked my own imperfections: the lack of money I'd brought to the marriage, my unhelpful politics and history of anxiety, the sad stigma of my mother's dislike.

I thought of Theodosia's advice about dealing with men who had had too much to drink at the Hermitage. I must find the reason in whatever his railing—and study what it would take to restore him to his best self.

What had I learned? He had been given command of Philadelphia but begrudged every expense in its management. Washington knew the importance of appearances and the place of grandeur in establishing the preeminence of a Patriot regime. He spent his wife's money freely, but if Benedict took so much as a ham from the storehouse, there was talk. Marrying me hadn't helped. I brought no assets, and now discovered my father had made our marriage conditional on further expense. The choice of Mount Pleasant was Benedict's, but he'd reached for that summit to please me.

We hadn't been married a week before the harping allegations of misconduct started again. Allegations I'd missed by skipping the papers. There could be no more news diet for me, and no more withholding of our problems by him, not if I had a hope of helping. It felt base—wrong and annoying—to have to worry about money when the world was on fire with war, but clearly, a major priority was income.

André had seen that Benedict was hard done by all the way from New York, and his letter had stressed the need for redress. It took pains to set down—and decipher—anything said in those letters. No word was wasted. And anyway, André was not one for empty sympathy. He had indicated not pity, but solidarity. He must mean something could—should—be done.

Chapter Twenty

Benedict woke from the binge with a thick head, foul breath, and a temper. By late afternoon he was suffering an attack of gout, incapacitated by excruciating pain and depression, and drinking again to relieve it.

"Go easy," I said gently. "It's doing you no good."

"Hair of the dog," he said ruefully, and I was glad to see his old smile again. "I'm sorry, Peggy. Forgive me? I drink to stop thinking, but I must look, and I do see. I lost the boys' mother, my store, my leg, took more blows to my head than I'll ever remember. I want to leave this post, but with any opportunity for profit considered suspicious, I don't know what I can do except fight and fail."

"If you did fight again, you'd be as brave and brilliant as you always were."

"You don't know that."

"I'm not having you leaving me. The question is what our next step will be. You've been injured, persecuted, fleeced, and we need an answer that's not the army."

He reached for his glass. I sighed.

A second day was lost in drink, a second evening in shouting, and a third day saw him defeated and ashamed, reaching for the bottle again.

"A controlled dose, Peggy. I need to feel better. I have friends who have offered to help, and they will, but I need to move carefully. It's not a good look, asking for money. Even accepting it can seem demeaning. There's expense in reassuring my friends I'm one of them. Lafayette, Schuyler, Washington, Hamilton—if he marries Eliza, as it seems he will—they're all of them extremely rich."

I felt the familiar pang of embarrassment about my nonexistent dowry. He took my hand.

"I don't want money for its own sake, but I'd like to look them in the eye as equals, be able to retire, put my leg up, when I'm ready, without us sliding into poverty. I want to keep helping the men who fought with me. I want to see friends and leave them easy I made it through all right. I don't want old comrades feeling sorry for me.

"There are ventures, speculations, good ones, under discussion, but they all take credit, and with the trial hanging over me, securing credit is not the business it was. The constant throbbing in my leg makes me feel impaired, out of time. I feel as trapped as I did in Saratoga, all those months with my shattered leg in a box and the incessant rain on the tent. It was like sitting in my own coffin waiting for the end, unable to turn, to sit up, without the stitches splitting and unmanning me again."

He looked up at me with such boyish worry, I loved him with fresh force.

"I'm afraid I'm turning coward, Peggy."

"You are not. But you shouldn't need to be back in active battle. You've done enough. The Patriots had no legend 'til they had you!"

"They had several. And plenty who gave their all. And Peggy, I did hope to kill two birds with one stone, in granting the pass to recover goods the British had seized."

"Isn't that efficiency? A quality prized in a city administrator? You did nothing criminal?"

"Nothing."

"Actions you feel beneath you?"

"No."

"Anything not done by every man in high command?"

He hesitated.

"I was damned if the British spoils would go to waste. The goods felt like bounty, won on high seas, ours to claim."

"A pirate's sense of justice?"

"Just for a minute."

"I can forgive it, in the cut and thrust. But Benedict? Is there anything you haven't told me? I can't help you prepare your defense if you don't share the full story."

"Franks wanted out," he said.

"Franks? I can't imagine anyone more loyal—to you or the cause."

"A moment of doubt at a time of great pressure. Allowable for anyone, and immediately forgivable in him. He was in anguish about money—hadn't been paid in a year—and I offered to help him transition to civilian life, suggesting he trade in surplus stock, before realizing we'd be in breach of a piece of new legislation. He understood at once, never suggested we persevere once we understood the deal to be illegal, and in fact he said seeing me want to help him had changed his mind. He recommitted to the military."

I nodded, satisfied, and glad of the devotion he inspired from Franks, a man anyone could see was the furthest thing from slippery.

"It should be allowable to look to one's own survival, provide for dependents, without that suggesting insufficient commitment to the cause."

"It should be—would be—if Congress would only get men fairly paid."

"Is it a problem of money, or will?"

"Both. We're tapped out. We can't afford to be entrenched enemies of a market as key as Britain. We can't afford independence if the Continental currency doesn't buck up. Most of us owed by Congress know we'll be lucky to receive the interest, only a fool would harbor hopes of seeing the principal. Some are rich enough to swallow it, but there are men who've financed this revolution with a full heart who will die in debt—and political division makes us shamefully slow to pay veterans whose basic needs can't wait."

And then he was off again, lamenting decisions made by Reed himself that wouldn't meet any public standard for decency.

I considered Atty in the mirror as she unpinned my hair in the dressing room later that evening. "How is your family, Atty? Has your father recovered? Typhus, wasn't it?"

"It is. Mrs. Arnold, he won't mend, and my mother can't work for nursing him. As it is, my work's all that's between them and penury."

"Well, as long as I'm alive, I'll see you're done right by."

Atty brushed, long steady strokes, meditative. I loved the way the light made a halo of her hair. "Why is it," I asked, "when women have been stepping up and surviving as widows, providing for their families, running entire estates for years during the Crusades, there still exists this stubborn myth about the male as sole provider? Women as ornament and homemaker—"

"That's only your lot, Mrs. Arnold, if you'll forgive me saying. The likes of us don't think twice about a life of labor. We pitch in."

"Is there any limit, do you think, to a woman's contribution? What do you make of Joan of Arc?"

"The martyr? They'd have her in an asylum today."

"I believe she's still the youngest in history to lead an army, of either sex."

"Hats off."

I smiled and made a gesture I hoped took in the chaos of the last few days.

"I'm sorry, Atty, when you're contending with so much. What would help? Would a husband?"

Our eyes met in the mirror. "It's not a given, Mrs. Arnold, best I can tell."

The fourth night I lay beside him staring at the ceiling. This pattern of drinking into a fury, raving all night, and suffering for two or three days would not do. The waste of time alone offended me, and already I missed the freedom to make hours of the day my own.

Benedict snored so violently I was amazed he stayed sleeping. I gently rolled him onto his good side, where after a brief pause, he continued snoring as before.

I took out my writing set from my nightstand. The one thing I knew I could do was throw a party. It was only fair to lend what I'd learned to my husband's cause. I would show my love and his detractors it had not been irresponsible to finish the house. The home was now appropriate to a governor general's status, and it was time to make the investment pay. Washington should hear the stories told by Franks and every good soldier still standing. They all should have a boost to morale. I would help Benedict extend his influence, build bridges to making a living on the far side of governing and fighting. Marrying me had added to his pressures, and that I had to make right. It was for me to help him make money now.

I began making a list.

The next morning, I ran Benedict a deep, near-scalding bath sprinkled with sandalwood oil and brought him a tray of breakfast and a beer as he steeped in it. When he'd eaten, I whisked away the tray, stripped, and climbed in with him to tell him the plan.

"We'll throw a party in honor of General and Mrs. Washington on the occasion of their visit to Philadelphia. It's what this house and a governor general are for. Guests: General and Mrs. Washington—"

"Naturally—"

"I met him once when I was fourteen. He won't remember."

"Want to bet?"

"The Marquis de Lafayette."

"The boy general. Up to his eyes in lace."

"Alexander Hamilton."

"Caribbean lothario. I will be watching him with you."

"General Schuyler."

He paused. "He's been under a cloud of suspicion for some time. Though he at least had the privilege of a trial against trumped-up charges not a million miles from mine, and cleared his name. People are starting to look askance again, since his eldest married an Englishman—"

"Didn't they elope? Such a love match can't count against him? And with Eliza now talked of in the same breath as Hamilton . . ."

"Yes, all right, Schuyler, and his daughters. He's been a steadfast supporter. Who else?"

"His Excellency and First Lady Reed."

"No."

"She's not *all* bad."

"He's satanic."

"But to fixate on him only engenders bitterness. And perhaps we haven't tried as hard as we could? I know not everything I've said and done around the pair of them has been helpful. How about we try one last push, together, an Arnold charm offensive?"

"You think better of people than you should. The last time I invited them to a party they hanged Carlisle."

I felt the weight of all the death there hadn't been time to grieve.

"I still think it's important he sees you hosting Washington—and not inviting them risks reducing you to his level. They are right next door . . . Reed wouldn't dare not attend if Washington is a guest. If we haven't done everything to appease him before the court martial, we might regret it—"

"All right." He sighed.

"The Cartwrights?"

"Spies confirmed he's supplying the British with munitions."

"Poor Mrs. Cartwright," I said, running a line through their names. "Will they be all right?"

"More than most. Unless the Militia Man gets them in his sights. If wise, they'll wait out the war over the border."

"The Chews?"

He shook his head. "I'm sorry, Peggy. I know you're fond of May, but since Germantown—no. We'll include General and Mrs. Knox if she's not too pregnant for a party. Good woman, Lucy. You'll like her. Franks, Varick, a few other officers and wives."

"And William, and Neddy and Betsy, Theodosia, and my parents—"

"Will they come?"

"Probably not. But I want to try, and the rest will, I bet. We can do this, Benedict, I can do this. You only need to put on that magnificent uniform and show up."

I was on a mission, intent on helping Washington see what Benedict meant for Philadelphia, and how beloved he was. I hired the choir of soldiers from our wedding for one or two nostalgic stag hops and military songs and dances, and a quartet drawn from the Mischianza orchestra for the minuets—and arranged for flowers on every surface in a theme of buff and blue. It made me uneasy, spending more on credit, but distress over offending fellow citizens or jealous politicians was eclipsed by my concern Washington and his all-star generals should not go wanting. We had to show them Benedict had the city in hand. Any embarrassing shortfall—any misstep at all—would be mocked, and reported, and lead to God knew what consequence for the Patriots.

"You're irresistible." He kissed me as I closed the door behind the deliveryman who'd brought my rented chairs. Would I be though? Lafayette had met Marie Antoinette! I tried rehearsing little French witticisms, and that only made me more anxious. Why hadn't I spent more hours practicing verbs when I had time?

Most good food was still hard to find in the city, but Benedict worked his magic. We'd serve salmon with tarragon, new potatoes whose skin burst at the first prick of a fork, asparagus and peas, stone-cold French rosé, and a new discovery: Joseph Priestley's sparkling spring water which tickled the tongue.

Chapter Twenty-One

Standing at the top of the steps with Benedict, I watched our guests arrive. A dozen of Washington's Life Guard, a uniformly glamorous group of officers, matched in build and features as thoroughly as a corps de ballet, stood tall as the commander in chief's vehicle pulled to a stop. Seeing the elegant cavalcade of carriages behind them, I squeezed Benedict's hand in childish excitement. He smiled down at me, as handsome as he'd ever been, as our rented footman announced General Washington. Who wouldn't find this fun?

His Excellency was tall, pink cheeked, and heavily powdered, with lively, intelligent eyes and an informal way about him which was an immediate relief. He gave a slightly grimacing smile, admitting he was suffering some discomfort with new teeth. Martha was little, with a pretty, plump décolleté. She exuded capable, pleasant energy—the safest woman in the world from making a mistake of taste.

They were both disarmingly warm with me, greeting Benedict as their treasured friend. Washington teased him, "I knew your wife long before you, Arnold. We go way back. Of course I remember that face at fourteen," before moving on into the room, a gracious and practiced political team. Hamilton and Lafayette were next, hugging Benedict like brothers, and I saw my husband's pleasure in their mock box and feint.

Hamilton was ridiculously good-looking, with thick, sandy hair and a smooth, tanned, exquisitely chiseled face. He called me "the object of two entire armies' admiration," lids lowered over those famously alluring, almost violet eyes, and adjusted the hilt of his dress sword to punctuate the point.

Lafayette was surprisingly gangly, not much older than me, and ten times as expensively dressed.

"*Charmante*," he said decidedly, as he bent his rather generous forehead to kiss my hand.

"An honor," I said, withdrawing prematurely as he dove in for a third kiss. The potential misfires in those mingled Colonial and European greetings were a minefield. You'd have thought the virus might have spared us the confusion of possible embraces, but it hadn't.

Behind him were dear Neddy and Betsy and Uncle William, all of whom I hugged hard, before urging them to go in and find a drink. Benedict introduced me to a jovial General Knox, fat in a way that absolutely suited him, and full of fantastic flattery for me. I met General Schuyler and his eldest daughter, Angelica, as beautiful and spirited as everyone said, and there too was lovely Eliza.

"Well done, Peggy!" she said, looking around the room. "This all looks just the thing!"

"Well done indeed," Esther added, unnecessarily, taking her arm.

I gave a deep curtsy and wide smile to Reed, which seemed to surprise him, just as I saw Theodosia and gave a small cry of delight. We inspected each other on outstretched arms and hugged again. She looked wonderful.

I moved constantly that evening, between checking preparations, fleeting greetings, ensuring the wine flowed fast enough, and once the dancing began, whirling from one set of arms to the next. Hamilton and Lafayette felt like boys beside Benedict, but beautiful boys, and I spent a lot of the evening laughing with the two of them.

I saw it was different, the spirit with which male attention had to be deflected now that I was married. I felt older, finally, than my eighteen years—more knowing, and more intent on showing Benedict that however hard I danced, I was good as gold and his alone.

He and I barely talked to each other the first half of the evening, but I was aware of his presence all over the room, and whenever in range, we reached for a brief touch. I kept light eyes on him as the evening advanced, hoping he'd stay civil and affable, and go easy on the drink.

I passed Theodosia chatting happily with Hamilton—he had made a second home of her house—as, it sounded, had Aaron Burr. Benedict was talking intently but apparently contentedly with Washington and Knox, Franks beaming at his side. I was proud of my husband being back on form.

"How is Burr?" I asked. "I haven't seen him since childhood."

"Circumspect as ever." Hamilton smiled.

"You know his own mother called him a dirty, noisy, sly boy shortly before she died? That seemed a terrible thing to say of one's child! I felt he must need my protection and was predisposed to fall in love with him, the tragic orphan, even before we met. I was seven, he perhaps eleven."

"What a sweet little girl you must have been—"

"I'm afraid I irritated him enormously with my sympathy."

"Do you think he knew his mother's verdict?" Theodosia said.

"Would we say she was mistaken?" Hamilton laughed as he bowed and made a beeline for Eliza.

Lafayette took over as my dancing partner, though "Believe me, I am very bad at it!" I was fascinated to talk to him, one of the richest men in France, to whom peasants had been obliged to pay taxes all his life.

I asked him how he came to support the cause, and delighted in his heavily accented English:

"I can recall no time in my life when I did not love stories of glorious deeds or have dreams of traveling the world in search of fame. At eight I tried to slay a beast terrorizing local livestock. And you, Mrs. Arnold, have you yourself dreamed of fame? I think you are ascending that way—"

"Oh no," I said, "I only ever sought to impress those I knew and thought it right to admire. Even at my most ambitious, I only dreamed of securing the good opinion of a very small circle. Although there was a time I had in mind that might include the King—"

Lafayette laughed. "A superior sort of snobbery then."

"The best! Tell me about Marie Antoinette?"

"The one time I danced with her, I'm afraid I made her laugh. In derision."

"I must be very provincial, then, to think you dance quite well."

"Can you think of a better incentive to improve than her ridicule? Laughter rebounding round the suddenly silent court, echoed by her flock of empty-headed pigeons."

"Are the ladies at Versailles very enamored of our cause?"

"*Mais oui*! They adore *les insurgents*! And there's pleasure provoking their ancient enemy. Louis was five when his father was driven off this continent by the British. He wants the satisfaction of his Canadian and Caribbean colonies back."

"Fathers and sons!"

"Families! I'll tell you a secret, Mrs. Arnold, I was at dinner with the King's younger brother, the Duke of Gloucester, when the colonists began their armed rebellion. The Duke declared, 'The colonists have every right to revolt against my brother' and swore they had his full support."

"What a thing to hear!"

"When I first learned of the quarrel, my heart was enlisted!"

"Did your parents object?"

"My father died when I was twelve, but my father-in-law tried to prevent me—"

"How did you manage him?"

"I was obliged to be disagreeable to preserve my independence."

"A condition always worth a struggle."

Theo kissed me. "They're all in love with you!" she whispered. "Does your husband know how lucky he is?" She narrowed her eyes. "Is he worthy?"

"Oh, Theo. I came with nothing—not a cent, not a penny." She shook her head and took my face in her hands. "You've no idea."

"Is everything all right, do you think? There are card tables, and desserts through there."

"Peggy, it's perfect. Every detail so considered. The guest bathrooms are the most elegant I've seen. You've made a still life of every surface."

William came to claim a dance as Benedict and Martha went gliding past.

"My dear, you're in your element. The general's looking good on that leg. I'm glad to see it, but I hear talk of his returning to the front lines, and he really shouldn't be fighting again. He's taken too many blows, the man's half-stitched together. Perhaps it's not my place, but I can't help feeling something of a paterfamilias at times . . . What he needs is gentle exercise with the weight off—swimming. In warm water, ideally!"

"What of your work, William? How are conditions at camp?"

"You should come see. A visit from you would be a great boost to morale."

I told Hamilton my uncle was suggesting warm-water therapy and asked about his upbringing in the Caribbean.

"You must see it. Pink sand, clear water. There are many days I want nothing more than to make a brilliant exit and get back there."

"Are you on about de island again?" Angelica teased, as she came to sit down and take a sip of his wine.

"You're too good at that."

"The accent?"

"All of it." Hamilton looked at Angelica like he wanted to eat her, quite different from the tentative reverence with which he watched Eliza.

"I feel a little like Cinderella," I told Betsy, as the night got later, "in that the wine will run out by midnight if the guard keep drinking it at this rate and then the shine will come off everything."

General Schuyler, one narrowed eye tracking Hamilton, urged me to bring Benedict to visit his family in the Hudson Valley. "New York State owes your husband a great debt. I hope to incentivize him to settle near us—"

"Do come," Angelica said. "We'd have fun."

"That's decided then." Her father beamed.

Everything was unfolding as if to instructions.

Toward the end of the evening I found myself together at a table with George and Martha. They were like marvelous surrogate parents, performing their own marriage a little for my benefit.

"My dear, what good you've done," Martha said as Benedict went to bring more wine from the cellar. "The limp's now barely visible!"

Washington agreed. "Time to get that asset back in battle."

"He needs a boost from you, George," Martha chided.

"As ever, I find my wife is quite right."

"I know we'd be grateful to have the court martial behind us," I said, as Benedict sat heavily down.

"Delay in the present case is worse than death . . ." he groaned, a little in his cups. "I want no favor! I ask only for justice. Let me beg of you, sir. If your Excellency thinks me a criminal, for heaven's sake let me be immediately tried and, if found guilty, executed."

"Arnold, Arnold. The trial is trivial." Washington waved the matter away like gnats and turned to me. "The nation owes your husband a great deal."

"He's certainly made a statesman's choice in his wife," Martha said. "Why not have Mrs. Arnold host Count Gerard and the French delegation, George? Show him the best of Philadelphia and see about securing that loan."

"Arnold doesn't approve of us moving from indebtedness to England to dependence on France. 'Monkeys swinging from branch to branch' was, I believe, your phrase."

"I don't like shrugging off the King only to start celebrating the Dauphin's birthday."

"Accepting a little assistance is not dependence," Martha said briskly. "Mrs. Arnold here will be a great inducement. And any standoffishness by Arnold will only ensure the overture doesn't look too desperate."

"*Then* can I have him back in active command?"

"I'd take command of the navy," Benedict said, "to which my being wounded would not be so great an objection."

Washington protested his ignorance "in marine matters," which I found a little unsettling, given the size of the British fleet, and expressed a vague wish that "abilities like yours may not be lost to the public."

Martha looked to me. I could only open my palms.

"We'll have you back in no time, Benedict," she said decidedly. "Suitably honored and pride restored."

Amazing to be privy to the Washingtons' decisions and trusted in the advancement of their plans! I caught Theo's eye and shared a smile of astonishment. Her knuckles met mine in a tiny bump, our arms by our sides.

Here we were, at the center of everything.

Chapter Twenty-Two

By dawn, everyone had left but Benedict, Knox, Neddy, and Franks, sprawled around the library fire, drunk and still drinking. With the party largely cleared I was ready to head to bed. I could tell from his tone that Benedict was being ribald, and as I passed the door with the carafe of water I knew I'd need by morning, I heard him slurring, "I have known pleasures in my life, gentlemen, but let me tell you, none, not a woman, compares to Peggy there—"

"Shut up and come to bed!" I called, and the three guffawed.

Clearly, men didn't feel intimate details need stay inside a marriage.

We duly hosted the French delegation as requested, and to the extravagant standard required.

Rayneval was considerate and easy with me, but the ladies in his retinue were as intimidating and highly ornamented as I'd feared. Spectacles in satin, embellished with rosettes, their faces immobilized by makeup.

"Come, Mrs. Arnold," Rayneval said, taking my arm. "I suspect we'll be friends. Tell me. You've had the fortune of knowing some exceptional men."

"I have! And you too, sir. What stories you will have to share when you are able."

"For my posthumous memoirs! You're right. What a time to be alive. Progress is underway—here as there, I think. Idealists, reformers challenging cynical old interests. Many necessary corrections might be made."

I liked him, which I hadn't dared hope I'd do. At dinner, my eyes darted around the table, rapidly scanning to be sure everyone had what they wanted. The table looked beautiful; I wished for a minute André were there to capture it. Benedict looked calm, and sober. I was relieved to see how pleasantly and firmly he deflected the expert, concerted flirting of the French.

Rayneval followed my gaze.

"A pity he's mired in this cesspit. They say Reed has his thumb on the ballot box and a rifle in the other hand. In France your husband is as famous for his bravery as his attempts at fairness in your city. A rare something on which the French and the British can agree . . ."

But after three days' almost obscene feasting, the delegate was still deflecting Benedict's attempts to secure a loan.

"Saratoga increasingly looks like a fluke, and without you leading the army, General, there is not the necessary confidence the Patriots will prevail. King Louis has risked enough—"

"With his help we could finish," Benedict insisted. "Without it, we face another horrifying winter at Valley Forge. Men will starve, and freeze to death before spring, and it won't make a difference if they are soldiers or prisoners of war—"

They bargained on, and still the most the French would concede was equivocation.

The women were clever but willfully silly. Conversation cycled through fashion, travel, slander. The trick was not allowing the banter to flag. To believe whatever position one assumed—at least for the duration of making a point—and afterward to shrug as if to say *probably.*

By the time I went to bed each night, I felt drained to the dregs.

"I like his manner," Benedict said. "He's kind, as well as wily, and ready to entertain everything."

"Except saying yes. You don't find him evasive?"

"A negotiator at his level is obliged to be agile, say nothing that's not reversible. If we weren't in a supplicant role, I know I could work with him."

"You're thinking you will?"

"A joint venture: an investment scheme to build on this goodwill. Rather than cravenly ask for loans, offer a new avenue to both our nations' enrichment."

"What are you thinking?"

"The Caribbean. I know the waters. My own ships did lucrative trade from New Haven before war got in the way. Plenty of British holdings there to target."

"Wouldn't that escalate the war rather than end it?"

"A tactic to help them see the appeal of peace. I could be admiral of a joint fleet, Colonial and French forces, taking on the merchant and British navy ships around Barbados and Bermuda."

"Washington didn't sound very interested in naval adventures?"

"He's got enough to contend with here. But this would help him. The enemy would never see us coming. They'd surrender. We'd take over. Govern Bermuda! There's a handsome mansion, Peggy. If it's still standing. And if not, we'll build a better one. We'd live beside turquoise waters between Britain and America, hosting travelers as they crossed either way."

"Not too many visitors." I yawned again.

"A sea journey makes a useful filter."

"Theodosia could come. If she ever wants to find that husband of hers."

"If he survives our attack."

"Locating him after all this time only to find you'd killed him would be embarrassing."

"I'll try to avoid it. But, Peg, the boys would love it there too. Soft pink sand, crystalline water. We could be happy, away from Philadelphia, from Reed—walking hand in hand at sunset, our children running barefoot on the sand."

"I approve this plan," I said, and he went back down.

I said a brief prayer for the scheme. It felt the perfect convergence of talents and interests. I snuggled under the covers, smug to think my husband could command forces at sea as well as on land.

I woke later to hear Benedict writing at the little bedroom desk. His pen moved with such a rapid patter and scratch he made the whole desk rumble. I fell back to sleep, satisfied well-starred plans were astir.

In the morning, I asked how the conversation with Rayneval had gone.

"Well, as far as I could tell. He saw the merit in the scheme. Asked sensible questions. Appeared satisfied with the logistics. His only concern seemed to be you, wasted in a Caribbean backwater."

"Any indication when they'll leave? It's like being visited by a plague of locusts."

"He said they'd sail soon as the wind's behind them. Could be tomorrow."

"Good." I swung my legs out of bed. "You were busy in the night," I said, tapping the stack of letters set on the table.

"I wrote to Washington, Congress, and the French naval office," he said.

"Such alacrity—"

"I've slept on them, and I'm sending them. Peggy, this is the answer. I don't want to add to your anxieties, but we have to act. Hearing Rayneval's perspective last night only confirms it. The currency is near worthless, morale worse. We can't sit by while we drift into defeat. With this scheme I can fill Patriot coffers, and ours, do what I do well, and see Washington wins."

We had waved goodbye to the French and taken to bed in relief when we were startled by a hammering at the front door.

Benedict was instantly out of bed and in full battle mode. If his horse had been by the bed, he'd have leaped on it. Telling me to stay where I was and lock myself in, he thumped down the stairs.

I heard men's voices, Benedict's protest, and Mrs. Green's distress. I couldn't leave them to it. Opening the door, I saw it wasn't, thank God, a mob, but creditors, repossessing china on which I'd paid no more than the deposit. It was appallingly close. If the ambassador had seen, that would have given an unhelpful impression of our side's fortunes hard to overcome. Benedict's agitation was clear; I couldn't afford high feeling. I ran down and laid a calming hand on the hard, heaving back.

"Let them take it. It served its purpose. We won't need it in the Caribbean."

Benedict submitted the receipts I'd tallied to Congress, but until we were reimbursed, we were in worse shape. I returned a lot of the furniture, wretched for the carpenters, and with it gone, the house lost its feeling of shelter. Though Benedict's leg was inflamed back to agony by gout and he badly needed to rest, he was too agitated for inaction. It was difficult to sit in those denuded rooms and think of those we owed and not seek solutions.

I returned a lot of the dresses to Stansbury, asking him to resell them now that they'd served their purpose, and saying I was sorry I wouldn't be the good customer he needed, not foreseeably.

"Don't forget your lifelines, Peggy. You have friends who want to help."

Reed presented a motion on the floor to remove Arnold from command. Uncle William was the lone dissenting vote, and the whole reckoning was postponed again.

As days passed without repayment, Benedict threatened hourly to resign, but I talked him down, persuading him it would look petulant and be risky without knowing our next step. He was sleepless and fitful, and I hated to see his painful pacing. He couldn't chase Washington for a formal response on the Caribbean scheme so soon, but I suggested he send a report on the French visit and request a few days' leave—adding a short postscript about Bermuda. It cheered him up to be in touch with Washington on a new and hopeful front and he entrusted the letter to Franks with some of his old flourish.

I asked what he'd like for lunch. "We have leftovers enough for a year."

"Do we have a dining table?"

I smiled. "We do not."

Washington promptly granted the leave, but made no mention of the Caribbean. Benedict was concerned, but not unduly. It couldn't be a small decision, for Washington or the French. But it was miserable to be stuck in place waiting for his word on our fate and a trial date. Better we were on the move.

"Let's get out of the city," I said.

"You're right. We can pay that visit to Schuyler. He's taken such a kind interest in our future. You'll like the Hudson Valley. We can see my old friend Beverley Robinson too."

"And stop in and see William on our way out of town?"

It was meant to be an uneventful reprieve.

I dressed plainly for the camp, daring to imagine I might be some practical help. I packed more extravagantly for the stint with General Schuyler and his well-dressed daughters.

As we rolled on our way, I asked Benedict to tell me about the other women he'd seen accompany their husbands to the front.

"There were some marvelous women in the mix. Not ladies per se, but exemplary."

I laughed as he described wives hoisting their skirts above their waists to wade through the icy water, others loading guns. "Some would come to see to the laundry, and the cooking. And then there were those who understood, stirred after battle, their men would be tempted if they weren't there. Forgivable, I think—where consensual."

"It can't always have been consensual," I said.

"Battle can bring out the animal in a man. Atrocities happen in every army. I never saw it under my command. But we've all heard reports."

"Lord Rawdon seemed to revel in the risk of ravishment. He made Staten Island sound lethal for any girl straying farther than her garden gate."

"That tells us more about Rawdon than reality. The British ran a tight ship. I can believe there were isolated incidents, but insubordination would be subject to court martial, and we'd have heard.

"The women who joined us helped hold the men to a higher standard. There were some who knew their man might flinch from killing when it came to it, and made themselves useful enough for the pair of them. There was one woman, Molly Pitcher, they said, who took over the cannon fire after her husband died. She fired all night, his body beside her. Possibly apocryphal, but a helpful legend."

It was humbling to hear of feats I couldn't pretend for one second I'd ever achieve. I might manage a bandage, but I'd probably make a performance of it.

Chapter Twenty-Three

THE FIRST GLIMPSE OF VALLEY FORGE WAS NOT ENCOURAGING. TENTS IN tatters, men missing limbs abandoned on stretchers in full sun. Benedict's input was wanted on a hundred urgent matters. He entrusted me to Major Franks while we waited for William to finish surgery and followed his officers into a modest headquarters.

Trailing around with Franks, I saw the conditions were worryingly squalid. After all the British resources I'd seen in Philadelphia—expensive uniforms—polished weapons—it was alarming to see the scraps we were working with here.

The precariousness of our situation—Benedict's warning about borrowed time—began rising like a panic. The heat and stinking latrines and risk of disease were one thing. When temperatures started to drop, it would be hard to imagine how anyone here—Bean among them if he got to enlist as he wished—could survive.

Franks pointed out the bright fire of liberty in the boys' eyes. I wasn't always certain it wasn't fever I saw burning, but the belief that had brought them here was a beautiful thing, and the idea that defeat by the enemy or inadequate supplies from their own side would ever disenchant them felt more cruelties they must be spared.

Determined to set aside my selfish and unhelpful anxiety, I bent to comfort a young infantryman and found myself confronting a mass of weeping blisters. The open sores were sticking to his rough covering, and I asked if I could change the bed. The doctor told me brusquely there was no sense near skinning him, not near the end as he was. I stared at him dumbstruck, dense about accepting there was nothing to be done.

I knelt beside the boy, feeling my stomach buckle at the reek of soiled sheets. Stroking the hair plastered to his head, I told him how brave he was being. I held a handkerchief balled in my spare hand but raising it to my face felt rude. I told myself to imagine he was Bean or Henry, and to be the comfort I'd want given to them.

He whimpered like a small boy, begging for release. I tried to bargain through the tears that had started to fall. I swore to God I'd never sin again, not even in thought, if only this boy's life could be spared. I'd been far too sporadic in calling on God to feel anything other than a fraud, but I kept on praying, swearing I'd accept any number of disfiguring scars—a pox on both our faces—if only he could live. After an hour of willing him to survive, he died.

I hadn't seen a lifeless body so close since my brothers' death and felt hurled back through time. My failure to save him seemed to make the loss of Benedict's boys unavoidable. My tears were then out of all proportion with who the poor infantryman was to me, and I cried harder to think I was disrespecting him by mingling remembered and anticipated loss with the sorrow he deserved. Where was the mother to mourn him? Would she even get to bury him? Where would I be if Bean and Henry were lying, bleeding and frightened, in some field? My legs felt like a loosely strung puppet's. I didn't trust them to stand, but I was in the way by then and there was nowhere to rest in the pestilent air.

From what felt a great distance, I saw Major Franks peering at me with concern. I willed myself to have the level head and strong stomach needed. I told myself to imagine Esther Reed was watching—her and Eliza and the great Martha Washington—and bent to attend to a boy with a dreadful musket wound to the ear.

I could smell the iron in his blood. The air was sweet with sick and shit. Men were pressing in on us from all sides, each more injured than the last. While I tried to keep my features and breathing steady—longing to be a worthy niece to William—I could feel hysteria becoming more insistent. Major Franks put a hand on my left shoulder, shook his head, and squatted to his haunches beside me, his expression appalled, whether out of reverence for the patient or at my excessive distress, I couldn't tell.

Young sons run through, because of a uniform which by the end would be cut off. Bean and Henry given rough burial before the letter would even reach us. The idea this could continue was lunacy.

And yet, and yet, I must steel myself to hate the enemy. Boys like these were dying at the hands of men I'd met—men I'd danced and laughed with. Redcoats had killed them, with musket balls and bayonets. It was André's side which did this. Benedict's and William's which might do this to him. Thoughts blew through me, and I could tell from Franks's face I must look demented.

I started darting about the camp, unable to settle anywhere for fear the anxiety would overwhelm me. I was crying, and retching, from the smell and the fear. I was desperately trying to keep my face from the patients and breathlessly relaying my thoughts to an ever more alarmed Major Franks.

He insisted we find William, but my uncle was still mid-surgery. We found him diligently restitching a soldier's shin, cut open from knee to heel. I tried to focus on his sewing skill but all I could see was leg of lamb. The extent of the suffering was staggering. I felt the room tunneling as it does in the inevitable prelude to a faint, heard Franks cry, "Look to the lady!" and the next thing I knew I was back in the carriage.

"Try not to speak, Mrs. Arnold. Breathe. There."

It was better in privacy, with a sip of cool water from Franks's flask, but I was mortified to have failed so spectacularly in the face of all that pain. I was ashamed of my vanity in dressing the part, thinking I'd be equal to it, only to be undone. Some ministering angel I'd made.

William shushed me gently, rubbing my shoulders, while Franks rattled off reassurances. "Good, Mrs. Arnold, you must not give it another thought."

"It was wrong of me to suggest you come," William said. "Worse to leave you to it. There are sights today to turn the stomach of even this grizzled old medic!"

He took my hand and continued offering dogged, cheerful nonsense. "Just to see a lovely young lady such as yourself gave many a lad hope. Nobody wanted you rolling up your sleeves and dealing with their fluids, believe me!

Your father never had the stomach for blood either." He winked. "Don't worry so, Peggy. Looking after this country we love will take all sorts. You have light. You have quickness. You'll find other arenas in which to put that delightful force of yours to work."

When Benedict rejoined us I told him I had not done well, but I was now myself again, thanks to William and the exemplary "nurse" I'd had in Franks. Franks was so particularly masculine a man, the silly nickname stuck.

When at last we reached our lodgings, I took a long bath in the evening sunlight, soaping the camp from my hair while Atty took every scrap I'd been wearing to wash.

Once I'd dressed, I went down to join the men. The inn was beautifully furnished, with thick Turkish carpets and downstairs a glittering bar with walls papered pale ochre and gray. I was shown down wide wooden steps to a private dining room where Benedict and Franks were waiting. They looked wonderful by candlelight, in their crisp uniforms, and the thought of their kindness made my eyes smart. Benedict's head was in the wine list, but Franks caught the risk of tears. He coughed. "I dare say, Mrs. Arnold, seeing your empathy today was humbling."

"Less empathy than fear, I'm afraid. It was what I'd wanted—what I asked to see—only, in the face of it, I lost confidence there was any narrative which could redeem—" I glanced at Benedict. "Of course, I quickly remembered. The noble liberty which makes sense of it all."

"The soldier's heart acquires its armor, but seeing your own intense connection with our boys, I feel ashamed of how hardened I've become. But now you've seen the horror, Mrs. Arnold, the test of all we are that it is, you can better understand how unusual a man you have in the general. You are both the pattern of Patriots. I don't say it to flatter, it's a fact."

"Psshh. Let's drink to you, Franks. To Nurse."

Later, the men stayed at the table as I made my way to bed. I felt my luck in being protected by them, cushioned by every comfort in that inn, but I couldn't sleep for images from the camp.

Much later I heard them taking leave of each other at the bedroom door. Benedict's voice was a little slurred, but I heard only goodwill.

"Thank you for your help today, Franks."

"It was my great honor." Franks paused. "In that condition, sir, Mrs. Arnold gave utterance to anything and everything on her mind."

"Did she?"

"Nothing of consequence, General, but it occurs to me we must be scrupulous over what is said in her hearing. We cannot risk inadvertently exposing any military secrets to the enemy, should she suffer such an attack again in the wrong company—"

"No indeed Franks. I should like to assign you the particular duty of protecting her from now on; see to her safety, general welfare, her health, whenever I cannot be present. I'd like you to attend her should another such . . . indisposition occur. She has suffered from childhood with nervous disability, but should not be with strangers when in the grip of that paroxysm—what would we call it?"

"A very great anxiety? A dreadful attack?"

"Exactly. Well, good night."

"Good night, sir."

I lay awake again, long after Benedict, ashamed to think I was being a liability again and impatient to make amends.

Chapter Twenty-Four

We passed quickly through tense New Jersey and treacherous no-man's-land, encountering straggling bands of refugees and mercenaries. I saw a girl of five or six who seemed entirely on her own. I spun to look back at her, wanted to get out, gather her up, but Benedict worried the carriage would be mobbed if we stopped. Competing compassion and anxiety about our own safety pulsed the whole way. It was wrong the value placed on Benedict's life, and my own, was higher than that of a child alone on the road, but I was intent now on finding a way to use our luck and prominence for the good.

After an hour the roads fell eerily quiet, and the air smelled scorched. We rolled through village after village, Indian settlements, apparently completely abandoned. Crops, houses, chattels burned. Outside the ruins of a hut, a simple stool lay on its side by a cooking pit, nearby a small wooden toy on wheels along with an improbable pair of spectacles. Everywhere the smell of charred buildings, and meat.

"Where is everyone? Who did this?"

"Sullivan and Clinton's expedition."

"Clinton?"

"Not that Clinton—George. I'm afraid this was done on Washington's orders. The 'total destruction and devastation of their settlements. No entertaining peace talks until the people were erased. Forty villages. Five thousand took shelter with the British at Niagara—'"

"Five thousand people forced to flee? Everyone else killed?"

Impossible to fathom the suffering that had led to this dreadful silence. A few buff and blue soldiers stood watch, saluting Benedict as we passed.

"What's left to guard?"

"The land was cleared for resettlement. Spoils of the victors," Benedict said.

"Who would live here, on the ashes of that?"

"Valuable land, Peggy. It is the way it is."

"It doesn't have to be!"

Philip Schuyler's family lived on a large estate on the outskirts of Rhinebeck, with a view of the Hudson Valley and the Catskill Mountains beyond. A private road took us past their millhouse, a stream-fed lake, a summer stage André must have loved, multiple barns, and a hamlet of cottages so pretty I'd have been happy in any of them.

"I could live like this," I said.

"Lady of the manor?"

"I was thinking more leaning on a Dutch door feeding the geese."

"In a milkmaid dress?"

I swatted him.

"Rustic simplicity is not an old man's game. A tooth falls out, a leg gives way, you want money to fix it."

"We'd have William. Lady of the manor sounds terribly feudal."

"Lord of the manor is Schuyler's title."

"Is it really? Does he use it?"

"I have to hope not. He talks of gifting me a parcel of land, Peggy. You know how I'd love to settle a community, offer a secure, productive place for my former soldiers to work. Tenancies for those who want them. Good living and a fair wage for all. With land, and that Caribbean capital, it's not impossible."

We passed perhaps thirty slaves harvesting crops and repairing the road, and with an eyebrow Benedict acknowledged the picture here was far from perfect.

General Schuyler was on the steps to welcome us with his family, the always gorgeous Angelica; her husband, Jack; Eliza; Peggy; Cordelia; and three heartbreaker little boys. There was armor and glamour in all that family.

Benedict and I had been given a room high in the house, off a thickly carpeted landing lined with books, which opened onto three children's bedrooms and a nursery. It was a dream of family living.

Before dinner, we gathered at the foot of the stairs with glasses of champagne while Schuyler struck a pose at the halfway landing. He chimed his glass with a fork to silence the chatter. I was struck by the family crest above his head, which read: "Semper fidelis."

Benedict stood to Schuyler's side, looking his splendid self, but shadowed about the eyes.

"On behalf of the grateful residents of New York State, it is my honorable duty to present General Benedict Arnold, a man I'm proud to call my friend, a tract of land, free and clear of all incumbrances."

Benedict ducked his chin modestly and shook Schuyler's hand. When he made it to me through the backslapping and applause, I wondered why he didn't look happier.

"Specifics," he muttered.

"Where is it then? The land?" I asked as we undressed later for bed.

"Up past Lake Champlain," he said dismissively.

"What's wrong?"

"It's Loyalist property, Peggy."

I felt sick. "We can't do that! Move in on someone's misfortune? What luck or kindness could we expect from life then? What happened to the family it belongs to?"

He shook his head. "I don't know. It didn't feel appropriate to ask, in the moment. But other such settlers have been massacred lately."

"No. Just no. Let's hold out. It can't be impossible to make an honest living."

* * *

"We thought we'd go by West Point on our way south," Benedict told Schuyler as we took our leave the next day. My husband looked tired and preoccupied, older than I'd seen him, in the morning light.

"They named the fort there for him," Angelica said. I glanced up at Benedict, charmed he'd never mentioned it.

"Fort Arnold?" Schuyler winced. "Not what it was. No back to it."

* * *

I felt depressed after the visit, sad that our hopes of Schuyler had been disappointed, and worried about Benedict's spirits.

I lay with my head in his lap, watching a shoal of starlings swoop and mass, forming and dissolving shapes so intentional it felt there must be some guidance for us, if only I could divine it.

Benedict woke me as we approached the fort.

"Many consider it the most significant post in America, since it controls one of the narrowest sections of the Hudson, the river connecting British-occupied New York to their possessions in Canada. We've slung a vast chain across the water just south of the fort, strong enough to stop the King's troops and supplies on their way upriver, is the idea."

Approaching from the north, we had a superb view of the soaring cliff west of the Hudson. I saw what could pass for the features of God in the rock face, while from the hills to the east a mass of beeches and oaks met marshes reaching to the glittering shore.

Another bend in the river, and there was West Point, rearing invincible from the basalt like a mighty stalagmite.

Beverley Robinson's house lay on a high meadow beneath Sugarloaf Mountain with wide views across the Hudson to the fort. It was a glorious position, and a handsome house, but the rooms had the weathered energy of a home frequently let to guests. Robinson himself had a wide, attractive face and sharp bright eyes. Warm with Benedict and chivalrous with me, he hoped we'd find his home "commodious."

I was glad to stand and breathe fresh air after being cooped up queasy with the motion of the carriage, but Benedict's leg was swollen from sitting so long. Robinson established him on the terrace with his leg up and a cool drink he held to his temples, and walked me out across the lawn, to the mouth of a steep wooded path which telescoped through high grass and an arch of branches to the river.

I smelled sea salt on the breeze and wondered aloud could I be right when so far from the ocean.

"The Atlantic," Robinson explained.

I looked at him in confusion, which he enjoyed.

"This river flows both ways."

How neat, I thought, looking up and down its expanse, crosshatched with currents.

As Atty tightened my corset that evening, I gave an involuntary yelp at the sudden tenderness in my breasts. My body knew before I did. Atty too, apparently. Her eyes were ready for mine in the mirror.

"It's early yet," she said. "Better not to think on it until you're further along."

I was quiet during dinner, nursing the secret of new life inside. Afterward, I leaned, calm and replete, against the rail on the terrace, looking out across the warp and weft of the water at the elegant silhouette of a heron, a cross on a distant church steeple, as the sun set in a fiery red glow.

"It really is magnificent," I said, turning from West Point back to the men.

"From *here*," Beverley quipped bitterly.

"It's what the Tower of London is to England," Benedict said, though his pride was subdued. "The crown to the King."

Robinson snorted. "How did you find Schuyler?"

"Wearing the war well."

"I should say so. There's a man who looks after his luck. Steeped in capital now. Angelica married to a man set to be the sole supplier to the Continental Army, Eliza to Washington's right hand. While I'm having to work ten times harder for ten times less, toiling up and down the Hudson collecting diminishing rents."

"No difficulty obtaining the passes through occupied territory, even lately?" Benedict asked.

"I have a back channel. A back channel I guard with my life."

Benedict met my eyes in brief amusement.

"How's business with you, Arnold?"

Benedict winced. "The value of the dollar plummets daily."

"Partly because the British are printing counterfeit currency and flooding the market."

"That sounds a low trick," I said.

Beverley shrugged. "Another nudge to completion. They want this done, my dear. Which doesn't change the fact the Patriots are out of money and luck. For all the rich symbolism of West Point, conditions inside are dire. A third of it derelict and Fort Arnold itself largely destroyed by fire. Your legacy neglected, Arnold. Insulted!"

"It's hardly for want of trying."

"Loyal to the end, General? Has nothing you have seen begun to erode your conviction in the unique virtues of Patriotism? I'm only saying *unique*. What's the word on the street in Philadelphia?"

Benedict admitted there were more and more congressmen and soldiers telling him true independence was impossible, and the best outcome was a reconciliation with Britain now that the key principles they'd all fought for had been conceded.

"Here, here," Robinson said, sounding every inch an English MP.

Gazing at the Hudson, snaking out of sight toward New York, my mind looped out to André, looking forward to a time he could join us for a view and light like this, along with the lateral thinking and lively conversation we loved. I was craving his voice and laugh again—longing to hear from him, without the risk and fiddle of invisible inks.

Robinson started on the indecision which plagued Washington.

"The man has lost more battles than he's won."

"He means to win, Beverley, and he has the resources to go the distance."

"Is it a happy marriage, do you think, beyond the shared aim?"

"I thought I saw real love—" I protested.

"Every relationship has its transactional aspect," Robinson said, watching us, "even if that's not clear until it's years in arrears!"

"Transactional relationships make the world go round." Benedict shrugged.

"They're what's wanted to span the Atlantic," Robinson said. He refilled our wine.

"To peace!"

"To peace," we agreed, raising our glasses, while the moon rose and lit a sparkling path across the Hudson.

"It looks like a fairytale castle," I said. "Makes me want to make a wish."

"If magic did it, that would do!" Robinson laughed and stood. "I'll leave you love birds to it," he said, with a last, complacent glance at the view. "See you in the morning."

We talked on, my hands resting on my belly, as the moonlight faded, outlining the fort against the milky indigo sky, and the stars began to shine.

Chapter Twenty-Five

"What did you think of him?" Benedict asked, as we were driven away the next morning. The white band of mist above the river evaporated, revealing its sparkling, shifting pink and silver.

"Very friendly, but a little too smooth? I can see how some people might consider him shifty—"

"Certainly alert to opportunity."

"Yes," I said. "Perhaps I was too harsh. It seems there's no way of living a minute in this conflict without someone maligning your intentions."

"Good thing he's scrupulous about keeping that back channel clean!"

It was a relief to be home and no longer in motion, but as soon as we opened the door, all the worry and need for news rushed in. Benedict was greeted with a stack of bills, no trial date, nothing from the French naval office, no reimbursement from Congress, but a letter from Washington.

I had to consciously unclench my fingers as I watched him read.

The letter was genial but made no mention of any of the open questions between them: not the Caribbean scheme, not the trial date, not the redress of debts.

Instead, Washington wrote to express his thanks for our service with the French delegation and reiterated his wish to have his best general back in active service in time for a second winter campaign to take Quebec.

"Quebec? Again?"

"Of course I'd like to finish it, avenge Montgomery, all who died. But we could not have tried harder with better men. I gave it everything. To attempt it again in winter, knowing there's no money to pay the troops? It would be criminal insanity."

"What's behind this then?"

"Lafayette's ambition? The Dauphin's revenge? Or deliberate misinformation—a test? I don't know." He tossed the letter down and pressed the heel of his hands to his eyes. Fighting a rising tide of nausea, I held the letter to the light, wondering if there might be more between the lines.

"It is a blow he doesn't acknowledge your hopes of the Caribbean," I said, frantically swallowing saliva, "or the navy, but the letter is not without consideration. There's honor in his offer, and acknowledgment of the misery you've endured here. That's a start?"

"I'm sick of the disingenuous cheer and all he leaves unsaid."

He reached for a bottle, rapidly unstopped it, and poured a fist of whiskey. My stomach lurched. I didn't want to tell him I was pregnant to stop him drinking. Or to find out that didn't work.

Afraid we might fight, I went riding in Fairmount Park. A gentle canter, nothing reckless. With every face I passed, I tried to calm down. Everyone in existence had been born at some point. It wasn't childbirth I was frightened of, though. It was the life that lay ahead for my child, and whether I could do right by it.

I didn't want to raise a son or daughter in raids and riots and retaliation, waking morning after morning to worry what had happened overnight and what today would bring.

I had sworn to André I would not bring a baby into war and I wanted to keep my promise.

Was it pride to imagine I had a choice? *Beauty queen dreams of peace*, Odie had said, but having been to Valley Forge, I couldn't feel the impulse for peace was naive.

Benedict was sleeping off the whiskey when I got back, so I went to visit Stansbury, glad to have some business for him.

"These will be needing letting out," I said, dropping an armful of dresses on the counter.

"Oh congratulations, Peggy! How are you feeling?"

"Fine. Tired. Tense."

"The entire city is on edge."

He took a sip of tea.

"You might write to our friend for provisions for the baby? Fabric's not easy to come by locally. Prices are exorbitant here. New York's a different story."

"How is the major?"

"Rising like a comet. He's got the top spot in British intelligence now. First time in history there's even been such a role."

"I'm glad for him."

"He and the general have more equivalent standing now. I imagine he's thankful for that."

"It never occurred to me he'd worry."

"Benedict would have felt it, in reverse. Everyone in the military is obsessed with rank."

"What is it he's actually doing?"

"His first priority is compiling what they've got, cataloging the backlog of incoming information in a dedicated intelligence book. Next to run rings around the enemy."

"It's like a surprise I keep having to realize, that we're his enemy, Benedict and me. I can't seem to fathom it."

"André, as your friend, would want Benedict to prevail. Professionally, he'd have to hope he fails. That or become so frustrated with the headwinds he'd be tempted to defect . . ."

"Don't joke," I said nervously.

"Well, my dear," Stansbury said, holding his cup up to the light where the translucence could be admired, "just one of endless hypothetical scenarios it's André's job now to entertain. The British are looking for a way the colonists might climb down, find a peace both sides can swallow. The Patriots are dreading what this winter will bring. The loss of life, and what that does for commitment."

He stood to look out of the window with a shiver. "I always found fall such a beautiful season, but now the trees browning feels alarming. I must be getting old."

* * *

"Where were you?"

"Stansbury's," I said, saliva rising in my throat. "Minimal expense. Only alterations."

Despite the nausea, pregnancy was manifesting as an expanding resolve, a rising well of conviction making me almost mystical in my thinking. In the baby, finally, I had found absolute allegiance, the insulation of a side I'd never second-guess. I felt as if I were following welcome orders.

"My love, bear with me, but I have a suggestion, something that made me feel better when I felt my own walls closing in. It made me despair, the idea of not being able to make myself understood—or heard. Life didn't—doesn't—feel worth living if we can't speak freely, in privacy, to those we love and that love us. I learned to write in code."

"Stansbury?"

I nodded.

"To André?"

"Initially. We've said nothing of consequence. The point is only to know communication's possible. To have privacy, in the event of interception. What can't be said, can't be done—

"I'm not even saying you write to anybody! Only, I think that a new skill, a fresh weapon in your arsenal, might give you a renewed feeling of strength just as you've hit what feels this towering wall. Washington's true thoughts are hidden behind a fortress as tall as Frontenac. Perhaps your being able to use code could come to help him, in time? I don't know what to make of him not trusting you except someone has got in his ear. It's something I can do for you, besides nagging you to rest that leg."

"We have men for cipher. There's no honor in it."

"You never asked your men to do something you wouldn't. What if you were away and the house were raided and I were forced into hiding and needed to reach you without giving my location away? Wouldn't you want me to have that ability? What if you were sailing into danger and a letter came to light with information about enemy intentions which you could not decipher when you might have learned how from me? How can it be a bad thing for you to know more of what's been said? Doesn't every battle rely on scouts and privileged troop movements? Better than begging a messenger's discretion, code ensures secrecy. How is it more ignoble than publishing articles under false names, as Reed the Militia Man does all the time?"

I was abruptly interrupted by a surge of vomit, dispatched into a plant pot. Having handed it off with many apologies to Mrs. Green, I turned back into the room to see Benedict's alarm. My anxiety reliably got into him, and he felt it tenfold.

"Please don't worry, my love. I'm not so agitated as all that. I think in fact I'm pregnant."

Benedict's hug lifted me off my feet, before setting me down in a rush of alarm he'd been too rough. Laughing, I told him I felt fine, but I was touched to see him solicitous, turning his focus from the problems that dogged us to our happiness.

When Benedict came up to bed, I set aside the Blackstone and candle and flung open the covers so he'd join me.

"How are you feeling?" he said tenderly, his brow creased.

"Very well." I laughed. "Come and see."

"You should be resting," he said as I reached for him.

"I'm not feeling very delicate."

Later, as his breath steadied into sleep, I pulled the Blackstone back onto my lap, along with a pencil and paper, and trying not to disturb him, wrote him a line in cipher.

I love you, my husband. We are in this together.

"Why aren't you asleep?"

I kissed the top of his head.

"I find it relaxing, training my all my focus on a puzzle rather than thinking. It helps me quiet my mind."

He didn't move, but I felt him approaching cautiously, watching with studied indifference initially, and then scooching up on the pillows to focus, as I wrote another line in numbers.

Let Me Help.

"Show me how it works."

I lit another candle for his side of the bed, and feeling the old pleasure I got from instruction, gave him my note, and the dictionary, and showed him how to count. Three numbers unlock each word. The first gives the page. The second spells the line. The third the word itself.

I loved seeing how assiduously he leaned into the effort, his frown of concentration and sweet eagerness to learn.

He kissed me when he read what I'd written, and mastering the key did lend him new strength. It gave a charge to us both.

"I'll write nothing which could betray our men," he said, once we'd fallen back exhausted and lay face to face.

"I know. The point is to help them."

"I may never use it."

"I know," I said again, snuffing the candle. "But Stansbury will relay what you say, should it come to it."

"Don't unman me, Peggy."

"Benedict, I couldn't if I tried."

"Don't write to André again, not without telling me."

He'd conceded for me. I could give him that.

"I won't. I promise. Perhaps we write together—"

"I won't be rushed."

"My love. You've seen how it works. There's nothing hasty about it."

He smiled ruefully. "A check on my temper then—"

"They say that in any new language one's character is different."

"Would you alter me?"

"No, my darling. Only keep you invincible."

It was a hot October day soon after when everything came to a head. All afternoon I was fighting sickness as I took dictation from Benedict, appealing for relief from Congress for one veteran after another, while sporadic disturbances reached us through the open window. Men were shouting about food shortages, resentful that farmers' output was being commandeered by Congress for the French before it could reach the city residents who needed it.

The temperature rose when counterprotestors arrived on the scene, calling for death to enemies of America. Criticism of Congress was taken for Loyalism, and the anger on both sides spiked.

At four, Franks ran in to report a Patriot crowd was gathering at the home of Mr. Wilson, the lawyer across the High Street who had defended Carlisle and Roberts. Armed with hammers and iron bars, they were smashing the shutters and denting the front door. Benedict immediately grabbed his coat.

"You are not going out there," I cried. Franks took one look at the resolve on his face, turned to me with apology, and opened the door so Benedict could bolt out.

"Lock the doors and stay upstairs," he shouted behind him. "Keep back from the windows."

I ran to the first floor with Atty, where we could see the scene more clearly. I'm not sure I'd ever loved Benedict as much as I did then, watching him half run, half limp right into the thick of the crowd, palms bared, hands raised, appealing and beseeching for calm.

His presence settled the men for a second—I could see the affection they held him in—the moment in which they were tempted to let him lead and resolve their problems. He was offering to go to the stores, find the truth of the stockpiling, see that goods the city needed were released. Then a woman started shouting about Loyalist pigs, and resentment rekindled. A shove ignited the riot, and again men were pushing forward, pummeling fists and wielding hammers.

Benedict and Franks fell out of sight beneath a scrum of men's backs.

The mob sank into the house, the door clearly breached. I dreaded to think what they were doing to Wilson, his wife, their children. I heard shots fired from inside the house, while men beat at the windows and drummed at shutters with whatever they had at hand.

I jumped as our own front door rattled. Atty screamed. I clamped my hand over her mouth, kissed her forehead in apology, and whispered she should go to her room, lock herself in.

I slowly closed every shutter, locking all but the one with the unimpeded view. What if Benedict never came back? What if the mob got to me? The

Militia Man had spent more energy whipping up resentment of Benedict than he had of Wilson. It wasn't *if* then, it was *when*. The door banged again, and I stifled a tiny sob, then heard the laughter and jeers receding, as the breakaway mob seemed to move on.

Summoning the courage to go to the ground floor and check the back door, I took the fire poker with me and crept, peering past my five-month belly, settling one foot then another slowly down.

I considered running across the garden to lock the gate in the far wall, but what if it was stormed before I reached it? I'd be trapped, and the back door open to Atty inside. I wondered if Esther was in her own house, with her small children, as terrified as me.

Ground floor secured, I returned upstairs, keeping the poker close, some part of me still worrying I was overreacting. I stood stock still, trying to decipher the muffled shouts and shots and screaming from the Wilsons', stroking and soothing my pregnant belly while swiping aside every insistent image of Benedict not making it out alive.

After what felt an hour, I heard a huge thundering of hooves and whinnying and cracked open the shutter. A massive militia led by Reed pulled up short outside Wilson's door. Still on horseback, he smashed rioters from above with the butt of his musket, fired a shot above his head, and under close cover, pushed inside the house surrounded by his guard.

One after another the rioters were yanked out, some kicking, some injured. Pulled roughly aside, they had their hands roped by militia, while the shooting continued inside.

I was readying myself for widowhood, raising a fatherless child among only enemies, when then suddenly there was Franks, and behind him, Benedict. My relief turned to indignation when I saw my husband had been arrested. Reed was personally shoving him from the building in a tethered mass of prisoners being marched away to gaol. Benedict met my eye for a moment as he passed beneath the window, but didn't risk a movement which might draw attention to me.

All evening, he didn't return. I took Atty a simple supper but couldn't swallow myself. I spent the night sleepless, pacing, tossing, or turning. Even in that fear, there was a still clear voice beside me, telling me this worry, this war, could not go on.

However it had happened, in becoming a military hero and then trying to stay afloat, Benedict had made an antagonist in Reed he would never appease. I couldn't fault a veteran desperate to prosper—and I needed a provider—but whatever little dodges Benedict had made, those were not going to be forgotten. I loved my husband for giving money to the orphans of soldiers who'd fought with him, and I didn't begrudge a penny to any one of them, but I didn't know who I'd appeal to if I was penniless myself, and I didn't want to wait until I was in that fix to try.

I stared out at Reed's house as the sun came up. Would he be waking now, beside Esther, feeling the reliable compulsion to make men miserable fill his veins? Did he think of me, his neighbor, through the wall? Was he enjoying this?

For a minute, I wished I'd never got pregnant and given Reed another target. For a minute I wished our neighbor were dead. It was unraveling me, the intimacy, his enmity, and that couldn't be. I wouldn't stand for it. Not before doing everything in sight while I could.

So I wrote. I didn't need Blackstone, or secret inks; we had established our language when it came to this, and I would risk nothing that a suspicious eye could take to signal guilt.

Mrs. Arnold presents her best respects to Captain André, is much obliged to him for his very polite and friendly offer of being serviceable to her and assures him that her friendship and esteem for him are not impaired by time or accident.

I followed with a simple shopping list, millinery bits and pieces of the sort André had said it would be his pleasure to find for me in the stores of New York City (without adding anything provocative or disloyal about shortages with us), culminating in a final item: *diaper cloth for nappies.* He would not mistake the significance; there was no escaping it. He would remember our conversation and know my settled intention. He would hear I needed him. He would feel me in reach.

I summoned a messenger and sent it to Stansbury. I'd broken a promise to Benedict, but in extremes he'd surely forgive. I felt immediately stronger being in touch with André again, believed my family safer, just for his knowing of the baby's existence.

I understood a little of the spider's patient satisfaction, turning a first precarious thread into a second, a tensile triangle, and from there a net of incredible, barely detectable strength. I'd have liked a less sinister image, but it was spiders which came to mind. I'd been frightened of them as a child, always calling others to take them outside, but I was to be a mother now and would do what needed doing.

At eleven I heard someone at the door and the jolt felt seemed enough to make me miscarry the baby. It was only Franks, telling me Benedict was alive, uninjured, still in jail, awaiting processing.

"Were there casualties?"

"Several dead, many wounded."

"Wilson? His family?"

He shook his head. "I don't know. It was chaos."

It was unbearable, the powerlessness of Benedict, outrageous he'd be unable to get due process. Being detained in a cell would have brought back his old horror of confinement, and I hated to think what that might be doing for his situation there.

When Benedict finally returned, I pummeled his chest, cross with the worry released, before collapsing in his arms.

Neither of us had slept or eaten since before the riot, so I made a simple lunch for us and Franks and Atty, who for the first time since I'd known her showed a face stained with tears.

"We need further protection," I said to Benedict, later in bed. "I watched you out there, wading in unarmed without a thought for yourself—or anyone else.

And then Reed? I've come to hate him Benedict, which frightens me, almost as much as the idea of losing you."

He held my face in his hands and kissed it.

"Promise me you'll get a guard?" I said, pulling away. "If they can target a lawyer like Wilson—a man only working to maintain a normal standard of justice—"

"None of this is normal now."

Benedict did apply for a guard, only to be told he'd have to apply to Reed personally, as president of the Supreme Executive Council, for permission.

"There is no protection for an honest man," Benedict said with finality.

He was right, but I felt the churn of doublethink. We weren't perfect. We had our shadows too. I had fantasized about someone assassinating Reed—in the fantasy there'd be no retaliation—and the risk to Benedict felt greater since I had.

I knew I was ready to be ruthless in pursuit of harmony. That I would be, as soon as I found my opportunity.

Chapter Twenty-Six

The winter proved everything the Patriots had feared, the worst in a hundred years. Snow, followed by freezing rain, followed by ice, week after week, so that every road and river was a rink. There were daily stories of wagons falling into ditches, passengers found stiff and blue by morning; babies dying of cold in their cribs; soldiers so cold and hungry they waded through miles of snow drifts to break into a farmhouse store, only to be shot there.

I craved any lightness in those pages and shared a laugh with Benedict when we read that in frozen New York harbor, captives had walked off their prison ship to freedom onshore.

Finally, we got a date for his court martial, and on December 20, after many hours' rehearsing his defense while pacing in front of my chair, Benedict put on his best blue and buff and, armed with a week's worth of shirts, set out in deep snow for New Jersey.

I swaddled my feelings, in case I made him incapable of performing or leaving at all.

The trial would be presided over by Patriot Major General Robert Howe, an old friend of Benedict's, and begin December 23. Franks would be a key witness, riven with guilt that his moment of indecision had given the prosecution part of their case. I was still reassuring him repeatedly when it came time to leave.

It would be just me and Atty and my great convex belly that holiday season. Franks sent a message after a few days telling me Benedict had defended himself brilliantly and Sergeant Matlack, the young man Reed had claimed was terminally offended by Franks's blasted barber errand, had completely caved. Every hostile witness collapsed in contradictions or recanted. General Knox and all present expected Benedict to be imminently acquitted.

I had never missed my husband as I did that Christmas, but I spent it dreaming of what we'd be doing this time next year, in health, in peace, in plenty, with our baby.

All through New Year's and past Epiphany the trial continued. I thought of Benedict constantly, picturing him under the inn's low ceilings, drifts up to the windowsills, a warm fire in the grate. I knew his cross-examination was strong, and if he just resisted sounding arrogant, he could expose every last lie to the jury. Franks's evidence would help him; it said everything best about Benedict, the instinct to help a fellow veteran and his readiness to respect the law.

Finally, on January 21, it was time for Benedict's closing statement. He had testimonials ready, from Washington and from Congress, and a good script, I knew.

I liked to think of him walking those boards, his handsome face, deep, melodious voice, and quick wit. I hoped he would be his best self. Strong, self-deprecating, allowing himself a little contempt for the lies, but wry, rather than testy.

He was found guilty of a single charge (granting an illegal pass for recovering goods from the ship the British had raided) and acquitted on all the rest. Nothing he had done had comprised an attempt to defraud the public or injure or impede the war effort. The one fault was exposed for what it was, a momentary imprudence.

Reed left in a fury, and Benedict galloped home in happy relief.

"It's over," he said, kissing my fingers in turn.

"We're just starting here," I said, as my first contractions began.

Benedict sat with me, until the midwife said it was time, and he stepped outside. I felt my insides unhinge, agony expanding, and the baby slip from me.

Once the midwife had cleaned and wrapped him, she took our boy out to Benedict to hold while she swabbed and tidied me. Atty helped me into a fresh nightdress, remade the bed and my hair, and showed Benedict back in.

He settled the baby in my arms, and I looked with astonished love at his perfect features, feeling the immense tide of my love rise as his tiny fingers gripped mine.

My milk came in quickly, and after the initial outrageous pain, I loved the little miracle of keeping my baby alive, the tugging feeling of feeding, the satisfaction of meeting his needs. I wanted him with me, and since I'd learned ladies at Versailles went without a wet nurse, I felt justified in trying.

We decided we'd call him Edward, after my father, but Eddie for now.

The first week, the three of us existed in a bubble of milky love. Gazing at the baby, kissing the tiny crescents of his cuticles, listening to his breathy sleeping while the logs crackled, hissed, and settled, Benedict beside us, exonerated at last.

And then betrayal came. General Washington issued a public reprimand of Benedict, dripping in superciliousness.

The commander in chief would have been much happier in an occasion of bestowing commendations on an officer who has rendered such distinguished services to his country as Major General Arnold; but in the present case, a sense of duty and a regard to candor oblige him to declare he considers his conduct in the instance of the permit as peculiarly reprehensible, both in a civil and a military view, and in the affair of the wagons as 'imprudent and improper.'

Tender as we'd been, it finished us.

Part Three

Chapter Twenty-Seven

I LEFT EDDIE WITH ATTY, AND TOOK BREAKFAST TO BENEDICT IN BED. Perching on the coverlet, heel tucked under me, I said, "One way or another, life as we've known it is over."

He looked at me carefully. "You're anxious?"

I shrugged. Always. He could see I was.

"For mankind or us particularly, at this minute?"

"Both," I answered. Pouring him coffee, as sunlight dappled the bedroom ceiling, I sketched the strategy tentatively, almost playfully. Speaking rapidly, in whispers, at tangents, worried what I was suggesting was already obvious, or not clear.

"Some men would say 'My country first and then my family,' but as a new mother, I feel differently. I think a father's family should be his priority, and if every father's was, the country ought to take care of itself."

"'For himself and all.'"

"Exactly! Your old motto. What would mine be? 'Security. Harmony. Good company.' Is that terrible to admit? That's the order in which they came to me. One thing is clear: Exposing a child to unnecessary danger feels unforgivable; ending the war does not.

"I have no more tolerance for it. You have no more appetite for command. You are not meant to be a soldier anymore, let alone in charge of half the army. You have given enough; the conflict needs decision."

"What do you propose?" he asked.

"It is only a suggestion," I said. "I see a problem. Finding a way to address it releases me from a feeling of obligation. That's how my mind works. It is, of course, for you to choose."

"Get on with it," he said.

"Can we agree British resources far outweigh anything in the possession of the Patriots, and yet they are as desperate as we are for the war to end?"

"We can."

"Can we agree there is no world in which neighbors being enemies makes sense?"

I leaned over and took his hand.

"If you were as pivotal to ending the war as you have been in fighting it, you would be indispensable in establishing the terms of the peace. You would have the ear of the King, could speak for the colonies, and honor everything that is best in America. You would defend these states, ensure no heads on spikes."

"You would have me forfeit the good opinion of my friends, Peggy? Betray everybody?"

"Not everybody. You would have the gratitude of every soldier's mother, here and there."

I paced at the end of the bed.

"George III or George Washington? Two sides of the same coin—both leaders to whom we owe a debt, both flawed men. Yes, the King can be a comical abomination—and yes, the British have been greedy and abusive in their policies. Granted too, there was a magnificence and justice to the Patriot rhetoric the world had never seen. Those words will hold men to a higher standard forever—and independence, God grant it, will come. But I detest the persecuting energy of Reed, the bickering negligence of Congress, and I can no longer pretend I believe our rights so sanctified they justify another hour of war. I am certainly not willing to live or risk losing my child's life under a debased, selective definition of liberty. To see 'freedom' used as a cynical tool of tyranny.

"Perhaps, in time, you could help spread Jefferson's best principles among British subjects. See that they are given some of the written and systematic protections we've welcomed in America. British decency can only go so far. Take their moderation and habeas corpus and marry it with the best of our rebel energy. Abolish slavery! Celebrate Quakers. All the labyrinthine hierarchies of class and twisty English byways could be straightened out by the space and air and commitment to equality here."

Was I a female Iago, whispering lies to a warrior with wounded pride? Was I warping his will to mine? A wife wants what her husband needs. Does a monster worry it's a monster, though? This one did.

He was silent, and I thought I had misjudged. A cleverer wife would have made him feel the idea was his.

"Benedict, the weight of your influence could end this." I brandished the copy of Mather, never far from my side. "We have 'much occasion for doing good.' Isn't it wrong then not to try?"

He had me check the letter over for errors, but the only detail I questioned was the alias he'd chosen: Monk.

"The man who turned against Cromwell, assisting the King in getting back on the English throne."

"How apt."

He grimaced, taking no pleasure in the invention. Stifling my own riddling misgivings, I tucked Eddie in with him, bolstered with pillows on all sides, while I took the letter to Stansbury. Joseph shuttered the shop immediately.

I held the envelope out.

"This is either unforgivable or the most moral option."

Stansbury exhaled, his eyes tired but bright.

André's reply was crisp and uncomfortably condescending. With "all possible respect," he welcomed the overture but determined it better Monk defect in place and wait for an opportunity to throw a battle the King's way.

Benedict was livid. There was no way he could rig a victory in the thick of active combat without putting thousands of men's lives at risk. He would sooner fall on his sword.

Of course, there had to be talk of rewards—the real Monk received a dukedom from the grateful King—but to offer Benedict the rank of brigadier for such a sin was insulting.

I could see it was also offensive to Benedict's pride that André didn't think it sufficient for the colossus he was simply to change sides, but, I argued, the British couldn't rush to trust at first approach, and though I believed André would have guessed at once who Monk was, he might not have known for sure.

I could see too André would need a more spectacular, decisive turn than a simple declaration of changed allegiance. Although word of General Arnold's quasi-religious conversion would be heard in every house in the colonies, it might not make such a loud report that it would finish the war for good.

Benedict's anger at André made him look askance at me.

"I told you I believed he would honor his word, Benedict. I didn't promise you flattery. My love, he's obliged to be tactical. His suggestion was one step. Now he looks to you."

This time he dictated his message, roundly rejecting André's proposal, while I transcribed it into code, heart sinking, Eddie in a basket at my feet.

Benedict then felt compelled to seek reassurance from Washington, hoping if he kept his options open, Providence would give direction.

"It will," I soothed. "You've burned no bridges. Just wait."

And so he hedged, responding to Washington's suggestion of a second assault on Quebec with a request to meet, and to André and Clinton letting them know there was talk of such a renewed Canadian attempt.

The double-talk felt nauseating, though I knew that was weak of me. I'd vaguely imagined once André and Benedict were in touch, my part would fade, leaving me free to plan a welcome reception for peace. Instead, I saw I'd need more flint to go the distance.

Benedict looked tired and drawn at dawn next day as he prepared to leave for Washington's headquarters, and I made a guilty fuss with his breakfast. In trying to help, I had exposed him to further hurt and confusion, and vertiginous risk. I resented Washington too, even while hoping he'd come through. I still wanted to believe Benedict's service would be honored.

As he told it, Benedict rode without break to Washington's New Jersey encampment, until his leg was screaming, enough he was afraid the skin would burst and blood seep through his breeches. Immediately spotting his commander in conversation with Lafayette and Hamilton, he galloped up to them and demanded to talk to Washington in private.

In his tent, Washington apologized for the public dressing down he'd given Benedict, explaining Reed had threatened to withhold all further funding for the troops if he didn't make the statement. He hadn't felt able to risk it. At Dobb's Ferry that week he'd seen soldiers devoid of bread, tents, shoes, and ammunition. He had been forced to dismiss all would-be recruits because he could not feed them.

"There has never been a stage of the war in which the army's dissatisfaction has been so general and so alarming."

While Benedict listened, feeling his leg would bleed out through his boots, Washington talked again of his disgust with Congressional squabbling and dysfunction.

"But by further fighting you might begin to regain esteem: I give you a choice of the two wings of the army. Gates will take whichever you don't want."

Benedict would not have believed his faith in Washington had farther to fall. To hear him speak of needing to *begin* to build a nation's esteem, after being one of the first to fight and giving all he had. His contempt settled into cold sediment.

Hamilton and Lafayette were at the flap of the tent, audibly speculating over Benedict's stunned silence.

"Was there a further injury to the head reports neglected to mention?"

"No suspicion of syphilis, I trust?"

"That would be monstrous injustice to Mrs. Arnold!"

Washington shushed the pair's teasing and urged them come in and help him persuade their old friend to come back where he was needed.

Benedict asked Lafayette, "You're intent on Quebec?"

In the look Lafayette exchanged with Washington, Benedict saw they were not, and felt fresh resentment that Washington would have dissembled.

"What news of the French?"

"Expected off Rhode Island any day."

"I'll believe it when I see it. We've been starving citizens for a rumor of their troops all year. What else?"

"The lobsterbacks have been flinging their money around," Hamilton offered.

"Nothing new there," Benedict said, feeling his eyelid flickering with guilt. Washington, sensing his discomfort, mistook it for unease at Hamilton's arch intimations.

"Blunt talk only for Benedict!" Washington said and clarified: "The British offered me an earldom."

"A city named after him!" Hamilton derided.

"A Colonial city," Lafayette scoffed loyally. "When only the capital of an independent United States of America will do, and for that, we do not need their permission!"

"Only their surrender," Washington said, with what felt to Benedict like bluster.

As he prepared to depart, the four men stood for a moment watching the troops set about their scant evening meal.

Benedict felt a wave of nostalgia which threatened to sink him.

"So, which is it," Washington asked him, clapping his back, "left or right flank?"

Part of Benedict longed to pick and commit, to pretend he had it in him, but he thought of his pain, the many ways that injury could let the side down, and of what the British would ask of him if he did resume military command.

"It can't be either. My injuries allow no question of my commanding in battle yet, and to keep on with the suggestion only humiliates me." (I worried as he relayed the conversation he'd have sounded peevish then, though I shared his frustration.) "Have you considered the naval scheme?"

Washington looked at him sorrowfully. "You looked so well on horseback."

"And dancing with your wife," Hamilton said. "How is Mrs. Arnold?"

"Very well. Mother to a new son—"

Lafayette laughed. "Arnold, you dog! How injured can you be? Compliments, General!"

The men had drunk a round, teasing and congratulating, so that Benedict felt his soul would cleave in two. Seeing him off, Washington said he begged Arnold would continue to consider his request.

* * *

Benedict sent word to André the French were soon to arrive at Rhode Island—promptly encouraging Clinton to call off an attack on Washington himself at Morristown. I was glad to think Benedict had inadvertently averted that threat, but the double-dealing felt increasingly sordid and excruciating, the furthest thing from the beautiful big gesture needed to deliver us.

I missed Theo. Longed to gallop and run. Craved a world in which I could go riding alone, without fear of man or militia. The garden would have to do. I picked a sprig of rosemary and turned it in my fingers.

I knew what was wanted. The question was what would work.

I wouldn't deliberately risk a single life. But I'd sacrifice principles. I might shrink from it, but I couldn't afford to be squeamish. If I could see a way my death would help, I hoped I'd be brave enough to take it, but securing peace need not mean martyrs yet.

In the moment the plan came to me I felt a mixture of hope and fear stronger than anything I'd ever known. I'd thought childbirth had shown me what full force was, but this moved through me like a tidal bore.

Once the answer had occurred to me, it felt inevitable, even late. The solution so clear that ignoring it felt wrong, ungrateful to nature and my Maker.

I almost laughed at the of-courseness, running back to the house. Scraping the mud from my boots, I examined the idea with as much diligence as I'd been equipped with and tried for more. Satisfied I couldn't see an objection, I was ready to have Benedict consider it. If it was a bad strategy, he would see that, and I would be happy to stand corrected—grateful to be protected from myself.

Even if Benedict approved, the plan would be vetted by André, reviewed by Clinton, possibly the King, and anyone else with the necessary security clearances. It would never come to anything if men who knew worlds more than me didn't agree it should.

Benedict might flinch, but he had overcome bigger challenges to do good before. Given the state of the place, capturing the castle needn't be fatal for anybody, and as a symbol, West Point had no rival. Benedict could act in a way which felt unworthy of him in order to achieve a noble legacy. It would be the greatest tale told about him yet.

"I think I have it, Benedict, our one shining stroke—"

He sighed. "And just what do you propose?"

"Take control of West Point and give it to the British."

He pulled away from me in horror.

"None of them would suspect me for a second."

"That is what gives the plan its power. They cannot suspect you because they fail repeatedly to give you your due. And you will make new friends, at the highest level. You will have the friendship of Clinton, André, Lord Carlisle, the King!"

"My men— Franks—"

"Look how he longed to resign! He would have, if he could have seen a clear, clean path to make a living. You'll be rescuing him—all of them—from more thankless suffering. I love Franks as you do. I would rest easier knowing he is safe—"

"The dead—"

"Benedict. I cannot believe the dead want more loss following them. The only possible way to honor their sacrifice—and the pain of those who loved them—is to do everything in your power to put an end to this."

He frowned. "It is not mine to give, Peggy."

"It will be! It could be! You will tell Washington the truth. Again. That you are not fit for command in the field but would defend the keys to the Hudson. This is it, my darling! The unanswerable gesture. It was you who showed me: West Point is as indelible a symbol of these colonies as there is. Only Washington's face could rival it, but I wouldn't see him harmed for anything. Him nor anyone! You will secure command of the fortress, and you will arrange it so that no one is hurt. Send every hothead on patrol the night of the handover. It will all be over before a drop of blood is shed."

"And what if he betrays us?"

"André? He would not. What are the odds of an opportunity like this? Of which as much could be said? With one fell swoop—one full swipe—which is it?—all three of us will be on the same side, heroes in Britain and thanked by every peace-seeking person alive. Nobody who has died will have died in vain.

Every one of them will have helped bring us to the point where we can achieve peace with a gesture that has all the hallmarks of art!"

"Or—"

"My love. I understand the compulsion to keep options open. I have, to an exhausting extent, tried for that all my life. But we are out of time for the infernal *ors* and *ifs* and *buts*. If our child is not a deadline, what will be?"

He stilled for a moment, his tired, magnificent face remaining difficult to read, and then into his eyes came a glint of longing and just as quick, decision.

"Win-win?" he said.

I felt my heart lighten with relief.

Chapter Twenty-Eight

Benedict had more whiskey than was ever ideal, and before even hearing back from Washington if command of West Point would be agreeable, he wrote to André offering the fortress.

There followed an agonizing wait, in which I worried about his impulsive judgment, and mine, and made him promise he'd run every future letter by me.

I worked in the garden, glad of the high wall between me and Esther, and played with the baby. By six each night, Benedict was ready to lose himself in drink. I begged him to play backgammon, managing that way to slow the refills and engage him in a playful way. With every move we flexed our luck and calculation—and one of us would always win, which was good enough for me. Washington responded,

> *Arnold, Command of West Point is beneath your dignity! There is nothing there to command, apart from a store of insensible munitions and a few sick and injured soldiers! My friend, you would be wasted. Mend your leg and take either flank—*

Benedict didn't express any frustration with me, though I felt plenty with myself. His tension manifested in his head. The plates in his skull felt they were splitting. Masking my own rising alarm, I massaged his scalp and urged more patience. "Washington always takes forever to make up his mind. This is typical. Write again. He'll come round."

Privately, I resented Washington for tormenting my husband again. Would it kill him to give the man his wish! But I felt a certain surrender too, as long as I couldn't see more I could do. When I found Benedict downstairs, drunk and sobbing before dawn, I saw such fatalism wasn't enough.

"I don't remember why I ever let them lionize me. For taking lives? Sometimes I think I eat dirt from Congress, all of them, because I agree with their low opinion. I wasn't qualified for governing. I liked Washington's idea, a chance to contribute while my leg healed, but it was vanity to agree. I shouldn't be trusted with anything: My mother knew it.

"Washington wants me dead. Why else send me back to the front when he knows my leg is spent? I'm more useful to him a dead hero than a compromised, crippled embarrassment. He asks for my suicide. Perhaps he's right."

This was not tolerable. Rapidly clearing empty bottles and scattered backgammon pieces, I had an idea.

Beverley Robinson had mentioned Chancellor Robert Livingston was the official directly responsible for West Point. It was him I needed to see. I'd watched women in need secure my own husband's assistance and I knew what to do. I waited until Benedict and Franks were out and invited him to tea. I dressed carefully, wanting to be attractive but not overt about it, and decided last minute to leave Eddie's rattle where it was on the table beside his seat, while Atty kept the baby occupied out of sight.

Tall, blond haired, with the well-bred features of that entire landed tribe, he made no secret of being intrigued.

"What is it I can do for you?" he asked.

"Colonel Livingston, it's kind of you to come, and I hope I don't offend you if I ask for your discretion. It's delicate."

He quirked an eyebrow and looked at me with naked relish.

"My husband does not have the strength in his legs he did. He hoped to make a useful contribution as governor—"

"I believe he did—"

"Thank you, but politics are not altogether his métier—"

"That speaks well of him."

"Yes, but we find ourselves in a bind. He longs to be of service and yet cannot accept his Excellency's generous invitation to command half the army. If you saw how swollen and mottled his leg can get, the misery of that infirmity—"

He winced with slightly prurient sympathy.

"You'll understand I'd sooner have him serving in a capacity which shows more tact."

I poured his tea and passed it to him. Here was another one under the powerful spell of breasts.

"I'd like to kill two birds with one stone—without hurting so much as a feather."

I saw him take up the silver rattle and turn it in his hands.

"I need our son to look up to his father. I'd wish him to see Fort Arnold a credit to the family name. Your own name is forever associated with the best of settlers."

Too much? No, he seemed to think the compliment only fair observation.

"What would you think about offering the general command of West Point, allowing him to restore it to the strength it ought to represent? Give him an opportunity to serve which won't add insult to his injury?"

Livingston was pleased to think of the prestige Arnold would confer on his pet project and promised to write to Washington.

Hannah, visiting, arrived as he was leaving, clocking my appearance with a rolled eye.

"Trust me," I said. "It's for your brother."

She didn't believe me, clearly, but Benedict was delighted when I told him what I'd done.

"My partner in greatness!" he exclaimed. I was disconcerted. Did he know the line came from *Macbeth*?

Within the month, Benedict was expected at West Point to take up his command.

Although there was no word back yet from André, high on my influence with Livingston and the relief of seeing Benedict freed from Philadelphia politics and responsibilities, I was inclined toward optimism. "Perhaps your letter never reached him? Perhaps a misfire is the best result! You can restore West Point to strength, sit out the rest of the war in your renovated fortress, and make no more enemies." I comforted myself further with the knowledge we'd soon be hundreds of miles away from Reed and under the protection of a West Point guard.

It was agreed that Benedict would go on ahead and get living quarters settled, while I packed up the house in Philadelphia and had Eddie inoculated. We couldn't have him living in a community of soldiers without taking that step. When it came to the journey, Franks and Atty would come with us, and bonus of bonuses, we'd break our journey with Theodosia in New Jersey.

I went to Stansbury to say goodbye and asked after André.

"Busy beyond belief, I think."

"I gather he must be," I said. "He owes Gustavus word—"

Stansbury clicked his heels.

"I swear you're getting taller, Peggy Arnold. Gustavus?"

"The latest alias. Led the Swedes to independence and was elected King."

He whistled. "One up from a duke."

"I don't love seeing how the two of them become when in negotiating mode," I confided. "There's a prickish feeling of competition—"

"Perhaps unavoidable, given you're in the middle?"

"God," I groaned, "I'll be so glad when this is over."

The night before Uncle William came, I felt such a desperate sense of dread and attachment to Eddie, it seemed a portent. Fear of inoculations might be superstitious, and mean a poor grasp of statistics, but it wasn't entirely irrational. There were people who had died in the wake of theirs, others who'd become irreversibly sick. What if my mother had been right and it wasn't worth the risk? It would be too cruel to lose my baby by my efforts to protect him.

There was a lot of coming and going from Reed's house in the night and I worried he had discovered Benedict had left—or worse still, got hold of his letter to André and was gearing up for my arrest, using me and Eddie as hostages, bait to lure his favorite victim back.

After a sleepless night I showed William in.

"How goes it with the poor men at camp?"

I saw a tiny flicker of irritation with my pity.

"Spirits are excellent," he insisted. "Conditions a little better."

I held Eddie, his chubby little legs kicking to find traction on my lap, wondering if my uncle would be grateful to return to the peacetime practice of medicine. Surely no doctor would want a world of unnecessary injuries, not when there would always be interesting work. William kept up a brisk chatter as he set out and cleaned his sharps, putting my mind at rest with stories of Lady Mary Wortley Montagu, who had seen inoculation done in Turkey and been the first woman in England to request it for her daughters. "Female pioneer!" he exclaimed, as he deftly nicked Eddie's skin. The baby wailed in outraged pain, and my own eyes filled, as William carefully spread infected pus from a slide into the scrape.

"Sorry," I said of my tears. "Turns my insides out."

"Natural, my dear. Mrs. Washington wouldn't even hear of it when I did Jackie. Said she'd rather not know!"

"Esther Reed died last night," he went on conversationally.

"What? My God—"

"Dysentery."

"I can't believe it!"

"Picked it up visiting the Pennsylvania Militia. The troops are riddled with it."

I felt the old childish *how* in the face of grief. Impossible to think.

"So young!"

"Thirty-four."

"Her poor children," I said, reeling. In some ways, it threw me to feel so moved.

I had wanted to prove to Esther there was something useful I could do, and now I never would. There was the selfish fear for my own mortality the death of a near contemporary will bring on, too. Was it Esther I grieved for, or myself?

How terrible though, to think of dying in such misery and indignity. How agonizingly sad, to know she was leaving her children behind.

It was hard to imagine the force she had been gone out. She felt vividly present, insistently with me, as the newly dead do, and all day my thoughts circled her. She'd come to mind, I'd think of seeing her, and remember, with fresh force, she was gone, and then I'd ruminate on all the ways I'd failed her and wonder why it had not felt possible to be a better friend. Was it as simple, as shameful, as not having liked her style? It had felt more a primal aversion. I wondered if that magnetic repulsion had steered my fate. I had gravitated as instinctively toward Theo as I had away from Esther. I liked Theo, trusted her, liked and trusted myself with her. Not so my neighbor. I wondered now if those instincts were something I could have tried harder to resist.

Esther had been so single-minded in her commitment, an admirable advocate for soldiers, and a devoted ally of her husband all her days. How different my life would have been if I'd had that same unilateral conviction in the Patriots from the beginning, and an attitude which didn't make Reed feel an unforgivable nightmare of a man. Could her death now inspire me, if Benedict went on at West Point, the letter to André miscarried, to become a steadfast Patriot wife? Had Esther occupying that territory meant no room for me? Was my sense of pride so big?

It never occurred to me we wouldn't have more time. A chance to find some stability in our antipathy, civility, short of being friends, or enemies. If Reed had gone first, would she have softened? Would I? Ridiculous that just as death reminds us of our powerlessness, we start bargaining, as if we're prepared to accept someone dying, but imagine there might yet be substitutions.

"I felt strangely affected by Esther's death throughout Eddie's two-week seclusion.

"Are you sure you won't stay with your parents?" William asked when he came to check the baby for fever before our departure. "I worry you might be imagining a fabulous castle, tapestries and blazing fires, when you're in for a cold and lonely highland ruin."

"Benedict needs me."

Once we'd delivered peace, it would be different. I'd have so much more than mother and wife to give.

Chapter Twenty-Nine

Everything is wanting . . . in this poverty-struck place. There's not a farthing to be got from Congress and none in the treasury. The garrison will be in a wretched uncomfortable situation next winter.

Benedict explained West Point forces consisted of fifteen hundred soldiers, short on supplies and completely missing discipline. William and Washington had not been wrong. Clearly, my fantasy of looking after the fort and waiting out the war was not an option. We couldn't live there. I relayed the conditions he described to Stansbury, dogged by a sickening feeling of betrayal. This wasn't our old fun gossip, for all I knew the end goal.

Benedict's next letter said he'd temporarily rented Beverley Robinson's house and we could join him there. He gave minutely detailed instructions for our journey.

You must by all means get out of your carriage in crossing all ferries and going over all large bridges to prevent accidents. Bring your own sheets to sleep in on the road to avoid dirty ones and to prevent disagreeable apprehensions and perhaps something worse. Bring your own tea and sugar, some meats, tongues or ham, and send a light horseman on early every morning to have dinner provided for you. Put a feather bed in the light wagon which will make an easy seat, and you will find it cooler and pleasanter to ride in when the roads are smooth than a closed carriage.

It was sweet to see him bossy in his worry.

Hannah brought Bean and Henry to say goodbye.

"I'm sorry you can't come with us, Hannah. Perhaps when the boys have finished their schooling—and the fort has been restored."

"As you have neither purling streams, nor sighing swains at West Point, 'tis no place for me. Nor do I think you will be long pleased with it."

She'd decided I was a silly flirt then, which was unfortunate, but I couldn't tell her what I'd been about with Livingston, not yet.

She had the right to feel resentful, after the decade she'd spent looking after Benedict's boys on her own, but I hoped when we'd delivered peace, she'd be a little less acerbic.

Bean was very somber taking leave of Eddie, while Henry made him giggle with peekaboo. Bean stood close and leaned against me, breathing heavily. I said I was sorry he couldn't join us at the fort just yet, but their father was making important repairs so that one day he could give them a proper tour. And very soon now I hoped we'd be back in Philadelphia, living at Mount Pleasant, where there would be room enough for all of us and more.

I asked Franks to kindly remove the iron boot scraper, and when I'd cleaned it, gave it to Bean and Henry.

"Here, this comes from Mount Pleasant. When we all return, we'll set it back in place and be grateful every time we cross the threshold that we're together."

Bean took the heavy object solemnly.

Benedict wrote again to tell me he had at last heard from André. Reassured he was in position to deliver the fort, the British were willing to confirm a price for his services: twenty thousand pounds.

I felt pretty unpleasant, reading that. It was another André I saw, in this coldly negotiating tone, and a queasy thing to see a price put on my vision for peace. A tension was inevitable, I guessed, whenever a well-meant endeavor met commerce, and of course I knew we needed money, but such an exact sum threw a harsh light on the whole endeavor, and I felt heavy and dirty with the treachery.

At last, I would see Theodosia in her own home. For all the risks on the road and nagging unease, I was exhilarated to show her the baby, and proud to have conceived a creative contribution worthy of her.

The Hermitage was a pretty, gabled stone house set back from the road, with a wraparound porch, trimmed with bay and lavender. I hoisted Eddie from the carriage. Soggy as he was, I knew he wouldn't be a size I could lift him for long and savored every minute of his solid little body against me. A gravel path led from the carriage through arbors of September roses. To the left, a lovely unkempt walled garden sprawled with beds of vegetables, fruit cages, herbs, and medicinal plants.

"You did all this!" I cried, as Theodosia emerged from the house.

She ran into my arms, followed by her mother and children, and we had a lot of embracing and exclaiming over babies.

"How are you? You look well—"

"Do I? I've decided it's all too frightening and the only possible remedy is not to worry a single minute more."

We had a family supper, with Franks and Atty too, chicken and mushroom pie and vegetables from the garden. "We continue to have all our favorites," Theodosia said, when I exclaimed over the meal. "Only in slightly smaller portions."

"Moderation in all things," her mother said, clearly not for the first time.

Theodosia's mother took Edward on her knee so Atty and I could eat and mashed for him his first tiny taste of carrot and pea on her finger while telling stories of their guests.

"I'm nosy enough to enjoy the glimpses of character and habits the work gives."

"What sort of things?"

"Ink on the bedding," Theo said. "You get that with writers. Irritating, but they don't mind if they return and find themselves assigned the old, blotted sheets. Officers can't seem to stop combing their hair or polishing shoes and tightening corners. Discipline bordering on nervous disorder."

Later her mother took the children upstairs so that Theo and I could catch up.

"You're managing well?"

"I can't replace their father, but I ask men I trust to teach them things which might keep them safe, how to fire catapults, climb trees, be all sorts of strong. My mother's a good shot. She'll see they can handle a gun before long."

"Maybe they'll never need one."

She laid both hands on the wooden table and said it made her angry her girls had never known a day now without anxiety, and she was afraid she couldn't pay for college, and without a proper education, how would her sons have any choice but joining the military? She laughed sadly. "And there was I saying I wouldn't worry—"

"It's not tolerable," I said. "Not any longer."

"What are you up to?" she asked. "You're pregnant with some scheme."

"Even now, friends are doing everything they can—"

I was struck again by how more than usually beautiful she looked. Her hair and eyes shone.

"Are you in love, Theodosia Provost?"

She gave a guilty grin.

"You are! Do I know him?"

"Aaron Burr—"

"No!" I cried. "I know him—knew him—as a child!"

"Yes," she hesitated.

Awkward memories mingled with reassurances left unspoken, but I was too glad Theodosia was happy to mind. Also slightly scandalized.

"How did it come to be?"

"He's a regular caller. At a certain point, I suppose we choose what feels our best defender. Or succumb to instincts it's impossible to resist!"

"What will happen if ever your husband returns?"

"I have no idea," Theodosia admitted. "But then none of us have known what will happen for the longest time. Meanwhile, I remain very careful. I know you won't tell a soul."

"Of course I won't. He's good to you?"

"He is. And there's fun in the secrecy. As far as anyone else is concerned, our relations are entirely respectable. In company, we're far too well-behaved to arouse suspicion, though I long to steal a kiss in the corridor. He leaves with the other officers and then returns through the window."

"No!"

Theodosia laughed. "He's gentle with my children. Promises me a child of our own, when we can."

"Does your mother support you?"

"Do you approve, Ma?" Theodosia called to the next room.

"I do." Her mother smiled, appearing in the doorway, and I had to be careful not to stare at the laughing love and trust between them.

"And what about you, Mrs. Arnold? How is the general?"

"I'm longing for reunion. There's so much news to hear." I paused. Not to confess felt churlish after the confidence she'd freely offered. "Just between us?"

"Peggy—" Theodosia reproved.

"If all has gone as planned, he and André will be meeting this week—teaming together to secure a lasting peace."

Her eyes widened.

"It needs to work," I said, fear spinning like a planet inside me.

Theodosia took my shaking hand. I sank back and closed my eyes.

"Picture yourself in a year. Where will you be?"

"In a garden, a late-summer tea. You. Me. Peace in the faces I see. Benedict and André, lounging at rest. Eddie chuntering happily at my feet. We're free." I blinked, laughed. "Thank you. That was helpful."

"You must be excited to see André again. How long's it been?"

"Two years, four months."

Theodosia laughed. "I always found him rather frightening," she admitted.

"André?"

"I'm always afraid a man with such an elevated aesthetic will be revolted by the flaws in me."

"Theodosia, he loves and admires you so much! You'll see. At tea next year!"

We talked on until dawn. Theodosia needed to know I didn't think her immoral.

"My husband hasn't written in several years—"

"You've seized happiness, and I see no harm in it," I said.

"But then again, it's blind spots we can't see." She laughed.

I wanted reassurance in turn. Was there vanity in the scheme? Or selfishness?

"If you were motivated most by appearances and self-interest, Peggy, you would not have done this."

I laughed, uneasily. In floating the idea of Benedict turning, had I forced change or only been ready when it came?

"If he hadn't suffered as he had, would I have seen the chance for what it was? Did the plan exist, objectively, independently of us? If I'd let it pass us by, would someone else have been given the same opportunity?"

"I don't think we see second chances, if they're not ones we need."

"Is it meant to be? That, I suppose, is the question."

"We can't ever know," Theodosia said.

"I know. I just wouldn't want to say, 'I don't know what I was thinking.'"

"It seemed a good idea at the time?"

We laughed, but I sank my face in my hands before emerging.

"Perhaps that is the best that can ever be said."

"In all this chaos and confusion, yes. It's the energy of intention—"

"Benedict talks about the *rectitude* of his intentions."

Theo put her head on one side.

"I know." I winced.

"But you love him."

"I do, and sometimes that slightly pompous ballast is what keeps him afloat. So I can't hate it. And look at what he has to put up with from me, a nervous liability—"

"I think you've shown impressive equilibrium. A little panic at times is natural, world as it is—"

I slept well. Better than I would for many weeks.

I felt delicate when I woke, queasy with all I'd revealed, and a little the worse for the wine we'd shared. Dogged by anxiety about Benedict and André's meeting, I worried now that it came to leaving her what Theo would really think. Drinking had made our conversation free, sincere—enjoyably snobby too. The morning after, I felt guilty of everything we'd judged and teased in others. My skin felt thin, stomach vulnerable, and I was eager to get on the road.

At King's Crossing, where the river narrows dramatically, we climbed down to deal with the checkpoint and wait in a thin strip of shade for the ferry. All official scrutiny made me uneasy. Even Franks blandly acknowledging the river's majesty made me feel guilty. I swiveled away from General Washington's Newburgh headquarters and prayed for the safe conclusion of the plan.

The baby started to fuss, absorbing my agitation and probably last night's wine in my milk. I took off both our stockings and, holding him under his arms, swept him through the water while Atty pretended to come for his toes. He laughed again and again in delight.

A dark cloud turned the silver water dark storm gray, flat and free of sparkle, and suddenly I could only picture my shame and failure, the contempt of friends, the danger.

I felt better once we were crossing the water, feeling the precious river breeze, and seeing the infinite configurations in the water's currents.

I tried to train my mind on what it would be like to return to this spot the next time, the war over. No checkpoints, no suspicion. We would find a secluded spot of our own, sun ourselves on rocks, and Benedict could teach Edward—and me!—to fish and swim.

Safely on the east bank, we embarked on the last stretch north to Garrison. Edward sat on my lap, clutching a finger on each of my hands with his fat little fists. I pointed out Bear Mountain and the highlands where the first maples were turning, with just a hint of pink before the russet that would come. I showed him lighthouses, islands, and ospreys in their massive nests on the cliffs above the river. I promised him glimpses of deer, mountain lions, beavers, and raccoons, if he was very patient and still.

"It's as lovely to listen to you as it is look at you," Franks said. "Rare in the species."

The guilt rose again like bile. I prayed he'd thank us in the end.

I was awed into silence by the sight of West Point from the south. For an immobilizing minute which felt like a stroke, I couldn't grasp why we'd doubted the Patriots. Why hadn't we waited? In suffocating confusion, I could not remember why it had felt necessary to risk all we had. Had we panicked? Our sense of time warped by all the loss and worry?

"I'm the King of the castle, and you're the dirty rascal," I tried to sing to Edward, but faltered.

Cantering the baby on my lap, I conjured contempt for my selfishness. It would have been wicked to cling to my own security, holed up in a fortified hill with a guard of one hundred, consigning everyone else to risk when I had power to bring the conflict to an end.

The last thing Benedict needed was me careening between hope and terror. I touched the Mather in my pocket, borrowing—robbing—its strength a little longer.

By the time we arrived, I had a violent headache and longed to lie down. Benedict was standing in the driveway and opened the carriage door, leaping up to us, before we came to a standstill.

"Your leg's looking better then!"

"It is," he said. "A good month walking these hills. Oh, what a sight for sore eyes, Peggy. Thank God you're here."

He kissed me hard. I caught a brush of unfamiliar whiskers. It was unlike him not to be perfectly shaved, and I saw the toll of alcohol and sleepless nights in his eyes. I was determined never to nag him, but that didn't stop me estimating with some impatience the soothing and grooming it would take to have him back at his best.

Franks teased the general that he had turned into a complete soldier in the weeks he'd been gone. "On campaign you won't see a chin for beard all winter," he told me, his instinct always to lighten the atmosphere.

"Just don't go asking anyone else to fetch a barber," I said.

Benedict led me all over the premises, describing his official duties when servants could hear us, updating me with snippets in moments we were alone.

He had stayed up too late reading back issues of the newspapers in Robinson's library, perversely interested in accounts of his former acts of bravery. He had sent his troops on purposeless reconnaissance missions up to the highlands, the steep granite palisades above us, leaving the fortress largely unmanned. He fussed constantly about the state of the chain strung across the river to keep the British at bay, shuttling about the water at all hours to scope out possibilities for Clinton's advance while filing flimsy reports about the defenses. It sounded risky and bordering on suicidal already, and I looked at him sideways, wondering if part of him was hoping for discovery.

On September 14 Washington had written him, "*You will keep this to yourself, but tomorrow I'll pass through Peekskill, and rely on your protection.*"

I stared at him in shock. "You didn't betray him?"

"He was never actually in danger. There wasn't time for the British to do anything with the information—but relaying it to André did the trick. He finally committed to a meeting in person."

"You've met then?"

"Oh yes."

I exhaled as he continued. Benedict had left the house near midnight, with only Richard—

I looked quizzical.

"A slave of Beverley's, discretion itself." He gave a little nod to a tall dark man under a straw hat steadily stacking firewood in the far field, who returned the gesture with a noncommittal inclination of his head.

"He'd wrapped the blades of his oars in sheepskin to muffle all splashing."

"And André?"

"Took a tender from the British sloop *Vulture*, anchored a little way south, leaving Clinton waiting on board. Rowed himself north. Cloaked.

"We met on the riverbank at Haverstraw. Striking how young he looks? I'd expected to find more wiliness in the eyes of Britain's preeminent spy."

He saw I didn't like his tone. "I was surprised he wasn't more guarded. He was so far from jaded, I almost felt protective, as I would toward a young officer on my own side."

"You are on the same side," I reminded him.

Benedict nodded, and I saw him list a little, reckoning over again with all he was leaving behind.

He described how he'd dragged his own boat with a couple of powerful heaves out of sight, and turned to help André with his own, before leading him to the wooded hilltop where they could talk privately. They had sat on tree stumps, faces in shadow, using the brandy to stay warm, not wanting to risk lighting a fire.

He told me he'd requested a contingency, some sum he'd be paid even in the event of failure.

"Failure?"

"He was fully convinced of the reasonableness of my proposal: ten thousand pounds sterling for my services, risk, and the loss which I should sustain in case a discovery of my plan should oblige me to take refuge in New York. Although commissioned to promise me only six thousand, he said he would use his influence to see it be ten."

I didn't want to hear this quibbling over numbers. The meeting sounded so stealthy—of course it had to be—but hearing the story while still sticky and grubby from our journey made me feel contaminated. And I was troubled, all this talk of *I* and not enough of *us*.

Benedict was becoming almost lyrical. Clearly, he had been as seduced by André as everybody always was. He gestured to demonstrate how André had looked at the landscape like a painter. Talked of capturing the scene when he could.

"All well, the meeting will be worth the painting—hanging in a palace across the Atlantic and gracing the finest American galleries, in time."

It was strange, to be standing in a place of such beauty while feeling so uneasy. The high meadow grass shivering in the breeze, the river's currents rippling silver and amber, the fortress looming on the far shore, all of it felt tainted with guilty fear.

"We drank to you," Benedict whispered, reaching for my hair.

I didn't want gallantry. I wanted assurances all was in order.

"And to peace?"

"Several times. And to Washington and the King!"

They had continued talking, and drinking, as the light came up, weighing eventualities, anticipating hazards, the flask passing back and forth between them. Benedict had handed over the plans and talked André through the approach, which aspects were defenseless and might be taken by a handful of men without loss. I could feel my confidence falling, dread rising, thinking of the bluster and posturing that would have come with drink. Benedict made a big thing of his having insisted any remaining guards be taken alive.

"But that was never in question," I said, testy with fear.

I hadn't let myself think how I'd feel if soldiers were to die as a direct result of the plan. I felt another wave of horror at the risks.

"André memorized the plans? Destroyed them?"

"He hid them securely in his stockings."

I stared at him. He rubbed the stubble on his chin with the back of his hand.

"I thought it important he have evidence of my commitment for Clinton, and he wanted to be sure the plan would survive him, should something happen."

"To André?"

"Nothing is impossible," he said, and again I stared at him stupidly. He must know that bad befalling André was.

"The British control most of the territory south of his ship," he said, as if that were consolation, "so I don't anticipate difficulty moving up the necessary troops. They should be here any day."

"Any day?" I couldn't stand the feeling of uncertainty and exposure any longer.

"Any day now, yes. André drank more than he's used to, that was clear," Benedict said, with something too like a roguish chuckle. André would never have kept pace with Benedict, who could sink a barrel and function and must have done if the state of him today was any indication. As it was, they'd both been in a fog of cognac by morning. I wanted to shake my husband for that.

We moved into the orchard, instinctively seeking the cover of those orderly rows, but I was further unnerved to see rosy windfall apples left to rot, the definition of squandered luck. Wasps were lazily investigating, and the smell of fermentation would be forever associated with fear in my mind. I felt I was having to coax the most important details from my husband while he lingered on unhelpful boasts. He was nervous, smirking, the furthest thing from reassuring.

"He made it safely back to his ship?" I prompted.

"Not quite." Benedict explained they'd been preparing to launch André's tender back to the *Vulture* when they were startled by a sudden volley of gunfire. "André turned quite white. Terrified," he said.

"Well, no wonder."

"After the initial shock, it became clear it was James, another of the Livingston clan, an old comrade of mine who now commands King's Crossing, firing a cannon from his garden at the British ship. Gave the *Vulture* a good hammering."

Benedict and André had been forced to watch as Clinton, his ship in tatters, retreated south.

"André was stranded in daylight? Where is he now?"

Benedict said he'd sent Richard for another of Beverley's accomplices, a man named Joshua Hett Smith, instructing him to take André overland south.

"Through British-controlled territory?"

"They have the river," Benedict explained, "but the banks include some neutral areas. He'll have had to navigate a stretch of no-man's-land and a slice of Patriot territory, but neutral, yes, for the most part—"

It always confounded me there could be neutral areas in war, and since neutrality was possible, that war wasn't avoidable overall.

Benedict explained he'd given André a pass under the name of John Anderson to ensure safe passage through the Patriot holdings, trusting he'd have no difficulty in stretches controlled by the British.

"And in neutral?"

"He should be left alone."

I sighed tersely. It sounded far from watertight.

Franks came striding into view, and Benedict called a hearty greeting, insisting he join us for dinner that evening along with a few other friends.

"Must we have company?" I smiled tightly. Franks promised me he'd do all the talking, shoulder the load as much as he could for me.

"Yes, my darling, you must rest," Benedict said, running a slow, proprietorial hand over my back. Franks turned his head from the intimacy, missing my miniscule flinch. Had I become headstrong, intolerant of Benedict, after these weeks alone? The comfort of the baby had been meeting all my need for touch.

"Perhaps I will lie down before our guests arrive."

In the bedroom, I assured Benedict he'd made the right choice in renting Beverley's place, while making a quick mental inventory of all the room's inherent hazards. An unforgiving stone floor. Shutters with hinges to pinch little fingers. There was the height of the bed, to which Eddie was bound to migrate later that night. Sharp corners on the low table. And all the time the question yelling through my head: *Had André made it safely back?*

Benedict was running through the guest list, apologetic, irritatingly solicitous, but he'd thought it important we appear relaxed and hospitable to the local grandees. There were so many in the neighborhood wanting to meet me. Tonight, we'd be joined by Colonel Lamb, who had fought and been captured at Quebec, and now commanded West Point artillery; Joshua Hett Smith, star of last night's drama, entrusted with André's safe delivery back to the British; plus Franks and Colonel Varick, Benedict's other aide, whom I'd met briefly at our party, and Dr. Eustice, the fortress physician.

Benedict also let me know the household was now on notice to host General Washington and his retinue as they came through the region from the north in three days' time.

"What?"

"It won't come to it."

He kissed me, promising the reassurance of an update once Hett Smith arrived. "Who is this character, Hett Smith?"

"He's a supple sort of fish, a seasoned go-between. You might not find him the most agreeable, but he's a necessary evil."

"Evil?" I pulled myself together. There was no time to be spooked. "Does he know that I know about the plan?"

"We didn't discuss it, but it's more than his life's worth to betray any knowledge himself."

Benedict massaged my shoulders, explaining, as if suddenly some sort of expert, "All enterprises of this sort necessitate association with insalubrious persons. Think of Joshua as a brief kink on the road to victory."

"If he has delivered André to safety, I'll be happy to welcome him," I said, feeling tension making a shrew of me. I removed my earrings, watching Benedict in the mirror.

"You liked him then, André?"

"I see why you do," he said.

"And he looked well, considering?"

"You'll soon see for yourself."

"Before Washington gets here?"

"Well before."

Chapter Thirty

BENEDICT HAD A REST IN OUR BED WHILE EDDIE AND I HAD OUR BATHS and Atty unpacked. He woke only once we were dressed and settled, and I had the baby on my lap, his little stout legs buckling and wavering, as I showed him the view of the river from our bedroom window.

"What a picture," Benedict said, dropping a kiss on the baby's forehead.

"Nobody told me what a joy it would be."

"I'm not sure every woman thinks it is. You're a very different mother from mine. Always warning of perdition. Years before it would come to pass!" The shadow fell over his face that I hated. Protectiveness welled within me, along with impatience with the bleak joking when what we needed was strength and belief.

"She would have been proud of you," I said stubbornly, "and your love of country, thinking of what's right for all, not what's best for either faction"—while another voice in me was wondering, *Could it be she'd seen this coming?*

It was only nerves causing this irritation. The enormity of our commitment, and the terrible ways it could be tested, frightened me.

"She'd never forgive me failing."

I cut in briskly.

"Well, I'm afraid my love is unconditional. For you and the baby."

Was it? I wondered. For Eddie, yes, no question. And surely for Benedict too. I turned the baby's beaming, oblivious, innocent face toward me. What could a child ever do that a mother couldn't forgive? Nothing, if I did my job right.

"I would die for him," I said simply. "I would save him over everything. When I think of Esther's talk of giving up her children rather than see the enemy prosper!"

I brought Eddie's face to my own and smooshed my lips on his. "Of all impossible things," I said, in the silly voice I had only for him.

I looked at Benedict. "Did you hear she had died? Esther?"

"No. Christ." He shook his head. "Reed will miss her. Poor sod. Well, R.I.P., Esther—"

"Yes, rest in peace."

He looked at me a beat.

"I mean it. Even if I did find her tricky to like. The idea of a restless spirit is unsettling, and a wicked one at large, actively alarming! There's nobody I don't hope rests in peace."

"Even Reed?"

"Especially Reed. He I rather wish just would."

Franks knocked to say Hett Smith was waiting downstairs. "Damn it, he's early!" Benedict muttered, heaving himself into his boots, and, to Franks, "Stick him in the library. I'll be right down!"

Seeing my face, he tried to revert to nurturing. "Don't concern yourself with the details, my darling."

André's safety was hardly a detail, but there was no time to argue.

"Go," I urged, praying Hett Smith had good news. "I'll settle the baby and join you."

Scanning the corridor for servants, I listened at the library door. The wood near my face was sticky with fingerprints, sloppy rental standards I'd have to see to before André and Clinton arrived.

"Your remedy, General." The sneer was audible, as was the glug of a generous pour.

"All as it should be?" Benedict asked stiffly.

I couldn't bear the suspense a second longer, and let myself in.

Joshua Hett Smith was a short man with pale, watchful eyes and an insolent smile.

"Ah," Benedict said, "Joshua, may I introduce—"

"You may indeed. High time, Mrs. Arnold. Your husband doesn't do well without you."

He addressed himself directly down my dress. Every underhand thing about him rang such an immediate alarm I actually shivered.

"My wife, Mrs. Arnold. Joshua Hett Smith, brother of William, chief justice of New York. Beverley assured me Joshua here can lay hands on any supplies you need."

"That I can," Hett Smith said. "A man with a wide acquaintance, I am. Get things done." He tapped the side of his nose slowly, drink still in hand. "Which will be invaluable to you, Mrs. Arnold, given the quantity and quality of company you'll be expecting in the coming days."

He managed to spin even the blandest sentence with insinuation or sarcasm. "How's the 'injury,' General? Good supply of port wine in your rented cellar to help with that. More where it came from too. Very convenient position for you, this, given the *circumstances.*"

The man was as good as suggesting Benedict was a malingerer.

"I'm afraid I interrupted you," I said pointedly to Benedict. "You have military business I think—"

"Yes," Hett Smith said, savoring our attention. "Is all as it should be? There's a question. Although, we did have to deal with a few changes in plan."

He took the slowest sip of whiskey in history.

"The major had, as you'll recall, made only a scanty concession to secrecy—his uniform barely hidden by his cloak—so I judged it better we avoid the full glare of daylight and took him to my house to wait. Furthermore"—another sip—"I insisted that if I was to accompany him under the alias Mr. John Anderson, man of affairs, he had to disguise himself as such a civilian and ditch the scarlet."

"That can't have sat well with André. His express wish was to do his duty as a uniformed officer," Benedict said.

"We can't all have what we want, now can we? Given the degree of personal risk which I was myself taking above and beyond what was expected, negotiated, and agreed, I required him to be flexible himself. We'll set off later tonight."

André was still stuck in hiding then, nearby.

Franks knocked and entered, with a look at Hett Smith which told me Nurse was no fan of his, to let us know our other guests had arrived. He re-introduced Major Varick, who wore a tense expression and alarmingly high color, along with Dr. Eustice and the colonel.

Benedict became horribly hearty, laughing too readily and interrupting everything our guests said. I could see Franks and Varick exchange glances, expressing misgivings about Benedict along with Hett Smith.

I had not hosted a dinner party since having Eddie, and though I knew he was in good hands with Atty, his cries, heard clearly through the floorboards, brought milk pricking to my breasts. My bodice contained any leakage, but the pressure was painful, and I was distracted by worry that the stain could seep through. Thinking of André, a hostage of sorts to this creep Hett Smith, didn't help.

We endured long-winded descriptions of minor medical advances from Dr. Eustice and smiled dutifully through Varick's stilted but familiar stories of Benedict's heroics.

The fish was dry to inedible. We were all struggling to swallow.

"Is there not a sauce?" I asked the cook, only to be told baldly, no, there was none. I apologized to the table. Franks protested I'd only just arrived; I could hardly be expected . . . Benedict, upset to be implicated, vastly overreacted to the challenge, wrenching back his chair and making for the kitchen, bellowing for butter.

I was longing for a drink after the previous evening's excesses, Theodosia, but with a rising feeling of chaos, I wanted every wit about me.

With Benedict gone, Hett Smith refilled his own glass and hovered the bottle over my own with an impertinent expression.

"No, thank you."

"You don't care for drink, Mrs. Arnold?"

"Not just now."

He proceeded to pour, regardless. "Do you good." He winked.

Franks pushed back his chair in agitation.

"The lady said no."

Hett Smith shrugged, then drained and refilled his own glass.

"You shouldn't close the door on any vice, not completely. Only makes it more powerful."

He held the bottle a little higher, waggled it at me, before topping himself to the brim.

Benedict returned with some oil he claimed was olive, but the fish had long gone cold. Eating it in a little slick of what was clearly cheap vegetable oil did nothing to improve it.

Hett Smith was the only one enjoying himself. He winked as he told me we had friends in common, including a certain Major André.

"Is that so?" I asked, while he pattered a tabletop drumbeat with his fingers. The drink was the only thing on the table there was a lot of, and I gestured that the other guests should help themselves.

"Shame about the sauce. If I'd known, I could have brought you butter. Would you adjudge, Mrs. Arnold, provisions in Philadelphia were more plentiful under the British or the Patriots?"

Benedict seemed to think the best plan was to match this vile man drink for drink and was becoming more belligerent by the minute. Varick, honor bound to defend the dignity of his commanding officer's house, glared hotly at Hett Smith. The confusion of drink caused a series of excruciating crosscurrents, while Franks tried to steer the conversation to safer territory, asking Dr. Eustice about the readiness with which he was acquiring bandages.

Eustice quoted the cost in American dollars, which Hett Smith provocatively dismissed as worth no more than an English penny. Varick insisted he could not sit by while he impugned the Patriot currency. Hett Smith retorted he had no stomach for hearing him defend it.

"You dishonor a general of the Patriot Army, sir!" Varick growled.

I sat rigid with mortification while Benedict, laboring his breathing like a bull close to charging, bellowed at Hett Smith, "You heard him!"

Scared of alienating the one man on whom André depended, a drunk who could compromise us all, I good as cried, "I beg you, gentlemen, please drop the matter!"

"I'm sorry, Mrs. Arnold," Varick said. "But I cannot stay at this table while Hett Smith does."

Varick rose to leave, followed by Hett Smith.

"I know when I'm not wanted—I'll be getting back. I need to attend to a special guest of my own," he said, throwing me a leer so villainous it ought to have been comical.

Arnold also left the table, calling Franks into his office and loudly haranguing him for his role in the argument. That left me with the appalled doctor and Colonel Lamb, all of us finishing our dinner to the sickening chink of cutlery, straining to think of something to say, while the argument raged next door.

"If I asked the devil to dine with me, the gentleman of his family should be civil to him," Benedict shouted.

Varick warned, "You will suffer, General, by this improper intimacy with Hett Smith. His insolence and ungentlemanlike conduct to Mrs. Arnold, in speaking impertinently to you before her, was unacceptable. The man's a damned rascal, a scoundrel, and a spy!"

"Illiberal language," Dr. Eustice regretted, "for a lady to hear."

As soon as I could politely manage it, I saw him and the colonel off, horrified at how fast standards were falling.

Franks and Varick were behind me as I closed the front door. Varick was such a high color now I asked if he was running a fever.

"May I?" I asked, and with the back of my hand established he was boiling hot.

"You need to get to bed," I said.

"We sleep at the fort, over the river."

"You're not crossing the water tonight, Varick. Not with this temperature. Franks, can you show me where to find clean sheets and a spare bed?"

As I billowed the sheets over him and tucked them tight, Varick and Franks took turns telling me all the reasons I must prevail upon the general to break off contact with Hett Smith.

"I worry he's trading illegally, Mrs. Arnold, and we cannot risk another court martial."

"No, Nurse, we can't," I agreed. "I see exactly what you mean. The man has a very regrettable aspect."

"Don't let the general give up. He kept me in the fight when I was wavering, and I want to do the same for him. He's tired—we're all of us tired—but it's no good giving the enemies on our own side fuel. One second with eyes off the ball and it's fatal."

I smiled sadly, promised to talk to Benedict, wished goodnight to Franks, who was off back to the barracks, and said I'd return to check on Varick before I went to bed myself.

I took a deep breath and rejoined Benedict.

All the patience I'd meant to marshal evaporated when I saw how much more whiskey he'd drunk.

"Are you trying to be undone, Benedict?" I whispered harshly, my tone an uncomfortable reminder of my mother. "You could scarcely have tried harder to distress Franks and Varick. I insist you apologize for your cavalier language and promise them never to visit with Hett Smith again. I can't believe the recklessness with which you provoked that man with André still not safe behind British lines!"

"Clinton is sailing north," he assured me. "At least, I've had word of a major British embarkation on the Hudson from New York. That must mean André safely reached his mark. They're on their way, Peggy! Oh Christ, what have we done?"

"Shh, shh," I soothed, stroking his hair as if calming a horse.

"Think of Eddie, Bean, and Henry. Think of your men."

"You goaded me to this."

"We did it together—"

He threw off my hand and lurched across the room. Conscious of the ease with which I'd been able to hear him through the door, I whispered would he please come and sit still?

Steadily, I repeated the arguments we both needed to hear.

"We're delivering an outcome as favorable for Americans as it is for the British. It might be irritating to submit to the King, but we have shown all power has limits. The world will know the British could not prevail, not without high-level Patriot help.

"Once the heat of these years is behind us and the King can save face, America will come fully of age and make an amicable break. Independence without acrimony. Ongoing trade alliances, so many shared interests. Meanwhile, we'll get a new Congress. See that nasty partisanship doesn't triumph and define us. This may be the least bitter route to realizing the truest Patriot vision there could be. Try to trust the currents—I know they feel like rapids, but we are so nearly free!"

When his breathing finally settled into sleep, I laid him out on the sofa, covered him with a blanket, checked Varick, who was still boiling steadily, and made for bed, where I could give my own anxieties free rein without inflaming Benedict's.

Hett Smith seemed the worst of it, crass and reckless. And yet André had chosen to use him, too. I found myself questioning for the first time André's own loyalty. It was dizzying the extent of our risk. What if he had been manipulating me? What if what the British wanted was Benedict humiliated? Seizing West Point and exposing Benedict as a traitor could dismay the Patriots into defeat. And if the British betrayed Benedict, there would be no need to see he was safe or paid.

I couldn't believe it though, no. André didn't have that in him. Benedict was right about his essential innocence. The risks Benedict and André were running were equilateral, and somewhere along the line were mine. There had to be protection in that triangle.

Hett Smith had not revealed the plan to Franks or Varick, however close it felt he came. Neither did the two of them suspect Benedict of more than risky trading.

My husband was a celebrated strategist. André the pinnacle of British intelligence. They must know what we were doing.

The arrow had been fired. Tomorrow it would meet its mark or wobble to a drop that disgraced us all.

Chapter Thirty-One

The next morning was one of those blue-sky days which make the sudden arrival of trouble feel like a cosmic joke. I woke under the heavy canopy, luxuriating for a second in the warmth of the covers, while savoring the first fall chill and faint smell of woodsmoke through the open window. Benedict had evidently slept in his study, and I sat up as Atty brought Eddie to be fed. Out of the window, the Betsy Ross flag snapped and billowed in the breeze.

I heard Benedict's voice hectoring the cook downstairs. If he was tense, I must be all easy confidence. André and Clinton would be with us soon, and what a welcome they must have. The thought of André waking under this roof, stirring, just across the hall, the exhalation we'd all be free to make, meeting downstairs for breakfast—

I touched my hip bones, for the reliable indicator of my weight they gave me. I was not as slim as I'd been when I'd last seen him, but the new curves would have to compensate. Benedict arrived with a cup of tea. The baby stopped sucking to smile up at him. Benedict sat beside me. He'd been up early, shaved, and bathed, his breath was fresh, and I was just suggesting he might put Eddie down and come back to bed so we could begin the day again, when urgent hooves on the gravel announced the approach of a messenger. I felt fear on my skin like a wasp's wing.

While Benedict went down to greet the unexpected arrival, I gathered up Eddie, still latched, and went to the open window, shielding myself with the shutter.

Squinting in the morning sun, the messenger declared he had come from his Excellency at Hartford that morning, and brought word that Washington, Hamilton, Knox, and the Marquis de Lafayette, along with a party of ninety, would be arriving for breakfast with us within the hour.

I staggered back into the room in shock, dislodging poor Eddie, who gave an outraged wail. Washington! Two days early!

It felt like time itself was accelerating and the motion was sickening. Downstairs Benedict was ominously silent. What if Clinton and André arrived at the same time as Washington's party? What if all of them were at the same table? It was still easier for me to picture a civilized historic treaty in the room beneath me than anyone's violent capture. What if we declared the Beverley Robinson House neutral territory, our own Dobb's Ferry, and let the peace talks begin right here?

The development had to be an opportunity. All would be well. All must be well.

I sat back on the bed, heart pounding, while Edward finished feeding.

It didn't help me feel on top of things, having that precious little appendage attached at my breast.

I hadn't seen a single one of the visitors since before Eddie was born, and I was not past caring what I wore.

Nothing too elaborate, not while entertaining at breakfast. The very late notice the general had given would excuse a little dishevelment, though remembering Hamilton's lovely, lazy smile as he'd adjusted his sword back at our party, I had to make a little effort.

Benedict came bursting back in, Atty at his heels for Eddie. There was no opportunity to speak privately, so we were forced to perform.

"What are the odds?" I smiled.

Benedict answered with the wry raise of an eyebrow I loved, and for a moment I let myself believe in him.

Atty took Eddie away for his morning bath while Benedict set off for the stables to be sure all grooms were on duty to see Washington's one hundred horses could be fed and rested.

I began moving rapidly about the house, ferrying silver from the keeping room to the dining table, folding linens, and bringing peaches and beer, fresh bread, and bacon to the table.

The reluctant cook was little help, but the extended visit from the French had trained me for this.

I wanted Washington to think well of me personally, as well as of Benedict, to remember this breakfast as a pleasant, civilized feast, nurture, as the war was all but over. Conceding would be a bitter pill for him, at least initially, but I told myself he too would come to feel relief.

Somehow, I willed myself to believe that if the breakfast I served was perfect, the day could still go well. Brought together, the men, all good and reasonable as I'd seen, would talk and surely reach agreement.

Hearing a shout of greeting, I checked the fire wasn't smoking but burning busily in the grate; adjusted the blinds so that sunshine would hit the linen, polished silver, and cut flowers without blinding anyone as they ate; and took a quick cloth to the sticky fingerprints on the door before rushing upstairs to dress.

Through the floor I heard Benedict welcoming Hamilton.

"Washington, Knox, and Lafayette aren't far behind me. The Frenchman hates to be late, but since Washington teased him for being in love with your wife, along with every other young man in the army, pride obliged him to give that the lie and join the general in inspecting defenses before breakfast."

Benedict retorted that would give Hamilton a head start with the bacon, but his humor sounded forced. Though I knew I should be grateful he wasn't a smoother liar, I did wish in that minute he was.

I heard the creak of the buttery door again as Benedict stepped out of the dining room to receive word from another messenger, then an urgent murmur and another creak as he returned. Benedict now was giving his flustered regrets, Hamilton his easy assurances. I heard my husband order a horse and then his rapid, painful ascent to our bedroom.

He dispatched Atty with one look and, shutting the door behind him, took my shoulders in his hands.

"Peggy, that was Commander Jameson's messenger." He handed me the paper. "Major André of the British army is a prisoner in my custody . . ."

A wave of terror lifted me. "What happened?"

"Unclear," Benedict said. "I had a message from Hett Smith first thing saying he was safely on his way. Now suddenly he's being sent to me under armed guard, while suspicious papers in his possession are on their way to Washington."

"What will you do with him when he gets here?"

"I can't be here! Peggy, it's not for him you have to fear!"

"Hamilton is here to arrest you?"

"No. He seems to have no idea. My confusion must have been apparent—but guilt doesn't occur to him. I don't have long. If the plans reach Washington while I'm still in range, I'm done for. I must make my way to Clinton and the British ship—"

"But if Clinton is close? Already on his way? He might liberate the fort before the papers even arrive—" I was a fool with the last of my hope.

"No, Peggy. Clinton will not be coming any closer. André is in captivity. The plans are en route to Washington and he's moments away." He thrust a leather correspondence folder into my hands. "Burn every last letter. Deny everything. I'll send for you, as soon as I can."

Reality was outrunning me now. I nodded rapidly, hands shaking, the first fat tears rolling down my cheeks.

He knelt beside the bed, took Eddie's little head in his hands, and kissed it.

Franks knocked on the bedroom door to announce Washington's advance guard was in sight. A hundred and sixty horses—a thundering nightmare bearing down—and the general himself front and center.

It was the end of every hope.

Benedict kissed me, muttering his love, but I could not look at him. I kept my eyes closed as I heard him half limp, half drop the height of the stairs, and reeling at the abandonment, cringed to hear his excuses to Hamilton:

"I must hasten to West Point to prepare for the reception of the general!" Then I watched from the window as he swung into the saddle and galloped into the mouth of the tunneling path that led to the landing place, where his oarsmen would be ready with the barge.

My husband, the hero.

In a minute which seemed a year, I considered my situation. Benedict had left us. Eddie and I were at the mercy of men about to learn we were their enemy. We faced the threat of death and the certainty of a disgrace which would reverberate for generations.

Frantically I pulled the letters I'd sent Benedict and those from André from the folder, and with Hamilton still creaking in his chair on the floor beneath my feet, I shoved them in the fire.

It was a slow smolder with nothing like the heat it needed. I opened the window to fan the flames, scrunched every last letter into a ball, set them individually ablaze, and stabbed at them frantically with the poker.

I heard footsteps on the stairs and imagined they were here to arrest me, to hang me as a spy. In the panic of a thousand thoughts, I stood too rapidly, the picture closed in, and I fell unconscious to the floor.

I had barely hit the rug before Atty was beside me, exclaiming her concern. I kept my eyes closed while my senses returned, the relief of that brief oblivion over too soon. I'd have welcomed years without responsibility—rest, no pressure, nuns susurrating in starched linen seeing to my care.

"Where's the general, ma'am?"

"Gone," I moaned.

"Where, for heaven's sake?" Atty asked.

"Gone, forever—"

Atty helped me to the window for air, where, with a quick glance to check for stray embers and ink-stained scraps, I steadied myself on the windowsill in time to see Washington, Lafayette, and Knox bringing their horses to a halt, outriders fanning behind them. They were an impressive spectacle, those horsemen, moving beautifully in the saddle, and as a team.

These men, sure as history, would be cast in bronze on rearing stallions, their images towering from plinths in the finest parks, while everything but Benedict's traitoring would be erased.

The shining flanks of their mounts rippled, along with the wind through the trees, as they listened to Hamilton describe my husband's abrupt departure for West Point to prepare for their reception.

"What of Mrs. Arnold?" Lafayette asked.

"She awaits."

The men glanced at my window, and I darted back from sight.

Atty was doggedly sweeping curls of singed paper, God love her.

What were my options? Pretend innocence, but what if they had evidence of letters between André and me? What if André, under arrest, had confessed? Say I knew, but had begged Benedict not to do it? Our marriage might be annulled, and the support of these men assured. But what of Eddie—raised out of legal marriage, raised in disgrace?

I could try to escape. In disguise? With check points at every turn? Not plausible, and never without Eddie. And with him, what stealth or speed was possible? We were one unwieldy, slow-moving creature, while Benedict had galloped off at will.

I could kill myself, but I had no rope, no poison. Impossible, and unforgivable.

Why had nobody told me how completely a baby would tether me to life, whether I wanted to hold on or not? While Eddie lived, I had no escape, and he must simply never die.

How much could I trust those men downstairs if they suspected me? They looked noble, liked to think themselves merciful, but they were killers, and their fight wasn't over. I thought of the Six Nation Indians whom Washington had ordered eradicated. The insistence not one man, woman, or child be spared. If Benedict had achieved anything, it was to expose Patriot vulnerability. How angry would that make them? Whether they believed me or not, what revenge would they seek, when instead of finding Benedict, a regimental inspection, and multiple-gun salute over at West Point, they found the fort empty and gathered what had been intended by the plans? Even if Washington was inclined to clemency, there were men he chose to keep close who were not.

Was there any room for hope? Incredible reversals had happened already this morning. This was the mother of setbacks, but it wasn't yet eight. My luck might turn again.

I sent Atty down to invite the men inside. Seeing her hesitate, I was impatient. "They're no more than men, Atty. Generals, like any other."

I soon heard her settling them down to breakfast.

"Please don't stand on ceremony, sirs. Help yourselves. My mistress is momentarily indisposed."

Ludicrous, the little distance between my bed and the cross beams above their table. I heard the gallant dismay with which the men learned I would not be joining them, every elegant expression of consideration for my health, and the low, ribald laughter which broke out on Atty's departure from the room.

The four of them finished breakfast and stood to set out for West Point. I had fresh hopes of escape when I heard Hamilton volunteer to stay.

"It seems a little disrespectful that we'd all eat and leave when Mrs. Arnold will be down any minute?"

Washington conceded with some arch remark about his selflessness, and hooves were soon cantering away.

I heard Hamilton throw a log on the fire and sit back down.

I could not afford to be guilty. They could hang me, bayonet my baby. He must not feel a moment's fear or pain. He would not come to harm. If I lost Eddie, I would spend my remaining days in the sin of despair, a spent shell waiting for death. And if I died while he lived, he'd be orphaned, raised either in ignorance of us or punished by the shadow of an executed mother and a disgraced and hated father. He would feel that stigma, be in its bondage, all his life. Only I could instill pride in his parents, love him like a mother, make him strong. I needed to commit, to him, to life. All in. I would draw on my real loss and shock and horror, every fear, every weakness, my ignorance and wickedness, and all my sorry hopes, and from that boiling, roiling brew I'd make it so my being to blame was unimaginable.

There was further risk in that. If I wasn't convincing, I failed again, and that meant more disgrace, more hatred, even Eddie's contempt down the line. Hating me would be a burden I'd spare him for anything. I'd come too far, too long, to give up now. I had an obligation to see this life through. God would judge—people too—but I had to try.

I kissed Eddie and asked Atty to take the baby, my tears already falling.

"Dear Mrs. Arnold, I hate to see your distress, let me find the general—"

"He's gone, Atty. Said he was leaving us, never coming back," I began to whimper. It was exploratory—intentional, but also natural, finally to give in. He had abandoned me. The worst had happened. I turned my face to the wall, away from Atty's worry. I could not let her honest affection break the spell. And I needed her reactions real. There could be no well-meant attempt at acting by her, God bless her. I had to get this right. I'd lose her love if she thought I'd lied and I couldn't bear that.

I reached for the fear I had been keeping tied up inside me and lit it like kindling.

My sob was a spark catching in dry brush. All the worries of the war went up like fire after a drought. I fed the flames with years of stories of horror and the memory of every one of my lies. The truth was I could not be trusted. I had released a plan whose failure had catastrophic ramifications for everyone I loved. I was disgusted by my own arrogance, launching consequences far beyond my imagining. We were ruined. It was my fault, and that nightmare would never end. Thoughts caught like resin, twigs spitting and popping until whole branches exploded, shooting nimble sparks from tree to tree.

I was hysterical now, sobbing hard enough I couldn't breathe. Atty ran for Major Franks.

"Here now, it's Nurse, Mrs. Arnold— Hush now! Please, dear lady, tell us what's wrong."

Franks's kindness only made it worse. He was no longer in Benedict's service and any minute now would realize he owed me nothing. How could he not see? I lashed myself with every instance of his sweet consideration and cried harder still.

"I haven't a friend left in the world—" I choked out, disgusted to sound so pathetic even as my life depended on it.

"You are surrounded by friends," he protested, "Let us help you. You have your husband. Your family. You have me."

The thought of my parents, Neddy and Betsy, Hannah, Bean, and Henry made me cry in pure pain.

Franks went to fetch Dr. Eustice. I heard him cry, "For God's sake, hurry, the lady will die."

My vision was flashing with horrific images, severed limbs, the conviction something even more despicable was about to happen and I was responsible.

Atty ran to the window as another messenger arrived outside. I held my breath and scooched to the back of the bed, hugging my knees and straining to hear as he was shown in to Hamilton downstairs, explaining he had missed Washington on his way from Hartford and followed him here.

The rustle of papers. Expletives from Hamilton. More galloping. The generals returning. Hamilton rushing out to greet them.

Washington's bark of shock, his horror and astonishment.

"Treason, of the blackest dye! Who now can we trust?"

I lay rocking on the bed. Knox called for lockdown. Hamilton shouted he'd catch Benedict. Footsteps coursed through the rooms.

Washington was making a command center of the dining room, marshalling emergency defenses for West Point. Lafayette dictated orders for the entire Continental Army to be ready for deployment at a moment's notice.

Franks arrived back. I could hear the murmur of his low, warm voice at the door with Atty, and then he was beside me.

Tactfully averting his eyes from my state of undress, he informed me gently in his no-nonsense way that Benedict had been involved in a plot to surrender West Point to the British, that he had escaped and was on his way to New York.

I startled like an animal, insensible, tried to dart from the room. Dr. Eustice blocked the stairwell as I tried to head down it, half-naked, restrained only with a struggle by Atty and Franks. At the foot of the stairs, I took in Lafayette's lively interest and poor Washington's appalled embarrassment as he tried to approach.

Seeing that famous face coming toward me triggered a new flight of fear. I ran back for Eddie, scooping him out of his cot and scurrying to the very back of my bed, where I sat bolt upright, kicking at the covers with my feet, clutching the baby close and cowering from the general, who had followed me in concern. Possessed by guilt, both out of my mind and diabolically aware of my situation, using everything real and every bit of artifice in my arsenal, I felt a hot fizzing pressure building in my head, and I pressed my knuckles to my temples to stop it.

"Where is your husband, Mrs. Arnold?" Washington asked. I stared wildly, unhinged by the fact I had no clue. He could be dead by now for all I knew.

Washington took a step toward me, and I was genuinely terrified he'd take Eddie. I turned to Franks in horror. "He comes to kill my baby—"

"No! Dear Madam, no!" Franks soothed. "This is your old friend and his Excellency. He means no such thing." He told the doctor to keep hold of me, and Atty to take Eddie safely to her room.

Washington retreated downstairs to consult with Knox. Franks covered me with the quilt, and followed him, while Dr. Eustice gave me a draught of something which made my limbs leaden but could not stop my mind from turning. I felt a wicked spirit, able to hear what Franks was saying while I lay flat out and staring.

"I am most solemnly and firmly convinced, your Excellency, that General Arnold never confided his detestable scheme to her. He could not have ventured to do it. He was too aware of her warm patriotic feelings—she is so completely an American, sir, and moreover too sensitive to any unpleasantness. Her nerves being what they are, she says all she thinks. I swear she was ignorant of his schemes."

I was ashamed to have Franks defend me. And to be taking the time of a doctor who had men who needed him. I thought with a cry of William. This he'd never forgive.

Knox was now arresting Franks! As Arnold's long-term aides, he and Varick were of course under suspicion; he hoped they understood. I wept to think they were in danger, my Nurse and loyal defender, and Varick, with his fever, who had tried so hard to steer Benedict right.

Was this the horror of the mind Stansbury had described? Guilt felt like demonic possession. As if I'd let evil in. By feigning madness, disrespecting it, it had come for me. However bad I was, I knew I had to hold on to the inner witness, the curious eye which could watch my undoing. I must tell myself I was only going through the motions of insanity, however crazed I felt.

Lafayette came up.

"Ah, my most unhappy Mrs. Arnold. You did not know a word of this conspiracy?"

"Nothing," I gasped. "My husband told me, moments before going away. He said he was flying, never to come back—" My voice sounded unnaturally high. Sobs got the better of me.

Atty interrupted. "He left her here lying quite unconscious. When she came to herself, she fell into frightful convulsions and completely lost her reason. We did everything we could to quiet her."

I whispered with sudden terror. "Murderer! You will murder my husband!"

Atty soothed me back to bed and apologized to the poor marquis.

"Not at all, not at all," he murmured. "The horror with which her husband's conduct has inspired her is a credit to her. I feel only the deepest sympathy for the dear lady, surely the most unhappy of women."

With a last lingering look, he left me to rest.

Chapter Thirty-Two

After several hours' interrogation, Franks came back up to say he and Varick had convinced Washington they had not been involved. Franks blamed himself for not giving more credence to doubts he admitted he'd been having for some time. He murmured he suspected we'd shared a mutual misgiving about the influence of Hett Smith.

"Repellent individual," I said.

Seeing that my fit had subsided, Franks sat beside me and told me all he had gathered of the plot, and its foiling.

As he began I thought of his relish for telling stories about Benedict when we'd first met.

André had woken Hett Smith before dawn: it was time to cover the last five miles of neutral territory to the British line. He'd submitted to Hett Smith's insistence that he cover his uniform with civilian clothes, but told his host he'd go the last stretch alone. He'd made it half the distance when a sudden footfall brought the muzzle of a musket to his face, a patrol of chancer militiamen emerging from the woods. They were a mixed lot, and he'd had to calculate fast. Maintain the civilian pose and risk robbery, proceed with Benedict's pass, or give his true identity? Seeing his accoster's filthy uniform was the green greatcoat of a Hessian, André had flicked his borrowed jacket aside, revealing a flash of scarlet.

"Stand down, men," he had said. "I'm a British officer on the business of the King."

"Did the coat fool you, sir? I had it from my captives."

They were Patriots, released only days ago from the British.

The letter of safe passage signed by Benedict would have diffused the threat, but it was too late to try that now.

That surplus confession—had he panicked, or acted with an excess of his unhelpful integrity, that beautiful, improbable purity leaving him fatally ill-equipped?

We had been a few feet from succeeding!

As it was, the men saw their opportunity to make off with a good pair of British boots and dragged André into the brush to strip him. Beneath the boots, they'd found distended stockings, and within those Benedict's drawings.

The discovery was a windfall bigger than the bandits knew what to do with. After some deliberation, they manhandled André to the command near Tarrytown, delivering him into the custody of Lieutenant Colonel Jameson.

Jameson could see the secreted papers looked dodgy, but he was confused by the pass from Benedict and completely unable to conceive of his beloved general being disloyal. Torn between two courses, he chose both, directing André back to Benedict at the Robinson house under armed guard, while sending the damning papers here to Washington.

Before André's party could travel far in our direction, Washington's beadiest spy, Benjamin Tallmadge, had arrived on routine patrol, and hearing what had happened, immediately grasped Benedict's guilt. He secured André in a Tarrytown gaol before galloping on to Washington's headquarters.

Still, a terminally divided Jameson had felt compelled to alert Benedict to all the morning's suspicious activity and dispatched a messenger to put him in the picture, the very man who arrived exactly as Benedict and Hamilton had sat down for breakfast.

Approaching the fortress across the water, Washington, Lafayette, and Knox had been met by an eerie feeling of abandonment. There was no parade, no ceremonial gunfire, nobody even to help them disembark. They had climbed the steep cliff steps to the fortress courtyard only to be met by long shadows and eerie silence. Benedict wasn't there to welcome them, and nor was anyone else. It occurred to Lafayette they might be about to be ambushed. At last, some unprepossessing character shuffled out to introduce himself as the presiding officer, telling them General Arnold hadn't been seen at West Point these last few days.

Meanwhile, Franks told it, the men from Benedict's barge had almost revolted when he ordered them to row for the *Vulture* with all force, but they too felt compelled to obey their commander and took him far enough he could clamber onto the British ship.

Benedict had been last seen waving a white handkerchief as his boat approached the *Vulture*—a flag of truce so he could board. On deck, he had loudly declared his loyalty to King George III and bowed to Clinton. He shouted down to his oarsmen, promising them amnesty if they would join him. "I'm afraid they let him know where to put that offer," Franks said.

I cringed to think of Benedict feeling the contempt of men who had worshipped him, and of Clinton's sarcastic courtesies. He would detest Benedict for failing. Never forgive him for endangering André.

But would he kill him for it?

I hid my face in my hands, tears and apologies falling again. Franks summed up my bleak situation with such typical candor I had to smile.

"You have lost absolutely everything on which your happiness depends, Mrs. Arnold. It's natural you'd despair."

Later in the afternoon, Hamilton arrived back with letters from my husband, one for Washington and one for me, which had been sent ashore by a flag from the *Vulture*.

Atty brought word that, if I permitted, Washington wished to bring me the correspondence himself.

I tossed the covers from me, catching the acrid scent of my fear. I washed rapidly and cranked open the window, seeing that Atty the saint had already swept the fire. I arranged myself in a clean nightdress back in the bed.

Washington was too tall for that house. He stooped as he came in, bowed, and professed himself glad to find me so much more myself. He seemed to have recovered from his own shock, smiling as he said, "I hope it will help you to know that I have, in accordance with my duty, done all in my power to have your husband arrested. And, not having succeeded, it gives me great pleasure to assure you of his safety."

It was remarkable, the force he presented, the palpable admiration and hopes of so many men carried with him. Light seemed literally to shine more brightly in the room with him in it. How had I missed all he was?

"I'm sorry," I said, with a gesture meant to contain all yesterday's scenes and the extent I'd added to his difficulties.

"Distress is only reasonable, Mrs. Arnold, in the face of unsuspected transactions such as will astonish posterity. Now, though, you are admirably composed, and I shall share with you the letter I've received from your husband:

'On board the Vulture, September 25, 1780.

Sir,—The heart, which is conscious of its own rectitude, cannot attempt to palliate a step which the world may censure as wrong. I have acted from a principle of love to my country since the commencement of the present unhappy contest between Great Britain and the colonies. The same principle of love to my country dictates my present conduct, however it may appear inconsistent to the world, who very seldom judge right of any man's actions.'

I did not like his self-righteous tone. My cheeks burned, I kept my eyes down.

"'I have no favor to ask for myself, I have too often experienced the ingratitude of my country to attempt it—'"

We both looked sideways at that.

"'—but, from the known humanity of your Excellency, I am induced to ask your protection for Mrs. Arnold, from every insult and injury that a mistaken vengeance of my country may expose her to. It ought to fall only on me; she is as good and as innocent as an angel—'"

I covered my face with my hands.

"'—and incapable of doing wrong. I beg you let her either return to Philadelphia or to me in New York as she may choose. From your Excellency I have no fears on her account, but she may suffer from the mistaken fury of the country . . .'"

I started. Images suddenly of mobs with pitchforks, the whoops of hunters with quarry cornered. Washington was going on:

"'In justice to the gentlemen of my family, Colonel Varick and Major Franks, I think myself in honor bound to declare that they, as well as Joshua Hett Smith, Esq. (who I know is suspected), are totally ignorant of any transactions of mine.'"

I didn't like Hett Smith bundled in, contaminating Franks and Varick by proximity. Benedict made a closing plea for the release of André, confessing he had been traveling under his flag and only forced into disguise against his will.

It took all I had not to ask what Washington intended for his prisoner as he handed me the separate letter Benedict had enclosed for me.

His kindness was its own punishment. There was no escaping his dignity, his decency, the inevitability of his prevailing in the end.

* * *

My letter from Benedict felt written for the benefit of anyone who might read it as much as for me:

> *Thou loveliest and best of women. Words are wanting to express my feelings and distress on your account, who are incapable of doing wrong yet are exposed to suffer wrong. I have requested his Excellency General Washington to take you under his protection and permit you to go to your friends in Philadelphia—or to come to me. I am at present incapable of giving advice. Follow your own intentions. But do not forget that I shall be miserable until we meet. Adieu—kiss my dear boy for me. God Almighty bless and protect you, sincerely prays, Thy affectionate and devoted, B. Arnold. Write me one line if possible, to ease my anxious heart.*

Relief he was safe gave way to anger. He had known Washington well; how could he have allowed me to misjudge him so badly?

We had mocked Washington before, his pomposity, pink cheeks, and that oddly big bottom, his formality and relentless eye on posterity. Those insults were jokes on us now. It had been easy for me—so often flooded with emotion—to mistrust the dispassionate commander—until I saw him navigating this crisis.

I understood now how people came to feel devotion, how reassuring the surrender to such a figure could be. By some miracle, the colonies had been sent the leader they needed, a man who, however he was lauded, would never agree to be the American King so many wanted, a man who would surely eventually check the fresh tyranny of figures like Reed.

Knox came in then, such a different profile from the other men, rotund and amiable and full of sympathetic fluster.

"What a business this is. The greatest and strangest betrayal in modern history. I don't like to think of it. I met André myself, you know—"

I hadn't known, but was curious, and Knox I liked already.

"Yes, my dear! We spent a very pleasant evening early in the war—talked all night—and it was only leaving the inn I realized his affiliation. Remarkable thing. And of course, I know your husband very well—"

He was flustered briefly by the unspoken *or thought I did*, before tactfully continuing. "He was good enough to see my life—I should say my wife, Lucy—and toddler, not much older than your boy, safely into Philadelphia after we took—retook—the city. Not a man on the planet I'd have trusted more with the task. And at his court martial, he defended himself so effectively I swore all charges would be cleared. That gift to likeably annihilate the liars! All of which is to say, you mustn't reproach yourself, dear girl. We all thought the world of him, none of us could have known.

"And I reproach myself my dear: I knew he was under pressure—enough to break any man—we all did—but in the constant hurly burly I didn't ask—didn't take the time—to find out how he was really managing, what he was thinking . . . Who's to say how that might have helped? Or if more might have been done to relieve him of worry about money."

What might have been avoided if they had talked honestly? If his friends had known how desperate Benedict had been not to humiliate his sons, leave them half-educated, as he had been? If they had listened, intervened against Reed? The slights had festered in my husband, eaten at him like infection, and it had all been so unnecessary.

Perhaps he had overreacted to his own father's example. Perhaps I had.

Knox gave my hand on the bedspread a rapid pat.

"Now I mustn't monopolize you. There are far more handsome men wanting to alleviate your anxiety—not that I'm suggesting that's your priority."

We exchanged an awkward smile, and I thanked him.

Hamilton came by next, as I was feeding Eddie. Was it only curiosity, or were they competing, petitioning me? One after another, jostling for place in this story, pointless, voiceless as I'd be.

He sat on the end of the bed, seemingly unaware he was shifting a little nearer all the time.

"My dear, Mrs. Arnold, I'm glad to gather you feel a little better. You know, I went in pursuit of your husband but was much too late. Seeing his lovely young bride, I can hardly regret having failed in my mission. Though a traitor to his country and to his fame, a disgrace to his connections—"

I gave a little cry and raised my hand, beseeching him to stop. Eddie looked up in shock to have his milk stopped and started to fuss.

"I hate to see you so"—Hamilton stared—"so frantic with distress for the loss of a husband you tenderly loved."

I lifted my breast back so Eddie could continue.

"Such a fond mother." Hamilton sighed, his tenderness and desire very evident. I kept my eyes on the baby.

"And Major André, hey. What a fellow. I can understand how Benedict became susceptible. I told Eliza—who I know would send you her best. I told her I wished I could be André myself, to be able to charm her as he would *in every sense*—"

He was elsewhere, imagining God knows what.

"How is Eliza? Have you set a date? She's a wonderful woman."

He looked at me in surprise, his mind evidently still in his reverie. The confusion he felt between thoughts of André, mention of Eliza, and discovering himself closer to a half-dressed woman than was right should have been funny.

Lafayette also came back, lamenting the happier times when we had danced and my tact at how badly he did.

"I hate to see you so distressed, but I cannot be sorry we are here, able to give you comfort and the mercy you deserve."

I heard the pair of them later murmuring in the corridor.

"It was the most affecting scene I ever was witness to," said Hamilton. "Would have pierced insensibility itself."

"Her face and youthfulness make her so interesting . . ." Lafayette agreed.

A wicked part of me was sorry Benedict had lived. A traitor's wife could only be exiled; a traitor's widow might have a second act. The idea of him dying, or suffering, was unthinkable. I could not go there. But I was not above imagining a reality from which he had been dispatched.

The next morning, I woke early, groggy from whatever the doctor had ordered, but grateful to have slept at all.

It was not yet dawn and the house was quiet. I watched sunrise dim the moon, and the pink river turn gray blue. For the first time the Hudson's beauty seemed cruel.

If my thoughts strayed, my nerves threatened to undo me again, so I willed myself to think only of the details immediately in my control.

Washington was for now persuaded of my innocence; I had that.

I wasn't safe though, not so long as André was in captivity: His interrogation might already have revealed my complicity.

I didn't believe he'd deliberately expose me, but given the blunder of his capture, I couldn't be confident he wouldn't let a detail slip. What if General Washington got hold of André's intelligence book? Or the letters Benedict and I had sent to him?

If Washington came to suspect I'd been dissembling with him yesterday, he would be within his rights to kill me. If he found out Benedict had gone as far as to plan his own capture—that we might have had him ambushed in our house—well, I knew there were limits to his decency.

He must never suspect.

When Atty brought water, I told her the men should be served a second day's breakfast, laying out every good thing I'd had in mind for Clinton and André. Atty had grown in confidence, bringing a little flourish to her interactions with the great men now.

Meanwhile, I washed, pinned my hair, and changed into one of the nightdresses Stansbury had made. What of him, and of Odie? Could André ensure they were protected even if he was released? Would he have logged their names along with ours?

Once the men had eaten, I summoned one after the other of those founding fathers to apologize.

"Dear Lafayette. I would like to say sorry for the state you found me in yesterday. I hope I might briefly seek your counsel on my best strategy of protection for my son."

"It would be exceedingly painful to General Washington if you were not treated with the greatest kindness."

"But Lafayette, there might be limits on the extent even of his Excellency's influence—in his absence. You know the sentiments of the people and of the Assembly of Pennsylvania. Your influence and your opinion, emphatically expressed, may prevent me from being visited with a vengeance which my son at least does not deserve."

"General Washington will protect you," he assured me. "As for myself, you know that I have always been fond of you, and at this moment you interest us all intensely. We are certain you knew nothing of the plot, and you have my assurances, Madam, we will do all in our power to ensure that message is disseminated and secures your safety."

Hamilton next. I confided to him that "added to my other distresses, I am very apprehensive the resentment of the country will fall upon me (who is only unfortunate) for the guilt of my husband."

Hamilton too tried to persuade me that my fears were ill founded. He declared he wished himself my brother, to see to it I was forever defended.

"I beg you, let me give you proof of my friendship! Could I forgive Arnold for sacrificing his honor, reputation, and duty, I could not forgive him for acting a part that must have forfeited the esteem of so fine a woman. At present you almost forget his crime in your misfortunes, and your horror at the guilt of the traitor is lost in your love of the man. But a virtuous mind cannot long esteem a base one, and time will make you despise, if it cannot make you hate."

"I do despise the bribery and corruption," I said honestly, "base arts to accomplish what I would wish were done in a more manly way."

Hamilton leaned forward and lowered his voice. "In truth, the authorized maxims and practices of war countenance almost every species of seduction as well as violence, and the general who can make the most traitors in the army of his adversary is frequently most applauded. This is the fate of war."

He was so like André. Principled, but supple too. He saw the hypocrisy, and all that typically went unsaid—and was clear on the need there'd be to perform national outrage too.

I thanked him. I had almost pulled it off. Now there was just the commander left to see.

Washington said he would do as my husband had asked and give me this choice: return to my father's home in Philadelphia or join Benedict in New York City.

My dismay was real. Neither prospect inviting.

"My dear," he said kindly. "What will you do? Make for your parents?"

"Won't Joseph Reed kill me, if I do?"

"Reed? No! Assuredly not."

Even if I didn't resent Benedict, I could not see going to New York without forfeiting Washington's goodwill. A girl betrayed as I'd been could only be wanting her family. Philadelphia it must be.

"I will take the baby to my parents," I said, leaning back on the pillow. "Thank you."

"I'll see to it."

He talked me calmly through the logistics. Word would be sent ahead (my stomach contracted picturing my parents' reaction). Franks would accompany me, along with Eddie and Atty, and we would break our journey in New Jersey, with a stop at Theodosia Provost's. Beverley Robinson would be releasing us from our tenancy. And a new commander would be found for West Point.

"More than that, I cannot say, but I wish you well, my dear, and hope we'll meet again in happier circumstances."

I maintained my composure while he was with me, but as soon as the door closed, I cried as if I'd just left my Maker.

He would soon remind me he could be merciless too.

Chapter Thirty-Three

Preparing for our departure, gathering Eddie's clothes and comforters, something caught my eye on the floor by my bed. It was a playing card. A joker. Probably it had been set aside from a fresh deck on our journey from Philadelphia, but it felt like the signature of a trickster, a sinister wink at more trouble to come.

Richard arrived to carry down my luggage. I admired his quiet composure, his tact and dignity, and I wondered where he put the fury he must feel. What did we look like to him? Pale-faced fools with our cloaks and maps and plans—all in a hurry for money and the mirage of no worries. Drawing lines on a map and making it so, moving troops like checkers, scheming in secret, dodging anything resembling bondage, while speaking as if we were at risk of it and benefiting from all those still in it. I thought again of those nuns. It would be nice to have some systematic recourse to penance and forgiveness.

I thanked him and gave him a look which I hoped conveyed my respect and regret. And then I felt ashamed again, asking him to condone me.

I settled into the carriage and hoisted Eddie onto the seat beside me. Washington's familiar slave, William Lee, appeared, and my stomach plunged, fearing a change of heart from the commander. He could use me or the baby as a pawn for the return of Benedict. He could detain me, given André's evidence. I would take anything he dealt except separation from my son.

But Lee had only come to help Franks with the horses. I didn't breathe until the wheels began to roll.

At the mouth of the drive, we met a column of a hundred men on horses turning in. Up front was Tallmadge, behind him a mounted prisoner with hands tied: André! On his way to be interviewed by Washington.

I saw his beautiful face, head bowed, rallying in surprise at seeing me. His eyes searched mine, mine his, seeking reassurance, trading apologies. He gave the saddest, sweetest smile, and before I could blink, he had passed me.

He would be under my roof tonight, so nearly exactly as anticipated, making one more mockery of my dreams.

It was an exhausting journey back to New Jersey, traveling with no hope through a military presence heavier than ever. I felt like a veteran with nothing left, and then more shame, for making the comparison. People in the street we passed hissed, and five times Franks was turned away when trying to buy food. The public were reacting to Benedict's betrayal with almost manic Patriotism, women fashioning their hair into tricorns and flags abounding.

Finally, Franks returned with a basket of bread and cheese.

"Compliments of a Mr. Reed—"

"That was the name? Our savior?"

It would be so easy to go mad for real. The joke of all the shared names: Howe and Howe. Clinton and Clinton; Carlisle and Carlisle. I was one of an entire tribe of Peggys in the colonies. My mother's namesake from the moment I was born. There wouldn't be another Benedict Arnold christened though, I'd bet, not for centuries, if ever.

Theodosia helped me out of the carriage. I hugged her, making some disparaging reference to the state of my appearance.

"Really? Given all that's going on?"

Theodosia's mother embraced me too and said she'd take Eddie while we girls settled in.

"Thank you."

She nodded at her daughter. "There was a brief time I cared for her every need. It's my treat when I can still help."

I felt a little fresh stab of self-pity at the prospect of my reception by my parents, but there was comfort, for all my fear and remorse, in being back in a household of strong women, surrounded by the understated loveliness of all things Theodosia. I felt as mute as I had been voluble on my last visit, and grateful to my friend, who busied herself with Eddie so that he wouldn't be disquieted by the slack-armed, blank-eyed mother I'd become.

"Sorry, Theo."

"No. You must be wiped out—"

"I never felt so tired. All these months straining and afraid, and for this, worse than nothing. It feels like grief after a long disease—"

"Oh Peggy, you won't go to Benedict? Isn't that better than your parents?"

"It wouldn't be wise. In Washington's eyes—"

"You did well to get out of there—"

"I'm not proud of how. Not proud of any of it. What would you have done differently?" I asked.

"I might have worked a bit harder at Washington before enlisting André. You had such favor from him."

I nodded. "I saw a break and found that I could. Obviously, an unreliable moral compass—"

"Peggy, you can worry all your life you won't get things right, hesitate at every crossroads forever. At a certain point you commit to a path and try it."

"I think I'd been obsessed with André. Infatuated. Ready, honestly, to have him on any terms. I think the war made me a bit insane, on top of the boys going. I was desperate to make sense of all that history. Let nothing lost go to waste—"

"Losing anyone young throws off your sense of time, and then war, foreshortening everything—"

"Benedict was so steadying—made me feel safe—held. Let me believe myself a good person. Truly beautiful. Hah. And when he was compromised, I didn't like it."

"Drunk?"

"Undone, at times. Haunted. He'd killed forty men, Theo. Boys. Imagine them laid out before you. The horror of it. And Reed kept coming for him.

Every day. The papers, the charges, the threats. I felt I was on a runaway horse, just longing to get off. And when Washington let Benedict down, I wanted to help him, and selfishly, to feel him have the upper hand again. Because when the power left him, it frightened me. I didn't know how to be me, seeing him not himself. I worried he'd succumb to despair, or pickle himself with drink. I didn't trust myself to take care of him, not reduced like that, a big infant twice my age. I wanted him strong. Loved him confident. All I could think was with peace would come freedom, from all the fighting and fear, and he could build, and sail and trade and be my maximum man. And then once I was pregnant, all my dreams of peace felt only right and reasonable and newly urgent too. I wanted protection, more shelter than I felt from Benedict, who couldn't get Reed off his back, make Congress pay him or Washington listen, and all the time just over there was André, at the top of his game, trying to end it, sympathetic to me, solicitous of Benedict. Stansbury had taught me code, and when I saw West Point, and had the notion, floated it. Hoped to help—"

"I see that."

"Five more minutes, and André would have made it."

The evening was finally bringing relief, with our shoes discarded and toes tucked under us, when suddenly the dogs were barking and Aaron Burr appeared, his patrician figure filling the door to the little sitting room and casting a long shadow where we sat.

"Peggy Shippen Arnold. Fancy finding you here."

I stood out of respect, feeling naked in my stockinged feet.

"Good to see you, Aaron. All you've achieved since we last saw each other—"

He gripped my shoulders and kissed the air by both my cheeks before addressing himself exclusively to Franks, who was hovering behind him protectively, establishing the latest regarding Benedict.

"Major. Was he paid?"

"I believe so, sir. They say twenty thousand—"

"In the event of success. Less, for failure."

Burr looked down at me. "Five thousand, I'd wager, along with an infinite fund of British scorn. And André?" he asked. "Tallmadge has him?"

"Yes, sir. As we left, he was arriving with General Washington for questioning."

"Tallmadge and André must have a lot to discuss. British intelligence won't recover from this."

"No, sir."

"Tallmadge sees all manner of men in his line, but I bet he hasn't met a spy as disingenuous as André." He looked again at me. "Or as good-looking?"

"Nathan Hale was a handsome man," Theodosia observed, trying to keep the conversation light.

"Another man too memorable to have been a sensible choice for a spy," Burr winked. "Again with the theatrical bent."

"That flamboyance makes sense," Theo said. "An interest in performance, disguise, a knack for memorizing lines."

"Painstaking detail and a steady head would better serve in that game."

"For a man who gave his life, Hale was oddly ambivalent," Theodosia said. "He wrote that while he felt a great state might arise in America, he was not always convinced the Patriots would be within their rights to deliver it."

"Do you remember the case of Nathan Hale, Peggy?" Aaron asked, as if my hearing were impaired. "He was entrapped in conversation, tricked into confessing his allegiance, caught behind enemy lines in disguise."

"Yes."

"And you remember the sequel?"

"Well, yes. He was hanged. But André was apprehended in the line of duty. Benedict gave him the pass. Franks said he didn't choose to be disguised—"

Burr interrupted me and turned to Franks. "Right, Major. Enough playing nursemaid. You have standing to recover back at camp. I will personally see that Peggy is deposited with her parents."

It felt fair that everything be taken away, but hard to do justice to my gratitude to Franks while Burr looked on with contempt. Franks stammered his good wishes and it was all I could do not to cry.

I was mortified by Aaron's dislike, and sorry for Theodosia's sake he didn't think better of me.

Once Franks had gone, he yawned, stretching his arm along the back of the chair he shared with Theodosia.

"What was Benedict thinking writing down the plans? Why was André not clever enough to memorize them? Nothing of consequence can be written down when it might be intercepted. Even private journals might fall into the wrong hands."

"I did wonder the same thing," Theodosia said.

Burr looked at his watch and sighed, a pantomime of the busy man. Theo saw the gesture but seemed to forgive it. She was clearly all-in.

"When it comes to secrets, better even than code is conversation," he said. "Everything then is deniable. I can't imagine how Benedict missed the memo. Never write anything down which might show a man's hand. For instance, one wouldn't write 'Peggy is a stupid woman,' but one might say so."

I stood and said goodnight. Theodosia followed. "Don't mind him, Peggy. He feels the betrayal, naturally, and can't help the acid asides. He has such discipline about avoiding risk, he can't forgive more dangerous plays."

"If you can, would you see if you can help Stansbury and Odie?"

"Don't punish yourself, Peggy. Don't feel less than—" She gave a tiny gesture to Burr downstairs, the concessions, and compromises. "We're all of us sinners."

"Yes, but you're so much better at being shameless about it!"

She laughed.

"The pitiful thing is I'd envisioned this visit in the event of success. I'd rehearsed the thanks I'd give you for the encouragement and friendship which helped me see peace achieved. I wanted to be some credit to you. To impress Aaron."

"You can't waste your days in guilt and remorse. I have had enough nights like that, torturing myself over mistakes big and small, but this life is very short, and we cannot spend it stooping under our shame with stricken expressions. You can be sorry for the outcome, but not the intention. I am proud of you. Most people look at the world only to see how they might get advantage. Your ambition was—"

"Stupid and vain—"

"Beautiful and brave."

"I was wrong, to be so vague about the details. I left him to it—the baby my alibi against responsibility. I knew Benedict's exhaustion and volatility might mean risk. I feared some precaution might get missed. Perhaps if I'd listened to the visceral antipathy I felt meeting Hett Smith and insisted Benedict personally protect André—"

"It's only reasonable you left arrangements to the men. Anything else risked oversteering. It was chance bandits betrayed André, and his error, not any mistake of your own."

"The dreadful thing is that in trying to protect Eddie, I've made him more vulnerable than he's ever been—"

"It's not impossible you'll come to feel glad you were thwarted. This world's so topsy-turvy—"

"Will you look after the baby, Theo, if anything happens to me?"

"Peggy, don't. It won't—"

"Theodosia?" Burr was summoning her to bed.

She went to join him. I heard them behind the door.

"You could have been kinder, Aaron. I fear for her, and Benedict."

"Washington's not going to make a martyr of her, or Arnold," Burr said. "But the price of her husband's life will be her first love's neck."

Leaving Theodosia was the hardest departure yet. I knew on some level I'd never see her again, and my head ached like it would break.

"Good Luck, Godspeed, and God bless," she said, with three kisses, as we waited for Aaron. "And write to me? If ever you need reminding?"

"Not to be bitter? I didn't imagine that commitment would be so tested."

"It might face worse pressure yet," Theo said, and I winced.

"Treason doth never prosper—what's the reason? If it doth prosper, none dare call it treason."

"Bloody Crambo," I said, and we laughed. "Thank you. For everything. I think I remember every word you've ever said."

"Oh, don't do that," she laughed. "I can't!"

I embraced her a final time, both our cheeks wet with tears. After a last squeeze, I stepped back, straightened my shoulders, and climbed into the carriage, where she passed Eddie to me.

Burr sat opposite, peering under his lids, the ghost of a smile on his lips, feigning sleep, as we rattled through New Jersey.

We'd no sooner reached the turnpike than the air yellowed and stilled; the clouds bruised first orange then deep mauve. Turkey vultures circled in the eerie light. The ominous pause before a downpour. The gathering pressure I had felt was obviously not only in my head.

At the first massive clap, Burr opened his eyes. I snuggled Eddie under my cape and threw a shawl around Atty as the rain began to fall in heavy curtains, lashing so hard and fast we could not see a thing.

It was a storm so severe and so timely, such a punishing piece of pathetic fallacy, in a novel I'd have rolled my eyes at the device.

We pulled over under a large yew, the road washing out before our eyes. Poor sodden Atty clambered inside the carriage, and Burr moved over to sit beside me. The driver explained there could be no proceeding without risking the horses losing their footing and tipping the carriage into a ditch.

"We're sitting ducks," Burr said. Fair game, I thought, for any Indians Washington had left living.

Burr insisted the driver make slowly for the nearest inn rather than linger in what was very dangerous territory. With a curse he took no trouble to keep from me, the driver complied, and we rolled blindly forward along the potholed road, while I imagined any minute a vengeful face would appear grinning at the carriage window to do as he would with us, and Burr kept his eyes on me. His attention on that painfully slow stretch of road became more persistent.

When at last we pulled into the carriage courtyard, Burr said we'd be wise to disguise my identity.

"Your husband is now the most wanted man in America." He actually licked his lips. "Prudence insists we present as a married couple."

"Or I could be your sister," I said. "A friend of your wife—"

But he snatched my hand and held it fast in his lap, making his intentions revoltingly apparent. The contempt in it, for me, for Eddie, for Atty. For Theodosia! He smiled, confident I'd never upset Theo by telling her. Knowing, if I told anyone else, the stigma would stick only to me. I was meant to feel how far I had fallen. Atty was meant to see. I held myself rigid, the hand he held in his lap clenched closed while the driver went in to inquire about rooms, returning to let us know they had one double. Burr climbed down and, with ironic courtesy, raised a hand for mine. I clambered down, Eddie under one arm, Atty's eyes locked horrified on mine.

When we reached the inn's entrance, I begged him, rain streaming down my face, for the sake of Theodosia and my parents, who had taken him in as an orphan, that he leave me in peace.

In his parting gesture that was pure Burr, he gave the innkeeper my real name.

"Well then, I must entrust the defector general's wife to you, sir. I'm sure you'll show Mrs. Arnold every courtesy she's right to expect." And with that he retreated to the carriage.

It was me, Atty, and Eddie then, alone in hostile territory. Fear of violent reprisal was not hysterical. I could not expect the respect I'd had from the four generals out here.

"Ready the top floor suite for Mrs. Arnold," the innkeeper said with a slow smile for me and a wink to the sullen serving girl.

Twenty long minutes later she was ready to lead me there. Conversation stopped at each table as we passed, and we were shown up back stairs to a dank room high in the house.

My candle caught dead flies on windowsills, mouse droppings along the baseboard. Atty and I shared a cold supper of lardy bacon, soggy broccoli, and apple pie (a slice I'd swear had been rescued unfinished from another plate) and settled Eddie into the center of the bed, where we lay flanking him to stop him from rolling onto the nail-spiked floor.

The pillows had long since lost all plumpness and smelled of dirty hair, regret, and furtive desire. The place was filthy with every dispiriting detail Benedict had tried to guard against on our journey to West Point.

The innkeeper knocked abruptly at our door and in a sardonic drawl regretted to say my reputation had preceded me and, in his courtyard, they were chanting for Margaret Arnold. If I'd be so kind as to follow him, I'd find abundant and painful evidence of the popular indignation against my husband. He thought it better I should address the gathering, rather than risk them storming his building or burning it down.

I put on my cloak, tucked Eddie under it, and instructed Atty to barricade herself in and make a rope of the filthy sheets so that in the event of fire, she could climb out of the garret window.

I followed our host to the front door. My legs threatened to buckle when I heard the size of the crowd angrily chanting my name. The innkeeper pushed open the door and introduced me with clumsy flourish to the torch-wielding mob, who fell into an uneasy, shifting sea of quiet, out of which erupted the odd haranguing shout.

They had a crude and ugly effigy of Benedict, which they lowered, though not out of sight. I saw as many women as men, and plenty of children, blood up, eyes glistening at a chance to vent their frustration on the common object they had in me.

To my surprise, I felt myself getting stronger in the face of my name. Though my fear of their hate was real, I felt possessed by a calm and practical understanding that maternal devotion would be my best defense. The picture of innocence assailed was in my repertoire after all.

So I was deferential to the crowd and told them the truth, up to a point. I said I understood their outrage. I was aware my son and I were dependent on their mercy. I begged them to believe my mortification, and my shame, and my regret at my husband's betrayal, and I prayed for their kindness tonight.

Judging that enough—both overcome, and acting overcome—I stepped inside, while the innkeeper conferred with the ringleader. I took Eddie back to Atty, made a sling for him and tied it to her, and told her to wait by the window and be ready if the crowd tried to breach our door.

I could hear outbreaks of shrill insults and low hollering for revenge on the traitor Arnold. I heard the innkeeper pleading for his property and the answering obscenities—and, gradually, fading chants for me. After what felt hours, the host returned. It seemed my "sad face and sorrowful air had touched the hearts of the people. With a delicacy and consideration honorable to the American character, they would postpone the exhibition until after our departure."

He offered me a drink with him; I declined.

Back in bed, keeping vigil as Atty and Eddie slept, I felt the wind getting up again, whipping the rain against our window. Buffeted by gusts, I felt chivvied from the bed, from the inn, which itself felt tipped downhill. I wasn't wanted, there or anywhere. The wind seemed to try every window until it settled into the dull roar of steady heavy rain, a downpour so relentless I worried it would collapse the roof.

I made myself brave thinking of Benedict's long winter through the woods to Quebec. The catastrophe of his failure there and what it must have been to make the thankless march home.

I would hold it together for Eddie.

Chapter Thirty-Four

Leaving the inn the next day, the leader of my little party for the first time in my life, I allowed myself a small surge of excitement. I had dodged a bullet from that crowd, repelled Burr, and escaped Washington. Forward motion alone was a relief. And whatever else, this was an adventure.

With every mile we traveled nearer Philadelphia, I felt the confidence in my competence recede and the old childhood shame and fear take root. I was returning at nineteen, in ruin and disgrace, a lower-class citizen than I'd left, an unwelcome guest in the house I'd once dared be impatient to leave. All my happiness at marrying Benedict, my pride in having the protection of a general, heckled me now.

Every control post, every ragged band of militia, every sign of strain and deprivation on the passing faces mirrored my failure.

I felt propelled back in time, against nature—uncomfortably redependent on my parents. Guilty, too, that my presence in the house could be dangerous for them. Tensions would be higher than ever in Philadelphia, and I could imagine Reed's ecstasy of outrage at Benedict's defection. He would want his satisfaction now.

It was a further kind of torture to realize the worst place I could be was the only place I could go.

It was dark by the time we pulled outside the house, and my parents came to the door together. I was touched to see how they'd aged over the last year and felt a flood of love.

They hurried me into the hall and closed the door, my father muttering about furious neighbors. "The public clamor is high."

"Anger toward the two of you," Mother clarified as she took my cloak.

"Generally better you're not seen," Father confirmed.

Eddie woke, blinking, and I propped him up in my arms to face them. My father gave a brief, unguarded smile, but my delight was soon stifled by the fuss Mother was making about the difficulty in accommodating Atty.

"There's no place for her here, Peggy. We hired a new girl."

"Please, Mamma, she can sleep in my bed. Don't send her out tonight—"

"Don't worry on my account," Atty said kindly. "I can go to my family."

"Please," I said. "At least until morning—"

"It's better for Atty herself she's not seen here," Father said. I asked him if he could please loan me something for her severance, after all the time and kindness and courage she'd shown, and he retreated to his office to fetch payment. The whole transaction made me ashamed of myself, and I thought my heart would break seeing Atty say goodbye to the baby, and to be saying another final farewell myself.

As Father shut the door on her, I felt my last tether had been cut.

We were all quiet during supper.

My father reached over. "It's good to have you safely back."

A portcullis clanged down in my mother.

"How do you imagine Benedict will be faring?"

"He's a British brigadier now. He'll fight for their side."

"You say that as if it's a good thing."

"He's alive. He has work. But no, no, it's a disaster, I know. I'm sorry. I was trying to put a better complexion on it. I know I've been a disappointment, brought you shame, and danger, and I'm so sorry. Perhaps I overstate the good trying to compensate—"

"You'll remember where to find your room. I left a copy of the paper you ought to see."

With a look at her husband that left him in no doubt he should follow her, she went upstairs.

"You must have met a lot of interesting people?" my father said, turning back from the door.

"Yes," I said, inadequately.

On my bed was *The Pennsylvania Packet* of September 30, 1780:

Our correspondent concludes with a remark on the fallacious and dangerous sentiments so frequently avowed in this city that female opinions are of no consequence in public matters.

The Romans thought far otherwise, or we should not have heard of the Clelias and Cornelias and Anias of antiquity; and had we thought and acted like them we should have despised and banished from social intercourse every character, whether male or female, which could be so lost to virtue decency and humanity, as to revel with the plunderers of their countrymen. Behold the consequence. Col. Andrie under the mask of Friendship and former acquaintance at Meschianzas and Balls opens a correspondence in August 1779 with Mrs. Arnold, which has doubtless been improved on his part to the dreadful and horrid issue we have described, and which but for the overruling care of a kind Providence, must have involved this country and our Allies in great distress, and perhaps utter ruin.

I had done my hair in childish braids, one of the few styles I could manage without Atty, and a pathetically transparent bid to appeal to my parents' earliest affection, when my father came to tell me that Reed had been calling for my removal. He and Neddy had prevailed on the Council for now to concede I could stay in the city on condition I renounce all contact with Benedict for the remainder of the war.

"Not one letter, Peggy—you understand?"

I nodded numbly, one fat tear staining the paper as I turned to reading Washington's statement on Benedict's defection in *The Packet*. He declared "the discovery of Arnold's plot evidence the liberties of America are the object of divine protection."

I was trying to fathom my indefinite sentence, suspended between child and wife and widow, under parental house arrest, when Neddy and Betsy arrived to see me. Introducing them to the baby gave a little distraction from the unbearable kindness and sympathy in their eyes. I was unraveling to infancy myself and didn't trust myself to speak. Once we were all seated, I looked to them to take the lead with news from their own lives. Instead, Neddy began with André, talking steadily and quietly, sharing everything he knew.

"After being interviewed by Tallmadge, he was transferred to a prison in Tappan, free to read and draw and talk, visited by friends, and kept abreast of every development. He'd admitted, 'I am too little accustomed to duplicity to have succeeded.'"

Clinton appealed for André's life, saying of Washington "he seems a moderate man."

Washington sent the major breakfast from his own table every morning during his captivity.

New York's Loyalist governor, Robertson, had met with Patriot Major General Nathaniel Greene in neutral Dobb's Ferry to discuss André's fate.

Greene had been heard to exclaim, "Good God, what a *Coup manqué*! Had it succeeded, all agree it would have finished the rebellion immediately."

"Benedict volunteered to trade places," Neddy added.

I looked up in surprise. Was that self-sacrifice? Had I made him despair, in choosing to go to my parents instead of him? Did he know he wouldn't hear from me? That no word of his would reach me here? Was my husband about to die? André to live?

"Did Clinton say yes?" I managed.

Neddy shook his head.

"I imagine he was tempted, but felt Britain must be seen to honor its agreements with informers. They wouldn't want to deter future defectors."

"What will Clinton do with Benedict then?"

"He will pay out the reward, but Benedict will be their mercenary, fighting for the King against the men he once led, as long as the war lasts, as long as he lives."

Eliza had written Hamilton appealing for her old friend's life. Beverley Robinson also tried to intercede. Tallmadge, André's supposedly supremely cynical counterpart, had become so deeply attached to his prisoner that he'd admitted he could remember no instance when his affections had been so fully absorbed in any man.

André was closely informed of every effort at intervention and of the Patriots' convening at Tappan to decide his fate. He wrote to Clinton securing compensation for his mother and sisters, and to Washington, pleading, if there could be no reprieve, to be executed as an officer—by firing squad—not hanged like a spy or common criminal. Washington could see no way around the fact André was captured in disguise, and therefore decreed he must be executed as spies are executed, by standing them on the back of a cart with a noose around their neck.

Time passes so strangely in shock. Facts relayed in seconds I'd reckon with the rest of my life.

"You're sure? Not a cruel rumor—"

"I'm so sorry, Peggy. He was admired by his Patriot captors, as much as by the whole British presence in America. I know I've never met his like and won't again. Nobody wanted him to die, but there was no mercy the commander could justify. When it was clear there would be no reprieve, the major faced the end with calm curiosity and bravery, always wanting to put his friends at ease, to lift spirits with a gentle joke. He extemporized his final night, talking as he always did with his love of life, his gentle, funny, original poet's soul. He was devoid of artifice, natural in a way which won the affection of even the most weary and cynical men."

"His final night?"

"I'm so very sorry, Peggy. They took him from the stone house in which he was confined. André, most elegantly dressed in his full regimentals, marched more than a mile from his prison to the place of execution with as much ease and cheerfulness as if he had been going to an assembly room, saluting the mounted Continental officers that lined his route and making a particularly courteous bow to the members of the board that had condemned him. An army wagon was placed under a tree in the middle of the field. When he first saw the gallows, his legs buckled, just for a second. He stepped backward to steady himself, and the officers murmured some explanation of protocol. He said gently, 'I know. I know. It is only I detest this mode.' He gave a last strong stride up onto the wagon and once he was squarely under the gallows, he placed the rope around his own neck.

"Colonel Scammell, presiding, told André he might speak to the spectators, at which the major looked out into our faces, acknowledging all present—and with a lightness, almost a smile, he said, 'Bear me witness that I meet my fate like a brave man.'

"He took from his pocket two white handkerchiefs; with one he tied his own blindfold with perfect firmness, the other he gave to the marshal, who pinioned his arms. And then the wagon was immediately moved from under him.

"His body was placed in a coffin and buried at the foot of the gallows.

"Hamilton said, 'Never, perhaps, did any man suffer death with more justice, or deserve it less.' Clinton calls it murder.

"It's done, Peggy. He's at rest."

Neddy had ridden through the night to tell me. The courage in that. The risk he'd taken. My sister hugged my heaving shoulders from behind while Neddy held out a folded paper.

"He drew a quick self-portrait after that last breakfast. He said he hoped he had been the loyal friend to you that you'd been to him."

In the picture, André sat at a writing table, his legs lightly crossed, one elbow resting on the back of his chair, his body arranged with careless grace. The weight of the moment was there in his face, but he held his head straight.

At dinner, against all convention, I sat the baby on my lap like a shield.

"He makes a fine Edward," Father declared with satisfaction.

"I named him for you," I said, "and for you, too, Neddy."

"He looks rather like William," Mother said.

"Hardly any Benedict at all!" I said lightly. Only Neddy smiled.

My mother sighed. "If only you had never married that man."

Regretting the wedding, even as I held their grandchild in my arms, felt wrong to the cosmos. As my defenses rose, I felt my feelings for Benedict stir.

"I was always so fond of the major. Do you remember how you cried for him?"

I found myself silently appealing to Betsy as I had as a child. My mother didn't miss it.

"If only you had made clear it was serious, with André, we would have been delighted to help you. You might have married him and gone to New York. But you moved so quickly from one to the next. Sad, to think what might have been. Still, you always admired the English, and now in some twist of fate we find you're married to an English brigadier!"

There was an archness about her needling, a female competition I didn't understand. How had I ever come to provoke her?

"Too dreadful that it should only be Major André that pays. You must feel that injustice very much, Neddy. I expect they're *baying* for Benedict—"

"Nobody, I know, would wish to deepen Peggy's distress at a friend's fate. It was General Washington's decision that the major should die. His decision as to the means. And his decision to free Peggy given her innocence, thank goodness."

"Of course, Neddy, but Peggy bears responsibility for the introduction. And her general, for exposing an associate so—"

"In fairness, had the Major lived, he would have faced uncommon criticism," Neddy said. "He made some staggering mistakes."

"I did take that risk. I do share the blame," I said.

"Well, we all share it now, Peggy."

"I'm sorry!"

I lurched back from the table, toppling the decanter, staining the tablecloth, and flooding my mother's plate. Every abject mess she'd expected.

I saw I'd forever now be an unwelcome guest, compromised beyond redemption.

I took Eddie for his rest, and when he was down and sleeping soundly, unfolded André's last picture.

He was dead, because of me.

I had taken pleasure picturing the three of us together. Envisioned a big, boundless freedom, life beyond the binaries, artists luxuriating in a peace of our own design. I had believed we deserved to be happy. Dreamed we'd succeed.

Infernally greedy half-breed, never one thing or the other and always wanting both. Stupid, stupid, stupid woman.

Of all the hours my failure shamed me, none came close to this.

Betsy came to find me and dug out the old gold spoons.

"Sorry, Betsy. To not see you in so long and then return pathetic. Why can't I please her? Don't I mean to? I do. Listen to me. I'm nearly twenty and you'd never know it. I have been more grown up since."

"I know that, you lovely girl. Think of that party! All you did."

"How pathologically averse to conflict must I be, to have risked all I did for peace—"

"You must never speak of it, Peggy. Never admit your involvement. Not outside this house. Reed could kill you. Promise me?"

"I promise. I'm so sorry. You deserve much better than me, you and Neddy."

I heard my mother's tread on the stair, the singsong insistence with which she called my and Betsy's names.

My parents had decided we'd attend the citywide rally to protest my husband's actions and assert our patriotism: a public display of being onside.

"What's your silly mamma done?" My mother cooed to Eddie, retying his smock before the parade. "Who's my best boy? Who loves his Grandmamma so?"

Thousands had massed in the streets of the old city, women buying chestnuts and children grotesque little souvenirs. My mother, holding Eddie, pressed ahead, while I tried to keep them in sight, holding my breath to keep the crowd's stale breath and sour sweat at bay.

I had to stand, flanked by my parents, and watch as a papier-mâché Benedict was paraded our way. The puppet was a vast two-faced Janus, and as it leered and scowled, bobbed and twisted above our heads, I felt hemmed in, trapped in that recurring dream where I needed to run but my legs failed me.

With a whoomph, the effigy was lit. Shielding my eyes from the flames, I felt the heat on my hand. I gave an involuntary cry of dismay as Benedict's face flared, buckled, and warped, grotesquely distorted by the fire. Red light shone in the jeering faces of neighbors, some of whom had clearly recognized me.

Was it possible I'd die in these flames? That my lifelong preoccupation with Joan of Arc was some terrible presentiment about the way I'd end? I was longing to take Eddie and run, but it would have taken a tug-of-war to wrest the baby back now. Moving would only draw attention to us. I looked at my father and saw his eyes were watery and tired, exhausted. All those years I had understood his ambivalence but been frustrated with his lack of commitment. Now I felt the full force of his strain and endurance.

His gaze slid away from mine.

The effigy spat embers while men thwacked and stabbed it with poles. They tossed the replica from man to man, each outdoing the other in defiling it, until the puppet was smashed and sodomized to a pulp, then they looked up for fresh prey. The mob was moving like a muscle intent on trouble, and I felt if I met the wrong pair of eyes the crowd would dismember me.

I spun back for Eddie. My mother had him pressed to her chest and met my look over his head. I felt all the childish instinct for reassurance, but whatever was shining in her eyes—whether it was triumph, embarrassment, an old abandonment—ended any expectation of help.

If it came to it, my parents could not defend me, and nor should they. I was only endangering them. I took my son then, hoisting him high on my hip. Flicking forward my hood to cover both our heads, I edged my way through the crowd to the house.

Reed had raided Benedict's house and Stansbury's, and Patriot agents in New York had somehow got hold of the list I sent André, which Reed had printed, alongside a letter I'd once written to May Chew in which I'd been rude about Esther.

The following morning, the committee issued a written edict on my fate. My mother received it, her face white, hands shaking, and as we met each other's eyes, I believed it must be a death sentence.

Handing Eddie to her, I kissed her trembling cheek, took the letter to my father in the library, and sat across from him. He leaned back in his leather chair, laid his hands on the desk for a moment, then sliced open the paper.

The careful lawyer read slowly and carefully, both hands holding the paper to the desk. I sat on my hands and considered the will he might make for me. Neddy and Betsy would have the baby. I wouldn't let Eddie near Burr.

It was such a pleasant room. As he read, I glanced at the window seat, the faded piping around the cushion where I'd sat from the youngest age. Outside, I could see the smooth, piebald trunk of the plane tree, and beyond it the gardens where I'd toddled so often after Betsy and later chased my brothers. A starling alighted on a branch, cocked its head at me, and flew free. The low slanting rays of the morning light lit the leather-bound law journals to either side of my father's chair.

Knowing Eddie had now reached Betsy and Neddie and safety, I found I was ready to consider my death. I was no saint or martyr, but it didn't feel unfair a person working to stop war should face a fate soldiers met each day.

Perhaps with my death Reed might finally be appeased.

Philadelphia, Friday, Oct. 27, 1780
The Council, taking into consideration the case of Mrs. Margaret Arnold (the wife of Benedict Arnold, an attainted traitor, with the enemy at New York), whose residence in this city has become dangerous to the public safety; and this board being desirous, as much as possible, to prevent any correspondence and intercourse being carried on with persons of disaffected character in this State and the enemy at New York, and especially with the said Benedict Arnold, therefore, Resolved, That the said Margaret Arnold depart this State within fourteen days from the date hereof, and that she do not return again during the continuance of the present war.

Father set the paper down and raised his milky blue eyes to mine.

"Is there any legal appeal to be made?"

"I don't believe so."

"Banished then?"

"That's the sum of it."

I saw his submission as he was confronted with the limits to his power—and the scale of my disgrace.

My mother cried in my arms, as she never had, and though I hated to feel the sobs rack through her, it was good to hold each other, to murmur my love, and find the old gold spoons for her.

"I'm sorry I made you feel it wasn't enough to be like me—"

"Oh no, Mamma. I'm sorry. Sorry I wasn't the daughter you hoped I'd be."

That night I dreamed I'd somehow become unmarried and had to choose whether to marry Benedict again. I did.

My mother had propped the drawing André had made of me on my dresser. I set it beside his self-portrait and glanced at him as I pulled my old trunk from under the bed. I hated that he'd been hanged when he'd wanted to be shot; hated the war which had taken him off course and my hubris in a scheme which had led to his death. I wished I had told him I loved him.

He had taught and inspired me at every encounter—by anecdote or example. He made every good thing believable. I would miss him and mourn him all my life.

Without the baby, I might have given in to the loss, crawled under the covers as I had when he'd left the city, but I had one more leg to my journey yet.

I'd need my stubborn streak now, at least until real courage came. It might be an unexamined, immature anger that drove me, but I still had that, and given the fix I was in, I'd take whatever fuel it took.

Benedict didn't react to getting his leg half shot off by collapsing. He carried on leading. I had one little man in my unit, and I would do the same.

It was as if from a thicket a path had appeared. I'd been so shocked and angry, with myself and Benedict, when he fled. Watching his back, galloping down to the riverbank, I fell quite abruptly out of love. And I hadn't let myself remember what we'd had, the team we'd been.

He was in New York City. I would go to him. Together we could forge a life, if only for a little while. I looked around my old childhood bedroom. Even if the Council had let me stay, even if the mob let me live, I couldn't reattach to the vine.

It was infamy we'd live in now, but we could live it in company.

With Eddie on my lap, I wrote to Henry Clinton. Politely, hinting at the strain my presence had placed on my parents' household and given the city's unwelcoming edict, I wondered if he might be so kind as to permit me be reunited with my husband.

The reply came by return, enclosing a pass to New York City.

I put the two portraits André had drawn in my jewelry case, along with his lock of hair, and began to pack.

When I went to collect Eddie for bed, my mother seemed startled, literally blocking the path to the baby, though I could see him starting to fuss. It was such a blatantly territorial move it struck me for a second as funny. I tried to suggest Eddie might be getting hungry. She was immovable.

"Perhaps you could leave him with us," my father ventured. "Your mother has missed out on so much . . ."

Some elemental instinct kicked in. I pushed rudely past my mother and whisked the baby upstairs.

My fear was visceral, but when I considered, I was ashamed not to have questioned before if I deserved to keep him. After all the difficulty I'd caused, could I not give my parents that gift?

I wouldn't. I couldn't. Not and keep my sanity intact.

Chapter Thirty-Five

I WAS READY BEFORE DAWN, WATCHING THE STREET FOR ANY LAST-minute interference from officials or opportunists. First came a pale fade, leaching the darkness and lending a peach wash to the sky, revealing the facing houses, and then a thousand low beams of golden light flooded the city.

My parents were waiting as I carried Eddie downstairs. We stood looking at each other in the hall.

"I can't leave him," I said.

"I know."

"I'm sorry Mamma." I held him to her. "Say goodbye to Grandmother, Eddie. I love you, Mamma. I'll write, and we'll see you very soon. Soon as it's over."

She nodded briskly. We were both streaming tears.

"You have everything? We don't want Betsy troubled with shipping your belongings after our deaths."

"Mamma!" I laughed. "I'll see you well before then."

I wouldn't for a while, and the last time I did would not be a success.

I was to be escorted to the British line by my father. We passed Christ Church, its windows aflame in the morning light.

As we approached the border, he took my hand.

"I hope the one you love is well, Peggy. And I sincerely hope the little one may contribute to your happiness."

"Thank you, Papa. I hope to repay you," I said. "For all you've given me."

He nodded fast. "Just make it safely."

I held on to him with all my might.

Forever on, each time my children did something new or remarkable, countless times in any given day, my mind would swipe the air like a net for my parents' presence.

The journey to New York was fraught with familiar hazards but the road itself, the King's Highway, was one of the best in America, and initially for me, bowling along that smooth surface felt a relief. Only one possible direction of travel. No more ambivalence. A fascinating city to see, brisk with business, its bay studded with the elegant threat of battleships. And I couldn't deny I was excited to reconcile.

I felt nervous, though, pulling up outside number 3 Broadway and knocking on Benedict's polished front door. If I didn't find him here, I'd have nowhere.

"Who's there?"

"It's only me."

The door burst open, and there were his brilliant blue eyes searching impatiently for mine before he had me in his arms.

I was stilted with him at first—we were both a bit formal—but I was glad to see him clear-eyed and fit as he settled me with a glass of wine in the elegant sitting room. He laid Eddie on a rug on the floor so he could gaze in wonder at his son.

He wanted every detail of my journey, and as I relaxed into the telling, it was a relief to be with a mind that liked mine and saw with shorthand every detail.

"It was almost insulting, that they'd never suspect—"

"Pray they never do—"

"Will Robinson's slave face any consequence?"

"They'll never even question him."

"I like the house," I said, appreciating the kilims and antiques. "Have you met the neighbors?"

"Next door we have Clinton."

"Literally?" I laughed.

He nodded. "Cheek by jowl."

He looked up at me.

"I'm sorry, Peggy, inadequate as that will always be, for leaving you. If it's any excuse, I never doubted you'd manage as well as you did."

He gave me a speech that would have encouraged his men after defeat, pointing out the war was not—despite our best efforts—over. Given the disdain I felt for Reed's ongoing tricks and yesterday's obscene display, I could just about muster hope Benedict's adopted army would save the day, despite my high regard for Washington.

Benedict quirked an eyebrow. "With all due gratitude for his safe release of you, he has not let up in his hunt for me."

He then made me laugh describing his Excellency's attempts at vengeance. Washington had called on "Providence—or some useful low man—to revenge Arnold"—offering slaves by way of payment.

"You're serious?"

"One currency still in abundant supply."

A candidate had been identified, a man named Champe.

Champe had watched Benedict's comings and goings from 3 Broadway from the alleyway behind, and stalked him whenever he went out. Benedict had felt eyes on him but never saw the aspiring assassin's face. He knew the satisfaction it would give any Patriot to have his scalp and stayed armed wherever he went. After five days, Champe approached Benedict in a tavern and presented himself as a fellow defector from the Patriots. Benedict bought him a drink but stayed shtum. Champe apparently was not so confident in his own acting ability that he sought more conversation, but once Benedict had drained his ale and went to leave, Champe followed and sprang him in the street. Benedict had summoned the old man of action within, scaled a ten-foot wall to the right of the tavern, and slipped across the river, eluding capture, before making it safely home again.

We sent for Atty and soon ensured there would be another baby she could help with.

Choose life, I thought. Keep living right now.

When it came time to fight again, Benedict rose to the occasion in New

Jersey. It didn't surprise him to find he liked and admired the King's troops as much as he had Patriot men. He always did the best he could for the men he fought alongside, and he had a new spur now, knowing he'd face a slow, tortured death if captured. He had to leave the battlefield intact, or die trying. No more injuries. He could not, would not, be laid to waste and linger.

Stansbury and Odell came to see me my first Christmas alone with Eddie. They had found safe harbor in New York, and though subdued, and clearly short of money, they were spry and lively, exclaiming kindly over the baby and staying to share memories of our beautiful, brilliant friend.

They asked after Benedict too, and while I ordered a new wardrobe thanks to the salary he had from Clinton, I was able to give a good account.

"Keeping his head up. Dodging endless assassination attempts. Arresting Hercules Mulligan. Recruiting Beverley Robinson for André's successor. He fights with more commitment than ever, pride insists on that, while doing all he can not to kill a man."

Odell nudged my leg. "You know the reason they hate him is he held a mirror to society. A mirror they can't break. He showed what they don't want known. That we are almost all of us in at least two minds. A few fanatics on either end of the spectrum excepted, there are limits to anyone's commitment. And none of us know that we won't overthrow one regime only to pollute and contaminate the next ourselves. The Declaration was poetry. The politics are prose."

"I think that's unfair to prose." I smiled.

The official storyline—my utter ignorance of the plot—loyally repeated by Neddy Burd on behalf of my family for years, calcified. I often felt it was less believed than wielded to diminish my intelligence, but I kept my mouth shut.

I spent one evening in the summer of 1781 in conversation with Henry Clinton. He praised Arnold for the morale and strategy and strength he'd lent the British and talked of imminent victory. The prospects for American success he declared now "remote in the extreme." The Continental Army was widely believed to be on the verge of extinction.

"You'll never extinguish the spirit," I said.

"I wouldn't wish to."

We talked of what was in store for me in England. I admitted I found the prospect intimidating. "You should." Clinton laughed. "I do and I was born there! We judge everything, forget nothing. But you'll fit in."

"Is it true they don't like a man to rise there?"

"Ambition can be embarrassing. We prefer a doomed hero."

He was wrong about what was ahead in the war, as everyone in it was, more than once. The Patriots fought brilliantly. And with diminishing support in Parliament, insufficient supplies left British troops increasingly exposed, until Lord Cornwallis took the decision to call it a day, surrendering on behalf of his ten thousand men to Washington at Yorktown, yielding recognition at last that America's right to independence was bigger than the King's claim could ever be.

Cornwallis was exchanged for Henry Laurens, late president of Congress, who had been captured at sea and confined in the Tower of London. War never felt more like a game of chess to me.

For Benedict it could have been a double defeat, having staked his reputation to the losing side, but he was happy to stop fighting, and to see all his men free.

I was troubled to hear Quakers were terrorized for their pacifism, but glad to picture the pretty illumination of Philadelphia in celebration of peace.

As far as I was concerned, we had freedom from fear and a place to be.

In December, I saw Benedict off as he embarked with Lord Cornwallis for London. Cornwallis came to kiss my hand.

"The irony, Mrs. Arnold, is your husband's intervention did accelerate the end of the war, though not at all as intended. Patriot outrage at Arnold's defection was so widespread, it galvanized opposition to the King and helped tip the balance in Washington's favor."

"Happy he could help." I smiled.

I think they had a very enjoyable trans-Atlantic passage rehashing strategy, toasting old adversaries, and formulating new ideas for the reunion of empire to put to the King.

I was glad to travel by separate ship with Atty and the boys.

When our time came, seagulls shrieked and wheeled as the ship pulled out of port. I turned from the wake like a great ray tail, Manhattan receding in the distance, the war with it, to look forward, out over an unknowable ocean.

We were invited to court on arrival in London. The soaring Gothic perfection of Westminster Abbey and the unthinkably elaborate Houses of Parliament were everything André had promised me.

Ascending the steps of St. James's Palace for our private audience with the King, Benedict's arm in mine, I felt André at my other shoulder, and the sad spin on that old dream.

Flooded with familiar grief and guilt, I turned from the handsome brick courtyard back to the park, tipping back the tears, until I could face André's memory squarely again.

Queen Charlotte granted me a pension for services rendered, and King George another for my meritorious contribution before declaring Margaret Arnold the finest-looking woman in the country. I told them we would name our next son George in honor of him, and of Washington. They laughed. Fast friends, for all our differences, convinced the real interest and happiness of the former colony consisted in harmony with Great Britain, however that was configured. At lunch, we traded views on the nature of Americans. I suggested perhaps achieving independence always took a little hard-heartedness from the offspring, but that a good father could forgive severed ties and reach civilized relations from a natural distance.

We walked with the King and Prince of Wales through the park afterward, savoring the bobbing daffodils and magnolias heralding London's early spring and the parade of extravagant fashions and pampered pets, and from there Benedict and I took the carriage on alone to Westminster Abbey to see the marble memorial installed in André's honor.

We passed the canopied tombs of Kings and Queens, with their sloping stone feet resting on eternally patient dogs, passed the bust of Shakespeare, and just across the wide stone floor, below the vaulted arches, reached André's monument.

I took Benedict's hand, afraid seeing the nation's love and honor for André's romantic figure risked making my husband bitter, but he looked as simply moved as I was. We were conscious of onlookers recognizing Benedict, their titillation at witnessing this posthumous encounter between collaborators.

"He wouldn't want us creeping out of here, cringing like Adam and Eve out of Eden. He'd forgive us, Benedict, as completely as we forgive him."

"Even if we'd succeeded, West Point might not have been the last word, for all the absolute coup they say it would have been. Who knows what reprisals might have followed?"

"Awful thought," I said. "We trigger events beyond our line of sight all the time. Some days it's terrifying how little we know. Some nights we're right to feel we know as much as anyone alive."

"What can you do?"

"Strive to be good ancestors, trust our children to see further, try to be a little better all the time?"

"Not too good." He smiled.

"Not us."

That night I dreamed of running, unencumbered, no punishing corset or pinching heels, not a thought of mess or expense. Even as I ran, moss under my bare feet, ferns whipping my ankles, I knew I was sleeping, marveling at the fact I was at once in my bed in London and in my childhood woods in Pennsylvania, smiling in my sleep at my ease spanning the Atlantic, bridging distant places in my dreams.

Note

Contemporary commentators, including Washington Irving, couldn't conceive of Peggy's guilt.

It was not until the 1930s that archival reference to her pension by the King and Queen of England was discovered by Carl Von Doren and her role in the conspiracy was revealed.

She's been pretty well vilified ever since—the object of titillation, condescension, and scorn.

Peggy's voice struck me in the surviving correspondence as that of a wry survivor, and a much more interesting woman than the ravishing ditz or simpering schemer I'd found depicted. This fiction is my attempt at letting her answer her critics.

Benedict remains the one traitor every American can name. He's something of our national Judas or Satan, fixing the beautiful ideals and inspiring achievement of independence in place.

* * *

Soon after settling in London, Benedict and Peggy discovered St. Mary's Battersea, a pretty church on the tidal waterfront of the River Thames. The recently completed building must have felt familiar, reminiscent of the unpretentious elegance of Philadephia's churches.

The family joined a congregation of artists, botanists, and expatriate Americans. Peggy seems to have made friends wherever she went. Benedict not so much.

They had seven children together, the delight and pride of Peggy's life.

A lot about life after leaving America was sad and difficult: Benedict's quarrels and duels; his unsuccessful trade ventures, infidelity, and illegitimate child; the death of two of their seven children and the loss of Peggy's mother; and more changes of address than can have been welcome. When Benedict was dying of the gout which killed him, he asked to be buried in his blue Patriot uniform.

Peggy suffered "Dreadful Attacks" of anxiety and nagging health worries. She settled the maze of Benedict's debts with help from her father's investments on her behalf and with Neddy, her loyal trustee, and discovered the pleasure of ocean swimming at last.

She always worried about more war, but she never did get bitter. She died before her father, of cancer at forty-two, her daughter Sophia beside her.

When war did break out again between Britain and America, André's grave at Tappan was repeatedly desecrated, until in 1821 it was arranged his remains would be brought home to England and reinterred at Westminster Abbey. There his grave remains, steps from his marble monument, honored among England's greatest poets and soldiers.

Theodosia and Aaron Burr married and had one daughter. Notorious for killing Alexander Hamilton, Aaron Burr was also the disaffected vice president behind an alleged conspiracy to create a new American nation which he would have been the one to rule. He was repeatedly, unsuccessfully, tried for treason. His and Theo's daughter was tragically lost at sea.

Benedict and Peggy were eventually joined in St. Mary's crypt by their daughter Sophia, after her own marriage and adventures in India, and the grave now sits in a nursery school, flanked by colorful coat pegs, miniature furniture, and the chatter of toddlers. Church services continue upstairs.

A stained-glass window in the nave shares the grave's inscription:

The Two Nations Whom He Served in Turn in the Years of their Enmity have United in this Memorial as a Token of their Enduring Friendship.

Acknowledgments

With all love and thanks to my parents.

And huge gratitude to:

My late grandparents.

And parents-in-law.

My agent, Chad Luibl.

My publisher, Molly Stern.

My editors, Nicole Otto and Sarah Goldstein.

Emily Andrukaitis, Zoey Cole, Tracey Engel, Jenny Freilach, Lucy Kim, Christopher King, Sam Mitchell, Sierra Stovell, Julia Talley, Aaron Tichenor, Nancy Trypuc, Kevin Ullrich and the whole team at Zando.

My colleagues and clients, neighbors and friends.

The work of Isaac Arnold, Vernon Benjamin, Clare Brandt, Alexis Coe, Mike Duncan, Jack Kelly, David McCullough, J. E. Morpurgo, Thomas Paine, Allison Pataki, Nathaniel Philbrick, Alexander Rose, Nancy Rubin Stuart, Carl van Doren, and Lewis Burd Walker, along with the resources of JSTOR, the Internet Archive, the Benjamin Franklin Museum, the Philadelphia Historical Society, and Wikipedia.

Rose Billington, Maia Rossini, and Carole Sargent for generous reads at key moments.

The Mid-Hudson Library system, and each of its beautiful branches, along with all our incredible local booksellers.

Mostly though, to JBK for the help and encouragement, love and fun, and your kind, wise, inspiring minds. I am so grateful to live and have lived in company with you (and Mabel too).